THE LAW OF INNOCENCE

Heading home after winning his latest case, defense attorney Mickey Haller — The Lincoln Lawyer — is pulled over by the police. They open the trunk of his car to find the body of a former client.

Haller knows the law inside out. He will be charged with murder. He will have to build his case from behind bars. And the trial will be the trial of his life.

Because Mickey Haller will defend himself in court.

With watertight evidence stacked against him, Haller will need every trick in the book to prove he was framed.

But a not guilty verdict isn't enough. In order to truly walk free, Haller knows he must find the real killer — that is the law of innocence . . .

MICHAEL CONNELLY

◆

THE LAW OF INNOCENCE

Complete and Unabridged

CHARNWOOD
Leicester

First published in Great Britain in 2020 by
Orion Fiction
an imprint of The Orion Publishing Group Ltd
London

First Charnwood Edition
published 2021
by arrangement with
The Orion Publishing Group Ltd
London

A catalogue record for this book is available
from the British Library.

ISBN 978–1–4448–4740–6

Published by
Ulverscroft Limited
Anstey, Leicestershire

Printed and bound in Great Britain by
TJ Books Ltd., Padstow, Cornwall

To Dr. Michael Hallisey, the members of the Hartford Hospital Book Club, and all of those on the front lines — including Kacey Rose Gajeski, R.N. — who have risked themselves for so many others

A murder case is like a tree. A tall tree. An oak tree. It has been carefully planted and cared for by the state. Watered and trimmed when needed, examined for disease and parasites of any kind. Its root system is constantly monitored as it flourishes underground and clings tightly to the earth. No money is spared in guarding the tree. Its caretakers are granted immense powers to protect and serve it.

The tree's branches eventually grow and spread wide in splendor. They provide deep shade for those who seek true justice.

The branches spring from a thick and sturdy trunk. Direct evidence, circumstantial evidence, forensic science, motive, and opportunity. The tree must stand strong against the winds that challenge it.

And that's where I come in. I'm the man with the ax. My job is to cut the tree down to the ground and burn its wood to ashes.

PART ONE

TWIN TOWERS

1

It had been a good day for the defense. I had walked a man right out of the courtroom. I had turned a felony battery charge into a righteous case of self-defense in front of the jury. The so-called victim had a history of violence of his own that both prosecution and defense witnesses, including an ex-wife, were eager to describe on cross-examination. I delivered the knockout punch when I recalled him to the witness stand and led him down a path of questioning that put him over the edge. He lost his cool and threatened me, said he'd like to meet me out in the street, where it would be just him and me.

'Would you then claim I attacked you, like you have with the defendant in this case?' I asked.

The prosecutor objected and the judge sustained. But that was all it took. The judge knew it. The prosecutor knew it. Everybody in the courtroom knew it. I notched the NG after less than half an hour of jury deliberation. It wasn't my quickest verdict ever, but it came close.

Within the informal downtown defense bar, there is a sacred duty to celebrate a not-guilty verdict the way a golfer celebrates a hole in one at the clubhouse. That is, drinks all around. My

3

celebration took place at the Redwood on Second Street, just a few blocks from the civic center, where there were no fewer than three courthouses to draw celebrants from. The Redwood was no country club but it was convenient. The party — meaning the open bar — started early and ended late, and when Moira, the heavily tattooed bartender who had been keeping the tab, handed me the damage, let's just say I put more on my credit card than I would ever see from the client I had just set free.

I had parked in a lot on Broadway. I got behind the wheel, took a left out of the lot and then another to put me back on Second Street. The traffic lights were with me and I followed the street into the tunnel that went under Bunker Hill. I was halfway through when I saw the reflection of blue lights on the tunnel's exhaust-smoked green tiles. I checked the mirror and saw an LAPD cruiser behind me. I hit the blinker and pulled into the slow lane to let him pass. But the cruiser followed my lead into the same lane and came up six feet behind me. I got the picture then. I was being pulled over.

I waited until I was out of the tunnel and took a right onto Figueroa. I pulled to a stop, killed the engine, and lowered the window. In the Lincoln's side-view mirror a uniformed officer was walking up to my door. I saw no one else in the patrol car behind him. The officer approaching me was working alone.

'Can I see your license, car registration, and proof of insurance, sir?' he asked.

4

I turned to look at him. His name tag said Milton.

'You sure can, Officer Milton,' I said. 'But can I ask why you pulled me over? I know I wasn't speeding and all the lights were green.'

'License,' Milton said. 'Registration. Insurance.'

'Well, I guess you'll eventually tell me. My license is in my pocket inside my coat. The other stuff is in the glove box. Which do you want me to go for first?'

'Let's start with your license.'

'You got it.'

As I pulled my wallet and worked the license out of one of its slots, I reviewed my situation and wondered if Milton had been watching the Redwood for lawyers exiting my party and possibly too tipsy to drive. There had been rumors about patrol cops doing that on nights when there was an NG celebration going on, and defense lawyers could be picked off for a variety of moving-vehicle violations.

I handed Milton my license and then went for the glove box. Soon enough the officer had all he had asked for.

'Now are you going to tell me what this is about?' I asked. 'I know I didn't — '

'Step out of the car, sir,' Milton said.

'Oh, come on, man. Really?'

'Please step out of the car.'

'Whatever.'

I threw the door open, aggressively forcing Milton to take a step back, and got out.

'Just so you know,' I said. 'I spent the last four

5

hours in the Redwood but I didn't have a drop of alcohol. I haven't had a drink in more than five years.'

'Good for you. Please step to the back of your vehicle.'

'Make sure your car camera is on, because this is going to be embarrassing.'

I walked past him to the back of the Lincoln and stepped into the lights of the patrol car behind it.

'You want me to walk a line?' I said. 'Count backward, touch my nose with my finger, what? I'm a lawyer. I know all the games and this one is bullshit.'

Milton followed me to the back of the car. He was tall and lean, white, with a high and tight haircut. I saw the Metro Division badge on his shoulder and four chevrons on his long sleeves. I knew they gave them out for five years of service each. He was a veteran Metro bullethead all the way.

'You see why I stopped you, sir?' he said. 'Your car has no plate.'

I looked down at the rear bumper of the Lincoln. There was no license plate.

'God damn it,' I said. 'Uh . . . this is some kind of a prank. We were celebrating — I won a case today and walked my client. The plate says IWALKEM and one of those guys must've thought it was a joke to steal the plate.'

I tried to think about who had left the Redwood before I did, and who would have thought this was a funny thing to do. Daly, Mills, Bernardo . . . it could have been anyone.

6

'Check the trunk,' Milton said. 'Maybe it's in there.'

'No, they would need a key to put it in the trunk,' I said. 'I'm going to make a call, see if I can — '

'Sir, you're not making a call until we're finished here.'

'That's bullshit. I know the law. I'm not in custody — I can make a call.'

I paused there to see if Milton had any further challenge. I noticed the camera on his chest.

'My phone's in the car,' I said.

I started moving back to the open door.

'Sir, stop right there,' Milton said from behind me.

I turned around.

'What?'

He snapped on a flashlight and pointed the beam down at the ground behind the car.

'Is that blood?' he asked.

I stepped back and looked down at the cracked asphalt. The officer's light was centered on a blotch of liquid beneath the bumper of my car. It was dark maroon at the center and almost translucent at its edges.

'I don't know,' I said. 'But whatever it is, it was already there. I'm — '

Just as I said it, we both saw another drop come down from the bumper and hit the asphalt.

'Sir, open the trunk, please,' Milton demanded as he put the flashlight into a belt holster.

A variety of questions cascaded through my mind, starting with what was in the trunk and ending with whether Milton had probable cause

7

to open it if I refused.

Another drop of what I now assumed to be bodily fluid of some sort hit the asphalt.

'Write me the ticket for the plate, Officer Milton,' I said. 'But I am not opening the trunk.'

'Sir, then I am placing you under arrest,' Milton said. 'Put your hands on the trunk.'

'Arrest? For what? I'm not — '

Milton moved in on me, grabbing me and spinning me toward my car. He threw all of his weight into me and doubled me over the trunk.

'Hey! You can't — '

One at a time, my arms were roughly pulled behind my back and I was handcuffed. Milton then put his hand into the back collar of my shirt and jacket and yanked me up off the car.

'You're under arrest,' he said.

'For what?' I said. 'You can't just — '

'For your safety and mine I'm putting you into the back of the patrol car.'

He grabbed my elbow to turn me again, and walked me to the rear passenger door of his car. He put his hand on top of my head as he pushed me into the plastic seat in the back. He then leaned across to buckle me in.

'You know you can't open the trunk,' I said. 'You have no probable cause. You don't know if that's blood and you don't know if it's coming from the interior of the car. I could've driven through whatever it is.'

Milton pulled back out of the car and looked down at me.

'Exigent circumstances,' he said. 'There might be someone in there who needs help.'

He slammed the door. I watched him go back to my Lincoln and study the trunk lid for some sort of release mechanism. Finding none, he went to the open driver's door and reached in to remove the keys.

He used the key fob to pop the trunk, standing off to the side should someone come out of the trunk shooting. The lid went up and an interior light went on. Milton supplemented it with his own flashlight. He moved from left to right, stepping sideways and keeping his eyes and the beam on the contents of the trunk. From my angle in the back of the patrol car, I could not see into the trunk but could tell by the way Milton was maneuvering and bending down for a closer look that there was something there.

Milton tilted his head to talk into the radio mic on his shoulder and then made a call. Probably for backup. Probably for a homicide unit. I didn't have to see into the trunk to know that Milton had found a body.

2

Edgar Quesada sat next to me at a dayroom table as I read the last pages of the transcript from his trial. He had asked me to review his case files as a favor, hoping there was something I could see or do to help his situation. We were in the high-power module in the Twin Towers Correctional Facility in downtown Los Angeles. This was where they housed inmates on keep-away status as they waited for trial or, as in Quesada's case, sentencing to state prison. It was the first Sunday evening in December and the jail was cold. Quesada wore white long johns under his blue jumpsuit, the sleeves all the way down to his wrists.

Quesada was in familiar surroundings. He had been down this path before and had the tattoos to prove it. He was a third-generation White Fence gang member from Boyle Heights with lots of inked allegiance to the gang and the Mexican Mafia, which was the largest and most powerful gang in California's jail and prison systems.

According to the documents I had been reading, Quesada had been the driver of a car that carried two other members of White Fence as they fired automatic weapons through the plate-glass windows of a bodega on East First

10

Street, where the owner had fallen two weeks behind on the gang tax that White Fence had been extorting from him for almost twenty-five years. The shooters had aimed high, the attack intended to be a warning. But a ricochet went low and hit the bodega owner's granddaughter on the top of the head as she crouched behind the counter. Her name was Marisol Serrano. She died instantly, according to testimony I read from the deputy coroner.

No witnesses to the crime identified the shooters. That would have been a fatal exercise in bravery. But a traffic cam caught the license plate on the getaway car. It was traced to a car stolen from the long-term parking garage at nearby Union Station. And cameras there caught a glimpse of the thief: Edgar Quesada. His trial lasted only four days and he was convicted of conspiracy to commit murder. His sentencing was in a week and he was looking at a minimum of fifteen years in prison with the likelihood of many more beyond that. All because he had been behind the wheel on a drive-by warning-turned-murder.

'So?' Quesada said as I flipped the last page over.

'Well, Edgar,' I said. 'I think you're kind of fucked.'

'Man, don't tell me that. There's nothing? Nothing at all?'

'There's always things you can do. But they're long shots, Edgar. I'd say you have more than enough here for an IAC motion but — '

'What's that?'

'Ineffective assistance of counsel. Your lawyer

sat on his hands the whole trial. He let objection after objection pass. He just let the prosecutor — Well, here, you see this page?'

I moved back through the transcript to a page where I had folded a corner over.

'Here the judge even says, 'Are you going to object, Mr. Seguin, or do I have to keep doing it for you?' That is not good trial work, Edgar, and you might have a shot at proving that, but here is the thing: at best you win the motion and get a do-over, but that doesn't change the evidence. It's still the same evidence and with the next jury you'll go down again, even if you have a new lawyer who knows how to keep the prosecutor inside the lines.'

Quesada shook his head. He was not my client, so I didn't know all the details of his life but he was about thirty-five and looking at a lot of hard time.

'How many convictions do you have?' I asked.

'Two,' he said.

'Felonies?'

He nodded and I didn't have to say anything else. My original assessment stood. He was fucked. He was probably going away forever. Unless . . .

'You know why they got you here in high-power instead of the gang module, right?' I said. 'Any day now they're going to pull you out of here, put you in a room, and ask you the big question. Who was in the car with you that day?'

I gestured to the thick transcript.

'There's nothing here that will help you,' I said. 'The only thing you can do is deal the time down by giving up names.'

I said the last part in a whisper. But Quesada didn't respond as quietly.

'That's *bullshit!*' he yelled.

I checked the mirrored window of the control room overhead even though I knew I could see nothing behind it. I then looked at Quesada and saw the veins in his neck start to pulse — even beneath the inked necklace of cemetery stones that circled it.

'Cool down, Edgar,' I said. 'You asked me to look at your file and that's all I'm doing. I'm not your lawyer. You should really talk to him about — '

'I can't go to him,' Quesada said. 'Haller, you don't know shit!'

I stared at him and finally understood. His lawyer was controlled by the very people he would need to inform on: White Fence. Going to him would almost assuredly result in a Mexican Mafia — engineered snitch shanking, whether he was in the high-power module or not. It was said that the eMe, as it was more informally known, could get to anybody anywhere in a California lockdown.

I was literally saved by the bell. The five-minute warning horn before bed check sounded. Quesada reached across the table and roughly grabbed up his documents. He was through with me. He got up while still smoothing all the loose pages into a neat stack. Without a *Thank you* or a *Fuck you*, he headed off to his cell.

And I headed to mine.

3

At 8 p.m. the steel door of my cell automatically slid closed with a metallic bang that jolted my entire being. Every night it went through me like a train. I had been in lockup for five weeks now and it was something I couldn't and didn't ever want to get used to. I sat down on the three-inch-thin mattress and closed my eyes. I knew the overhead light would stay on another hour and I needed to use that time, but this was my ritual. To try to blank out all the harsh sounds and fears. To remind myself of who I still was. A father, a lawyer — but not a murderer.

'You got Q all hot and bothered out there.'

I opened my eyes. It was Bishop in the next cell. There was a grated air vent high up on the wall that separated our cells.

'Didn't mean to,' I said. 'I guess next time somebody needs a jailhouse lawyer in here I'll just pass.'

'Good plan,' Bishop said.

'And where were you, by the way? It was about to become kill-the-messenger time with him. I looked around, no Bishop.'

'Don't worry, homes, I had you covered. I was watching from up on the rail. I had your back.'

I was paying Bishop four hundred a week for protection, the payment delivered in cash to his girlfriend and mother of his son in Inglewood. His protection extended throughout the quarter of the high-power octagon where we were housed: two tiers, twenty-four single cells, with twenty-two other inmates presenting varying levels of known and unknown threat to me.

On my first night, Bishop had offered to protect me or hurt me. I didn't negotiate. He usually stuck close when I was in the dayroom but I had not seen him on the second-tier walkway rail when I gave Quesada the bad news about his case. I knew very little about Bishop, because you didn't ask questions in jail. His dark black skin hid tattoos to the point of making me wonder why he even got them. But I had been able to make out the words *Crip Life* inked across the knuckles of both his hands.

I reached under the bed for the cardboard file box that held my own case docs. I checked the rubber bands first. I had wrapped each of the four stacks of documents with two bands each, horizontal and vertical, with the bands crossing at distinct spots on the top sheet. This told me if Bishop or anyone else had snuck in and gone through my stuff. I had a client once who almost went down on a first-degree murder because a jailhouse snitch had gotten to the files in his cell and read enough discovery material to concoct a convincing but phony confession he claimed my client had made to him. Lesson learned. I set rubber-band traps and would know if someone had looked through my paperwork.

I was now facing a first-degree murder charge myself and was going pro se — defending myself. I know what Lincoln said and probably many wise men before him and since. Maybe I did have a fool for a client, but I couldn't see putting my future in any hands other than my own. So, in the matter of *The State of California versus J. Michael Haller*, the defense's war room was cell 13, level K-10 at Twin Towers Correctional Facility.

I pulled my motions packet out of the box and snapped off the rubber bands after confirming that the documents had not been tampered with. A motions hearing was scheduled for the following morning and I wanted to prep. I had three requests before the court, beginning with a motion to lower bail. It had been set at my arraignment at $5 million, with the prosecution successfully arguing that I was not only a flight risk but a threat to witnesses in the case because I knew the inner workings of the local justice system like the back of my hand. It didn't help that the judge handling the arraignment was the Honorable Richard Rollins Hagan, whose rulings in prior cases I had twice gotten overturned on appeal. He got some payback on me, agreeing with the prosecution's request to more than double down on the schedule that recommended a $2 million bail for first-degree murder.

At the time, the difference between $2 million and $5 million didn't matter. I had to decide if I wanted to put everything I had into my freedom or into my defense. I decided on the latter and took up residence in Twin Towers, qualifying for keep-away status as an officer of the court who had potential enemies in all of the gen-pop dorms.

But tomorrow I would stand before a different judge — one I believed I had never crossed — and ask for a reduction in bail. I had two other motions as well and now reviewed my notes so I could stand and argue before the judge instead of read.

More important than the bail motion was the discovery motion that accused the prosecution of withholding information and evidence I was entitled to, and the challenge to the probable cause of the police stop that led to my arrest.

I had to assume that Judge Violet Warfield, who had drawn the case on rotation, would put a time cap on arguments on all the motions. I would need to be ready, succinct, and on point.

'Hey, Bishop?' I said. 'You still awake?'

'I'm awake,' Bishop said. 'What's up?'

'I want to practice on you.'

'Practice what?'

'My arguments, Bishop.'

'That ain't part of our deal, man.'

'I know but the lights are about to go out and I'm not ready. I want you to listen and tell me what you think.'

At that moment the lights on the tier went out.

'Okay,' Bishop said. 'Let's hear it. But you pay extra for this.'

4

Monday, December 2

In the morning, I was on the first bus to the courthouse, having dined on a baloney sandwich and a bruised red apple for breakfast. It was the same breakfast every morning and it was served again at lunch for good measure. In my five weeks here we caught a break from it on Thanksgiving only, when the baloney was replaced with a slice of pressed turkey and served at all three meals. I was long past any revulsion with the food at Twin Towers. It was the routine and now I put it away quickly and easily every breakfast and every lunch. Still, I estimated that I had already lost between ten and twenty pounds during my incarceration and I looked at it as getting down to fighting weight for what would surely be the bout of my life.

On the bus, I was with thirty-nine other inmates, most of whom were heading to morning arraignment court. As a lawyer, I had seen the wide-eyed look of fear in clients when I met them for initial consultation at first appearances. But that was always in court and always with me calming and preparing them for what lay ahead. On the buses, I was surrounded by it. Men facing their first experience of incarceration. Men who had been in lockup many times before. Rookie or recidivist, there was a palpable sense

18

of desperation coming from all of them.

I found the bus rides to and from court to be my own moments of biggest fear. It was random selection when you were loaded on. I had no Bishop, no bodyguard. Should anything happen to me, the deputies were behind an iron grate at the front: the driver and so-called safety deputy. Their role would be simply to sort out the dead and dying when whatever happened was over. They weren't there to protect and serve, just to move people along in the underbelly of the justice system.

This time it was one of the modern buses with compartmentalized seating, the sight of which filled me with even more dread. The newer fleet was designed after there had been full-scale riots on buses that had raged out of control. With the Sheriff's Department responsible for the safety of inmates, the riots resulted in scores of lawsuits against the agency for failure to protect those who had been injured and killed. I had lodged a couple of those lawsuits myself and so was aware of the weaknesses of the old and new designs.

The new buses were sectioned off by steel fencing into seating compartments of eight inmates each. This way, if a fight broke out, it was contained to a maximum of eight combatants. The buses had five such compartments and were loaded back to front, filling the seats in the rear section first and so on. The prisoners were cuffed together four to a chain, with one group on either side of the aisle in each compartment.

This design also was the blueprint for a significant problem. Should the bus be in transit and a fight break out in the rear compartment, the unarmed safety deputy must unlock and move through five doors and four compartments — four tight spaces filled with inmates accused in some cases of violent crimes — to break up a fight in the fifth. The idea was preposterous, and to my thinking, the department's solution had actually doubled down on the problem. Fights in the rear compartments were allowed to play out until the bus got to its destination. Those who could walk off did and those who couldn't were tended to.

The bus pulled into the cavernous garage beneath the Clara Shortridge Foltz Criminal Justice Center and we were off-loaded and escorted into the building's vertical maze of holding cells that served its twenty-four different courtrooms.

As a pro se, I was entitled to some legal niceties not afforded most of the men and women who came off the buses. I was led to a private holding cell where I could confer with my investigator and stand-in attorney — the lawyer assigned as my backup to handle the printing, filing, and in some cases fine-tuning of motions and other documents produced as part of the case. My investigator was Dennis 'Cisco' Wojciechowski and the stand-in was my law partner, Jennifer Aronson.

Everything moves slowly in incarceration. My 4 a.m. wake-up at Twin Towers resulted in me getting to my private conference room at 8:40 a.m., a total travel distance of four blocks. I had brought one rubber-banded stack of documents with me

— the motions — and was spreading them on the metal table when my team was shown in by a detention deputy at nine sharp.

Cisco and Jennifer were required to sit across the table from me. No handshakes or hugs. The meeting fell under attorney-client privilege and was private. But there was a camera in one corner of the ceiling. We would be watched, but the camera carried no audio back to the deputy who monitored it — or so it was claimed. I didn't fully believe this, and during prior team meetings I had occasionally made a remark or issued an order designed to send the prosecution off on a wild-goose chase if they happened to be illegally listening in. I used the code word *Baja* in each statement to alert my team to the ruse.

I was in dark blue scrubs with LAC DETENTION stenciled across the front and back of my shirt. Like Edgar Quesada the evening before, I wore long johns underneath. I had learned quickly during my stay with the county that the early-morning bus rides and courthouse holding cells were unheated, and I dressed accordingly.

Jennifer was dressed for court in a charcoal-gray suit and cream-colored blouse. Cisco, as was his routine, was dressed for a sunset ride down the Pacific Coast Highway on his classic Harley Panhead, Cody Jinks blasting on his helmet stereo: black jeans, boots, and T-shirt. It appeared that his skin was impervious to the cold, damp air of the conference cell. That he was originally from Wisconsin might have had something to do with that.

21

'How's my team this fine morning?' I said cheerily.

Although I was the one incarcerated and wearing the jailhouse scrubs, I knew it was important to keep my people engaged and not worried about my predicament. *Act like a winner and you'll become a winner* — as David 'Legal' Siegel, my father's partner and the man who mentored me in the law, used to say.

'All good, boss,' Cisco said.

'How are you doing?' Jennifer asked.

'Better to be in the courthouse than the jail,' I said. 'Which suit did Lorna pick out?'

Lorna Taylor was my case manager as well as my sartorial consultant. This second duty extended from when she was my wife — my second wife, in a union that lasted only a year and preceded her marriage to Cisco. Though I would not be appearing this day before a jury, I had previously secured Judge Warfield's approval of a motion allowing me to dress in my professional clothes during all appearances in open court. My case had drawn considerable attention from the media and I didn't want a photo of me in convict garb going viral. The world outside the courthouse was a jury pool from which twelve people would be drawn to judge me. I didn't want them, whoever they were, to have already seen me in jailhouse blues. My carefully curated selection of European suits also added to my confidence when I stood before the court to argue my case.

'The blue Hugo Boss with pink shirt and gray tie,' Jennifer said. 'The courtroom deputy has it.'

22

'Perfect,' I said.

Cisco rolled his eyes at my vanity. I ignored it.

'What about the time?' I asked. 'You talk to the clerk?'

'Yes, the judge slotted an hour,' Jennifer said. 'Will that be enough?'

'Probably not, with argument from Dana. I might have to drop something if Warfield sticks to the schedule.'

Dana was Dana Berg, the Major Crimes Unit star prosecutor assigned to convicting me and sending me off to prison for the rest of my life. Among members of the downtown defense bar, she was known as Death Row Dana because of her propensity to seek maximum penalties, or, alternately, as Iceberg because of her demeanor when it came to negotiating pleas. The fact was that her resolve couldn't be melted and she was most often assigned cases where trial was inevitable.

And that was the situation with me. The day after my arrest, I had put out a media statement through Jennifer that forcefully denied the allegations against me and promised vindication at trial. It was most likely that statement that got the case assigned to Dana Berg.

'Then what do we drop?' Jennifer asked.

'Let's put bail on the back burner,' I said.

'Wait, no,' Cisco said.

'What? I wanted to go with that right out of the gate,' Jennifer said. 'We need to get you out of there and into unrestricted strategy sessions in an office, not a cell.'

Jennifer raised her hands to take in the space

where we were sitting. I knew that they would both protest my decision on bail. But I intended to make better use of today's time in front of the judge.

'Look, it's not like I'm having a great time at Twin Towers,' I said. 'It's not the Ritz. But there are things that are more important to accomplish today. I want to get a full hearing on the probable-cause challenge. That's number one. And then I want to argue the discovery issues. You ready on that, Bullocks?'

It had been a long time since I had called Jennifer by her baby-lawyer nickname. I had hired her right out of Southwestern Law School, which was housed in a former Bullock's department store. I had wanted somebody with a working-class law degree and an underdog's drive and fierceness. In the years since, she had proved me a genius, rising from associate counsel to whom I handed off low-money cases to full partner and trusted confidante who could hold her own and win in any courtroom in the county. I wasn't interested in using her as a mere filer of documents. I wanted her going toe to toe with Dana Berg on the prosecution's delays in discovery. This was the most important case of my career and I wanted her side by side with me at the defense table.

'I'm ready,' she said. 'But I'm also ready to argue bail. You need to be out so you can prepare for trial without needing a bodyguard watching your back while you're eating baloney fucking sandwiches.'

I laughed. I guessed I had complained a little

24

too often about the Twin Towers menu.

'Look, I get that,' I said. 'And I don't mean to laugh. But I need to keep payroll going and I just don't want to come out of this thing bankrupt and with nothing left for my daughter. Somebody's got to pay for law school, and it's not going to be Maggie McFierce.'

My first ex-wife and the mother of my child was a prosecutor in the District Attorney's Office. Real name: Maggie McPherson. She made a comfortable living and had raised our daughter, Hayley, in a safe neighborhood in Sherman Oaks — not counting a two-year stint in Ventura County, where she went to work for the D.A. while waiting for a political fire to burn itself out down here. I had paid for private schools all the way and now Hayley was 1L at USC after graduating from Chapman in May. That carried a steep price tag that fell solely to me to pay. I had planned for it and had it covered in savings, but not if I pulled the cash and put it into a nonrefundable bond just to spring myself loose to prep for trial.

I had done the math and it wasn't worth it. Even if we persuaded Judge Warfield to cut bail in half, I was still looking at needing $250,000 to buy a bond that really only amounted to three months of freedom. After all, I had refused to waive my right to a speedy trial and had the state on a clock — sixty court days within which to put me on trial. This meant that the trial was only two months away, in February, and the verdict would either give me back my freedom or permanently suspend it. On many previous

25

occasions, I had counseled clients to save their bond money and nut it out in Twin Towers.

Usually that was to make sure they had money to pay me. But now, that was the counsel I gave myself.

'Have you talked to Maggie about this?' Jennifer asked. 'Has she even visited you over there yet?'

'Yes, she's visited and, yes, we've talked,' I said. 'She says the same thing you say, and I don't disagree it would be better. But it's about priorities. Case priorities.'

'Look, you know that Lorna, Cisco, and I have all said we can defer paychecks till this is over. I really think this is a case priority and you need to reconsider. Besides, what about Hayley? You already missed Thanksgiving with her. You want to miss Christmas too?'

'Okay, duly noted. Let's see if there's time to get to it today. If not, we'll take it up in the next round. Let's move on past the motions. Cisco, what's happening with the review of previous cases?'

'Me and Lorna are through more than half the files,' Cisco said. 'So far nothing stands out. But we're working on it and making a list of possibles.'

He was talking about a list of former clients and enemies who might have the motive and wherewithal to pin a murder rap on me.

'Okay, I need that,' I said. 'I can't just go into court and say I was framed. A third-party-culpability case requires a third party.'

'We're on it,' Cisco said. 'If it's there, we'll find it.'

'If?' I asked.

'I didn't mean it like that, boss,' Cisco said. 'I just meant — '

'Listen,' I said. 'I've spent the past twenty-five years of my life telling clients that it didn't matter to me whether they did it, because my job was to defend them, not judge them. Guilty or innocent, you get the same deal and the same effort. But now that I'm on the other side of it, I know that's bullshit. I need you two and Lorna to believe in me on this.'

'Of course we do,' Jennifer said.

'Goes without saying,' Cisco added.

'Don't be so quick to answer,' I said. 'You must have questions about it. The state's case is more than persuasive. So if at any point Death Row Dana turns you into a believer, I need you to step up and step out. I don't want you on the team.'

'Not going to happen,' Cisco said.

'Never,' added Jennifer.

'Good,' I said. 'Then let's go to war. Jennifer, can you go get my suit and bring it in so I can get ready?'

'Be right back,' she said.

She got up and hammered on the steel door with one hand while waving to the overhead camera with the other. Soon I heard the sharp metal crack of the door unlocking. A deputy opened it to let her out.

'So,' I said, once Cisco and I were alone. 'What's the water temp these days down in Baja?'

'Oh, it's nice,' Cisco said. 'I talked to my guy

27

down there and he said high eighties.'

'Too warm for me. Tell him to let me know when it gets down to about seventy. That would be perfect for me.'

'I'll tell him.'

I nodded to Cisco and tried not to smile for the overhead camera. Hopefully, this last bit of conversation was intriguing enough to any illegal listeners to send them fishing for a red herring down in Mexico.

'So, what about our victim?' I said.

'Still working it,' Cisco said hesitantly. 'I'm hoping Jennifer gets more stuff in discovery today so I can run down his movements and how and when he ended up in your trunk.'

'Sam Scales was a slippery guy. Nailing him down is going to be tough, but I'm going to need that.'

'Don't worry. You'll have it.'

I nodded. I liked Cisco's confidence. I hoped it would pay off. I thought for a moment about my former client Sam Scales, the ultimate con man who had even conned me. Now the victim in the biggest con of all, I was set up for a murder that I knew was going to be a hard frame to break.

'Hey, boss, you okay?' Cisco asked.

'Yeah, fine,' I said. 'Just thinking about things. This is going to be fun.'

Cisco nodded. He knew it was going to be anything but fun, but he understood the sentiment. *Act like a winner and you'll become a winner.*

The cell door slid open again and Jennifer

came back in, carrying my court clothes on two hangers. I usually reserved the pink oxford for appearances before a jury, but that was okay. Just seeing the sharp cut of the suit kicked my mood up to a new level. I started getting ready for battle.

5

My suit fit me loosely. I felt like I was swimming in it. The first thing I told Jennifer when they moved me into court and took off the chains was to ask Lorna to go to my house, pick out two of my suits, and take them to a tailor to be altered.

'That's going to be kind of hard without you there to be measured,' she said.

'I don't care, it's important,' I said. 'I don't want to look like a guy in a borrowed suit in front of the media. That gets out to the jury pool and sends a message.'

'Okay, I get it.'

'Tell her to have them taken in a full size all around.'

Before she could respond, Dana Berg stepped over to the defense table and put down a set of documents.

'Our answers to your motions,' she said. 'I'm sure it will all come out in oral.'

'Timely,' Jennifer said, meaning it was anything but.

She started reading. I didn't bother. Berg seemed to hesitate, as if expecting a retort from me. I just looked up and smiled.

'Good morning, Dana,' I said. 'How was your weekend?'

'Better than yours, I'm sure,' she said.

'I think that would be a given,' I said.

She smirked and returned to the prosecution table.

'No surprise, she's objecting to everything,' Jennifer said. 'Including bail reduction.'

'Par for the course,' I said. 'Like I said, don't worry about bail today. We'll — '

I was silenced by the booming voice of Morris Chan, the courtroom deputy, announcing the arrival of Judge Warfield. We were instructed to remain seated and come to order.

I believed I got lucky when we drew Warfield on the case. She was a tough law-and-order jurist but she was also a former member of the defense bar. Oftentimes defense lawyers who become judges seem to go out of their way to show impartiality by favoring the prosecution. That was not what I had heard about Warfield. While I had never had a case before her, I had listened to the conversations of some of the other defense pros at the Redwood and Four Green Fields in the past, and the picture I got was of a judge who threw her pitches right down the middle. In addition, she was African American and that made her an underdog. Coming up, she had had to be better than the other lawyers. That demanded a mindset I liked. She knew full well the disadvantages I faced in trying to defend myself. My guess was that she would include that knowledge in her decisions.

'We're on the record in *California versus Haller* and we have a series of defense motions to consider,' the judge said. 'Mr. Haller, will you be offering argument or will it be your co-counsel, Ms. Aronson?'

31

I stood to reply.

'May it please the court,' I began, 'we would like to tag-team a little bit today. I would like to start with the motion to suppress.'

'Very well,' Warfield said. 'Proceed.'

Here is where it got tricky. I had filed what was technically a motion in limine to exclude evidence that had been unconstitutionally obtained. I was challenging the traffic stop that led to the discovery of the body of Sam Scales in the trunk of my car. If I won the motion, the case against me would probably be DOA. But it was a long shot to believe that a judge, even as impartial as I had heard Warfield to be, would throw such a wrench into the state's case. And that was what I was counting on, because I didn't want that to happen either. With any other client, I would want that ruling. But this was my own case. I did not want to win on a technicality. I needed to be exonerated. The trick here was to have a full-blown hearing on the constitutionality of the traffic stop that put me in jail. But I only wanted it in order to get Officer Milton on the stand so that I could draw out his story and lock it down under oath. Because I believed I was set up and that the setup had to have included Milton in some way, whether knowingly or not.

Carrying the printout of the motion, I walked to the lectern between the prosecution and defense tables. On the way, I casually checked the gallery and saw at least two people I recognized as journalists covering the hearing. They were the conduit I would use to get my defense out into the world.

I also saw my daughter, Hayley, in the back row. I assumed she was cutting class at USC Law but I couldn't be too upset. I had forbidden her to visit me in jail. I didn't want her ever to see me in jail scrubs and had gone so far as to leave her off my approved visitors list. So court was where she could see and support me, and that was not lost on me. I also knew that she was leaving the make-believe world of law school and getting a real education in the law by being here.

I threw her a nod and a smile, but seeing her now reminded me how ill-fitting my suit was. It looked borrowed and announced that I was a convict to all courtroom observers. I might as well have been wearing the scrubs. I tried to shake off these thoughts when I got to the lectern and I turned my attention to the judge.

'Your Honor,' I said. 'As the motion before the court states, the defense contends that I was set up and framed in this case. And that setup came into play with the illegal and unconstitutional stop by the police on the night I was arrested. I have re — '

'Set up by whom, Mr. Haller?' the judge asked.

I was thrown by the question. As valid as it might have been, it was unexpected from the judge, especially before I finished my argument.

'Judge, that is irrelevant at this hearing,' I said. 'This is about the traffic stop and whether it was constitutional. It — '

'But you are saying you were framed. Do you know who framed you?'

'Again, Your Honor, that is irrelevant. In

33

February it will be very relevant when we go to trial, but I don't see why I have to reveal my case to the prosecution while challenging the validity of the traffic stop.'

'Then continue.'

'Thank you, Your Honor, I will. The — '

'Is that a shot?'

'Excuse me?'

'What you just said, is that a shot at me, Mr. Haller?'

I shook my head, confused. I couldn't even remember what I had said.

'Uh, no, not a shot, Judge,' I said. 'I don't remember what I said but it was in no way intended to — '

'Very well, let's move on,' the judge said.

I remained confused. The judge appeared to be sensitive to anything she construed as a questioning of her skill or authority. But it was good to register this early in the process.

'Okay, well, I apologize if anything I said sounded disrespectful,' I said. 'As I was saying, I've filed a motion to suppress, challenging the probable cause to stop and the probable cause supporting a warrantless search of the trunk of the vehicle I was driving. An evidentiary hearing is required on the issues raised, with the attendance of the officer who stopped me and searched my vehicle. I would like to schedule a time for that hearing. But before we can do that, I have other matters that need to be addressed. My investigator has been trying for five weeks, Your Honor, to talk to the officer who stopped me — Officer Roy Milton — and has been unsuccessful despite numerous requests to him and the police department. I know we will be discussing our discovery motion later but, same thing, no cooperation from the D.A.'s Office in regard to the arrest. This is a continuation of the prosecution's effort since day one to prevent a fair trial from occurring.'

Berg stood up but Warfield held up a hand to prevent her from speaking.

'Let me stop you right there, Mr. Haller,' the judge said. 'That is a very serious accusation you just made. You'd better back that up right now.'

I composed my thoughts before proceeding.

'Your Honor,' I finally began. 'The prosecution clearly does not want me to question Officer Milton, and you can see this all the way back in the decision to go to a grand jury for an indictment and have him testify in secret instead of holding a preliminary hearing where I would be able to question him.'

In the California courts, a felony charge can advance to trial only after a preliminary hearing in which evidence of probable cause for the arrest is presented to a judge and the defendant is ordered to trial. An alternative to the preliminary hearing is for the prosecution to present the case to a grand jury and ask for an indictment on the charge. That was what Berg had done in this case. The difference between the two procedures is that a preliminary hearing is held in open court, where the defense is allowed to question any witness who testifies in front of the judge, while a grand jury operates in secret.

'The grand jury is a perfectly valid option for the prosecution to choose,' Warfield said.

'And it prevents me from questioning my accusers,' I said. 'Officer Milton was clearly wearing a body camera the night of my arrest, in keeping with LAPD regulations, and we have not been given that video. I also noted that there was a video camera in the police car, and we have not been given that video either.'

'Your Honor?' Dana Berg said. 'The state objects to defense's argument. He is turning a motion to suppress evidence in the case into a request *for* evidence. I'm confused.'

'So am I,' Warfield said. 'Mr. Haller, I allowed you to defend yourself because you are an experienced lawyer, but you are sounding more and more like an amateur. Please stay on point.'

'Well, then, I, too, am confused, Your Honor,' I said. 'I filed a legally sufficient motion to suppress the fruits of a warrantless search. Ms. Berg bears the burden of demonstrating the justification for the search. Yet I don't see Officer Milton in the courtroom. So unless the prosecution is about to announce a concession, Ms. Berg is not ready to defend against the motion. Yet Ms. Berg acts as though she is outraged and as though I'm supposed to merely argue and be done with it.

'Judge, the point is, I request an evidentiary hearing and an opportunity to prepare for that hearing after receiving the discovery I am entitled to. I can't properly and fully argue the motion to suppress, because the prosecution is violating the rules of discovery. I ask the court to table this for today, order the prosecution to fulfill its discovery obligations, and schedule a full evidentiary hearing on the motion at a time when witnesses, including Officer Milton, may appear.'

The judge looked at Berg.

'I know we have a discovery motion in Mr. Haller's stack,' Warfield said, 'but where are we on those items just mentioned? The video from the officer and the car. Those should have been turned over by now.'

'Judge,' Berg said. 'We had technical issues with the transfer of — '

'Your Honor,' I roared, 'they can't be pulling this *technical difficulty* excuse! I was arrested five weeks ago today. My freedom is on the line here, and for them to say technical issues have delayed my due process rights is patently unfair. They are trying to keep me from getting to Milton. Plain and simple. They did it when they went to a grand jury instead of a prelim and they are doing it again here. I have not waived my right to a speedy trial and the prosecution is doing anything and everything it can to push me toward a delay.'

'Ms. Berg?' Warfield said. 'Response to that?'

'Judge,' Berg said. 'If the defendant would stop interrupting me before I even finish a sentence, he would have heard that we *had* — that's past tense — technical difficulties, but they were cleared up and I have the videos from the officer's car and body cam to give to the defendant today. Additionally, the state objects to any suggestion that it is dragging its feet or

37

pressuring the defendant in any way to delay this case. We are ready to go, Your Honor. We are not interested in a delay.'

'Very well,' Warfield said. 'Turn the videos over to the defense and we will — '

'Your Honor, point of order,' I said.

'What is it, Mr. Haller?' the judge said. 'I'm losing my patience.'

'Counsel just referred to me as the defendant,' I said. 'Yes, I am the accused in this case, but when I am arguing before the court, I am *counsel* for the defense and I request that the court direct Ms. Berg to refer to me properly.'

'You are talking about semantics, Mr. Haller,' Warfield said. 'The court sees no need for such direction to the prosecution. You are the defendant. You are also the defense counsel. Same difference in this case.'

'Members of a jury might see the difference, Your Honor,' I said.

Warfield once again held her hand up like a traffic cop before Berg could voice an objection.

'No argument from the People is needed,' she said. 'The defense request is denied. We are going to continue this motion to Thursday morning. Ms. Berg, I will expect you to have Officer Milton here to be questioned about the traffic stop of Mr. Haller. I will be happy to sign a subpoena to that effect if needed. But rest assured that if he does not appear, I'll be inclined to grant the motion. Is that understood, Ms. Berg?'

'Yes, Your Honor,' Berg said.

'Very well, let's move on to the next motion,'

Warfield said. 'I have to leave the courthouse at eleven for an outside meeting. Let's press on.'

'Your Honor, my co-counsel, Jennifer Aronson, will discuss the motion to compel discovery.'

Jennifer got up and approached the lectern. I went back to the defense table and we lightly touched arms as we passed each other.

'Go get 'em,' I whispered.

6

The perks I received as a pro se inmate extended to the detention center, where I was afforded space and time for daily meetings with my legal team. I set these meetings Monday through Friday at 3 p.m. whether or not there were issues or strategy to discuss. I needed the connection to the outside, if only for the mental health maintenance.

The meetings were a hardship for Cisco and Jennifer because they and their belongings were searched coming in and going out, and the rule was that the team had to be in place in the attorney-client room before I was even pulled from the module where I was housed. Everything in the jail moved at an indifferent pace set by the deputies running the show. The last thing afforded an inmate, even a pro se, was punctuality. It was the same reason my wake-ups were at 4 a.m. for a hearing six hours later and only four blocks away. These delays and harassments meant that they usually had to present themselves at the jail's attorneys' entrance at 2 p.m. so that I might see them for an hour beginning at 3 p.m.

The meeting that followed the court hearing was more important than a mental health hour. Judge Warfield had signed an order allowing Jennifer Aronson to bring a disc player into the

40

jail for the legal-team conference so that I could view the videos that had finally been turned over by the prosecution.

I was late to the meeting because it had taken nearly four hours to bus me back from the courthouse to the jail. By the time they put me in the lawyer room, Jennifer and Cisco had been waiting nearly an hour.

'Sorry, guys,' I said as I was ushered in by a deputy. 'I don't control things around here.'

'Yeah, no kidding,' said Cisco.

It was the same setup as with the attorney room in the courthouse. They sat across from me. There was a camera that supposedly had no audio feed. The difference here was that I was allowed to use a pen when I was in the room to keep notes or handwrite motions to the court. I was not allowed to take a pen back to my cell because it could be used as a weapon, a pipe, or a source for tattoo ink. In fact, I was allowed a red-ink pen only, because it was considered an undesirable tattoo color should I somehow smuggle it back to my pod.

'Have you looked at the videos yet?' I asked.

'Only about ten times while we were waiting,' Cisco said.

'And?'

I looked at Jennifer with the question. She was the lawyer.

'Your recall of what was said and done was excellent,' she said.

'Good,' I said. 'Can you stand to watch it again? I want to take notes for the Q and A with Officer Milton.'

41

'Do you think that's the best way to go?' Jennifer asked.

I looked at her.

'You mean me asking the guy who arrested me the questions?'

'Yes. Might look vindictive to the jury.'

I nodded.

'It could. But there won't be a jury.'

'There will probably be reporters. It will get out to the pool.'

'Okay, I'm still going to write questions, and we'll make it a game-time decision. You should write up what you would ask and we'll compare tomorrow or Wednesday.'

I was not allowed to touch the computer. Cisco turned the screen toward me. He played the video from Milton's body cam first. The camera was attached to his uniform at chest height. The footage began with a view of the steering wheel of his car and quickly moved to him exiting the car and moving up the shoulder of the road toward a car I recognized as my Lincoln.

'Stop it,' I said. 'This is bullshit.'

Cisco hit the stop button.

'What is bullshit?' Jennifer asked.

'The video,' I said. 'Berg knows what I want and she's fucking with us even though she made the grand gesture of compliance in court today. I want you to go back to the judge tomorrow with a motion requesting the full video. I want to see where this guy was and what he was doing before I supposedly happened to cross his path. Tell the judge we want to go back half an hour minimum

42

on the body cam. And we want the full video before we go in for the hearing Thursday.'

'Got it.'

'Okay, go ahead with what they gave us.'

Cisco hit the play button again and I watched. There was a time code in the corner of the screen and I immediately started writing down times and notes to go with them. The traffic stop and what happened afterward was pretty much how I remembered it. I saw several places where I thought I could score points questioning Milton, and a few others where I thought I might be able to lead him into a lie trap.

Where I saw new stuff on the video was when Milton opened the trunk of the Lincoln and looked down to examine Sam Scales for any sign of life. I had been in the back seat of Milton's patrol car at that point, my view of the trunk limited and from a low angle. Now I was looking at Sam's body on its side, knees pulled up toward the chest and arms behind his back, secured with several wraps of duct tape. He was overweight and looked as though he was crammed into the trunk.

I could see bullet wounds in the chest and shoulder areas, and what looked like an entrance wound on the left temple and an exit through the right eye. This wasn't new to me. We had already gotten crime scene photos in the first batch of discovery from Berg but the video lent a visceral realness to the crime and the crime scene.

Sam Scales in life deserved no sympathy but in death he looked pitiful. Blood from his wounds had spread across the floor of the trunk and dripped out through a hole created by the bullet that had exited his eye.

'Oh, shit,' Milton could be heard saying.

And then he followed his exclamation with a low humming that sounded like a stifled laugh.

'Play that part again,' I said. 'After Milton says 'Oh, shit.''

Cisco replayed the sequence and I listened again to the sound Milton had made. It was almost like he was gloating. I thought it might be useful for a jury to hear.

'Okay, freeze it,' I said.

The image on the screen froze. I looked at Sam Scales. I had represented him for several years and through different charges and had somehow liked him even as I privately joined the public in their outrage at the scams he pulled. A weekly newspaper had once labeled him 'The Most Hated Man in America' and it wasn't hyperbole. He was a disaster con artist. Without showing a scintilla of guilt or conscience, he set up websites to take donations for survivors of earthquakes, tsunamis, mudslides, and school shootings. Wherever there was a tragedy that caught up the rest of the world in horror, Sam Scales was there with the quickly built website, the false testimonials, and the button that said DONATE NOW!

Though truly believing in the ideal that everybody charged with a crime deserves the best defense possible, even I could not take Sam Scales for very long. It wasn't that he had refused to pay an agreed-upon fee for the last

44

case I handled for him. The final straw came with the case I didn't handle — his arrest for soliciting donations to pay for coffins for children killed in a childcare-center massacre in Chicago. Donations poured into a website Scales had built, but as usual, the money went right into his pocket. He called me from jail after his arrest. When I heard the details of the scam, I told Sam our relationship was over. I got a request for his files from a lawyer with the Public Defender's Office, and that had been the last I had heard about Sam Scales — until he ended up dead in the trunk of my car.

'Anything unique on the car cam?' I asked.

'Not really,' Cisco said. 'Same stuff, different angle.'

'Okay, then let's skip that for now. We're running out of time. What else was in the latest discovery from Death Row Dana?'

My attempt to inject a little levity into the discussion fell on deaf ears. The stakes were too high for these two to make jokes. Cisco answered my question in the full-on professional tone that contradicted his look and demeanor.

'We also got video from the black hole,' he said. 'I haven't had time to go through it all but it will be my priority once I get out of here.'

The *black hole* was what regular downtown commuters called the massive underground parking garage located beneath the civic center. It spiraled down into the earth seven levels deep. I had parked there on the day of the Sam Scales murder, giving my driver the day off because I expected to be in trial all day. The prosecution's theory was that I had abducted Sam Scales the night before, put him in the trunk, and shot him, leaving his body there overnight and the next day while I was in court. To me that theory defied common sense and I was confident I could convince a jury of that. But there was still time between now and the trial for the prosecution to change theories and come up with something better.

Time of death had been set at approximately twenty-four hours before the body's discovery by Officer Milton. This also accounted for the leakage under the car that had supposedly alerted Milton and led to the grim discovery of the trunk's contents. The body was beginning to break down and decompose, and fluids were leaking through the bullet hole in the floor of the trunk.

'Any theory on why the prosecution wanted those angles in the garage?' I asked.

'I think they want to be able to say that nobody tampered with your car all day,' Jennifer said. 'And if the camera angles are clear enough to show the dripping of bodily fluids under the car, then they have that too.'

'We'll know more when I can get a look,' Cisco added.

A sudden chill went through me as I thought about how someone had murdered Sam Scales in my car, most likely while it was parked in my garage, and then how I had driven around with the body for a day.

'Okay, what else?' I asked.

'This is new,' Cisco said. 'We have a witness

46

report from your next-door neighbor, who heard the voices of two men arguing at your house the night before.'

I shook my head.

'Didn't happen,' I said. 'Who was it, Mrs. Shogren or that idiot Chasen who lives downhill from me?'

Cisco looked at the report.

'Millicent Shogren,' he read. 'Couldn't make out the words. Just angry voices.'

'Okay, you need to interview her — and don't scare her,' I said. 'Then you talk to Gary Chasen on the other side of the house. He's always picking up strays in West Hollywood and then they get into arguments. If Millie heard an argument, it was coming from Chasen's. Since it's a stepped neighborhood and she's at the top of the hill, she hears everything.'

'What about you?' Jennifer asked. 'What did you hear?'

'Nothing,' I said. 'I told you about that night. I went to bed early and didn't hear a thing.'

'And you went to bed alone,' Jennifer confirmed.

'Unfortunately,' I said. 'If I knew I was going to be tagged with a murder, maybe I would have picked up a stray myself.'

Again, stakes too high. Nobody cracked a smile. But the discussion of what Millie Shogren heard and from where she heard it prompted a question.

'Millie didn't tell them she heard the shots, right?' I asked.

'Doesn't say it here,' Cisco said.

'Then make sure you ask her,' I said. 'We might be able to turn their witness into ours.'

Cisco shook his head.

'What?' I asked.

'No go, boss,' he said. 'We also got the ballistics report in the discovery package, and it doesn't look good.'

Now I realized why they had been so somber, with me trying to cheer them up instead of the other way around. They had buried the lede and now I was about to hear it.

'Tell me,' I said.

'Okay, well, the one shot that went through the victim's head and that punctured the floor of the trunk was found on the floor of your garage,' Cisco said. 'Along with blood. The slug hit the concrete and flattened, so matching of the rifling was no good. But they did metal-alloy tests and matched it to the other bullets that were in the body. According to what we got in the package, the DNA is still out on the blood but we can assume that will be matched to Sam Scales as well.'

I nodded. This meant that the state could prove that Sam Scales was murdered in my home's garage at a time I had confirmed that I was at home. I thought about the legal conclusion I had offered Edgar Quesada the night before. I was now in the same sinking boat. Legally speaking, I was fucked.

'Okay,' I finally said. 'I need to sit with this and think. If you two have no more surprises, then you can get out of this place and I'll do some strategizing. This doesn't change anything.

It's still a setup. It's just a fucking good one and I need to close my eyes and figure things out.'

'You sure, boss?' Cisco asked.

'We can work it with you,' Jennifer offered.

'No, I need to be alone with this,' I said. 'You two go.'

Cisco got up and went to the door, where he knocked hard on the metal with the side of his meaty fist.

'Same time tomorrow?' Jennifer asked.

'Yes,' I said. 'Same time. At some point we have to stop trying to figure out their case and start building ours.'

The door opened and a deputy collected my colleagues for exit processing. The door was closed and I was left alone. I closed my eyes and waited for them to come get me next. I heard the banging of steel doors and the echoing shouts of caged men. Echoes and iron were the inescapable sounds of my life at Twin Towers.

7

Tuesday, December 3

In the morning I notified the dayroom deputy that I needed to go to the law library to do research on my case. It was ninety minutes before another deputy came to escort me there. The library was just a small room on *B* level where there were four desks and a wall of shelves containing two copies of the California Penal Code and several volumes containing case law and reported decisions of the state's supreme court and lower appellate courts. I had checked a handful of the books on my first visit to the library and found them seriously out of date and useless. Everything was on computer these days and updated immediately upon the change of a law or the setting of a precedent. Books on shelves were for show.

But that was not why I needed the library. I needed to write down my sleepless night's thoughts on the case and I was allowed to check out and use a pen at the library. Of course, Bishop had long ago offered to rent me a pencil stub that I could surreptitiously use in my cell, but I declined because I knew that before it got to me it would have come into the jail and been passed module to module in a series of visitor and inmate rectums. When not actually using the pencil, I would also be expected to hide it from the hacks in such a manner.

I chose the law library instead and set to work, writing on the back of the pages of a motion that had already been filed and dismissed.

What I put together was essentially a to-do list for my investigator and co-counsel. We'd had some setbacks in the early going — no cameras in the lot where I had parked the night of the Redwood party; no cameras that worked, at least, at my across-the-street neighbors'. My own camera on the front deck of my house did not pick up a view of the garage or street below. But I felt that there was still much that could be done to shift things and get momentum going in our favor. First and foremost, we needed to get full-data downloads off my cell phone and car, both of which were currently in police custody. We needed to file motions to examine these and retrieve the data. I knew that a cell phone was the best personal tracker on the planet. In my case, it would show that on the night in question, mine was in my home the entire night. Data off the Lincoln's navigation system would show that the car was parked in the garage all evening and night and through the estimated time of death of Sam Scales. This, of course, didn't mean I could not have slipped out in a borrowed car or with a co-conspirator to abduct Sam Scales, but then logic and common sense starts undercutting the state's case. If I had planned the crime so carefully, why did I then drive around for a day with the body in the trunk?

The car and phone data would be two powerful points to put in front of a jury and they

51

would also serve to corner the prosecution in regard to opportunity, a key building block of guilt. The prosecution carried the burden of proof and therefore would have to explain how I committed this crime in my own garage when it could not be proven that either my car or I had ever left the property.

Had I lured Sam Scales to the house and then killed him? Prove it.

Had I used a different vehicle to secretly leave the house to abduct Sam and then bring him back to place him in the trunk of my own car and then kill him? Prove it.

These were motions I would need Jennifer to research and write. For Cisco I had a different task. I had initially put him on a survey of my prior cases in search of someone who might want to do me harm: an unhappy client, a snitch, someone I had thrown under the bus at trial. Framing me for a murder was a bit extreme as far as revenge plots go, but I knew that I was being set up by somebody and had to leave no possibility unchecked. Now I would shift Cisco away from that angle of investigation and turn it over to Lorna Taylor. She knew my cases and my files better than anyone and would know what to look for. She could handle the paper chase while I put Cisco full-time on Sam Scales. I had not represented Scales in years and knew very little about him. I needed Cisco to background him and figure out how and why he was chosen as the victim in the plot to get to me. I needed to know everything Sam had his fingers in. I had no doubt that at the time of his murder, he was either scheming his next con or in the middle of it. Either way, I needed to know the details.

Part of vetting Sam Scales's life was to also vet him in death. We had gotten the autopsy report in the very first but thin wave of discovery from the prosecution. It confirmed the obvious, that Scales had died of multiple gunshot wounds. But we had received only the initial autopsy report put together after the examination of the body. It did not include a toxicology report. That usually took two to four weeks to complete following the autopsy. That meant the toxicology results should be in by now and the fact that they had not been included in the latest batch of discovery was suspicious to me. The prosecution might be hiding something and I needed to find out what it was. I also wanted to know what level of mental function Sam Scales was at when he was put into the trunk of my car, presumably alive, and shot.

This could be handled two ways. Jennifer could simply file a motion seeking the report as part of discovery, or Cisco could go down to the coroner's office and try to cadge a copy of it on his own. It was, after all, a public record.

On my to-do list, I assigned the job to Cisco for the simple reason that if he got a copy of the tox report, there was a good chance the prosecution would not be aware that we got it. This was the better strategy. Don't let the prosecution know what you have and where you are going with it — unless it is required.

That was it for the list. For now. But I didn't want to go back to the module. Too much noise, too many distractions. I liked the quiet of the library and decided that while I had a pen in hand, I might as well sketch out the brief on the motion to examine the cell phone and car. I wanted to hit Judge Warfield with it at Thursday's hearing so we could move expeditiously. If I outlined it for Jennifer now, she could easily have it ready to submit.

But just as I began, the deputy assigned to the library got a call on his radio and told me I had a visitor. This was a bit of a surprise because I could be visited only by people I had put on the visitation list I filled out at booking. The list was short and primarily contained the names of the people on my defense team. I was already scheduled to have a team meeting in the afternoon.

I guessed the visitor would be Lorna Taylor. Though she managed my practice, she was neither a lawyer nor a licensed investigator, and that precluded her from being able to join the afternoon sessions with Jennifer and Cisco. But when I was escorted into the visitor booth and looked through the glass, I was pleasantly surprised to see the woman whose name I had written last on my list as a long-shot hope.

Kendall Roberts was on the other side of the glass. I had not seen her in more than a year. Not since she had told me she was leaving me.

I slid onto the stool in front of the glass and picked up the phone out of its cradle. She picked up the phone on the other side.

'Kendall,' I said. 'What are you doing here?'

'Well,' she said, 'I heard about you getting

arrested and I had to come. Are you okay?'

'I'm fine. It's all bullshit and I'll beat this in court.'

'I believe you.'

When she had left me, she had also left the city.

'Uh, when did you get here?' I asked. 'Into town, I mean.'

'Last night. Late.'

'Where are you staying?'

'I'm at a hotel. By the airport.'

'Well, how long are you staying?'

'I don't know. I have no plans. When is the trial?'

'Not for, like, two months. But we're in court this Thursday.'

'Maybe I'll come by.'

She said it as if I had invited her to a happy hour or a party. I didn't care. She looked beautiful. I didn't think she had cut her hair since I had last seen her. It now framed her face as it fell to her shoulders. The dimples in her cheeks when she smiled were there like always. I felt my chest constrict. I had been with my two ex-wives for a total of seven years. I had spent almost as much time with Kendall. And it was good for every one of those years until we started drifting apart and she said she wanted to leave L.A.

I couldn't leave my daughter or my practice. I offered to make more time for travel but I wasn't going to leave. So, in the end, it was Kendall who left. She packed everything she owned one day while I was in trial and left me a note. I had put

Cisco on it just so I had the comfort of knowing where she was and that she was all right — or so I told myself. He tracked her to Hawaii but I left it at that. Never flew across the ocean to find her and beg her to return. I simply waited and hoped.

'Where did you come in from?' I asked.

'Honolulu,' she said. 'I've been living in Hawaii.'

'Did you open a studio?'

'No, but I teach classes. It's better for me not to be the owner. I just teach now. I get by.'

She'd had a yoga studio on Ventura Boulevard for several years but sold it when she started getting restless.

'How long are you here?'

'I told you. I don't know yet.'

'Well, if you want, you can stay at the house. I obviously won't be using it and you could water the plants — some of which I think are actually yours.'

'Uh, maybe. We'll see.'

'The extra key is still under the cactus on the front deck.'

'Thanks. Why are you here, Mickey? Don't you have bail or . . . ?'

'Right now they have me on five-million bail, which means I could get out with a ten percent bond. But you don't get that money back at the end, innocent or guilty, and that would be about everything I've got, including the equity in my house. I can't see giving all of that away for a couple months of freedom. I've got them on a speedy trial clock and I'm going to win this thing

56

and get out without having to pay a bail bondsman a dime.'

She nodded.

'Good,' she said. 'I believe you.'

The interviews were fifteen minutes only and then the phones would get cut off. I knew we were almost out of time. But seeing her made me think of all that was at stake.

'It is really nice of you to come see me,' I said. 'I'm sorry the visits are so short and you came so far.'

'You put me on your visitors list,' she said. 'I wasn't sure when they asked me and then they found my name. That was nice.'

'I don't know, I just thought maybe you'd come if you heard about it. I didn't know if it would make news in Hawaii but it was big news here.'

'You knew I was in Hawaii?'

Ugh. I had slipped up.

'Uh, sort of,' I said. 'When you left like you did, I just wanted to make sure you were okay, you know? I had Cisco check things out and he told me you flew to Hawaii. I didn't know where or anything like that, or if it was permanent. Just that you had gone.'

I watched her think through my answer.

'Okay,' she said, accepting it.

'How is it there?' I asked, trying to move past my gaffe. 'You like it?'

'It's been okay. Isolating. I'm thinking of coming back.'

'Well, I don't know what I can do from here, but if there's anything you need, let me know.'

'Okay, thanks. I guess I should be going. They said I only get fifteen minutes.'

'Yeah, but they just shut down the phones when your time is up. You think you'll come back to visit? I'm here every day if I'm not in court.'

I smiled like I was some sort of comedian hawking his stand-up act. Before she could answer, there was a loud electronic buzz on the phone and the line went dead. I saw her speak but didn't hear it. She looked at the phone and then at me and slowly put it back in its cradle. The visit was over.

I nodded at her and smiled awkwardly. She made a slight wave and then got up from her stool. I did the same and started walking down the line of visitor booths, all of them open behind the prisoner's stool. I looked through every window as I passed and caught a few glimpses of her moving parallel to me on the other side.

Then she was gone.

The hack asked me whether I was going back to the law library and I told him I wanted to go back to the module.

While I was being led back, I worked over my final view of Kendall on the phone. I had watched her lips as she spoke into the dead phone. I came to realize that she had said, 'I don't know.'

8

Officer Roy Milton was in uniform and sitting in the first row of the gallery behind the prosecution table when I was led into the courtroom. I recognized him easily from the night of my arrest. Following Sheriff's Department protocol I was manacled by a waist chain, with my hands cuffed at my sides. I was led to the defense table, where the escort deputy unchained me, and Jennifer, who was standing and waiting, helped me put on my suit jacket. Lorna had somehow gotten two-day tailoring done and the suit fit me perfectly. I turned toward the gallery as I shot the cuffs and addressed Milton.

'Officer Milton, how are you today?' I asked.

'Don't answer that,' Dana Berg said from the prosecution table.

I looked at her and she stared right back at me.

'Mind your own business, Haller,' she said.

I spread my hands in a gesture of surprise.

'Just being cordial,' I said.

'Be cordial with someone on your side,' Berg said.

'All right,' I said. 'Whatever.'

I did a 180 sweep of the gallery and saw my daughter in her usual spot. I smiled and nodded and she gave both back to me. I didn't see

59

Kendall Roberts anywhere but I wasn't expecting to. I had come to view her visit the other day as her fulfilling some sort of duty to me. But that was all there would be.

I finally pulled out my chair at the defense table and sat down next to Jennifer.

'You look good,' she said. 'Lorna did a good job with that suit.'

We had spoken earlier in the holding cell along with Cisco. But Cisco was gone now, with a full plate of investigative tasks to carry out.

I heard whispers directly behind me and turned to see that two of the reporters who had been covering the case from the beginning were now in their usual spots. Both were women, one from the *Los Angeles Times*, the other from the *Daily News*, competitors who liked to sit together and chat while waiting for court to start. I had known Audrey Finnel from the *Times* for years, as she had covered a few of my cases. Addie Gamble was new on the criminal courts beat for the *News* and I knew her by her byline only.

Soon Judge Warfield appeared in the doorway behind the clerk's corral and court was called to order. Before getting to the motion to suppress, I told the judge that I had a new motion to file with the court on an emergency basis because the prosecution was still not playing fair when it came to the rules of discovery.

'What is it this time, Mr. Haller?' the judge asked.

Her voice took on a tone of exasperation, which I found disconcerting, since the hearing

60

had just started. As I walked to the lectern, Jennifer carried copies of the new motion to the prosecution table and the court clerk, who then handed the documents to the judge.

'Your Honor, the defense just wants what it is entitled to,' I said. 'You have a discovery motion in front of you for data from my own car and cell phone, which the prosecution has not provided because it knows it is exculpatory and will show that I was in my house and that my car was in my garage when I supposedly went out and abducted Mr. Scales and then took him back to my house to murder him.'

Dana Berg immediately stood up and objected. She didn't even have to state her grounds for the objection. The judge was on it right away.

'Mr. Haller,' she boomed. 'Making your case to the media instead of the court is unacceptable and . . . dangerous. Do you understand me?'

'I do, Judge, and I apologize,' I said. 'Defending myself has taken me to some emotional depths I don't usually deal with.'

'That is no excuse. Consider that your one and only warning.'

'Thank you, Your Honor.'

But as I spoke my apology, I couldn't help wondering what the judge would do to me with a contempt citation. Put me in jail? I was already there. Fine me? Good luck collecting with me earning zero income while I fought a murder rap.

'Continue,' the judge instructed. 'Carefully.'

'Judge, the motion is clear,' I said. 'The state

61

obviously has this information and we have not received it. It appears that it is the practice of the District Attorney's Office to hold discovery and not share it unless it is specifically asked for by the defense, and that is not the way it works. This is vital information about my own property that I need in order to defend myself, and I need it right now, Your Honor. Not when the prosecution feels like it.'

The judge looked at Berg for a response and the prosecutor took the lectern, lowering the stem microphone to her level.

'Your Honor, Mr. Haller's assumptions are completely wrong,' she said. 'The information he seeks was acquired by the LAPD following the issuance of a search warrant, which took time to write and execute. The material that came from that search warrant was received by my office just yesterday and has not yet been reviewed by me or anyone on my team. I believe the rules of discovery allow me to at least review evidence before passing it to the defense.'

'When will the defense have this material?' Warfield asked.

'I would think by the end of the day tomorrow,' Berg said.

'Your Honor?' I said.

'Hold your horses, Mr. Haller,' Warfield said. 'Ms. Berg, if you don't have time to review the material, then get someone else to review it or turn it over blind. I want you to give it to the defense by the end of the day. That's today I'm talking about. And that's the workday. Not midnight.'

'Yes, Your Honor,' a chastened Berg said.

'Your Honor, I would still like to be heard,' I said.

'Mr. Haller, I just got you what you asked for,' Warfield said impatiently. 'What else is there to say?'

I went to the lectern as Berg stepped away. I glanced back into the gallery and saw Kendall sitting next to my daughter. That gave me confidence. I raised the microphone stem back up.

'Judge,' I began, 'the defense is troubled by this absurd idea that discovery does not need to be completed until a review of the discoverable evidence occurs. *Review* is an amorphous word, Your Honor. What is a review? How long is a review? Two days? Two weeks? Two months? I would ask the court to set out clear guidelines about this. As the court knows, I have not and will not waive my right to a speedy trial, and therefore any delay in the transfer of discovery puts the defense on an unfair footing.'

'Your Honor?' Berg said. 'May I be heard?'

'No, Ms. Berg, there is no need for you to be heard,' Warfield said. 'Let me make clear the rules of discovery in this courtroom. Discovery is a two-way street. What comes in must go out. Forthwith. No delay, no undue review. What the state gets, the defense gets. Conversely, what the defense gets, the state gets. Without delay. The penalty for violation is the disallowance of the material at the source of the complaint. Remember that. Now, can we take up the cause that this hearing was scheduled for? The motion in limine filed by Mr. Haller to essentially disallow the body in this case. Ms. Berg, you bear the burden of justifying a warrantless search and seizure. Do you have a witness to call in this matter?'

'Yes, Your Honor,' Berg said. 'The People call Officer Roy Milton.'

Milton stood in the gallery and walked through the gate and to the witness stand. He raised his hand and was sworn in. After he was seated and the preliminaries of identity were completed, Berg elicited Milton's version of my arrest.

'You are assigned to Metro Division, correct, Officer Milton?'

'Yes.'

'What is Metro's jurisdiction?'

'Well, we have the whole city, I guess you could say.'

'But on the night in question, you were working downtown on Second Street, weren't you?'

'That's correct.'

'What was your assignment that night, Officer Milton?'

'I was on an SPU assignment and was posted near — '

'Let me stop you right there. What is SPU?'

'Special Problems Unit.'

'And what was the special problem that you were addressing that night?'

'We were encountering spikes in crimes in the civic center. Vandalism mostly. We had spotters in the center and I was in a support car posted just outside the zone. I was at Second and Broadway, with eyelines down both streets.'

'Eyelines for what, Officer Milton?'

'Everything, anything. I saw the defendant pull out of the parking lot on Broadway.'

'You did, didn't you? Let's talk about that. You were stationary, correct?'

'Yes, I was parked at the curb at the southeast corner on Second. I had a view up to the tunnel in front of me and down Broadway to my left. That was where I saw the vehicle leaving the pay lot.'

'Were you assigned that position, or did you choose it?'

'I was assigned that general location — the top corner of the box we were putting over the civic center.'

'But didn't your position put you in a blind? The L.A. Times Building would block any view of the civic center, would it not?'

'Like I said, we had spotters inside — observers on the ground in the civic center. I was containment. I was placed in a position where I could react to anyone leaving the civic center on Broadway. Or I could come into the box if needed.'

Step-by-step she walked him through the pull-over and the discussion with me at the rear of my car. He described my reticence to open the trunk to see if the license plate was there, then his spotting the substance dripping from the car.

'I thought it was blood,' Milton said. 'At that point I believed there were exigent circumstances and that I needed to open the trunk to see if

65

someone was hurt inside.'

'Thank you, Officer Milton,' Berg said. 'I have nothing further.'

The witness was turned over to me. My goal was to build a record I hoped would be useful at trial. Berg had not bothered to show any video during her questioning, because all she needed to do was establish exigent circumstances.

But we had received the extended versions of both his body-cam and the car-cam video from the prosecution the day before and had studied them during our three o'clock at Twin Towers. Jennifer had the body-cam tape cued up on her laptop and ready to go now if needed.

As I walked to the lectern, I took the rubber band off a rolled printout of an aerial shot of the downtown civic center. I asked permission of the judge to approach the witness, then unrolled the photo in front of him.

'Officer Milton, I see you have a pen in your pocket,' I said. 'Would you mark this photograph with the position you had taken on the night in question?'

Milton did as I requested, and I asked him to add his initials. I then took the photo back, rolled and banded it, and asked the judge to enter it as defense exhibit A. Milton, Berg, and the judge all looked a bit bewildered by what I had just done, but that was okay. I wanted Berg to be puzzled about what the defense was up to.

I returned to the lectern and asked the court's permission to play both videos turned over to me in discovery. The judge gave her approval and I used Milton to authenticate and introduce the

66

videos. I played them back-to-back without stopping to ask any questions. When they were finished, I asked only two.

'Officer Milton, do you believe those videos were an accurate accounting of your actions during the traffic stop?' I asked.

'Yes, it's all there on tape,' Milton said.

'You see no indication that the tapes have been altered or edited in any way?'

'No, it's all there.'

I asked the judge to accept the videos as defense exhibits B and C and Warfield complied.

I moved on, once again leaving the prosecutor and judge puzzled by the record I was building.

'Officer Milton, at what point did you decide to initiate a traffic stop on my car?'

'When you made the turn, I noticed there was no license plate on the vehicle. It's a common capering move, so I followed and initiated the traffic stop when we were in the Second Street tunnel.'

''Capering,' Officer Milton?'

'Sometimes when people are engaged in committing crimes, they take the plates off their car so witnesses can't get the plate number.'

'I see. But it appeared from the video we just watched that the car in question still had a front plate, did it not?'

'It did.'

'Doesn't that contradict your capering theory?'

'Not really. Getaway cars are usually seen driving away. It's the rear plate that would be important to remove.'

'Okay. Did you see me walk down the street

from the Redwood and turn right onto Broadway?'

'Yes, I did.'

'Was I doing anything suspicious?'

'Not that I recall.'

'Did you think I was drunk?'

'No.'

'And you saw me walk into the parking lot?'

'I did.'

'Was that suspicious to you?'

'Not really. You were dressed in a suit and I thought you probably had parked a car in the lot.'

'Were you aware that the Redwood is a bar frequented by defense lawyers?'

'I was not.'

'Who was it who told you to pull me over after I drove out of the lot?'

'Uh, no one. I saw the missing plate when you made the turn from Broadway onto Second, and I left my position and initiated the stop.'

'By that, you mean you followed me into the tunnel and then turned your lights on, yes?'

'Yes.'

'Did you have advance knowledge that I would be leaving that lot without a rear plate on my car?'

'No.'

'You weren't there in that spot specifically to pull me over?'

'No, I was not.'

Berg stood and objected, saying I was badgering Milton by asking him the same question in different ways. The judge agreed and told me to move on.

I looked down at the lectern at the notes I had written in red ink.

'No further questions, Your Honor,' I said.

The judge looked slightly confused by my examination and its abrupt end.

'Are you sure, Mr. Haller?'

'Yes, Your Honor.'

'Very well. Does the state have recross?'

Berg also seemed confused by my questioning of Milton. Thinking I had done no damage, she told the judge she had no further questions. The judge shifted her focus back to me.

'Do you have another witness, Mr. Haller?'

'No, Your Honor.'

'Very well. Arguments?'

'Judge, my argument is submitted.'

'Nothing further? You don't want to at least connect the dots for us after your examination of the witness?'

'Submitted, Your Honor.'

'Does the state wish to argue?'

Berg stood at her table and raised her hands as if to ask what there was to argue, then said she would go with her written response to my motion.

'Then the court is prepared to rule,' Warfield said. 'The motion is denied and this court is in recess.'

The judge had spoken matter-of-factly. And I could hear whispers and sense the letdown of those in the courtroom. It was as though there was a collective *What?* from those in the gallery.

But I was pleased. I didn't want to win the

motion. I wanted to cut down the prosecution's tree at trial and win the case. And I had just made the first swing of the ax.

9

We came into the three o'clock meeting with good spirits, despite the surroundings. Not only had we accomplished what we wanted to get done and on the record in the court hearing that morning, but both Jennifer and Cisco said they had good news to share. I told Jennifer to go first.

'Okay, you remember Andre La Cosse?' she asked.

'Of course I do,' I said. 'My finest hour.'

It was true. *The State of California versus Andre La Cosse* might as well be etched on my tombstone at the end of my days. It was the case I was proudest of. An innocent man with the entire weight of the justice system against him charged with murder, and I walked him. And it wasn't just an NG. It was the rarest of all birds in the justice system. It was the Big I. My work in trial had proved him innocent. So much so that the state paid damages for their malfeasance in charging him in the first place.

'What about him?' I asked.

'Well, he saw something about your case online and he wants to help,' Jennifer said.

'Help how?'

'Mickey, don't you get it? You got him a seven-figure settlement for wrongful prosecution. He wants to return the favor. He called up Lorna and said he could go up to two hundred on bail.'

71

I was a bit stunned. Andre had barely survived the case while being held in this same place — Twin Towers — while we were in trial, and I had negotiated a settlement for him in compensation. I had taken a third, but that was seven years ago and it was long gone. He had apparently done better with his money and was now willing to chip off some of what he had in order to spring me.

'He knows he doesn't get it back, right?' I said. 'Two hundred out the window. That's a big chunk of the money I got him.'

'He knows,' Jennifer said. 'And he hasn't just been sitting on that money. He invested it. Lorna said he's into the whole crypto-currency thing and he says the settlement was only seed money. It has grown. A lot. He's offering the two hundred, no strings attached. I want to go in and set up a bail hearing. We get Warfield to knock it down to two and a half or three million — where it should be — and you walk out of here.'

I nodded. Andre's money could go for a 10 percent bond against the set bail. But there was a problem.

'That's very generous of Andre, but I don't think that'll get it done,' I said. 'Berg's not going to roll over and play dead on a sixty percent reduction on bail. I don't think Warfield will either. If Andre really wants to kick in, maybe we talk about using his money for expert witnesses, exhibits, and everybody on staff getting paid for the overtime they're putting in.'

'No, boss,' Cisco said.

'We thought about that,' Jennifer said. 'And

72

there's somebody else who wants to help. Another donor.'

'Who?' I said.

'Harry Bosch,' she said.

'No way,' I said. 'He's a retired cop, for god's sake. He can't — '

'Mickey, you got him a million-dollar settlement from the city last year and didn't even take a cut. He wants — '

'I didn't take a cut, because he might need that money. He's going to max out his insurance and then he'll need it. Besides, I set up a trust and he put it in there.'

'Look, Mickey, he can tap it or borrow against it,' Jennifer insisted. 'The point is, you have to get out of here. Not only is it dangerous in this place, but you're losing weight, you don't look good, and your health is at risk. Remember what Legal Siegel used to say? 'Look like a winner and you'll become a winner'? You don't look like a winner, Mickey. You can tailor your suits but you still look pale and sick. You need to get out of here and get yourself in shape for trial.'

'He actually said, 'Act like a winner and you'll be a winner.''

'Doesn't matter. Same thing. This is your chance. These people came to us. We didn't go to them. In fact, Andre said he came because he saw you on TV from that last hearing and it reminded him of himself when he was in here.'

I nodded. I knew she was right. But I hated taking the money, especially from Bosch, my half brother, who I knew needed it for other things.

'Not only that, but you need to get home for

73

Christmas and see your daughter,' Jennifer said. 'This no-visitation thing is hurting her as much as it must hurt you.'

She nailed me with her final argument. I missed my daughter, missed her voice.

'Okay, I hear you,' I said.

'Good,' Jennifer said.

'I think we might be able to knock the bail down to three million,' I said. 'But that's probably it.'

'We can cover three million,' Jennifer said.

'Okay, set it up,' I said. 'Don't give any hint that we can go up to three million. I want Berg to think we're coming in hat in hand. She'll think dropping bail a couple million will still probably keep me in stir. We ask for one million and she compromises at two or three.'

'Right,' Jennifer said.

'And one last thing,' I said. 'Are you sure Harry and Andre came in voluntarily with this? It wasn't the other way around?'

Jennifer shrugged and looked at Cisco.

'Scout's honor, boss,' he said. 'That's straight up from Lorna.'

I looked for any sign of deception and didn't see any. But I could tell something was bothering Jennifer.

'Jennifer, what?' I asked.

'On bail, what if the judge makes a monitor part of the deal?' she asked. 'An ankle bracelet. Can you live with that?'

I thought about it for a moment. It would be the ultimate invasion, having the state monitoring my every move while I was building my defense. But I recalled what Jennifer had said about spending time with my daughter.

'Don't offer it,' I finally said. 'But if it comes up as part of the deal, I'll accept it.'

'Good,' Jennifer said. 'I'll file the motion as soon as we get out of here. If we're lucky, we'll get before the judge tomorrow and you'll be home for the weekend.'

'Sounds like a plan,' I said.

'There's one other thing from Harry Bosch,' Jennifer said.

'What's that?'

'He said he also wants to help with the defense, if we want him.'

This was cause for hesitation. There had always been a low-level friction between Cisco and Bosch that stemmed from their origins as investigators. Bosch was retired now, but from law enforcement. Cisco was from the defense side from the start. Bringing Bosch on could be extremely useful because of his experience and connections. It could also throw off the chemistry of my team. I didn't have to ponder the offer long before Cisco ended my uncertainty.

'We need him,' Cisco said.

'You sure?' I asked.

'Bring him on,' he said.

I knew what he was doing. He was casting all friction or animosity aside for me. If it had been any other case, he would have said we didn't need Bosch, and that was probably true. But with my life and freedom on the line, Cisco wanted any possible advantage we could get.

I nodded my thanks to him and looked at Jennifer.

'Get me out of here first,' I said. 'Then we meet with Bosch. Make sure he gets everything from the discovery file, especially all the crime scene photos. He's good with that stuff.'

'I'm on it,' she said. 'Is he on your visitors list here?'

'No, but I can add him,' I said. 'He may have already tried to see me.'

I shifted my focus back to Cisco.

'Okay, Big Man, what've you got?' I asked.

'I got the full autopsy from a guy at the coroner's,' he said. 'You're going to like the tox report.'

'Tell me.'

'Sam Scales had flunitrazepam in his blood. That's what's on the report. You look that up on Google and you get Rohypnol.'

'The date-rape drug,' Jennifer said.

'Okay,' I said. 'How much was in his blood?'

'Enough to knock him out,' Cisco said. 'He wasn't conscious when they shot him.'

I liked that Cisco had said *they*. It told me he was all in on the theory that I had been framed and most likely by more than one person.

'So what does this tell us in terms of when he got dosed?' I asked.

'Not sure yet,' Cisco said.

'Jennifer, we're going to need an expert for trial,' I said. 'A good one. Can you work on that?'

'On it,' she said.

I thought about things for a few moments before continuing.

'I'm not sure it really helps us,' I said. 'The state's position will be that I dosed him, then abducted him and took him to the house. We still need to get into Sam Scales and where he was and what he was doing.'

'I'm on it,' Cisco said.

'Good,' I said. 'Let's talk about the garage next. Did Lorna get Wesley out to look at it?'

Wesley Brower was the installer I'd used to replace the emergency release on my garage door. This happened seven months earlier during fire season when a rolling brownout left my house without power. I could not open the garage door and was due in court on a sentencing. I had long misplaced the key to the emergency release. I called out Brower to get the garage open and he found that the keyed handle of the release pull was seized with rust. He still managed to get the door open, and I got to court — late. The next day Brower came back and installed a new emergency release system.

If my defense was going to claim that I was framed, then it would be my job at trial to explain to the jury exactly how that frame came together. And that would start with how the true killer or killers got into my garage to put Sam Scales in the trunk of my car and then shoot him. I had told my team to have Wesley Brower check the emergency release to see if it had been recently engaged or tampered with.

Jennifer answered my question by raising a hand and wagging it side to side to say she had good and bad news.

'Lorna got Brower out to the garage and he checked the emergency release,' she said. 'He determined that it had been pulled, but he can't say when. You put the new one in back in July, so all he can say is that it has been pulled since then.'

'How does he know?' I asked.

'Whoever pulled it put it back together after they got the door open. But they didn't do it the way he left it back in July. So he knows it was pulled — he just won't be able to testify when. It's a wash, Mickey.'

'Damn.'

'I know, but it was a long shot.'

The good feelings that we had started the meeting with were dissipating.

'Okay, where are we on the suspects list?' I asked.

'Lorna is still working on it,' Jennifer said. 'You've had a ton of cases in the past ten years. There's still a lot to go through. I told her I'd work with her this weekend, and with any luck you'll be out of this place and able to be there too.'

I nodded.

'Speaking of which, you should probably go if you're going to file something today,' I said.

'I was thinking the same thing,' Jennifer said. 'Anything else?'

I leaned across the table to talk in a low voice to Jennifer — in case the overhead camera had grown ears.

'I'm going to call you when I can get to a phone in the module,' I said. 'I want to talk about Baja and I want you to record it. Can you do that?'

'Not a problem. I've got an app.'

'Good. Then we'll talk later.'

10

It was almost an hour before they moved me back to the module. I found Bishop at one of the tables playing Mexican dominoes with a custody named Filbin. He gave me his customary greeting.

'Counselor,' he said.

'Bishop, I thought you had court today,' I said.

'Thought I did too until my lawyer put it over. Motherfucker mus' think I'm stayin' at the Ritz over here.'

I sat down, put my documents on the table, and looked around. A lot of guys were out of their cells and moving around the dayroom. The module had two phones mounted on the wall below the mirrored windows of the hack tower. You could either make a collect call on them or use a phone card purchased from the jail canteen. At the moment, both phones were being used and each one had a line of three men waiting. The calls cut off after fifteen minutes. That meant if I got in line now I would get a phone in roughly an hour.

I didn't see Quesada on my survey of the dayroom. Then I saw that the door to his cell was closed. Every man in the module was on keep-away status, but being locked up in a cell in a keep-away module was reserved for those inmates who were either in imminent danger or highly valuable to a prosecution.

'Quesada's on lockdown?' I said.

'Happened this morning,' Bishop said.

'Snitch,' Filbin said.

I almost smiled. Calling someone in the keep-away module a snitch was a bit like the pot calling the kettle black. The most common reason for segregating people in the module in the first place was that they were informants. For all I knew, Filbin was one. I didn't make it a practice of asking fellow inmates what they were being held for or why they were on keep-away status. I had no idea why Bishop was in the module and would never ask him. Sticking your nose in other people's business could have consequences in a place like Twin Towers.

I watched them play until Bishop won the game and Filbin got up and walked off toward the stairs leading to the second tier of cells.

'You want to play, Counselor?' Bishop asked. 'A dime a point?'

'No, thanks,' I said. 'I don't gamble.'

'Now, that's some bullshit right there. You gambling with your own life right now bein' in here with us criminals.'

'Speaking of that, I might be getting out soon.'

'Yeah? You sure you want to leave this wonderful place?'

'I need to. Gotta prep my case, and in here it's not going to happen. Anyway, I'm only telling you because I want you to know that I'll make good on our deal. I'll pay till the end of my trial.'

'That's mighty white of you.'

'I mean it. You've made me feel safe, Bishop, and I appreciate it. When you get out, you should look me up. I might have something for you. Something legitimate.'

'Like what?'

'Like driving. You have a driver's license?'

'I could get one.'

'A real one?'

'As real as they get, Counselor. Driving what? Who?'

'Me. I work out of my car and I need a driver. It's a Lincoln.'

My previous driver had been working off her son's debt for my representation and was a week away from completing that when I was arrested. If I got out, I would need a new driver, and I wasn't blind to what Bishop could bring in terms of intimidation and security in addition to the driving chores.

I checked the phone bank again. The line was down to two each. I knew I should get over there before it built up to three again. I leaned in close to Bishop and violated my own rule about getting into other people's business.

'Bishop, say you were going to break into a garage at somebody's house. How would you do it?'

'Whose house?'

'It's a hypothetical. Any house. How would you do it?'

'What makes you think I would break into a house?'

'I don't think that. It's a hypothetical and I'm picking your brain. And it's breaking into a garage, not the house.'

'Any windows or a side door?'

82

'No, just a double-wide garage door.'

'It got one of those pop-out handles in case of emergency?'

'Yeah, but you need a key.'

'No, you don't. Those handles you can pop with a flathead.'

'A screwdriver? You sure?'

'I'm sure. I knew a guy, that was his specialty. He'd drive around and hit g'rages all day long. Got cars, tools, lawn mowers . . . all kinds of good shit to sell.'

I nodded and checked the phone bank. One phone had only one man waiting. I stood up.

'I have to hit the phone line, Bishop,' I said. 'Thanks for the intel.'

'I got you, man.'

I walked over to the phones and got behind the single just as the man on the phone in front of him hung up angrily and said, 'Fuck you, bitch!'

He walked away and the next man stepped up to the phone. My wait ended up being less than two minutes, as the man in front of me called collect and the call either went unanswered or the recipient declined to accept the charges. He walked away and I stepped up and put my paperwork down on top of the phone box. I entered Jennifer's cell phone number for a collect call. While I waited for the electronic voice to tell her that she was receiving a collect call from the county jail, I studied the sign on the wall: ALL CALLS MONITORED.

Jennifer accepted.

'Mickey,' she said.

'Jennifer,' I said. 'Hold on while I make this announcement. This is Michael Haller, pro se defendant, talking to his co-counsel, Jennifer Aronson, under privilege. This call should not be monitored.'

I waited a beat, presumably for the monitor to move on to another inmate's call.

'Okay,' I said. 'Just checking in. Did you file?'

'I did. Notifications went out. Hopefully we get a hearing tomorrow.'

'Did you and Cisco get that Baja thing set up?'

'Uh, yes . . . we did.'

'The whole package? Travel, everything?'

'Yep, everything.'

'Good. And the money is ready?'

'Yes.'

'What about the guy, you trust him?'

There was a pause. I assumed Jennifer was realizing what I was doing with the call.

'Absolutely,' she finally said. 'He has it down to a science.'

'Good,' I said. 'I'll only get one shot at this.'

'What if they make you wear a bracelet?'

Jennifer had caught on fast. Her mention of the bracelet was pure gold.

'Won't be a problem,' I said. 'We can use that guy Cisco used on that other thing that time. He'll know what to do.'

'Right,' Jennifer said. 'I forgot about him.'

There was another pause while I thought about how to wrap it up.

'So, you'll have to come down, go fishing with me,' I said.

'I'll have to brush up on my Spanish,' she said.

84

'Anything else to talk about?'

'Not really.'

'Okay, then. I guess all I can do is wait on the hearing. See you then.'

I hung up the phone and stepped aside for the man who had lined up behind me. Bishop was no longer at the table where we had talked. I went up the stairs to the second tier and was halfway to my cell when I remembered my paperwork. When I got back to the phone bank, the documents were gone.

I tapped the guy who was on the phone on the shoulder. He turned to me.

'My paperwork,' I said. 'Where is it?'

'What?' he said. 'I don't have your fucking paperwork.'

He started to turn back toward the phone box.

'Who took it?' I said.

I hit him on the back again and he turned angrily toward me.

'I don't know who took it, motherfucker. Get the fuck away from me.'

I turned and scanned the dayroom. There were several inmates moving about the room or sitting in front of an overhead television screen. I looked at their hands or what was beneath their chairs. I didn't see my paperwork anywhere.

My eyes went to the cells, the bottom tier first and then the second level. I saw no one and nothing suspicious.

I moved to a spot below the mirrored glass of the hack tower. I waved my hands over my head to get attention. Eventually a voice came from the speaker below the glass.

'What is it?'

'Somebody took my legal papers.'

'Who?'

'I don't know. I left them on the phone box and then two minutes later they were gone.'

'You're supposed to take care of your property.'

'I know that but somebody took it. I'm pro se and I need the documents. You have to search the module.'

'First of all, you don't tell me what we have to do. And second, that's not going to happen.'

'I'm going to report this to the judge. She's not going to be happy.'

'You can't see me but I'm shaking.'

'Look, I need to find those documents. They're important to my case.'

'Then I guess you should have taken better care of them.'

I just stared up at the mirror for a long moment before turning away and heading to my cell. I knew at that moment that it didn't matter how much money it cost, I needed to get out of this place.

11

Dana Berg claimed she needed time to prepare her opposition to Jennifer Aronson's motion to reduce bail. That meant I got to spend another weekend and then some in my cell at Twin Towers. I waited for Tuesday like a man in shark-infested waters waiting for the rope that will finally pull him to safety.

I ate what I hoped would be my last jail baloney sandwich and apple on the bus to the CCB, then began my slow ascent through the courthouse's vertical jail to the holding cell on the ninth floor beside Judge Warfield's courtroom. I was delivered there shortly before my 10 a.m. hearing was due to begin, so there was no chance to convene ahead of time with Jennifer. My suit was brought in and I changed. Already tailored once, it was loose in the waist again, and it was mostly by this that I measured what incarceration had done to me. I was clipping on my tie when the courtroom deputy told me it was time for court.

The gallery was more crowded than usual. The reporters were in the same row they always took, and I also saw my daughter and Kendall Roberts as well as my would-be benefactors, Harry Bosch and Andre La Cosse — two men who could not have been more different but

87

were seated there together and ready to shell out their savings for me. Next to them sat Fernando Valenzuela, the bail bondsman ready to make the transaction if the judge could be swayed in my favor. I had worked with Valenzuela on and off for two decades and had at times sworn I would never use him again, just as he had sworn on occasion never to bail out another of my clients. But here he was, apparently willing to let past grievances go and accept the risks of posting a bond for me.

I smiled at my daughter, winked at Kendall. Just as I was about to turn to the defense table, I saw the courtroom door open and Maggie McPherson enter. She scanned the gallery, saw our daughter, and slid in next to her. Hayley was now sitting between Maggie and Kendall, who had never met. She was making introductions when I took my seat next to Jennifer at the defense table.

'Did you ask Maggie McFierce to be here?' I whispered.

'Yes, I did,' Jennifer said.

'Why would you do that?'

'Because she's a prosecutor and if she says you won't flee, then that will carry a lot of weight with the judge.'

'Also a lot of weight with her bosses. You shouldn't have put that kind of pressure on — '

'Mickey, my job today is to get you out of jail. I'll use every tool I can get my hands on — and you would too.'

Before I could respond, Deputy Chan called the courtroom to order. A second later Judge

Warfield stepped through the door behind the clerk's station and moved quickly up the steps to the bench.

'Back on the record in *California versus Haller*,' she began. 'We have a motion to reduce bail. Who will be arguing for the defense?'

'I will,' Jennifer said, standing at the defense table.

'Very well, Ms. Aronson,' Warfield said. 'I have the motion before me. Do you have further argument before we hear from the People?'

Jennifer moved to the lectern with a legal pad and a stack of documents to distribute.

'Yes, Your Honor,' she said. 'In addition to the cases mentioned in the moving papers, I have additional case law here that supports the motion for a lower bail. This is not charged as a case with extenuating or aggravating circumstances and at no time has the state even hinted at an argument that Mr. Haller is a risk to the community. As far as being a flight risk, he has shown nothing since his arrest except the absolute intention to fight this charge and exonerate himself, despite this baseless attempt to hamper his pro se defense by keeping him locked up and unable to fully prepare his case. Put simply, the prosecution wants to keep Mr. Haller in jail because they are afraid and want to go to trial on a slanted playing field.'

The judge waited a beat in case there was more. Berg stood up at her spot at the prosecution table and waited to be recognized.

'Additionally, Your Honor,' Jennifer said, 'I do have a number of witnesses here who are willing to testify, if need be, to the character of Mr. Haller.'

'I'm sure that will not be necessary,' Warfield said. 'Ms. Berg? I see you are waiting to respond.'

Berg moved to the lectern as Jennifer vacated it.

'Thank you, Judge Warfield,' she said. 'The state opposes lowering bail in this matter because the defendant does have the means and motive to flee. As the court well knows, we are talking about a murder here, the victim of which was found in the trunk of the defendant's car. And the evidence clearly indicates the murder took place in the defendant's garage. In fact, Your Honor, the evidence in this case is overwhelming, and this gives the defendant all the reason in the world to flee.'

Jennifer objected to Berg's characterization of the evidence and her presuming what my state of mind would be. The judge instructed Berg to refrain from such speculation and to continue.

'Additionally, Your Honor,' Berg said. 'The state is considering adding a special-circumstance allegation to the charge in this case, which would render the question of bail moot.'

Jennifer shot up out of her seat.

'Objection!' she exclaimed.

I knew this was the battle line. An allegation of special circumstances — murder for hire or for financial gain — would bump the charge to the no-bail level.

'Counsel's argument is preposterous,' Jennifer protested. 'Not only is there no special circumstance that could be applied in this case, but the defense motion was filed last week, and if the state was considering a valid special circumstance allegation, it would have added it by now. The state is blowing smoke, hoping to stop the court from providing Mr. Haller's right to bail.'

Warfield's eyes moved from Jennifer to Berg.

'Defense counsel makes a good argument,' the judge said. 'What is the special-circumstance allegation the state is supposedly considering?'

'Your Honor, the investigation of this crime is ongoing and we are developing evidence of a financial motive,' Berg said. 'And as the court well knows, murder for financial gain is a special-circumstance crime.'

Jennifer angrily spread her hands wide.

'Your Honor,' she said, 'is the District Attorney's Office really asking for bail to be set on the basis of what evidence might be found down the line? This is incredible.'

'Incredible or not, this court is not going to consider what may lie in the future while making rulings in the present,' Warfield said. 'Do both sides submit?'

'Submitted,' Jennifer said.

'One moment, Your Honor,' Berg said.

I watched her lean down to confer with her second, a young attorney who wore bow ties. I had a pretty good idea what they were talking about.

Warfield quickly grew impatient.

'Ms. Berg, you asked for time to prepare for this hearing and I gave it. There should be no need for a sidebar with your colleague. Are you ready to submit?'

Berg straightened up and looked at the judge.

'No, Your Honor,' she said. 'The state believes that the court should be made aware that there is an ongoing investigation of the defendant relating to a plan to flee the country to Mexico, should he be released on bail.'

Jennifer stood up.

'Your Honor,' she protested. 'More unfounded allegations? Is the state so desperate to keep this man in jail that it trumps up an investigation into — '

'Your Honor,' I said, as I stood up. 'If I may address this allegation?'

'In a moment, Mr. Haller,' Warfield said. 'Ms. Berg, this better be good. Tell me more about this alleged plan to flee the country.'

'Judge, all I know is that a confidential informant in the jail where Mr. Haller is being housed revealed to investigators that the defendant has openly spoken about a plan to cross the border and flee, if he can make bail. The plan includes circumventing an electronic monitor should the court order that as part of a bail reduction, and co-counsel is fully aware of this. The defendant has gone so far as to invite her down to go fishing.'

'What do you say about that, Mr. Haller?' Warfield asked.

'Your Honor, the prosecution's claim is false on multiple levels, starting with the alleged confidential informant,' I said. 'There is no CI. There are only the jail deputies listening in on

92

privileged conversations and then feeding what they hear to the prosecution as intel.'

'That's a serious allegation, Mr. Haller,' Warfield said. 'Do you care to enlighten us with your knowledge?'

The judge gestured toward the lectern and I stepped over.

'Judge Warfield, thank you for the opportunity to bring this matter before the court,' I began. 'I have been incarcerated at Twin Towers for six weeks. I elected to go pro se and defend myself with the help of my co-counsel, Ms. Aronson. This meant meetings with my team in the jail as well as calls from the community phones in the K-10 module. These meetings and calls are not supposed to be monitored in any way by law enforcement or anyone else. The privilege is supposed to be sacrosanct.'

'I hope you are going to get to a point soon, Mr. Haller,' the judge interjected.

'Arriving there now, Your Honor,' I responded. 'As I said, the privilege is sacrosanct. But I became suspicious that that was not the case at Twin Towers and that somehow what was said in my meetings and phone calls with co-counsel and my investigator was getting back to the D.A.'s Office and Ms. Berg. And so, Your Honor, I set up a little test to either prove or disprove my theory. On a phone call with my co-counsel, I announced that I was having a call with counsel under privilege and stated that the call should not be monitored. But it was. And I spun a story that just came out of Ms. Berg's mouth almost verbatim.'

Berg stood to speak and I gestured with my hand as if to say *your turn*. I wanted her to respond because I would then hang her with her own words.

'Your Honor,' Berg began. 'Talk about incredible. The defendant's plan to flee is revealed in court, and his response is to say, 'Yes, but I was just kidding. I was just testing to see if anyone was listening.' That's a confirmation, Your Honor, and reason alone not to reduce bail in this matter but to raise it.'

'Does this mean that counsel for the People acknowledges listening to the privileged call?' I asked.

'It means no such thing,' Berg shot back.

'Excuse me!' the judge boomed. 'I'm the judge here and I'll ask the questions, if you don't mind.'

She paused and stared down hard, first at me and then at Berg.

'When exactly was this call, Mr. Haller?' she asked.

'About five forty p.m. Thursday,' I responded.

Warfield shifted her focus to Berg.

'I would like to hear this phone call,' she said. 'Is that possible, Ms. Berg?'

'No, Your Honor,' Berg said. 'Privileged calls are destroyed by the monitors because they are privileged.'

'Destroyed after they are listened to?' the judge pressed.

'No, Your Honor,' Berg said. 'Privileged calls are privileged. They are not listened to once they are established as protected conversation with

94

counsel or others under the rules of privilege. The calls are then destroyed. That is why it is not possible to confirm or refute counsel's outlandish allegation, and he knows it.'

'That's wrong, Your Honor,' I said.

Warfield swung her eyes back to me and squinted them down to slots.

'What are you saying, Mr. Haller?' she asked.

'I'm saying we were running a test,' I said. 'Ms. Aronson recorded the call and that recording is available to the court right now.'

The air momentarily went out of the room while Berg recalculated.

'Your Honor, I am going to object to any playing of a tape,' she said. 'There is no way to validate its legitimacy.'

'I disagree, Judge,' I said. 'The tape begins with the jail system's collect call announcement, and more importantly, you will hear the exact words and story Ms. Berg just revealed to the court. Now, if I were to make a phony tape, how would I know exactly what she was going to say in court?'

Warfield registered that for a few moments before responding.

'Let's hear the tape,' she said.

'Your Honor,' Berg said, panic creeping into her voice, 'the People ob — '

'Objection overruled,' Warfield said. 'I said, let's hear the tape.'

Jennifer came forward with her cell phone, placed it on the lectern, and bent the stem microphone down to it before pushing the play button on the recording app.

95

Without my instruction Jennifer had been smart enough to record the call from the start, including the electronic voice saying she was receiving a collect call from the L.A. County jail. After the call was over, she had also added her own tag, announcing that the call had been a test to see if L.A. County authorities were violating my privilege rights.

The call was convincing. I wanted to see Berg's reaction but could not pull my eyes away from the judge. Her face seemed to grow darker as she heard the parts of the conversation that Berg had said came from an informant.

When the tape ended with Jennifer's tag, I asked the judge if she wished to hear it again. She said no, then took a moment to compose herself and her verbal response. As a former defense attorney, she had probably always had reason to be suspicious about the monitoring of calls from jailed clients to their lawyers.

'May I address the court?' Berg said. 'I did not listen to that call. What I represented to the court earlier was the truth as it was told to me. The sheriff's jail intelligence unit provided a report that gave me the information and said it came from an informant. I did not knowingly lie to or mislead the court.'

'Whether or not I believe you doesn't matter,' Warfield said. 'A serious intrusion upon the rights of this defendant has occurred, and there are consequences for that. There will be an investigation, and the truth will come out. In the meantime, I'm ready to rule on the defense motion on bail. Any other argument, Ms. Berg?'

'No, Your Honor,' Berg said.
'I didn't think so,' the judge said.
'May I be heard, Your Honor?' I asked.
'There is no need, Mr. Haller. No need.'

12

A small group of friends, colleagues, and loved ones were there to greet me when I stepped through the inmate release door at Twin Towers. They erupted in cheers and applause as I came through. The media was there too, and they filmed me as I went down the line, hugging and hand shaking. It was embarrassing but felt good at the same time. I was breathing free air again and wanted to revel in it. One of my Lincolns was there at the curb, ready to go — obviously not the one Sam Scales had been murdered in.

Harry Bosch and Andre La Cosse were last in the well-wishers line. I thanked them both for being willing to stand up for me and put up their money as well.

'We got off cheap,' Bosch said.

'You played that perfectly in court,' La Cosse added. 'As usual.'

'Well,' I said. 'Twenty-five K apiece is still a lot of money in my book, and I will pay you guys back sooner than you think.'

Both men had generously agreed to put up as much as $200,000 each to pay for a 10 percent bond. But Judge Warfield was so enraged by the obvious eavesdropping on my jail calls that she dropped bail from $5 million to $500,000 as punishment for the wrongdoing. Unfortunately, she also ordered me to wear an ankle monitor, but this did not dampen the news that my two sponsors only had to put up a fraction of what they had offered.

It was a good day all around. I was free.

I took Andre aside for a private moment.

'Andre, you didn't need to do this, man,' I said. 'I mean, Harry's my brother. There's blood there, but you're a client, and I hate like hell taking any of the money you earned with your own blood.'

'Yes, I did,' he said. 'I had to do it. I wanted to do it.'

I nodded my thanks again and shook his hand. As I did so, Fernando Valenzuela walked up. He had missed the cheering section.

'So, don't burn me on this, Haller,' he said.

'Val, my man,' I said.

We bumped fists.

'When I first heard that shit in court about Mexico, I thought, *What the fuck?*' Valenzuela said. 'But then, man, you had it wired. Good show.'

'Ain't no show, Val,' I said. 'I had to get out.'

'And now you are. I'll be monitoring you.'

'I'm sure you will.'

Valenzuela moved off and the others crowded around me again. I looked for Maggie but didn't see her. Lorna asked what I wanted to do.

'Meet with the team? Be by yourself? What?' she asked.

'You know what I want?' I said. 'I want to get in that Lincoln, open all the windows, and just drive out to the beach.'

'Can I go?' Hayley asked.

'Me too?' Kendall added.

'Of course,' I said. 'Who's got the keys?'

Lorna put the keys into my hand. Then she handed me a phone.

'The police still have yours,' she said. 'But we think we have all your contacts and email on this.'

'Perfect,' I said.

Then I leaned down and whispered to her.

'Let's get the team together later,' I said. 'Call Christian at Dan Tana's and see if we can get in. I've been eating baloney for six weeks. Tonight I want steak.'

'You got it,' Lorna said.

'And ask Harry to come,' I added. 'Maybe he's had a chance to look at the discovery file and will have something to say.'

'Will do.'

'One other thing: Did you talk to Maggie in court? She kind of disappeared, and I'm wondering if she's pissed off at us for bringing her there as a character witness.'

'No, she's not mad. Once the judge said she didn't need any testimonials, she told me she had to get back to work. But she was there for you.'

I nodded. It was good to know.

I unlocked the Lincoln with the remote and walked around to the driver's side.

'Fall in, ladies,' I said.

Kendall gave up the front seat to Hayley and took the back. That was nice of her and I smiled at her in the rearview.

'Eyes on the road, Dad,' Hayley said.

'Right,' I said.

We pulled away from the curb. I worked my way down to the 10 freeway and headed west. At that point it was time to put up the windows so we could hear one another talk.

'How do you feel?' Kendall asked.

'Pretty good for a guy still charged with murder,' I said.

'But you're going to win, right, Dad?' Hayley asked urgently.

'Don't worry, Hay, I'm going to win,' I said. 'And that's when I'll go from feeling pretty good to feeling pretty great. Okay?'

'Okay,' she said.

We rode in silence for a few moments.

'Can I ask a dumb question?' Kendall said.

'There are no dumb questions when it comes to the law,' I said. 'Only dumb answers.'

'What happens next?' she said. 'Now that you're out on bail, will the trial get delayed?'

'I won't let them delay it,' I said. 'I have them on speedy trial.'

'What exactly does that mean?' Kendall asked.

I looked over at my daughter.

'You're One-L,' I said. 'Why don't you answer that?'

'I only know the answer because of you, not law school,' Hayley said.

She turned to look back over the seat at Kendall.

'If you're accused of a crime, you're entitled to a speedy trial,' she said. 'In California that means they have ten court days from your arrest to hold a preliminary hearing or seek an indictment from a grand jury. Either way, you then get formally arraigned on the charges and the state must take you to trial within sixty calendar days or drop the charges and dismiss the case.'

I nodded. She had it right.

'What are calendar days?' Kendall asked.

'That just means workdays,' Hayley said. 'It's sixty days excluding weekends and holidays. My father was indicted and arraigned right before Thanksgiving — November twelfth, to be exact — and the sixty days push us into February. They count two days at Thanksgiving and a whole week from Christmas to New Year's as holidays. Then you add in Martin Luther King Day and Presidents' Day, when the courts are closed. It all adds up to February eighteenth.'

'D-Day,' I said.

I reached over and squeezed Hayley's knee like the proud father I was.

The traffic was flowing and I took the freeway all the way to the curving tunnel that dumped out onto the Pacific Coast Highway. I pulled into a lot that served one of the beach clubs down there and got out. An attendant came walking toward us. I reached into my pocket but realized all the belongings from my pockets the night I was arrested were in an envelope I had handed off to Lorna so I could shake hands and hug people.

'I don't have any money,' I said. 'Either of you have a five we can give this guy for ten minutes on the beach?'

'I got it,' Kendall said.

She paid the man and we all walked across the pedestrian and bike paths and across the sand toward the water. Kendall took off her heels and carried them in one hand. There was something very sexy about her doing that.

'Dad, you're not going to jump in, right?' Hayley asked.

'Nah,' I said. 'I just want to hear the waves. Everything sounds like echoes and iron where I've been. I need to wash it out of my ears with something good.'

We stopped on a berm that was just above the wet sand where the surf washed in. The sun was slinking down toward the blue-black water. I held both my companions' hands and said nothing. I breathed deeply and thought about where I had been. I resolved at that moment that I had to win the case because there was no way I was going to go back into lockup. I would take all extreme alternatives to that.

I let go of Hayley's hand and then pulled her close.

'All this about me,' I said. 'How are you doing, Hay?'

'I'm good,' she said. 'What you told me about first year being a bitch is true.'

'Yeah, but you're smarter than I ever was. You'll do fine.'

'We'll see.'

'How's your mom? I saw her in court, and Jennifer said she was going to vouch for me if needed.'

'She's good. And, yeah, she was ready to speak up for you.'

'I'll call her and thank her.'

'That would be nice.'

I turned and looked at Kendall. It almost felt like she had never left me for Hawaii.

'And you?' I said. 'You doing all right?'

'I am now,' she said. 'I didn't like seeing you in the courtroom.'

I nodded. I got that. I looked out at the ocean. The pounding of the waves seemed to echo in my chest. The colors were vibrant, not the gray of my last six weeks. It was beautiful and I didn't want to leave.

'Okay,' I finally said. 'Time's up. Back to work.'

The traffic was not as kind heading in the opposite direction. It took almost an hour to get Hayley to her apartment in K-town after she turned down my invitation to dinner in favor of her weekly study group. This week's subject: The Rule Against Perpetuities.

After dropping her off, I stayed on the curb and called Lorna. She told me that dinner was set up at Dan Tana's at 8 p.m. and that Harry Bosch would be in attendance.

'I think he has something to discuss,' Lorna said.

'Good,' I said. 'I'll want to hear it.'

I disconnected and looked at Kendall.

'So,' I said. 'The dinner with my team is at eight and it sounds like they really want to work and discuss the case. I don't think — '

'That's okay,' she said. 'I know you want to get to it. You can just drop me off.'

'Where?'

'Well, I took you up on your offer. I've been at your place. Is that okay?'

'Of course. I forgot, but that's great. I want to go there anyway to change. This is the suit I was arrested in. It doesn't fit anymore and it smells like jail to me.'

'Good, then. You'll be taking off your clothes.'

I looked at her and she smiled provocatively.

'Um, I thought we were broken up,' I said.

'We are,' she said. 'That's why this is going to be so much fun.'

'Really?'

'Really.'

'Okay, then.'

I pulled the Lincoln away from the curb.

13

Somebody once said that a person's favorite restaurant is where they know you. That might be true. They knew me at Dan Tana's and I knew them: Christian at the door, Arturo at the table, Mike behind the bar. But that didn't obscure the fact that the kitschy Italian joint with checkered tablecloths served up the best New York strip in the city. I liked the place because they knew me, but I liked the steak even better.

When I pulled up to the valet, I saw Bosch standing outside the restaurant's front door by himself. He was at the smoking bench but I knew he didn't smoke. After turning over the car keys, I walked over. I noticed he had an inch-thick file tucked under his arm. The discovery file, I assumed.

'You're the first one here?' I asked.

'No, they're all in there,' he said. 'Table in the back corner.'

'But you're here waiting for me. Is this where you ask me if I did it?'

'Give me a little more credit, Mick. If I thought you did it, I wouldn't have put up the money.'

I nodded.

'And nothing in that file changed your mind?'

'Not really. Just made me think you've got yourself in a pretty tight box.'

'Tell me about it. Should we go in?'

'Sure, but one thing before we're with the others. Like I said, somebody really put you in a box here, and I was thinking that you may want to run this out for as long as you can. You know, drop the speedy trial thing . . . take your time with it.'

'So much for the vote of confidence.'

'It is what it is.'

'Thanks for the advice but I'll pass. One way or another, I want this thing done.'

'I get it.'

'What about you? You okay? Still taking your pills?'

'Every day. So far, so good.'

'I like hearing that. And Maddie? How's she doing?'

'She's good. In the academy.'

'Man, the second generation, just like the first.'

'I thought Hayley wants to be a prosecutor.'

'She'll change her mind.'

I smiled at him.

'Let's go in.'

'One other thing. I just wanted to explain why I never came to see you in the jail.'

'I don't think you need to, Harry. Don't worry about it.'

'I should have visited, I know. But I didn't want to see you in there.'

'I know. Lorna told me. To be honest, I didn't even put you on my list. I didn't want you to see me in there either.'

He nodded and we went inside. Christian, the tuxedo-clad maître d', greeted me warmly and had the class not to mention that I hadn't been there in more than six weeks, even though he probably knew why. I introduced Bosch as my brother. Christian escorted us to the table where the others were waiting: Jennifer, Lorna, and Cisco. It was a table for six but with Cisco in the mix it was crowded.

The smell of food on the tables around us was almost overpowering. I was distracted by it and found myself turning and craning my neck to see what other patrons had ordered.

'You all right, boss?' Cisco asked.

I turned back to him.

'Fine, I'm fine,' I said. 'But let's order first. Where's Arturo?'

Lorna waved to someone behind me and soon Arturo was at our table with his order pad. It was orders of Steak Helen all around except for Jennifer, who wasn't a red-meat eater. She went with eggplant parmigiana on Arturo's recommendation. Lorna ordered a bottle of red wine for the drinkers, and I asked for a big bottle of sparkling water. I also told Arturo to bring bread and butter as soon as he could.

'Okay,' I said when we were alone. 'Tonight we can celebrate because I'm free and we knocked the prosecution down a notch or two in court. But that's it. No hangovers tomorrow because we go back to work.'

Everybody nodded except Bosch. He just stared at me from the opposite side of the table.

'Harry, you're dying to say something,' I said. 'Probably something bad. You want to start? You have the discovery file. Did you read it?'

'Uh, sure,' he said. 'I read the discovery and I also talked to some people I know.'

'Like who?' Jennifer asked.

Bosch looked at her for a moment. I raised my hand a few inches off the table as a signal to her to cool it. Bosch was long retired from the LAPD but he was still tightly connected. I knew that firsthand and did not need him to name his sources.

'What did they tell you?' I asked.

'Well, they're pretty pissed off over at the D.A.'s Office because of the way you sandbagged Berg,' Bosch said.

'They get caught cheating and they're pissed at us,' Jennifer said. 'That's just beautiful.'

'What's the upshot?' I said. 'What are they going to do about it?'

'For one, they're going to go after special circumstances like it's the holy grail,' Bosch said. 'They want to punish you for that stunt today, put you back in jail.'

'That's bullshit,' Cisco said.

'Yeah, but they can do it,' Bosch said, 'if they find the evidence.'

'There is no evidence,' Jennifer said. 'Financial gain? Murder for hire? It's ridiculous.'

'All I'm saying is they're looking,' Bosch said, staring at me as though the others at the table didn't count. 'And you have to be careful with your own moves.'

'I don't understand,' Lorna said.

'You raised hell about car and phone data,' Bosch said. 'I assume you need it to prove you never left your house. That might just end up

109

being evidence supporting that you paid somebody to grab Scales and bring him to you. That gets you close to murder for hire.'

'Like I said, bullshit,' Cisco said.

'I'm saying, this is how they're thinking,' Bosch said. 'It's how I would think.'

'Sam owed me money,' I said. 'Never paid me the back end on the last case and we sued him. What was it, Lorna? Sixty K?'

'Seventy-five,' Lorna said. 'With interest and penalty, it's over a hundred now. But we did it just to get a judgment and lien. We knew he'd never pay.'

'Still, they could point to that, make it look like murder for financial gain,' I said. 'If they could prove Sam had money, the lien would carry over in death.'

'Did he?' Bosch asked. 'Have money? They have a newsclip that says he ripped off ten million dollars through all his cons. Where'd it go?'

'I remember that article,' I said. ''The Most Hated Man in America,' they called him. It was exaggerated and didn't make me any friends, especially at home. But Sam was always on the con. He always had money coming in. It went somewhere.'

'But this is crazy,' Jennifer said. 'They think you would kill a former client for an unpaid bill? For seventy-five thousand dollars? A hundred thousand?'

'No, they don't think that,' I said. 'That's not the point. The point is, they're pissed and if they can push this into special circumstances, my bail

110

is pulled and I go back to Twin Towers. That's what they want. To fuck me over. To tilt the table their way. Doesn't matter if the added charge doesn't hold up later in court.'

Jennifer shook her head.

'It still makes no sense,' she said. 'I think your sources are crap.'

She looked pointedly at Bosch. He was the new guy, the outsider, and was suspect in her eyes. I tried to push past the moment.

'Okay, so how long do I have before they pull this shit?' I asked.

'They have to find the money and prove you knew about it,' Bosch said. 'If they get there, they'll drop the current charges and go back to the grand jury. Then they refile with special circumstances.'

'That will restart the speedy-trial clock and mean the money posted today for bond goes down the toilet,' Jennifer said. 'You go to jail, the bond is forfeited.'

'That's bullshit,' Cisco said again.

'Okay, well, we should be ready to go in to see Warfield the minute this all breaks,' I said. 'Harry, you let us know what you hear when you hear it. Jennifer, we'll need an argument. They're subverting speedy trial, maybe vindictive prosecution, something.'

'I'm on it,' Jennifer said. 'This makes me so fucking mad.'

'Don't let your emotions into it,' I cautioned. 'Let's not go in mad, let's make the judge mad. I saw some of that today when we played the tape. I know it took her back to when she was a

111

defense attorney. If the D.A. is doing this just to fuck with me, then Warfield will see it before we say it.'

Both Jennifer and Bosch responded with nods.

'Fucking cowards,' Cisco said. 'Afraid to go straight up with you, boss.'

I liked that my team seemed angrier about the prosecution's end run than I was. It would help keep them sharp in the days and weeks running up to trial.

I returned my attention to Bosch. I realized more than the others what an incredibly good break it was to have him in our court. I had taken his side the year before and now he was taking mine. But the moral support paled in comparison with what he brought as an investigator.

'Harry, did you ever work with Drucker and Lopes?' I asked.

Kent Drucker and Rafael Lopes were the LAPD leads on the case. They worked out of the elite Robbery-Homicide Division, where Bosch had worked until the end of his LAPD career.

'Never directly on a case,' Bosch said. 'They were in the squad but there wasn't a lot of crossover on things. They were good detectives, though. You don't get to RHD if you're not. The question becomes, What do you do when you get there? — rest on your laurels or keep chopping wood? The fact that they were assigned this case answers that one.'

I nodded. Bosch looked hesitant. I wondered whether he had heard more, something he didn't realize was valuable or was holding back until he could fill it out.

'What?' I asked. 'You have something else?'

'Sort of,' he said.

'Might as well get it out so we can discuss it,' I said.

'Well, one of my last cases at RHD, I had an investigation where there was a financial fraud involved,' Bosch said. 'A guy was embezzling funds, got found out, killed the guy who found out to shut him up. Pretty clean but we couldn't find the money. His lifestyle showed nothing. He wasn't spending it, he was hiding it, so we hired a financial forensics analyst to follow the money. Help us find it.'

'Okay,' I said. 'Did it work?'

'Yeah, we found the money offshore and made the case,' Bosch said. 'I bring it up now because my partner from back then is still on the job in RHD. She told me that Drucker came to her and asked for the contact info for the financial forensics guy.'

'We should look into getting our own,' Jennifer added.

She wrote a note down on a small pad on the table in front of her.

'Let's look again through our files on Sam's past cases,' I said. 'Maybe there's something in them with info on how he moved and hid cash. Harry, anything else?'

I looked over my shoulder for Arturo. It wasn't that I was starving, but I couldn't wait to have a real meal for the first time in six weeks.

'Just on the discovery file,' Bosch said. 'I've

been through the photos and the autopsy. It was all pretty self-explanatory, no surprises. But then I saw this.'

He was looking through his copy of the discovery and pulled out two documents and a crime scene photo. He handed them around the table and waited a moment until everyone had a look and they came back to him.

'The autopsy report stated that the victim's fingernails were scraped for samples of what looked like dirt or grease,' he said. 'Then the lab report came in, identifying the substance as a combination of vegetable oil, chicken fat, and some sugarcane — cooking grease, according to the report.'

'I saw that in the discovery,' I said. 'Why is it significant?'

'Well, when you look at the crime scene photos, you see that all of this guy's fingernails were dirty with this stuff,' Bosch said.

'I'm still not following,' I said. 'If it was blood or something, I could — '

'I looked at this guy's rap sheet,' Bosch interjected. 'He was strictly white-collar cons. Internet mostly. And now he's got grease under his nails.'

'So, what does it mean?' I pressed.

'Maybe he was working as a fucking dishwasher,' Cisco said.

'I think it means he was into something completely new,' Bosch said. 'What that means to the case, I don't know. But I think you should request a sample of the fingernail grease for your own testing.'

'Okay,' I said. 'We can do that. Jennifer?'

'Got it,' she said.

She wrote it down. I was about to pass the baton to Lorna to see what she had come up with on the review of my past cases. But Arturo brought the steaks to the table at that moment and I kept my mouth closed until we were all served. I then started devouring my strip like a man who has eaten only apples and baloney sandwiches for a month and a half.

I soon became aware that I was being watched by the others. I spoke without looking up at them.

'What, you never seen a guy eat a steak before?' I asked.

'Just never seen one eat it so fast,' Lorna replied.

'Well, stand back, I might order another,' I said. 'I need to get back to my fighting weight. Since you take so much time between bites, Lorna, why don't you tell us where we stand on my enemies list.'

Before she could answer, I glanced over at Bosch to offer an explanation.

'Lorna has been going through the old case files and drawing up a list of enemies, people who might have wanted to do this to me,' I said. 'Lorna?'

'Well, the list so far is short,' Lorna said. 'You've had your problem clients and there have been some threats, but very few who we think have the skills, smarts, and general wherewithal to pull together a frame like this.'

'It's a sophisticated frame,' Cisco added. 'Your

115

run-of-the-mill client could not do this.'

'So, who could?' I asked. 'Who's on your list?'

'I've been through everything twice and came up with only one name,' Lorna said.

'One name?' I said. 'That's it? Who?'

'Louis Opparizio,' she said.

'Wait, what?' I said. 'Louis Opparizio . . . ?'

The name rang a loud bell in my memory but I needed a moment to place it. I was sure I'd never had a client named Louis Opparizio. Then I remembered. Opparizio wasn't a client. He was a witness. A man from a mob-connected family who straddled the line between criminal enterprise and legitimate business. I had used him. I had cornered him on the witness stand and made him look like the guilty party. It drew the jury's attention away from my client and on to Opparizio. Compared to him, my client looked like an angel.

I remembered an encounter I'd had with Opparizio in a courthouse restroom. I remembered the anger, the hate. He was a bull of a man, built like a fireplug, and his arms hung away from his body like he was ready to use them to tear me apart. He'd backed me into a corner and had wanted to kill me right there.

'Who is Opparizio?' Bosch asked.

'He's somebody I pinned a murder on once in court,' I said.

'He was mobbed up,' Cisco added. 'From Vegas.'

'And did he do it?' Bosch asked.

'No, but I made it look like he did,' I said. 'My client got the NG and walked.'

116

'And was your client really guilty?'

I hesitated but then answered truthfully.

'Yes, but I didn't know it at the time.'

Bosch nodded and I took it as a judgment, as though I had just confirmed why people hate lawyers.

'So,' he said then. 'Would Opparizio wanting to return the favor and pin a murder on you be out of the question?'

'No, not at all,' I said. 'What happened in court back then, it caused him a lot of problems and cost him a lot of money. He was a sleeper. He was trying to move mob money into legitimate fields and I sort of blew that up when I had him on the stand.'

Bosch thought about that for a few moments and nobody interrupted.

'Okay,' he finally said. 'Let me take Opparizio. Find out what he's up to. And Cisco, you stay with Sam Scales. Maybe we cross paths somewhere and then we know why this whole thing went down.'

It sounded like a plan to me but I was going to let Cisco decide. It seemed we were all looking at him, waiting, when he nodded his approval.

'Okay,' he said. 'Let's do it.'

14

I got home late and parked on the street. I didn't want to park in the garage and wasn't sure I ever would again. I entered to find the house completely dark. In that moment, I thought Kendall was gone. That she had realized, now that I was out, that she didn't want to live here with me again. But then I saw movement in the darkened hallway and she appeared. She was wearing just a robe.

'You're home,' she said.

'Yeah, it went late,' I said. 'A lot to discuss. You've been waiting in the dark?'

'Actually, I've been asleep since earlier. We never turned on any lights when we got here. We just went straight to the bed.'

I nodded that I understood. My eyes started adjusting to the shadows and the dark.

'So you didn't eat?' I said. 'You must be hungry.'

'No, I'm fine,' she said. 'You must be tired.'

'Sort of. Yeah.'

'But still excited about being free?'

'Yeah.'

I had woken that day in a jail cell. I was now about to sleep in my own bed for the first time in six weeks. My back on a thick mattress and my head on a soft pillow. And if that wasn't enough, my ex-girlfriend had come back and was standing in front of me with her robe open and nothing on underneath. I was still accused of murder but it was amazing how my fortunes had changed in a single day. As I stood there, I felt that nobody could ever touch me. I was golden. I was free.

'Well,' Kendall said, smiling. 'I hope not too tired.'

'I think I can manage,' I said.

She turned and disappeared into the darkness of the hallway leading to the bedroom.

And I followed.

PART TWO

FOLLOW THE HONEY

15

I had no illusions about my innocence. I knew it was something only I could know for sure. And I knew that it wasn't a perfect shield against injustice. It was no guarantee of anything. The clouds were not going to open for some sort of divine light of intervention.

I was on my own.

Innocence is not a legal term. No one is ever found innocent in a court of law. No one is ever exonerated by the verdict of a jury. The justice system can only deliver a verdict of guilty or not guilty. Nothing else, nothing more.

The law of innocence is unwritten. It will not be found in a leather-bound codebook. It will never be argued in a courtroom. It cannot be written into law by the elected. It is an abstract idea and yet it closely aligns with the hard laws of nature and science. In the law of physics, for every action, there is an equal and opposite reaction. In the law of innocence, for every man not guilty of a crime, there is a man out there who is. And to prove true innocence, the guilty man must be found and exposed to the world.

That was my plan. To go further than a jury verdict. To expose the guilty and make my innocence clear. It was my only way out.

To that end, December proceeded with

preparations for trial as well as prep for the anticipated move by the prosecution to recharge me and remand me back to a solo cell at Twin Towers. As the days until Christmas counted down, my paranoia rose incrementally. I expected the cruelest of moves by Death Row Dana as payback for the humiliation I had brought her in the last hearing — a Christmas Day arrest with courts closed for the holidays and me left unable to put our ready arguments before Judge Warfield until the calendar turned to the new year.

There was no evasive action that I could take. My current bail restriction forbade me to leave the county, and the ankle-mounted monitor broadcast my location to authorities twenty-four hours a day. If they wanted me, they could surely find me. There was no escape.

But no one came knocking. No one came looking for me.

I spent Christmas Eve with my daughter and she went to her mother's on Christmas Day. And I got an early dinner with her a week later before she went off with friends to celebrate the changing of the year. Kendall was with me the whole time and even told me on New Year's Eve that she was having all her belongings shipped back from Hawaii.

All in all, it was a great month of freedom and work in preparation for the trial that lay ahead of me. But it would have been better if I hadn't been looking over my shoulder the whole time. I began to think that I had been played, that Harry Bosch had been fed the false narrative of my re-arrest as the real payback. Dana Berg had made sure I would not be able to rest easy in my newfound freedom, and so she had the last laugh.

As far as the investigation into eavesdropping on privileged conversations at Twin Towers that Judge Warfield had promised, Berg escaped unscathed. The illegal activity was laid squarely at the door of the jail intelligence unit. A report that was leaked to the *Los Angeles Times* during the news-starved week after Christmas resulted in a New Year's Day exclusive on the front page that concluded that deputies had been listening for years to privileged conversations, the contents of which were then used to create tip sheets from nonexistent jailhouse informants. These were then turned over to police and prosecutors. It was one more black eye for the sheriff's jail division, which in the prior decade had been the target of multiple federal investigations. Horror stories had abounded of jail deputies staging gladiator fights, putting inmates in cells with enemies, using gang members to carry out punishment beatings and rapes of other prisoners. Indictments had come and heads had rolled. The elected sheriff at the time and his second-in-command had even gone to prison for turning a blind eye to the corruption.

Now the eavesdropping scandal promised more scrutiny and disgrace. Most likely the feds would be back in play and the new year was sure to bring a free-for-all for defense attorneys looking to overturn convictions in cases affected

125

by the illegal activity.

This caused me to double down on my resolve not to be returned to Twin Towers. Every deputy in the jail would know that the latest scandal that had befallen them was caused by me. I could clearly imagine the retribution that would be awaiting me if I went back.

I finally got a call from Harry Bosch. I had not heard from him since well before Christmas despite leaving messages of holiday greetings and requests for updates on his part of the investigation. I knew that nothing had happened to him — my daughter had reported seeing him at his house when she visited her cousin Maddie over the break. And now, finally, he called. He appeared not to be aware of my efforts to contact him over the past weeks. He simply said he had something he wanted me to see. I was still at home, having a second cup of coffee with Kendall, and he agreed to swing by and pick me up.

We drove south in his old Jeep Cherokee, the one with the squared-off design and the twenty-five-year-old suspension. Shake, rattle, and roll: the car shook every time its tires hit a seam in the asphalt, rattled with every pothole, and threatened to roll on every left turn as the aging springs compressed and the car tilted to the right.

He kept KNX news on and had the uncanny ability to engage in conversation while still keeping an ear on the radio and from time to time throwing comments on the news of the day into the conversation. Even when I turned the volume knob down to respond, he would then turn it back up.

'So,' I said, once we were down out of the hills. 'Where are we going?'

'It's something I want you to see first,' Bosch said.

'It's about Opparizio, I hope. I mean, you were working on him and then you disappear for like a month.'

'I didn't disappear. I was working the case. I told you you'd hear from me when I had something and now I think I do.'

'Well, I hope it's a connection to Sam Scales and the case. Otherwise you've been chasing a pipe dream.'

'You'll know soon enough.'

'Can you at least tell me how far we're going? So I can tell Lorna when I'll be back.'

'T.I.'

'What? They're not going to let me in with this thing on my ankle.'

'We're not going to the prison. I just want to show you something.'

'And a photo wouldn't do?'

'I don't think so.'

We drove in silence for a while after that. Bosch took the 101 south into downtown and then jumped onto the 110, which would be a straight shot down to Terminal Island at the Port of Los Angeles. There was nothing awkward or uncomfortable about the stall in the conversation. We were half brothers and comfortable with the silences. Bosch listened to the news and I tuned it out with thoughts about the case. We were going to trial in under six weeks and I still had no grounds for a defense. Bosch may have gone silent but at least he had something he wanted me to see. My other investigator, Cisco, had been staying in close contact, but his efforts to background Sam Scales had so far been fruitless. I figured I was a week away from doing the unthinkable: throwing aside my right to a speedy trial and asking for time, for a continuance. But I worried that such a request would reveal too much. It would show desperation, panic, and maybe even signal guilt — I would be acting like someone delaying the inevitable.

'Where the hell is Wuhan?' Bosch said.

His words rescued me from the downward spiral of my thoughts.

'Who?' I asked.

He pointed to the radio.

'Not who,' he said. 'It's a place somewhere in China. Were you listening?'

'No, I was thinking,' I said. 'What was it?'

'They've got a mystery virus over there, killing people.'

'Well, at least it's there and not here.'

'Yeah, for how long?'

'You ever been over there, China?'

'Just to Hong Kong.'

'Oh, right . . . Maddie's mom. Sorry I brought it up.'

'Long time ago.'

I attempted to change the subject.

'So, what's Opparizio like?' I asked.

'What do you mean?' Bosch responded.

'Well, I just remember, when I had him on the stand nine years ago, he was restrained at first but then out came the animal. He wanted to jump out of that chair and tear my throat out or something. He seemed more Tony Soprano than Michael Corleone, if you know what I mean.'

'Well, so far I haven't laid eyes on the guy. That's not what I've been doing.'

I looked out the window and tried to blunt my shock and upset. I then turned back to engage.

'Harry, then what have you been doing?' I asked. 'You had Opparizio, remember? You should've — '

'Hold on, hold on,' he said. 'I know I have Opparizio but it wasn't about putting eyes on him. This isn't a surveillance job. It's about finding out what he was doing and whether or not it somehow connects to Scales and you. And that's what I've been doing.'

'Okay, then stop with the whole mystery trip thing. Where are we going?'

'Just take it easy. We're almost there and you'll be enlightened.'

'Really? 'Enlightened'? Like divine intervention or something?'

'Not quite. But I think you'll like it.'

He was right about one thing. We were almost there. I looked around to get my bearings and saw that we had crossed the 405 and were just a few miles from the end of the Harbor Freeway at Terminal Island. Through the windshield and to the left I could see the giant gantry cranes that loaded containers on and off cargo ships.

We were in San Pedro now. Once a small

fishing village, it was now part of the giant Port of Los Angeles complex, serving as a bedroom community for many of those who worked on the docks and in the shipping and oil industries. It had once had a full courthouse where I appeared regularly on behalf of clients accused of crimes. But the justice complex was shuttered by the county in a cost-cutting move and the cases moved up to a courthouse by the airport. The San Pedro courthouse had now stood abandoned for well over a decade.

'I used to come down to Pedro a lot on cases,' I said.

'I used to come down when I was a teenager,' Bosch said. 'Sneak out of whatever place they put me, come down to the docks. I got tattooed down here once.'

I just nodded. It looked like he was reliving the memory and I didn't want to intrude. I knew very little about Bosch's early life beyond what I had read once in an unauthorized profile in the *Times*. I remembered foster homes and an early enlistment in the army, with Vietnam as the destination. This was decades before we learned of our blood connection.

We crossed the Vincent Thomas, the tall green suicide bridge that connected to Terminal Island. The entire island was dedicated to port and industrial operations, with the exception of the federal prison at the far end. Bosch exited the freeway and used surface streets to get us moving along the northern edge of the island and next to one of the deep port channels.

'Taking a wild guess,' I said. 'Opparizio has

130

some kind of smuggling operation here. Stuff coming in on cargo containers. Drugs? Humans? What?'

'Not that I know of,' Bosch said. 'I'm going to show you something else. You see this area?'

He pointed through the windshield toward a vast parking lot filled with plastic-wrapped cars fresh off the boats from Japan.

'There used to be a Ford Motor plant here,' Bosch said. 'It was called Long Beach Assembly and they made the Model A. My mother's father supposedly worked there in the thirties on the Model A line.'

'What was he like?' I asked.

'I never met him. Only heard the story.'

'And now it's Toyotas.'

I gestured toward the vast parking lot of new cars ready to be disseminated to dealers across the West.

Bosch turned onto a crushed-shell road that ran alongside a rock jetty lining the channel. A black-and-white oil tanker the length of a football field, including the end zones, was slowly making its way down the channel to the port. Bosch pulled to a stop by what looked like an abandoned railroad spur and killed the engine.

'Let's walk up to the jetty,' he said. 'I'll show you what we've got as soon as this tanker goes by.'

We followed an uphill walk to the top of a berm that ran behind the jetty as a barrier against high tides. By standing on top of it we got a solid view across the channel of the various

131

petroleum refining and storage facilities vital to the operations of the port.

'Okay, so this is the Cerritos Channel right here and we are looking north,' Bosch said. 'That's Wilmington directly across the water and Long Beach to the right.'

'Okay,' I said. 'What exactly are we looking at?'

'The center of the California oil business. You've got the Marathon, Valero, Tesoro refineries right there. Chevron is farther up. The oil comes in here from all over — even Alaska. Comes to port by supertanker, barge, rail, pipeline, you name it. Then it goes over there to the refineries and it gets processed and from there into distribution. Into tanker trucks and out to your local gas station and then into your own gas tank.'

'What's it all got to do with the case?'

'Maybe nothing. Maybe everything. You see that refinery at the end there with the catwalks around the tanks?'

He pointed to the right and at a small refinery with a single stack billowing a white plume of smoke into the sky. An American flag was draped around the upper section of the stack. There were two side-by-side storage tanks that looked to be at least four stories tall and were surrounded by multiple catwalks.

'I see it,' I said.

'That's BioGreen Industries,' Bosch said. 'You won't find Louis Opparizio's name attached to any of the ownership documents but he holds the controlling interest in BioGreen. No doubt about it.'

Bosch had my undivided attention now.

'How did you find that out?' I asked.

'I followed the honey,' Bosch said.

'What's that mean?'

'Well, nine years ago you were able to drag Opparizio through the legal wood chipper at the trial for your client Lisa Trammel. I pulled the transcript and read his testimony. He — '

'You don't have to tell me. I was there, remember?'

Another tanker was coming down the channel. It was so wide, it had little margin for error as it navigated between the jagged rocks that lined both sides.

'I know you were there,' Bosch said. 'But what you might not know is that Louis Opparizio learned a lot from getting pounded by you that day on the stand. Number one, he learned never again to be connected by legal documentation to any of his companies — legit or not. He currently owns nothing in his name and is connected to no company, board, or reported investment to anything. He uses people as fronts.'

'I'm damn proud I was able to teach him how to be a better criminal. How did you get around it?'

'The Internet is still a pretty useful tool. Social media, newspaper archives. Opparizio's father died four years ago. There was a service in New Jersey and a virtual visitation book. Friends and family signed in, and damn if the funeral home's website doesn't still have it online.'

'More like hot damn. You got lots of names.'

'Names and connections. I started tracing, looking for stuff out here. Three Opparizio associates are vested owners of BioGreen and make up a majority interest. He controls it through them. One of them is named Jeannie Ferrigno, who in the last seven years has risen from a Vegas stripper with a couple of possession pops on her record to part owner of a variety of businesses from there to here and back again. I think Jeannie is Opparizio's sidepiece.'

'Follow the honey.'

'Right to BioGreen.'

'This is getting good, Bosch.'

I pointed down the channel to the refinery.

'But if Opparizio has a secret ownership in businesses from here to Vegas, why are we looking at this one?'

'Because this is where the biggest money is. You see that place? It's not a typical refinery. It's a biodiesel plant. Basically, it makes fuel from plants and animal fat. It's recycling waste into an alternate fuel that costs less and burns cleaner. And right now it's the apple of the government's eye because it reduces our national dependence on oil. It's the future, and Louis Opparizio is riding the wave. The government is propping this business up, paying companies like BioGreen a premium on each barrel just to make it. That's on top of what they get for then going out and selling that barrel.'

'And where there's government subsidy, there is always corruption.'

'You got that right.'

I started pacing along the worn footpath on

top of the berm. I was trying to see the connections and how this could all work.

'So, there's a guy,' Bosch said. 'A lieutenant who runs the bureau at Harbor Division. I trained him twenty-five years ago when he came through Hollywood detectives as a D-one.'

'Can you talk to him?' I asked.

'Already did. He knows I'm retired, so I told him I was fishing around for a friend who is interested in BioGreen as an investment. I wanted to know if there were any red flags and he told me, yeah, there's a big red flag, an FBI flag on the place.'

'Meaning what?'

'Meaning he is supposed to take no action on anything that comes across his plate from BioGreen. He's supposed to alert the bureau and stand down. You understand what that means?'

'That the bureau's working on something there.'

'Or at least keeping an eye on it.'

I nodded. This was getting better and better in terms of building a smoke screen for trial. But I knew I needed to do more than provide smoke. This wasn't work for a client. It was for me.

'Okay, so all we need is a connection to Sam Scales, and we have something I can tee up in court,' I said. 'I'll call Cisco and see what he — '

'We already have it,' Bosch said.

'What are you talking about? Where does he connect?'

'The autopsy. Remember the fingernails? The scrapings showed vegetable oil, chicken fat, sugarcane. That's biofuel, Mick. Sam Scales had

135

biofuel under his fingernails.'

I looked down the channel at the BioGreen refinery. The smoke from the stack billowed ominously upward, helping to feed the dirty cloud that hung over the entire harbor.

I nodded.

'I think you found it, Harry,' I said. 'The magic bullet.'

'Just be careful you don't shoot yourself with it,' he said.

16

Bosch's discovery of BioGreen and its connection to Louis Opparizio and possibly Sam Scales served to kick-start the defense case by providing a focal point of investigation and strategy. The trip to Terminal Island was followed by an all-hands meeting the following morning at which tasks were delineated and assigned. Establishing a link between Scales and Opparizio was paramount and I wanted that to be the main focus of my investigators.

Locating Opparizio was another. He had insulated himself from direct ownership and control of the refinery operation and we needed to nail that down before trial. With no direct link we worked the secondary link: Jeannie Ferrigno. I told Cisco to put together a surveillance team in hopes that Jeannie would lead us to Opparizio, and then we would jump the surveillance to him. I wanted to be able to document for the jury that this man who held an undeniable grudge against me had an association with the man I was accused of killing. If we could make that connection, then I believed we had our frame.

The meeting ended with a lot of excitement. But for me the adrenaline ebbed quickly. While the investigators got the thrill of working in the

137

field, I focused through the weekend on what many lawyers abhor: reviewing the case files. The paper trail of a case is a living thing that grows and changes. Documents and evidence reviewed at one point could look different or take on new significance when reviewed through the prism of time.

It was important to know the case inside and out, but I could only accomplish that through repeated reviews of the case files. It had now been more than two months since my arrest and the files had thickened by the week with the dissemination of discovery material. I had read and reviewed it all as it came in but it was also important to take it all in as a whole.

By Sunday morning I had filled several pages of a legal pad with notes, lists, and questions. One page was a list of what was missing from the case. At the top was Sam Scales's wallet. It was not on the property report that described the clothing found on the body and the contents of its pockets.

No wallet. It was assumed that the killer — meaning me — had taken and disposed of it. This missing wallet was important to me because in the variety of scams for which I had defended Sam, he had never used his real name. It was the con man's way. Each con required a new personality so that he could avoid being traced after the victims woke up to the fact that they had been had. To this end, I knew that Sam was gifted at reinventing himself. I only represented him the times he got caught. It was unknown how many cons he had pulled off without detection.

The missing wallet in this case was important because after a month of diligent work, Cisco Wojciechowski had come up empty in his efforts to background Scales. It was a black hole. We had found no digital record of his whereabouts in the two previous years. The wallet would help if it contained the identification of his current persona. It also would help connect him to BioGreen. If he was working there or involved in some kind of scheme with Opparizio, his current identity would be key to tracing it.

It was only when I reviewed the case file for a third time on Sunday evening that I noticed a discrepancy that appeared to flip the case over and give me one more grievance to take to Judge Warfield.

After strategizing next moves, I called Jennifer Aronson and spoiled her dinner plans. I told her to draw up an emergency motion to compel discovery from the prosecution. I told her that the request should clearly state that the prosecution had been withholding vital evidence from the defense since the start of the case and that the evidence in question was the victim's wallet and its contents.

It was a provocative move and my guess was that Dana Berg would object to the accusation, and an evidentiary hearing would be quickly scheduled before Warfield. That was exactly what I wanted — a hearing presumed to be about a discovery dispute that would be about something else entirely.

I told Jennifer I wanted the request filed as soon as court opened in the morning and then I disconnected and let her go to work. I had not asked if the assignment intruded on her plans for the evening. I was only interested in protecting my own. Kendall had not gotten to the Musso & Frank Grill since her return from Hawaii. It had been her favorite restaurant and a place where we had shared many a martini and dinner in our first go-round. I was off martinis and all other alcohol now, but I had made a deal with her. Musso & Frank's on Sunday night in exchange for allowing me to hole up in my home office and work through the weekend. That work had paid off big-time and now I was looking forward to the night out as much as Kendall was. I passed the case baton to Jennifer and told her I would meet her at the Nickel Diner in the morning after she filed. I asked her to tell the whole defense team to come for breakfast so we could update one another on the prior seventy-two hours.

Despite having to witness many martinis being prepared, served, and consumed, I found dinner at Musso's a welcome distraction from thoughts on the case, if only for a few hours, and it pulled Kendall and me back toward the relationship we had shared for seven years before her departure for Hawaii. What drew me closest to her was her assumption that there would be no interruption in our relationship going forward. The idea that I could be found guilty of murder a month from now and be locked away in prison for the rest of my life had never entered her thinking or her discussion of our renewed life together. It was naive, yes, but also endearing. It made me not want to disappoint her, even as I understood that disappointing her would be the least of my problems if I didn't win the case.

'You know,' I said, 'being innocent is no guarantee of a not-guilty verdict. Anything can happen in trial.'

'You always say that,' she said. 'But I know you're going to win.'

'But before we make any great plans, let's get the verdict, okay?'

'It doesn't hurt to plan. As soon as this is over, I want to go somewhere and lie on a beach and forget all about this.'

'That will be nice.'

And I left it at that.

17

At breakfast the next morning Jennifer was the last to arrive. By then we had been around the table with team members reporting on their efforts since the last meeting. There had been little advancement, largely because of the weekend. Cisco said that he had had a surveillance team on Jeannie Ferrigno since Friday evening but there had been no sign of Louis Opparizio having contact with her. Meanwhile, Bosch told us that he was working his law enforcement contacts to try to determine why BioGreen was on the FBI's radar.

Jennifer had not heard the updates and asked a few questions to catch up.

'Is there any confirmation beyond his dirty fingernails that Sam Scales was somehow involved with BioGreen?' she asked.

'Well, not under that name,' Bosch said. 'I dummied in a call to check on employment for a car loan and they said they had no record of a Sam Scales working there now or ever.'

'What about the FBI?' Jennifer asked. 'Do we know what they're up to?'

'Not yet,' Bosch said. 'I didn't think we wanted to take a head-on approach to that question, so I'm sort of sniffing around the edges while trying to get a line on Scales.'

'I followed a tanker truck out of there Friday afternoon,' Cisco added. 'For the hell of it. Just wanted to see where it went. But he went through a security gate at the port and I had to hold back. About a half hour later, he comes driving out and goes back to the refinery. I think he either picked up or dropped off a load.'

'Are we thinking Sam Scales was driving a truck?' Jennifer said. 'What's the scam in that?'

'Maybe he went straight,' Cisco said.

'No,' I said. 'I knew Sam. He was never going to go straight. He was up to something and we still need to find it.'

There was silence for a few moments while I thought about what Bosch had said. I had spent the entirety of my career laboring in state courts and had few interactions with FBI agents or the federal government. Though Bosch had once been married to an FBI agent, I knew he had a history of antagonism when it came to his federal counterparts. The rest of my team were also outsiders when it came to the feds.

'We've got trial in a month,' I said. 'What do you think about switching to a head-on approach to the bureau instead of sniffing around the edges?'

'We can do that,' Bosch said. 'But you have to remember, the feds only respond to threat. Threat of exposure. Whatever they've got going down there, they want to keep it quiet and they'll only take you seriously if they see you as endangering their secrecy or their investigation. That's what a head-on approach is. You make

143

yourself a threat. That's how we always did it at the LAPD.'

I nodded and thought about that. Monica, one of the owners of the Nickel, brought over a variety plate of doughnuts to go with the pancakes and eggs we had already eaten. Jennifer, the only one who hadn't had breakfast yet, reached for the chocolate-frosted entry.

'Anyone want to share this?' she asked.

There were no takers. Jennifer continued.

'I was going to say we should file a Freedom of Information Act request,' she said. 'But those take forever. They probably wouldn't even acknowledge receipt until after your trial.'

I nodded in agreement and then changed my mind.

'We could do that but then back it up with a subpoena requesting files on Scales,' I said.

'The FBI can ignore a subpoena,' Jennifer countered. 'They don't have to answer questions about federal investigations in state court.'

'Doesn't matter,' I said. 'Just delivering the subpoena would be the threat Harry's talking about. They would be on notice that this is coming up at my trial. It might bring them out of the shadows. Then we see what we can get.'

I looked at Bosch for confirmation. He nodded.

'It could work,' he said.

'Let's do it,' Jennifer said.

'Jennifer, I know I'm putting everything on your plate,' I said. 'But can you add the subpoena and FOIA request?'

'No problem,' she said. 'The FOIA's probably

an online request. It'll be done by the end of the day. I'll work on the subpoena first. What are the parameters?'

'Sam Scales and any and all aliases,' I said. 'Then include Louis Opparizio and BioGreen Industries. Anything else?'

Jennifer received a call on her cell and got up from the table to take it outside. The rest of us continued to talk through the subpoena idea.

'Even if it does bring them out, I'm not sure what you'll get,' Bosch said. 'You know what they say: the FBI doesn't share. It eats like an elephant and shits like a mouse.'

Lorna laughed. It made me realize that Cisco had been silent through the whole discussion.

'Cisco, what do you think?' I asked.

'I think another way to get information about that place is for me to go down there and ask if they're hiring,' Cisco said. 'Maybe I get inside there and see what's going on — even if they don't hire me.'

'Put a hard hat on, and you look the part,' I said with a smile. 'But no. If they're running a con, they'd do a deep dive checking you out, and your name would connect to mine. I think I'd rather have you working with the Indians on Opparizio.'

Cisco called the men on his surveillance team the Indians. Political correctness aside, he likened them to the Indians in the old westerns who watched the wagon trains from the cliffs without the settlers having any clue.

'Well, ready to go if you need it,' Cisco said. 'Surveillance gets a bit boring, you know?'

'Then I'll tell you what,' I said. 'If you are okay leaving your team on Opparizio and Ferrigno, why don't you spend a couple days on Milton, the cop who pulled me over.'

Cisco nodded.

'I could do that,' he said.

'I still don't buy his story,' I said. 'If he was doing somebody's bidding, I want to know whose and why.'

'On it,' Cisco said.

'What about me, Mickey?' Lorna said. 'What do you need from me?'

I had to think fast about that. Lorna wouldn't want to be left out of the case.

'Uh, go back into our files on Trammel,' I said. 'Pull out anything that has to do with our background work on Opparizio. I don't remember everything, and I have to be ready to go at him again — if we ever find him.'

Jennifer came back to the table from her call but didn't sit down. She looked at me and held up her phone.

'We're on,' she said. 'Warfield set a hearing on the motion to compel for one o'clock today. She told Berg to bring her lead investigator too.'

I was surprised.

'That was quick,' I said. 'We must've struck a nerve.'

'That was Andrew, Warfield's clerk,' Jennifer said. 'We definitely struck a nerve with the prosecution. He said Death Row Dana got mad as hell when he called her.'

'Good,' I said. 'That'll make it interesting. We're going to put her lead detective on the

146

stand before she does.'

I checked my watch and then looked at Lorna.

'Lorna, how long would it take to get a couple blowups off crime scene photos?' I asked.

'Give them to me now and I'll put a rush on them,' she said. 'You want them mounted on a hard back?'

'If we can,' I said. 'More important just to have them for the hearing.'

I pushed my empty plate back and opened my laptop on the table. I pulled up the two crime scene photos I planned to display at the afternoon's hearing: two different shots of Sam Scales in the trunk of my Lincoln. I sent them to Lorna and warned her that they were graphic. It wasn't her delicate sensibilities I was trying to protect. It was the photo technician at the FedEx store that I wanted her to warn.

18

It felt good to enter Judge Warfield's courtroom through the public entrance rather than the steel door from the holding cell. But at the same time, the 'free man's' entrance put me in a heavy confluence of post-lunch returnees to the courthouse, including Dana Berg, who mad-dogged me on the elevator like an OG from lockdown. I ignored it and saved my own enmity for court. I held the door for her but she declined to say thanks.

The media twins were already in their usual spots when we entered.

'I see you alerted the press,' Berg said.

'Not me,' I said. 'Maybe they're just vigilant. Isn't that what we want in a free society? A vigilant press?'

'Well, you're barking up the wrong tree this time. They're going to see you get your ass handed to you by the judge.'

'For the record, Dana, I don't blame you. I actually like you, because you're fierce and focused. I wish all our government people were. But you have people working for you who are not doing you any favors.'

We split as we went through the railing. She went left to the prosecution table, while I went right to the defense table. Jennifer was already seated there.

'Anything from Lorna?' I asked.

148

'She just parked and is on her way,' she said.

'Hope so.'

I opened my briefcase and pulled out a legal pad I had worked on while doing final prep in the first-floor cafeteria. Jennifer leaned over to look at my scribbling.

'You ready?' she asked.

'Yep,' I said.

I turned in my seat and checked the gallery. I had sent a text about the hearing to my daughter, but it was last minute and I was unsure of her Monday-afternoon class schedule. I had not heard back from her and she was not in the courtroom.

Judge Warfield was ten minutes late starting the afternoon session and that gave Lorna enough time to get to the courtroom with the photo exhibits. We were locked and loaded when Deputy Chan called the room to order and Warfield took the bench.

I held my pad in hand and was ready to be called to the lectern — it was my motion, my prerogative to go first. But Berg stood and addressed the court.

'Your Honor, before Mr. Haller is allowed to stand up here and feed his completely unfounded claims to the media that he has invited to the hearing, the state would request that the hearing be moved in camera so as not to taint the jury pool that the defense is trying to reach with these wild and wholly unsubstantiated accusations.'

I was standing before she was finished and the judge cued me.

149

'Mr. Haller?'

'Thank you, Judge. The defense objects to the motion to move this hearing to chambers. Just because Ms. Berg doesn't like what she will hear is no reason to cover up what is said and presented. It's true that these are serious allegations but sunlight is the best disinfectant, Your Honor, and this hearing should remain open to all. Additionally, and for the record, I did not alert the media to this emergency hearing. I don't know who did. But it never occurred to me, as it apparently has to Ms. Berg, that a vigilant media would be a bad thing.'

I turned and gestured toward the two reporters as I finished. I saw then that Kent Drucker, the lead investigator on the case, had arrived and was sitting in the gallery row behind the prosecution table.

'Are you finished, Mr. Haller?' Warfield asked.

'Yes, Your Honor,' I said. 'Submitted.'

'The request for a closed hearing is denied,' Warfield said. 'Mr. Haller, do you have any witnesses?'

I paused. In a perfect world a lawyer never asks a question he doesn't know the answer to. That means a good lawyer never puts a witness on the stand whom he or she cannot control or draw the needed answers from. I knew all of that but still made the call to go against the received wisdom.

'Your Honor, I see Detective Drucker in the courtroom. Let's start with him as the first witness.'

Drucker went through the gate to the witness

150

stand and was sworn in. He was a seasoned investigator with more than twenty years on the job, half of it working homicides. He wore a nice suit and carried his copy of the murder book with him. If he was surprised I had called on him, he didn't show it. Since we were not in front of a jury, I skipped the soft introductory questions and got right to the heart of the matter.

'Detective, I see you brought your murder book with you.'

'Yes, sir, I did.'

'Would you mind going to the property report that was filed in regard to the belongings of the victim in this case, Sam Scales.'

Drucker opened the thick binder on the flat surface at the front of the witness box, leafed through it, and quickly found the report. I asked him to read it to the judge and he quickly ticked off items of clothing and shoes, as well as the contents of Scales's pockets, which amounted to some loose change, a set of keys, a comb, and a money clip containing $180 in twenties.

'Anything else in his pockets?' I asked.

'No, sir,' Drucker responded.

'Cell phone?'

'No, sir.'

'No wallet?'

'No wallet.'

'Was that notable to you?'

'Yes.'

I waited for more and got nothing. Drucker was one of those witnesses who would not give an inch more than what was required.

151

'Can you tell us why?' I said, not hiding my exasperation.

'It raised a question,' Drucker said. 'Missing wallet — could this have been a robbery?'

'But there was a money clip in his pocket, wasn't there?'

'Yes.'

'Didn't that undercut the robbery theory and raise the possibility that the wallet was taken for another reason?'

'It could have, yes.'

'It 'could have'? I'm asking if it did.'

'Everything was a question. The man was obviously murdered. There were a lot of possibilities as to motive.'

'Without a wallet and ID, how did you identify the victim as Sam Scales?'

'Fingerprints. There was a patrol sergeant on hand with a mobile reader. We got the ID pretty fast and it was more reliable than checking a wallet. People carry fake IDs.'

He had just unknowingly made a point that I intended to make.

'After you identified the victim as Sam Scales, did you do a criminal background check on him?'

'My partner did.'

'What did he find?'

'A long list of frauds, cons, and other crimes that I am sure you are familiar with.'

I ignored the barb and pressed on.

'Isn't it a fact that in each of those frauds, cons, and other crimes, Sam Scales used a different alias?'

152

'That is correct.'

Berg sensed that a kill shot might be coming and stood up and objected.

'Your Honor, this is a motion to compel discovery, and counsel is leisurely walking the witness through the entire investigation of the case. Is there a purpose here?'

It wasn't much of an objection but it did serve to knock me out of my rhythm. The judge admonished me to get to the point of my questioning or move on.

'Detective Drucker, knowing that the victim of this murder used different aliases, wouldn't it have been important to the investigation to recover his wallet to see what alias he was using at the time of his death?'

Drucker digested the question for a long moment before responding.

'Hard to say,' he said.

I knew with that answer that I would never get what I wanted from Drucker. He was too wary of me to ever break free of the short answers that imparted very little information of value.

'Okay, let's move on,' I said. 'Detective, could you turn to the crime scene photos in your murder book and look at photographs thirty-seven and thirty-nine.'

While Drucker found the relevant pages in the murder book, I quickly set up two portable easels in front of the empty jury box and on them placed the 24 × 18 blowup shots Lorna had gotten made that morning. Each was a photograph of Sam Scales lying on his side in the trunk of my Lincoln. The second shot was a little tighter than the first.

'Did you find the photos, Detective Drucker?'

'Yes, I have them here.'

'Do your photos thirty-seven and thirty-nine correspond with the blowups I have put up for the court to see?'

'Do they correspond? I'm not — '

'Do they match, Detective? Are they identical?'

Drucker made a display of looking down at his photos and then at the two shots I had put up on the easels.

'They appear to be the same,' he finally said.

'Perfect,' I said. 'Can you tell us for the record what the two photos depict?'

'They're both shots of the victim in this case in the trunk of your car. One of the photos is zoomed closer in than the other.'

'Thank you, Detective. The victim is lying on his right side, correct?'

'That is correct.'

'Okay, and can I now draw your attention to the victim's left hip, which is up toward the camera. Do you see the left rear pocket of the victim's pants?'

'I see it.'

'Do you see the rectangular-shaped distension of the pocket?'

Drucker hesitated as he realized where this was going.

'Do you see it, Detective Drucker?'

'I see some sort of pattern there. I don't know what it is.'

'You don't think that is indicative of a wallet in

154

that back pocket, Detective?'

'I couldn't know for sure without looking in that pocket. All I do know is that there was no wallet turned in to me by forensics or the Medical Examiner's Office.'

Berg stood and objected to the line of questioning.

'Your Honor, counsel is trying to create suspicion about the investigation of this case based on a pattern he sees in the victim's clothing. There is no wallet in that pocket because no wallet was recovered from the victim or the crime scene. The defense is using this issue, this ghost wallet, to distract the court and feed the media a conspiracy theory he hopes will get out to the jury pool. Once again the People object, first of all, to the hearing itself, and, second, to this being discussed in open court.'

She sat down angrily and the judge turned her eyes to me.

'Your Honor, that was a nice speech, but the fact remains that anybody with two eyes can see that the victim had a wallet in his back pocket. Now that wallet is gone and not only does it cast doubt on the investigation of this murder, but it puts the defense at a steep disadvantage because it is prohibited from examining the evidence that was in the wallet. Having said all of that, if the court will indulge me for five more minutes with this witness, I believe it will become abundantly clear that something was terribly wrong with this investigation.'

Warfield took her time before responding and this told me she was riding with me on this, not with the prosecution.

'You may continue with the witness, Mr. Haller.'

'Thank you, Judge. My colleague Ms. Aronson is now going to put the body-cam video for Officer Milton on the big screen. What we will show is the early moments of the tape, when Officer Milton uses the remote car key to pop the trunk.'

The video started to play on the flat-screen on the wall opposite the jury box. The angle was from the side of the rear end of the Lincoln. Milton's hand came up into the screen as he used his thumb to pop the trunk. The lid came up, revealing the body of Sam Scales. The camera started moving as Milton reacted.

'Okay, stop it right there,' I said. 'Can you back it up to the point where the trunk just comes open?'

Jennifer did so and froze the image. Milton had taken a safe side angle to the car as he opened the trunk, presumably because he did not know who or what was in it. This gave a two-second side view of the body, an angle the forensic photographer had not taken. It just happened to be captured by Milton's body cam.

'Detective Drucker,' I said. 'Can I draw your attention to the victim's rear left pocket again? Does what you see from this angle change your opinion as to whether the victim had a wallet in his pocket at the time the body was discovered?'

All eyes were on the video screen except mine. I even saw one of the journalists slide down her gallery bench to get a better angle on the screen.

The camera angle on the video clearly showed the back pocket of the victim's pants to be slightly open because of an object inside it. It was a dark object but there was a line of lighter color running lengthwise in the middle of it.

To me, it was clearly a wallet with the edge of a currency bill poking out of it. To Drucker, it was still nothing.

'No,' he testified. 'I can't tell for sure what that is.'

I had him.

'What do you mean by 'what that is,' Detective?'

'I mean I can't tell. It could be anything.'

'But you are now acknowledging that there is something in his pocket, correct?'

Drucker realized he had walked into a defense trap.

'Well, I can't say for sure,' he said. 'It could just be the lining of the pocket.'

'Really?' I said, full of disbelief. 'You are now saying that is the lining of the pocket?'

'I'm saying I don't know for sure.'

'Detective, can you go back to the property report you have in the murder book, and I'll ask my last question.'

The room waited silently until Drucker had it in front of him.

'Okay, sir,' I said. 'The property report lists where each item recovered came from, correct?'

'Yes, correct.'

Drucker seemed relieved to get an easy one. But I didn't let it last long.

'Okay, then,' I said. 'What does the report say

157

was removed from the left rear pocket of the victim's pants?'

'Nothing,' Drucker said. 'Nothing is listed.'

'No further questions,' I said.

19

Like a good prosecutor, Dana Berg was thinking of the trial down the road. Her cross-examination of Detective Drucker was not so much about winning the day as it was about winning the trial. She had to make sure that what went on the record today would not turn a juror against Drucker or the prosecution at trial. The smartest move she made was to ask for a ten-minute recess after I finished my direct. That gave her the space to huddle with Drucker and get a handle on what was transpiring here.

When court reconvened, Drucker had a completely different view of the photographs and video I had showed him.

I was not surprised.

'Detective Drucker, did you get a chance to review all of the crime scene photos of the victim during the break?' she asked.

'Yes, I did,' Drucker said.

'And did you draw any new conclusions about what you saw?'

'I looked at all of the photos we have of the body in the trunk and I now believe that there most likely was a wallet in the rear pocket of the pants at the time the body was in the trunk.'

I had to smile. Berg was going to make it seem as though the prosecution team had made this discovery and brought it to light.

'And yet your own property report says no

wallet. How do you explain that?'

'Well, obviously, the wallet was taken at some point.'

'Taken? You mean taken and misplaced?'

'Possibly.'

'Could it have been stolen?'

'Possibly.'

'When was the clothing that was on the body searched?'

'We didn't touch it while it was in the trunk. We waited for the coroner's people to arrive and then the body was removed from the trunk. We grabbed his prints with the reader and then the body was wrapped in plastic. After that, it was taken to the coroner's office for autopsy.'

'So, can you say at what point the clothing was removed and examined and the property inventoried?'

'That all falls under the coroner's duties. The body was prepped for autopsy the following day and I got a call from an investigator over there that I could swing by and pick up the property.'

'And did you?'

'Not right away. The autopsy was scheduled for the following morning. I waited to pick up the property then.'

'It wasn't urgent?'

'Not really. The coroner's investigator shot me an email with the property list. I noted that there was no wallet, and the other property didn't appear to be germane to the investigation.'

'You got that email when?'

Drucker looked up innocently at the judge.

'Can I refer to my records?' he asked.

'You may,' Warfield said.

Drucker flipped through pages in the murder book and then stopped to read.

'I have the email here,' he said. 'Got it at four twenty the afternoon after the callout.'

'So, doing the math,' Berg said. 'The first you knew that there was no wallet was about seventeen hours after you were called to the murder scene to begin the investigation. Correct?'

'Correct.'

'And during that time, you did not have custody of the victim's clothing or personal belongings, correct?'

'Correct. Anything could have happened to the wallet in that time.'

'It could have been stolen or misplaced?'

'Correct.'

'Did you take the wallet, Detective Drucker?'

'No, I never even saw it.'

'Did you intentionally hold it back from the discovery package I asked you to put together for the defense?'

'I did not.'

'No further questions, Your Honor.'

I had to give Berg credit. She had skillfully pulled Drucker from the credibility scrap heap and would live to fight another day with him at trial. He was dismissed from the witness stand and I told the judge I had no other witnesses and was ready to argue. Berg also said she was ready to go.

My opening salvo was short and to the point.

'Your Honor, we have a situation here where the state has mishandled a key piece of evidence, hidden their malfeasance from the defense, and now it is the defense that is left damaged by their failure. Whether or not their actions were intentional, my right to a fair trial has been more than infringed on — it's been trampled. I knew the victim. I knew his history and I knew his MO. He changed aliases the way some people change their shoes. The loss of this wallet, which contained the current identification of Sam Scales at the time of his death, has prevented my team from adequately being able to investigate the victim's activities and therefore learn of potential threats and killers.

'That is my argument if you buy their explanation of the wallet being innocently misplaced or stolen by someone skulking around the halls of the coroner's office. Personally, I don't believe any of it. This was an intentional effort to subvert a fair trial. This was the prosecution and police getting together and — '

Berg jumped up and objected to my casting aspersions on the actions and motives of the prosecution.

'This is argument,' I said. 'I can say whatever I want.'

'To a degree,' Warfield said. 'I'm not going to let you stray from what is on the record. I think you have made your argument. Do you wish to add anything else?'

Berg had effectively knocked me off the rails and the judge wasn't going to let me get back on.

'No, Your Honor,' I said. 'Submitted.'

'Ms. Berg,' the judge said. 'I hope you will be as succinct.'

Berg went to the lectern and began.

'Your Honor, the histrionics of defense counsel aside, there is no evidence that exists or was submitted here that indicates some great conspiracy to prevent a fair trial in the case and, most important of all, no evidence or indication of a plan to hold back or subvert the discovery process. Yes, the victim's wallet went missing, but it was defense counsel himself who brought this to light only this morning. To come here and cry foul play and conspiracy, counsel is simply grandstanding for the media, and the state asks the court to dismiss the motion.'

I stood to respond but the judge did not allow it.

'I think I have heard enough, Mr. Haller. I know what you will say and then I know what Ms. Berg will say in return. So, let's save the time, shall we?'

I got the message and sat down.

'The court finds the information revealed today to be very troubling,' Warfield continued. 'The state concedes that there was a wallet in the victim's pocket but it now cannot produce that wallet for examination by the defense. Whether the wallet disappeared through negligence or something more sinister, the situation still leaves the defense in a reduced position. As Mr. Haller has suggested, the wallet could have contained an alternate ID used by the victim. That in turn could lead to evidence supporting Mr. Haller's position.'

Warfield paused there and appeared to be studying her notes for a moment before continuing.

163

'At this time, the court doesn't know what the remedy is but is going to take forty-eight hours to consider it. And it will give the state those same forty-eight hours to either find the wallet or determine exactly what happened to it. I am continuing this hearing until Wednesday at one o'clock, and my suggestion to the prosecution is to not come back empty-handed. We are adjourned.'

Warfield then turned in her chair and stood up. She moved down the three steps from the bench quickly and gracefully, her robe flowing behind her as she reached the door leading to her chambers and disappeared.

'Good work,' Jennifer whispered in my ear.

'Maybe,' I whispered back. 'We'll see in a couple days. Did you get that subpoena printed?'

'Got it.'

'Let me go see if I can get her while she's feeling it for the defense.'

While Jennifer opened her briefcase to get the document, Berg stopped by the defense table on her exit.

'You really think I had something to do with that? That I even knew about it?'

I looked up at her for a moment, then answered.

'I don't know, Dana. All I do know is that from day one you've been trying to tilt the board so all the pieces roll to your side. So, give me a reason not to believe it. Go find the wallet.'

She frowned and walked away without a response.

'Here,' Jennifer said.

164

I took the subpoena and got up.

'I'm going to go,' she said. 'Let me know if there's a problem.'

'Will do. Let's talk tomorrow morning. And thanks for jumping on this today.'

'No problem. You'll get it to Cisco?'

'Yeah, but I think I'm going to go with him, see if I can rattle the cage a little bit.'

'Good luck with that. The FBI doesn't usually rattle.'

I walked over to Warfield's clerk and asked him to call the judge before she settled in to chambers and see if I could come back to get a subpoena signed. He reluctantly made the call and I could see the slight surprise on his face when the judge apparently told him to send me in.

The clerk opened a half door in his corral and buzzed me through the door to chambers. It led me into a hallway that was an extension of the clerk's domain, with file cabinets on one side and a large printer and worktable on the other. I passed through to another hallway, this one lined with doors to individual judge's chambers.

Warfield's was one down to the left and her door was open. She was behind her desk and had hung her black robe on a coatrack.

'You have a subpoena for me?' she said.

'Yes, Judge,' I said. 'A subpoena for records.'

I handed the document Jennifer had prepared across the desk. I remained standing while the judge studied it.

'This is federal,' she said.

'It's for the FBI but it's a state subpoena,' I explained.

'I can see that, but you know you're spinning your wheels. The FBI won't respond to a state subpoena. You have to go through the U.S. Attorney's Office, Mr. Haller.'

'Some would say that going through the U.S. A's Office would be spinning wheels, Judge.'

She kept her eyes on the subpoena and read out loud: "'All documents related to interactions with Samuel Scales or aliases . . .'"

Now she dropped the paper on her desk, leaned back, and looked up at me.

'You know where this will go, right?' she said. 'The circular file.'

'It may,' I said.

'You're just fishing? Trying to get a reaction?'

'I'm working on a hunch. It would have helped if I had had the wallet and a name to work with. Do you have a problem with my fishing, Judge?'

I was speaking to the former defense attorney in her. I knew she had been in the same position: needing a break and backing a long shot to get it.

'I don't have anything against what you're doing,' Warfield said. 'But it's a little late in the game for it. You have trial in a month.'

'I'll be ready, Judge,' I said.

She leaned forward, grabbed a pen from a fancy silver holder on the desk, and signed the subpoena. She handed it back to me.

'Thank you, Judge,' I said.

I walked to the door and she caught me before I could slip through.

'I cleared two weeks for jury selection and

trial,' she said to my back.

I turned around to look at her.

'If you try to fuck me by running it up to game time and then asking for a delay, my answer's going to be no.'

I nodded that I understood.

'Thank you, Your Honor,' I said.

I walked through the door with my long-shot subpoena.

20

Back in the courtroom the clerk told me I'd had a visitor who had been waiting in the gallery but the deputy had shooed him out because the courtroom was dark for the rest of the day.

'A big guy?' I asked. 'Black T-shirt, boots?'

'No,' the clerk said. 'A Black guy. Had on a suit.'

That made me curious. I gathered the materials I had left at my place at the defense table and then left the courtroom. Out in the hallway I found my visitor waiting on a bench outside the courtroom door. I almost didn't recognize him in the suit and tie.

'Bishop?'

'Counselor.'

'Bishop, what are you doing here? You got out?'

'I'm out, man, and ready to go to work.'

It then struck me. I had offered him a job when he got out of jail. Bishop read my hesitation.

'It's okay, man, if you don't have it. I know you got your trial and shit to worry about.'

'No, it's okay. I just . . . it's a surprise, that's all.'

'Well, you need a driver?'

'I do, actually. I mean, not every day but I need a guy on call, yeah. When do you want to start?'

Bishop spread his arms as if to display himself.

'I got my funeral suit on,' he said. 'I'm ready to go.'

'What about a driver's license?' I asked.

'Got that, too. Went to the DMV as soon as I got out.'

'When was that?'

'Wednesday.'

'Okay, let me see it. I'll have to shoot a photo of it and add you to the insurance.'

'No problem.'

He pulled a thin wallet out of a pants pocket and gave me a brand-new license. It looked legit to me as far as I could tell. I saw for the first time that his name was Bambadjan Bishop. I pulled my phone and took the photo.

'Where's that name come from?' I asked.

'My mother was from Ivory Coast,' he said. 'Her father's name.'

'So, I have to go out to Westwood to drop a subpoena. You want to start right now?'

'I'm here. Ready to go.'

My Lincoln was parked in the black hole parking structure. We walked over and I gave Bishop the keys and took the back seat.

We worked our way up to the ground-level exit and I paid careful attention to his driving skills as I gave him the rundown on how the job worked. He was essentially on call 24/7 but most of the time I would need him during weekdays only. He needed to have a phone I could text him on. No burners. No alcohol. No weapons. He didn't have to wear a tie but I liked the suit. He could shed the jacket whenever he was in the car. On the days I needed him he would have to get to my house, where the car was kept, and go from there. No overnight take-homes of the car.

'I got a phone,' he said when I was finished. 'It ain't a burner.'

'Good,' I said. 'I need the number. Any questions?'

'Yeah, what'm I getting paid?'

'The four hundred I was paying you for protection is now suspended because you're out and I'm out. I'll pay you eight hundred a week to drive me. There will be a lot of downtime and days off.'

'I was thinking a thousand.'

'I was thinking eight. Let's see how you do, then we can talk about a thousand. As soon as I get through this trial and am back to making money, we'll talk. Do we have a deal?'

'Yeah. Deal.'

'Good.'

'Where we going in Westwood?'

'The federal building at Wilshire and the 405.'

'With all the flagpoles out front.'

'That's it.'

We got out of the underground parking and Bishop worked his way to the 10 freeway and headed west without my having to issue instructions. That was a good sign. I pulled my phone and texted Cisco, telling him to meet me in the lobby of the federal building in Westwood.

What's up

On my way.

I put the phone away and looked at Bishop's eyes in the rear-view mirror.

'What do you want me to call you?' I said. 'I'm so used to calling you Bishop but that was in jail and maybe — '

'Bishop is good.'

'So when I was in there, I wanted to mind my own business. I didn't ask anybody anything. But now I have to ask you, what were you in Twin Towers for and how'd you get out?'

'I was doing a bullet on a probation violation. Normally they would have put me up at Pitchess but a guy from LAPD gang intel was working me and he didn't like driving all the way up there all the time. So I got lucky. Got a solo cell at T.T. instead of a dayroom cot at Pitchess.'

'So, those times you said you had court, you were actually off snitching to gang intel?'

He glanced at me in the mirror, picking up the tone in my voice.

'I worked him,' he said. 'He didn't work me.'

'So, you're not going to have to testify in a case?' I pressed. 'I don't want to make myself a target here, Bishop.'

'There is no case, Counselor. I worked it until my year was up and then I was out. If'n he comes around now, I can tell him to fuck off.'

His story tracked right. A bullet was a year and convicts serving a year or less usually weren't

171

sent to state prison. They served their short sentences in one of the county's stockades, and the Peter J. Pitchess Honor Rancho was the largest of them all.

'You're a Crip, right?' I asked.

'I was an associate,' Bishop said.

'Which set?'

'Southside.'

During my time with the Public Defender's Office I had represented defendants from probably every known clique and set of the Bloods and Crips, but that was long ago and no names of former clients came to mind.

'Before your time, but Southside guys supposedly took out Tupac in Vegas,' I said.

'That's the word,' Bishop said. 'But that was ancient history. None of those OGs were around when I was.'

'What were you on probation for?'

'Slinging.'

'So, why do you want to work for me when you could go back to your homies and sling dope? More money in that.'

'You know why, man. I got a girl and a kid now. I'm gonna get married and be done with all that.'

'You sure, Bambadjan?'

'You check me, man. You'll see. I never was a user and I'm outta that life. I'm gonna find a place up here to rent and never go back down there.'

Bishop transitioned onto the northbound 405 to get off on Wilshire Boulevard. The federal building rose seventeen floors next to the freeway, a building that looked like a giant gray tombstone.

Soon we were in the vast parking lot that surrounded it. I told Bishop to stay in the lot and that I would text him when I was coming out.

'This probably won't take too long,' I said.

'Paying your taxes?' he asked.

I didn't answer. I wasn't going to start telling him my business just yet.

In the lobby I saw Cisco waiting on the other side of the metal detector. He had brought Lorna with him. This was fine because she was a state-registered process server as well. California statutes required that all subpoenas be delivered by process servers or licensed private detectives. It was a safety rule designed to circumvent the possibility of lawyers or their clients serving subpoenas and other legal documents on the people they were engaged in disputes with.

Normally I would be nowhere near this subpoena delivery but I wanted to be there to make a statement. A statement I hoped would engender a response from the bureau.

I joined Cisco and Lorna after getting through the metal detector. We took an elevator up to the fourteenth floor, where the largest FBI field office west of Chicago was located. We somehow ended up alone on the elevator.

'You know they aren't going to accept this, right?' Cisco said.

'I know,' I said. 'I just want to make some waves, bang a few drums, and see what happens.'

'The FBI?' Lorna said. 'Don't count on them reacting at all.'

'Just have your phone ready,' I said.

Keeping with the rules, I handed Cisco the subpoena that Judge Warfield had signed. The elevator doors opened on fourteen and we saw a reception counter protected with thick glass like a bank teller's cage in a high-crime zone. A woman sat on a stool behind a slide-through drawer. She switched on a two-way speaker attached to the glass.

'Can I help you?' she asked.

Cisco leaned down to the speaker and read the name on the subpoena.

'I'd like to see the SAC, John Trembley,' he said.

'Do you have identification?' the receptionist asked. 'For all three of you?'

I pulled my wallet and dug out my driver's license and a business card — one of the old ones printed before the California bar made me remove 'Reasonable Doubt for a Reasonable Fee' from all of my advertising and marketing. Cisco and Lorna produced their IDs as well and we put all three in the drawer. The receptionist took her time studying them before responding.

'The special agent in charge doesn't see anyone without an appointment,' the receptionist said. 'I can give you an email you can use to reach out and set something up.'

Cisco held up the document with Trembley's name written on it.

'I have a subpoena here signed by a judge requesting documents from Agent Trembley,' he said. 'He needs to see it right away and I have to

174

confirm service or we could both end up in contempt.'

'All subpoena service goes through the U.S. Attorney's Office and they are located downtown,' the receptionist said. 'You should know that.'

'I do know that,' Cisco said. 'This is different. This subpoena has a clock on it.'

I leaned toward the speaker.

'Can you call Agent Trembley, please?' I asked. 'He'll want to know about this.'

The receptionist seemed annoyed by the request.

'Put it in the drawer,' she said.

The steel drawer slid out with our IDs, which we all collected. My business card was in the bottom. I took it and gave it to Cisco, who slid it under the paper clip attached to the multipage subpoena.

Cisco placed the subpoena in the drawer and it was immediately pulled in. The receptionist turned off the speaker while she pulled the subpoena out and looked at it. She then picked up a phone and made a call. The glass suppressed her side of a short conversation.

A few moments later a man in a suit stepped through a door behind the receptionist, took the subpoena, and only glanced at it as he opened a door and stepped into the waiting area.

'Agent Trembley?' I asked.

'No,' he said. 'Agent Eason. We don't accept subpoenas here.'

I nodded to the one in his hand.

'You just did,' I said.

175

'No, this has to be taken to the U.S. Attorney's Office,' he said.

Lorna raised her cell phone and took a photo of Eason and the subpoena.

'Hey!' the agent cried. 'No photos. Delete that now!'

'You're served,' Cisco said.

Mission accomplished, I reached back and hit the elevator button. The doors opened right away. I looked back at Eason.

'My card's there,' I said. 'Tell Trembley he can call anytime.'

We left Eason standing there, holding the subpoena. As the elevator doors closed I saw him glance through the glass at the receptionist. He looked both angry and embarrassed.

Back down in the lobby I gave Lorna and Cisco the news about Bishop.

'I just hired a driver,' I said.

We walked through the glass doors to the flag plaza.

'Who?' Lorna asked. 'I thought hiring someone was my job.'

'Bambadjan Bishop,' I said.

'What?' Lorna said. 'Who?'

'Is that the guy who had your back in Twin Towers?' Cisco asked.

'Exactly,' I said. 'He's out and I'm trying him out as a driver. I sort of promised him the job when I was in there. The protection money to his girlfriend now stops and I'm paying him eight bills a week to drive.'

'And you trust him?' Lorna asked.

'Not exactly,' I said. 'I need to make sure he's

legit. After the eavesdropping scam and now the wallet gone missing, I'm not going to be surprised by anything the other side pulls.'

'You think he's wired up for them?' Lorna asked.

'No indication of that but I want to be sure,' I said. 'That's where you come in, Big Man.'

'Where is he?'

'Out in the lot somewhere. I'll text him to come pick me up.'

'So you want me to bend him over the car or what?'

'I want you to search him for a wire but you don't need to prone him out. I think he'll cooperate. If he doesn't, then we know.'

When we got to the parking lot, I texted the number Bishop had given me and we waited. When the Lincoln pulled up, Lorna and I got into the back and Cisco squeezed into the front for the meet and greet.

'Bishop, this is Lorna and Cisco,' I said. 'Lorna manages the practice and she'll get with you about any paperwork you need to set up the job. And Cisco's my investigator and he needs to check you.'

'Check me for what?' Bishop said.

'A wire,' Cisco said. 'Just a little pat-down.'

'That's bullshit,' Bishop said. 'I ain't wearin' no wire.'

'I don't think you're wearing one either,' I said. 'But a lot of confidential conversations take place in this car. I need to be able to guarantee my clients that they are in fact confidential.'

'Whatever,' Bishop said. 'I got nothing to hide.'

Cisco turned in his seat and reached his big hands toward Bishop's chest. It took him less than a minute to make a determination.

'He's clean,' Cisco said.

'Good,' I said. 'Welcome to the team, Bishop.'

21

They came that night to my home. A knock so sharp that Kendall nearly shrieked. She was bingeing the last season of *The Sopranos* and was already on edge. I was sitting next to her on the couch, going through the files from the old Sam Scales cases I had handled.

I opened the door and a man and woman stood there. I knew they were feds before they said word one or showed their badges. They introduced themselves as agents Rick Aiello and Dawn Ruth. Over my shoulder they could see Kendall sitting on the couch and asked if there was a place we could speak privately. I stepped out through the front door and pointed to the table and chairs at the far end of the deck.

'Out here is good,' I said.

We moved toward the table, and the motion engaged the deck lights — two sconces on the wall and an overhead in the roof's eave. That told me that the motion-activated camera attachment had engaged as well.

We stopped at the high-top table but no one sat down. I broke the ice.

'I suppose this is about the subpoena we dropped off for your boss today,' I asked.

'Yes, sir, it is,' said Aiello.

'We need to know why you believe that the bureau would have any information on the activities of Sam Scales,' Ruth said.

I smiled and spread my hands.

'Does it matter now?' I asked. 'Aren't the two of you confirming it by showing up here at my house at nine o'clock at night? I thought the subpoena might cause some commotion and consternation, but to be honest, I wasn't expecting you guys till at least tomorrow, maybe Wednesday.'

'We're glad you think it's funny, Mr. Haller,' Aiello said. 'We don't.'

'No, what's not funny is me being charged with the murder of a guy who was being watched by the FBI,' I said. 'Maybe you can tell me — how did that happen?'

I was bluffing, hoping to get a confirmation or some indication I was on the right track with Sam Scales. But the agents were too smart for that.

'Good try,' Ruth said.

From the inside pocket of his standard-issue FBI blue blazer, Aiello pulled out a folded document and handed it to me.

'There's your stupid little subpoena,' he said. 'Wipe your ass with it.'

'What about my Freedom of Information Act petition?' I asked. 'I guess I can wipe my ass with that too, huh?'

'We don't expect to hear from you again,' Ruth said.

She nodded to Aiello and they turned back toward the steps. I watched them go and then, without thinking, I made a play for the camera.

'Or what?' I called after them. 'You know it's all going to come out at trial. I'm not going

180

down so you can keep your BioGreen case secret.'

Ruth pirouetted perfectly and came back toward me. But Aiello passed her on the outside and got to me first.

'What did you say?' he asked.

'I think you heard me pretty good,' I said.

He brought both hands up and shoved me backward into the deck railing, then moved in and held me leaning back over it, the street twenty-five feet below.

'Haller, you've been told,' he said. 'Any attempt by you to compromise a federal investigation that has zero to do with your . . . situation . . . is going to be met with a very harsh response.'

Ruth made an effort to pull her partner off me but she didn't have the weight or muscle.

'What's going on at that plant?' I asked. 'What's Opparizio got going? I exposed that guy for what he was nine years ago. You're kind of late to the game.'

Aiello put his own weight into leaning me farther over. It was a wooden railing and I felt it hard against my backbone. I was afraid the rail might give way and we would both fall to the street.

'Rick!' Ruth yelled. 'Let him go. Now!'

Aiello finally pulled me by the collar back onto steady ground and pointed at my face.

'You don't know what you're dealing with,' he said.

'Just barking up the wrong tree, huh?' I said. 'Is that what — '

181

'You're barking up the wrong planet, Haller,' Aiello said. 'Stay away from it. Or you'll bear witness to the power and might of the federal government.'

'Is that a threat?' I asked.

'It is what it is,' Aiello said.

Ruth yanked her partner away by the arm.

'Have a good evening,' she said.

She pulled him toward the steps. They passed Kendall, who now stood in the open doorway to the house, drawn from the television by the raised voices. I watched them go, this time deciding not to bother baiting them further. They descended the stairs to the street. I heard Ruth admonish Aiello in a tense whisper.

'What the hell was that?' she said. 'Get in the car.'

I heard the doors of their car open and close. Then the engine turned over and the tires shot gravel as they took off and drove down the hill.

'Who were they?' Kendall asked.

'FBI,' I said.

'What? What did they want?'

'To scare me. Let's go in.'

The first thing I did when I got back inside was go to my Ring camera app and check whether the confrontation on the front deck could be seen and heard clearly. It was all there, but the sound was sketchy in places. I had no doubt that it could be teased out by a sound expert if I ever needed it. I sent the video to Cisco and Jennifer so they would have copies. I also wrote a short note to accompany the file transfer: *Looks like we touched a nerve.*

182

I returned to my spot on the couch next to Kendall but found it hard to get back into the grind of going through the case files.

'What exactly did they want?' Kendall asked.

'I rattled their cage today,' I said. 'They wanted to rattle mine.'

'Did they?'

'Nope.'

'Good. You want to keep working?'

'Nah, I think I'm done for the night.'

'Then, let's go to bed.'

'Good idea.'

But the move to the bedroom was interrupted by Cisco, who called after viewing the video I had sent. I told Kendall I'd be in in a few minutes.

'That looked a little testy,' Cisco said.

'They definitely aren't happy with the subpoena we dropped on them,' I said. 'Whatever they've got going at BioGreen, they don't want us in the picture.'

'But we stay with it, right?'

'Right. You hear anything from the Indians after this morning?'

'I got a report on the sidepiece. Still no sign of Opparizio.'

'We have to find him. What about that other thing you were doing?'

'Yeah, I was going to fill you in tomorrow. There was nothing there tonight. No flags. After he left you at the house, he walked down the hill to Sunset, ordered food right there at Zankou Chicken, and waited for a ride. Then I see a car pull up and it's his girlfriend.'

'How'd you know it was his girlfriend?'

'Because I've been dropping off cash to her every week since you got popped.'

'Right. Forgot.'

'She had the kid in the car too. They picked him up with dinner and went home to Inglewood. And that was it.'

'He didn't make any calls?'

'A couple but I had eyes on him. They were social calls. He was smiling, animated — not like he was reporting in as a CI.'

'Still, if we get the chance, we should check the phone. Get the call log. I want to be sure.'

I realized that my tone indicated that I was disappointed Bambadjan Bishop didn't appear to be snitching for the prosecution or the police. And I guess I was. If he was snitching, I could use that to my advantage, plus get the ultimate payoff when it came time to expose the wrongdoing in court.

'I think after the jail surveillance thing and now the missing wallet, they'd be crazy to try to submarine us,' Cisco said.

'You're probably right,' I acknowledged. 'But stay on him one more night. You never know.'

'Done.'

'Okay, Cisco, thanks. We'll talk tomorrow.'

As soon as I disconnected, I thought about Bosch. I had not sent him the video of the confrontation with the two FBI agents.

I called him directly and he picked up after two rings.

'Hold on,' he said. 'Let me get clear.'

I heard the distinctive sounds of a casino in

the background: slot-machine bells, people shouting. Then it got quiet and Bosch said hello.

'It's Mick. Where the hell are you?'

'Vegas. You couldn't tell? I just checked in at the Mandalay.'

'What are you doing there? I thought you were working for me.' I immediately regretted my choice of words.

'With me, I mean.'

'I am. That's why I'm here. Following something.'

'Well, we struck a big nerve today with the bureau. Two agents just showed up here to tell me we're barking up the wrong tree with BioGreen while confirming that we're barking up the right tree.'

'They like to do that.'

'Well, I don't know what you've got there, but I want to put everything we have into finding out about how Sam was mixed up with Opparizio and BioGreen. I still think it's the magic bullet. It'll win the case.'

'Got it. I should be back by tomorrow night.'

'Are you going to tell me what you're doing?'

'Tracking Sam Scales. The last time he got caught was for a phony online fundraiser for the victims of the music festival shooting out here. Remember that? The shooter was actually here at the Mandalay.'

'Of course. Another senseless act of hyperviolence perpetuated by the easy access to high-powered weapons.'

'You're not an NRA guy, are you?'

'No, I'm not.'

'Anyway, the state of Nevada was all over these scams related to the shooting and grabbed Scales in L.A. They extradited him back here for trial and he cut a deal and did fifteen months for fraud up at High Desert.'

'I remember he called me from the can out there. Wanted me to rep him but I said no. But couldn't you have gotten all of this by phone? I need you back here.'

'Not what I'm doing tomorrow. High Desert State Prison is about an hour from here. Scales's cellmate is still there and I'm going to go up and talk to him. Got it set up for eight a.m. I'll head back to L.A. after that.'

'You think he has something?'

'He's serving a five-year sentence for major fraud. He was selling phony casino chips, took in a couple million before they caught him. Anyway, these two spent fifteen months together in a cell. I'm thinking they may have traded a few stories about things they did and were planning to do.'

'Perfect, they put a fraud and a con artist together in the same cell. That's some match,' I said.

'They usually try to keep white-collar guys together so they don't get picked off by the heavies.'

'Thanks for schooling me.'

'Sorry, I guess you know more about jails than I do,' Bosch said.

'I don't know if that's a dig or a compliment. You fly over there or drive?'

'Drove.'

'Okay, call me when you're heading back. And then I want to get everybody together Wednesday after court to figure out the next steps.'

'I'll be there.'

After disconnecting the call, I thought about things for a few minutes. I felt that the team was getting close to the big secrets of the case. We had a momentum that could lead us to truth and triumph. It was just a question of whether we would get there in time.

Kendall called down the hall from the bedroom.

'Are you coming to bed or not?'

I stacked all the files I had spread around and got up from the couch. I dumped the files into my briefcase and clicked it closed.

'Coming.'

I headed into the hallway and she was standing there in her bathrobe. I stopped short.

'Scared me,' I said.

'You know, this is what happened before,' she said.

'What did?'

'You know. You let your work take over your life. *Our* lives. Night and day. And then what we had disappeared. And here we are, back together, and already you're doing it again.'

I reached out and gently grabbed the robe's terry-cloth belt, which she had loosely cinched around her waist. I tugged it playfully.

'Come here. This isn't the same thing, babe. This is me. My case. I have to put everything into it or there might not be any future for us. We've got a month until trial. I just need you to

187

put up with this for a month. Okay? Can you give me that?'

I moved my hands up her arms to her shoulders and waited. She said nothing. She just looked down at the floor between us.

'You can't give me the month?' I asked.

She shook her head.

'It's not that,' she said. 'I can give you the month. But sometimes it's like you're talking to me like a juror, like you're trying to convince me you're not guilty.'

I let go of her shoulders.

'And what, you think I am?'

'No. I'm talking about the way you talk to me.'

'I don't know what you mean,' I said. 'But if you think I'm trying to play you, then maybe you should go to bed and I should go back to work. I have to figure out how to convince a real jury I'm not a killer.'

I left her there in the hallway.

22

Tuesday, January 14

I worked late and fell asleep on the couch. I had forgotten to attach the charger to my ankle monitor and it woke me at 8:15 a.m. with a sharp intermittent beeping that told me the device's battery would be dead in an hour. And I would be in violation of the terms of my bail.

I timed the beeps. At the moment, the alarm was on a five-second interval but I knew that would get shorter and the device would get ear-piercingly louder as the hour counted down. I couldn't casually go into the bedroom to get the charger without the alarm waking Kendall, who liked to sleep in most mornings. But with no choice in the matter, I timed my move, went swiftly into the room, and managed to plug the charging cord into the ankle device before the next beep. It appeared that Kendall had slept through. She was on her side, turned away from me, and I could see her arm moving with each rhythmic breath of sleep. I now had an hour to pass while the device charged, but I had left my phone, laptop, and briefcase in the living room. I could unplug the charger and race with it out of the room but I felt I was pressing my luck already. And if the alarm sounded again, it would definitely wake up Kendall.

The bedroom TV remote was on the bed within reach, having been left there by Kendall the night before. I turned on the flat-screen and immediately muted the sound. I switched on the closed captions and started reading the news. The House was planning to send articles of impeachment to the Senate for what everybody in the country knew was a nonstarter. But it was monopolizing the news feed. I watched and read captions for twenty minutes before another story broke in for a few seconds of airtime. It was a report on rising concerns in Asia after the mystery virus originating in Wuhan, China, was confirmed as having jumped borders to other countries.

I heard my phone ringing out in the living room. I checked my watch. It was now 8:45 and I believed the ankle monitor had sufficiently charged to the point where there would be no alarm beep if I disconnected it. I quickly yanked out the charging line and moved quickly to get the phone. I missed the call but saw it had come from Bosch. I called him right back.

'Mick, there's an issue with the cellmate,' he said.

'You're at the prison?' I asked.

'I'm here and I saw the guy. His name is Austin Neiderland, but he won't talk to me. Says he's got a name that will tell us all we need to know about what Sam Scales was into. But he wouldn't give me the name.'

'What's he want? He's got to be through his appeals by now.'

'He wants you, Mick.'

'What's that mean?'

'He said he would give only you the name. He knows about you. Scales must've told him that you were a good lawyer. Neiderland says he'll give you the name if you just come up, sign in as his lawyer, and talk to him. See if there's anything to be done on his case, I guess. He's still got two years on his sentence. That means he still has to do eighteen months.'

'You mean today? Come there today?'

'Can you? I'll set it up and wait here for you.'

'Harry, I can't. I've got an ankle monitor and bail restrictions. I can't leave the county.'

'Shit, I forgot.'

'What about a video connection? Can we set up something like that?'

'I checked and the prison only does it for court hearings. No teleconferencing interviews or attorney-client meetings.'

There was silence on the phone while I thought about this.

'So, what else did he say about this name?' I finally asked. 'I mean, what if we jump through all these hoops and he says, yeah, it's Louis Opparizio. Then we're nowhere. We already have that name.'

'It's not Opparizio,' Bosch said. 'I tried that name on him and got a read. He didn't know it.'

'Okay, so can this even be done today? I have court tomorrow. Even if I can convince the judge to let me go up there, I have to be back tonight — tomorrow morning at the latest. You think I can get in and out? It's a prison, and they don't like cooperating with defense lawyers.'

'Your call, Mick, but if you have to talk to the judge to get permission, maybe she can write you an order that gets you in.'

'Different states, Harry. She doesn't have jurisdiction.'

'Well . . . what do you want to do?'

'Okay, hold tight. I'll see what I can do. I'll call you back as soon as I know something.'

I disconnected and thought about the best way to approach this. Then I called Lorna and asked if there was anything on my schedule.

'Your first witness list is due today,' she said. 'But that's it. And then you have the continuation of yesterday's hearing tomorrow at one.'

'Okay, I already have a wit list ready,' I said. 'I'll send it in. I might be going to Las Vegas — if the judge lets me.'

'What's in Vegas?'

'A prison where Sam Scales last served time. I want to talk to the guy he shared a cell with.'

'Good luck with that. Let me know.'

I next called Judge Warfield's courtroom and got her clerk, Andrew. I said I wanted to set up a teleconference with the judge requesting that I be allowed to leave the county for the day to pursue a witness. The clerk said he would check with the judge and call me back. I reminded him that Dana Berg would need to be alerted.

While I waited, I decided to act as if I would gain the judge's permission and I booked flights on JetSuite out of Burbank to Las Vegas. The outbound left in two hours.

Thirty minutes went by with no return call

from the judge or her clerk. I called the court-room back and pushed for an answer. Andrew said the judge was okay with a teleconference but Dana Berg had not responded to a message left for her.

'Can the judge just talk to me, then?' I asked. 'This is time-sensitive. I can see this potential witness today only and need to know whether I can go. If you leave a message for Berg saying when the conference is taking place, my guess is she'll respond and be on the call. If you just wait for her to call back, we're going to be waiting all day.'

The clerk took what I said under advisement and said he would get back to me. Another twenty minutes went by and Andrew called, saying he was connecting me to a conference call with the judge and Deputy D.A. Dana Berg. My plane was leaving in seventy minutes.

Soon I heard the judge's voice on the phone.

'I think we have everybody here,' she said. 'Mr. Haller, you are asking for a deviation in bail restrictions?'

'Yes, Your Honor, just for one day,' I said. 'I need to go to Las Vegas to see a witness.'

'Las Vegas. Really, Mr. Haller?'

'It's not what you think, Judge. I won't be anywhere near the Strip. Sam Scales was last incarcerated at High Desert State Prison about an hour north of Las Vegas. His cellmate is still there and I want to talk to him. The prosecution has given us nothing through discovery regarding Scales's activities leading up to the murder. The cellmate could be an important witness for the defense. One of my investigators is at the prison as we speak. He said the inmate will only talk to me. I've booked an eleven forty flight to Vegas and a seven o'clock flight back.'

'That was a bit presumptuous, was it not, Mr. Haller?'

'No, Your Honor. I did not anticipate how the court would rule. I just wanted to make sure I could get there should the court allow it.'

'Ms. Berg, are you still with us? Does the prosecution object to the defense request?'

'Here, Your Honor,' Berg said. 'I would first like to ask the name of the inmate he is going to see.'

'Austin Neiderland,' I said. 'He's at High Desert State Prison.'

'Your Honor,' Berg said. 'The state objects to this travel outside of bail restrictions and maintains its original argument from the bail hearing. We believe Mr. Haller is a flight risk. More now than before because the closer we get to trial, the clearer it becomes to Mr. Haller that his conviction and permanent incarceration are certain.'

'Judge, the prosecution's statement is ridiculous,' I said quickly. 'I've now been out of custody for five weeks and I have done nothing but prepare for my defense, even with the handicap of being pitted against a prosecution that does not like to play by the rules.'

'Your Honor, there is no handicap and there is no evidence that the prosecution doesn't play by the rules,' Berg said forcefully. 'Defense counsel has been engaged since the beginning of — '

'Stop it, stop it,' Warfield shouted. 'I do not intend to start my day playing referee to you two. I'm growing very weary of that. Now, as to the request, has counsel explored the possibility of teleconferencing this interview?'

'Yes, Your Honor,' I said. 'Believe me, that would be the way to go, but my investigator told me the prison does not make that available for meetings besides court hearings.'

'Very well,' Warfield said. 'The court is going to allow Mr. Haller to interview this witness. I will make the appropriate notification to the bail and detention folks, and, Mr. Haller, you need to be back in this county by midnight tonight or Ms. Berg's prophecy will become true. You will be considered a fugitive. Is that understood?'

'Yes, Your Honor,' I said. 'Thank you. And if I could make one other quick request?'

'Here we go,' Berg said.

'What is it, Mr. Haller?' Warfield asked.

'Your Honor, I have the ankle monitor and I'm sure that's going to be a problem at the prison in Nevada,' I said.

'No way,' Berg jumped in forcefully. 'You can't be serious. We are not going to accept him taking off the monitor. The state — '

'I'm not asking for that,' I cut in. 'I'm asking for a letter from the court that maybe Your Honor's clerk could write up quickly and email me, explaining my standing — if it comes into question.'

There was a pause during which the judge was most likely waiting for Berg to object. But I thought the prosecutor probably believed she

195

had overstepped with her loud objection to removal of the monitor. She had overplayed and now was silent.

'Very well,' Warfield said. 'I will craft a note and have Andrew email it to you.'

'Thank you, Your Honor,' I said.

After the call, I contacted Bosch and told him I was coming. I told him to set up the appointment with Neiderland for 2 p.m. This would give me time to fly over and be driven up to the prison. I also told Bosch to keep an eye out.

'I had to give Neiderland's name to the prosecution,' I said. 'I doubt they'll be able to get anybody out there before me. But they may try to fuck with us somehow.'

'I'll stay right here,' Bosch said. 'Look out for anything strange. Call when you're getting close.'

A quick shower and shave later, I was in fresh travel clothes and ready to go. I downloaded and printed the letter from Judge Warfield and put it in my briefcase.

Kendall was awake and in the kitchen. There was a loud silence that she broke first.

'I'm sorry about last night,' she said. 'I know you need to put everything you've got into your defense. I was being selfish.'

'No, I'm sorry,' I countered. 'I was ignoring you and that should never be. I'll do better. I promise.'

'The best thing you can do for me is win your case.'

'That's the plan.'

We hugged it out, then I kissed her goodbye.

Bambadjan Bishop was sitting at the bottom of the stairs when I exited my house and locked the door behind me.

'Right on time,' I said. 'I like that.'

'Where're we going?' he asked.

'Burbank Airport. I'm flying to Vegas. Then you're free until eight tonight, when I come back. I'll need you to pick me up.'

'Got it.'

The JetSuite terminal was not on the commercial airfield at Burbank. It was hidden in a long line of private jet operators and hangars. The beauty of the little-known airline was that it operated like a private jet but provided commercial service. I got there fifteen minutes before my flight and it was no problem.

The sold-out flight carried thirty passengers into the air above the San Gabriel Mountains and then out over the Mojave Desert. I finally started to relax after the rush-rush morning.

I had a window seat and the woman next to me was wearing a surgical mask. I wondered if she was sick or trying to prevent becoming sick.

I turned and looked down on the vast nothingness below. The brown, sun-burned desert went in all directions as far as the eye could see. It made everything seem inconsequential. Including me.

23

Harry Bosch was waiting for me in front of the prison's main entrance. He met me at the door of my ride as I got out. The sun was blistering and I had forgotten to bring sunglasses. I squinted at him.

'Can I let this guy go and you drive me back to the airport?' I asked. 'Flight's at seven.'

'Yeah, no problem,' he said.

I made sure I had my briefcase, then tipped the driver and sent him off.

Bosch and I started toward the prison entrance.

'You go through the doors and then there's another door just for visiting attorneys. Head in through there and it should all be set. Neiderland is supposed to be in a room by two.'

'You can go through the attorney chute with me,' I said. 'You're — '

'No, I'm not going in with you. It'll just be you and him — attorney-client.'

'That's what I'm saying, you work for me as an investigator and that puts you under the privilege umbrella.'

'Yeah, but you're about to go to work for him and I'm not working for that guy.'

'What are you talking about?'

'I pick my cases, Mick. I don't work for criminals — that would undo everything I ever did in my career.'

I stopped and looked at him for a moment.

'I guess I should take that as a compliment,' I finally said.

'I told you at Dan Tana's that I believe you,' he said. 'I wouldn't be here if I didn't.'

I turned and looked up at the prison.

'Well, okay, then,' I said.

'I'll be out here,' Bosch said. 'You get a name from him, I'll be ready to go to work on it.'

'I'll let you know.'

'Good luck.'

I didn't get into a room with Neiderland until forty minutes later. The ankle monitor set off alarms with the jail staff as I had thought it might. The letter from Judge Warfield was deemed not good enough because it could have been forged. Somebody called the judge's office to confirm that she had granted permission for me to travel to Nevada but was told the judge was currently on the bench. It wasn't until Warfield took the midafternoon break and returned the call from chambers that I was led to the attorney-client interview room. I was running a half hour late and Neiderland looked angry when I arrived.

He sat in a chair across a bolted-down table from another chair. His hands were cuffed and a lead chain ran from his wrists to a ring bolted to the front of his chair, which in turn was bolted to the floor. Still, he tried to stand and yanked hard against the chain as I slid into my seat.

'Mr. Neiderland, I'm Michael Haller,' I began. 'I'm sorry — '

'I know who the fuck you are,' he said.

'You told my — '

'Fuck you.'

'Excuse me?'

'Get the fuck out of here.'

'I just flew here from L.A. because you told my — '

'Don't you fucking get it?'

He yanked his cuffed hands up until the lead chain snapped taut again. His hands were gripped as if around an imaginary neck. My neck.

'They didn't used to do this,' he said. 'Chain you down like this. Not with your lawyer. I didn't know. I didn't fucking know. You should be dead by now, motherfucker.'

'What are you talking about?' I asked. 'Why would I be dead?'

'Because I would've broken your fucking neck.'

He pushed his words through gritted teeth. He wasn't a big man or heavily muscled. He had thin blond hair and a sallow complexion — no surprise considering his current address. But the look of sheer hatred on his face was downright scary. My first thought was that somehow there had been a setup and he was working for Louis Opparizio — a hit man in an elaborate scheme to take me out. But then I dismissed it. The circumstances of my visit defied such a plan. And there was clearly emotion behind the hate on Neiderland's face.

'You were going to kill me,' I said. 'Why?'

'Because you killed my friend,' he said, again through clenched teeth.

'I didn't kill Sam Scales. That's why I'm here.

I'm trying to find the person who did, and you just wasted a whole fucking day of my time and my investigator's time. You may not believe me and I may even go down for it, but know this: there's someone else out there who did it and walked away. And by not helping me, you help him.'

I got up and turned to the steel door, raising my arm to pound on it. I was frustrated and angry and wondering whether there would be an earlier flight back so that my entire day would not be wasted.

'Wait a minute,' Neiderland said.

I turned back to him.

'Prove it,' he said.

'That's what I'm trying to do,' I said. 'And it doesn't help when I go off on a wild — '

'No, I mean prove it right here.'

'How do I do that?'

'Sit down.'

He nodded to the empty seat. I reluctantly sat down.

'I can't prove it to you,' I said. 'Not yet, at least.'

'He told me you betrayed him,' Neiderland said. 'Yeah, the famous Lincoln Lawyer. You went Hollywood when they made a movie about your ass and left all the people who counted on you in the gutter.'

'That's not what happened. I didn't go Hollywood. Sam stopped paying me. That was one thing. But the truth is, I just couldn't do it anymore. He was hurting a lot of people, taking their money, making them feel like fools. He got off on it, but I'd had enough. I couldn't take another case.'

Neiderland didn't respond. I tried again. I wanted to win him over because I still thought he could be helpful.

'You were really going to kill me?' I asked. 'With less than two years to go in here?'

'I don't know,' Neiderland said. 'But I was going to do something. I was mad. I still am.'

I nodded. I could feel the temperature in the room subsiding.

'For what it's worth, I liked Sam,' I said. 'He ripped off a lot of people, and that was hard to take, but somehow I always liked him. I just had to draw the line because what he was doing was reflecting on me in the media and at home. Added to that, he stopped paying me and that was the same as treating me like one of the fools he ripped off.'

'He outstayed his welcome with a lot of people,' Neiderland said.

I could see a door of communication opening.

'But not you?' I asked.

'No, I never abandoned him,' Neiderland said. 'And he never abandoned me. We had plans for when I got out of here.'

'What were they?'

'Find one big score and then disappear.'

'What was the score? Did he already find it?'

'I don't know. It's not like he could put it in one of his letters. Everything here is monitored — visitors, phone calls, letters. You're not even supposed to have contact with any ex-cons on the outside.'

'So, how did you communicate?'

Neiderland shook his head. He wasn't going to go there.

'Hey, I'm your lawyer,' I said. 'You can tell me anything, and they can't listen and I can't repeat it. It's privileged.'

Neiderland nodded and relented.

'He sent me letters,' he said. 'Posing as my uncle.'

I paused for a moment. I knew the next question and answer could change everything about the case. I also knew that when people make up stories, plays, and even cons, they usually salt their stories with truth. Neiderland had promised Harry Bosch a name if I came to the prison. Maybe that was the truth in his con.

'What's your uncle's name?' I asked.

'Was,' Neiderland said. 'He's dead now. His name was Walter Lennon. My mother's brother.'

'Did you ever send Sam letters — as your uncle?'

'Sure. What else is there to do in here?'

'And do you remember where you sent the letters?'

'He had a garage apartment in San Pedro. But that was three months ago, when he was alive. They probably put his shit out on the street.'

'Do you remember the address?'

'Yeah, I looked at a few of his letters this morning. The return was 2720 Cabrillo. He said it was small. He was saving and we were going to get something bigger when I got out. He said we'd buy a place.'

The vibe I was getting was that Neiderland

was talking about a romantic relationship without actually saying it. I realized that I had never known Sam Scales's sexual orientation because it didn't play a part in his crimes or our attorney-client relationship.

'Did he tell you how he was getting the money he was saving?'

'He said he was working at the port.'

'Doing what?'

'He didn't say and I didn't ask.'

To Sam, working a job meant working a grift. I wrote the name and address down on my legal pad. It would be considered work product and not discoverable.

'Anything else you think I should know?' I asked.

'That's it,' he said.

I thought about protecting the information I had just received — at least until we checked it out.

'An investigator from the LAPD might come to see you,' I said. 'They think I killed Sam and that's all they're worried about. Just remember that you don't have to talk to them. I'm your lawyer now, you can refer them to me.'

'I won't tell them dick.'

I nodded. That was what I wanted.

'Okay, then,' I said. 'I'm going to head back.'

'What about your trial?' Neiderland asked. 'Do you want me to testify?'

I wasn't sure how I could use him in my defense, or whether I could get the judge to approve it. Teleconferencing from prison to courtroom would probably put the jury to sleep.

There was also the question of conflict of interest. Neiderland was now technically my client — at least on paper at the prison.

'I'll let you know,' I said.

I stood up again, ready to bang on the door.

'Are you really going to find out who killed him?' Neiderland asked. 'Or are you just worried about proving you didn't?'

'The only way to prove I didn't do it is to prove who did,' I said. 'That's the law of innocence.'

PART THREE

ECHOES AND IRON

24

We got down to San Pedro by 9:30 the next morning. We drove separately. I was driven by Bishop because I needed to get to downtown before 1 p.m. for the hearing on the missing wallet. Bosch came in his old Cherokee and Cisco on his Harley. We convened at the house on Cabrillo that Austin Neiderland had put me onto. There was an APARTMENT FOR RENT sign on the front lawn. Bishop had been cleared by Cisco but you can never be 100 percent sure about anything. I didn't want him sitting in the Lincoln in front of the house. I told him to go get coffee nearby and wait for me to summon him when I was ready to go to court. I then approached the house with my investigators and knocked on the door. A woman in a bathrobe answered. I held up a business card and went with a script I had written in my head based on what I knew from Neiderland.

'Hello, ma'am, I'm Michael Haller, an attorney involved in the situation regarding the estate of Walter Lennon, and we are here to ascertain and review any property he left behind.'

' 'Estate'? Does that mean he's dead?'

'Yes, ma'am, Mr. Lennon passed in late October.'

'Well, no one told us. We just thought he took off. He was paid up through November but then December went by and no sign of him and no rent check.'

'I see the sign out front. You are rerenting the apartment?'

'Of course. He was gone and he didn't pay.'

'Are his belongings still in there?'

'No, we cleared him out. His stuff is in the garage. We wanted to dump it, but the law, you know. We have to wait sixty days.'

'Well, thank you for adhering to the law. Do you mind if we look at the property in the garage?'

She didn't answer. She closed the door about halfway so she could reach something behind it. She then came up with a remote control and reached out the door to click it.

'Third bay,' she said. 'It's open now. The boxes are marked with his name and stacked between the tread marks.'

'Thank you,' I said. 'Do you mind if we also look around the apartment? Just a quick check.'

She reached behind the door again and then handed me a key.

'Stairs are on the side of the garage,' she said. 'Bring it back when you're finished.'

'Of course,' I said.

'And don't mess it up. It's all clean. Mr. Lennon left it a mess.'

'How so? What kind of mess?'

'Like a tornado had hit the place. Broken furniture, his stuff thrown all over the floors. So don't be asking about his deposit. It barely covered what we had to do in there.'

'Understood. Do you mind one more thing? We'd like you to look at a photo to confirm that the Walter Lennon we are talking about is the Walter Lennon you are talking about.'

'I guess so.'

Cisco had pulled a photo of Sam Scales up on his phone. It was a DMV photo that had been released to the media after my arrest. He held it up to the woman at the door and she nodded after getting a look at it.

'That's him,' she said.

'Thank you, ma'am,' I said. 'We won't take long.'

'Just bring the key back,' she said.

We started with the apartment, which was a small one-bedroom flat over the garage. The place had been cleaned and prepped for a new renter. We weren't expecting to find anything in plain sight — especially since the landlord's description indicated that it had already been searched. But Sam Scales was a lifelong con artist who might have reason to hide things in his home that a quick search might miss. The lead on this went to Bosch, who'd had many years of experience searching the homes of criminals.

Bosch had brought a little tool bag with him. His first stop was the kitchen, where he was methodical about checking the underside of drawers, unscrewing and checking behind the kickboards beneath the cabinets, opening the insulation spaces in the refrigerator and freezer doors, and examining the light and fan assembly over the stove. When I realized how long his full

211

search might take, I decided to change things up. I left Bosch in the apartment while Cisco and I went down to the garage. I had to make sure I got to the courthouse in time.

There were two stacks of four cardboard boxes in the middle of the third bay — between the tread marks presumably left by renters' cars over time. The boxes were sealed and each was marked with the name Lennon and the date 12/19. Cisco started with one stack and I started with the other.

My first box contained clothes. There was a car in the second bay of the garage. I laid the clothes out on its hood and then went through each item, checking pockets, before returning it to the box.

The second box contained shoes, socks, underwear, and nothing else. I checked the shoes inside and out and found a set of lace-up work boots with oily debris stuck in the treads. It reminded me of the oily substance found under Sam Scales's fingernails.

I put the shoes aside and checked on Cisco. He was also dealing with clothes from his first two boxes.

My third box contained personal items, including toiletries, a plug-in alarm clock, and several books. I fanned the pages of each but found nothing hidden among them. They were all novels except for one book, which was a 2015 owner's manual for a Mack Pinnacle tanker truck. I knew this fit in with BioGreen but wasn't sure how. I set the manual aside on the hood of the car in the second bay.

My fourth box contained more of the same. More books and personal items, such as a drip coffee maker and several coffee mugs that were wrapped in old newspaper. A layer of unopened mail was at the bottom of the box, probably put there to further cushion the fragile glass coffeepot and mugs.

The mail was mostly junk with the exception of an AT&T phone bill and an unopened letter from Austin Neiderland with the return address Nevada's High Desert State Prison. I put the prison letter unopened back into the box. It was apparent from my interview with Neiderland that he didn't know what scam Sam Scales was into. I didn't think the letter would be of much use. Instead, I ripped open the phone bill to see if it included a list of numbers called, but it was a reminder notice that the prior bill was unpaid. There was a list of services Sam Scales was receiving but no list of calls.

Cisco was running one box behind me as he fanned the pages of books from his third box. I moved over and opened his last one. It contained three unopened boxes of Honeycomb cereal and a fourth box of Rice Krispies.

'Sam liked his cereal, I guess.'

I shook and examined each box to see if it was factory-sealed or Sam-sealed to hide something inside. I decided they were just boxes of cereal and moved on. Below the cereal were some bags of ground coffee and other unopened items from kitchen cabinets.

'Look at this,' Cisco said.

He held up a thin study manual for the

California commercial driver's license exam.

'It's got stuff underlined in it,' Cisco said. 'Like he was really studying it.'

'And I found an owner's manual for a Mack tanker truck,' I said.

'I'll say it again — maybe he was going straight. Being a trucker or something.'

'No way. For Sam, working a square job was worse than prison. He was working a long con. He could never go straight.'

'Then, what was it?'

'I don't know but we're getting close. This is why they stole the wallet.'

'Why?'

'The wallet had his current alias. That would have led here and then to BioGreen. They didn't want us getting there.'

'Who is 'they'?'

'We don't know yet. Maybe Opparizio. Maybe the FBI. They're set up on Opparizio and that place and didn't want the investigation compromised by a murder investigation linked to BioGreen. As soon as the LAPD ran Sam's prints that night, the bureau probably got an alert. They assess the situation and go grab the wallet before anybody looks at it. They come here, search the place, remove any connection. Sam is never linked to the Walter Lennon alias and the investigation never gets to BioGreen.'

'So you're saying they just stood by while you got tagged with the murder and were going to let you go down for it?'

'I don't know. It had to have been a plan hatched without a lot of down-the-road thinking.

Maybe they were just buying time to wrap things up on BioGreen. Then I blew up the schedule when I refused to waive a speedy trial. Instead of a trial in July or even later, it's February, and they didn't see that coming.'

'Maybe. A lot of maybes.'

'It's all speculation right now. But I think we're — '

Bosch entered the garage then and I stopped.

'Anything upstairs?' I asked.

'Clean,' he said. 'I found a false-floor storage space in the bedroom closet, but it wasn't hidden well and was empty. Whoever searched the place before would have found it.'

'How big?' I asked. 'Could a laptop fit?'

'Yeah, it could fit,' Bosch said.

'That's what's missing here,' I said. 'Sam used the Internet for his scams. I can't see him without a computer. Plus there's a phone bill in here for a full-service package including home Wi-Fi. Why get Wi-Fi if you don't have a computer?'

'So, we're missing a computer, a phone, and a wallet,' Cisco said.

'Exactly,' I said.

'What's in the boxes?' Bosch asked.

'Not much,' I said. 'A pair of boots with grease in the treads. We're almost finished.'

I went back to the last box and saw that the bottom was lined with various documents and paperwork — things that were probably stuffed into a kitchen drawer. There was an instruction manual for the coffee maker, a set of step-by-step directions for putting together an

Ikea table, and several opened letters from Neiderland. That Scales had kept them reinforced in me the idea that they'd had a romantic relationship.

There was also a trifold and stapled printout of a story from the *New York Times*. The headline read 'Bleeding the Beast.'

The story had a Salt Lake City dateline. I started reading and by the time I finished I knew that the story changed everything. And I knew that the printout was something I would need to turn over in discovery to the prosecution — if I took it from the garage.

I refolded the printout and dropped it back into the box. I picked up the Mack truck owner's manual and dropped it in as well. I then closed it up and stacked two other boxes on top of it.

I pulled my phone and texted Bishop, telling him to come pick me up.

'Okay, we're out of here,' I said.

'Wait,' Cisco said. 'You don't want to take any of this stuff?'

'We take it, we have to share it,' I said.

'Discovery,' Cisco said.

'Let them discover it on their own,' I said. 'They're not doing me any favors, I won't do any for them. Let's go. I have court.'

I checked Bosch as we walked out to see if he showed any signs of discomfort with my decision to leave everything behind. I didn't see a thing.

Bishop was pulling up out front as we emerged. I handed Cisco the key to the apartment.

'You mind taking the key back to the old

216

lady?' I asked. 'And get her name and contact info. To put on the witness list.'

'You got it,' Cisco said.

'Tell her we found nothing of value to the estate in the boxes. She can donate them or get rid of them any way she wishes. As soon as she wants to.'

Cisco looked at me and nodded. He understood what I meant. Get rid of the property before the police or prosecution finally find this place.

'I'll deliver the message,' he said.

25

Things had changed rapidly since the first hearing on Sam Scales's missing wallet. My outrage over the missing evidence and its impact on my case was now tempered by my team's findings of the last forty-eight hours. I believed I had learned the key secret of the wallet — the alias Sam was using in the last year of his life. And now I didn't want to share that secret with the prosecution until I had to. I certainly didn't want it to be pursued by a court order or continue to be an issue. This led me to approach the hearing in Judge Warfield's courtroom cautiously and with a plan to score points — especially in front of the reporters who would be there — but to let sleeping dogs lie.

Judge Warfield was again a solid ten minutes late coming to the bench for the afternoon session. This gave me time to update Jennifer on the morning's activities. I told her about the *Times* story from Salt Lake City and the need to keep the knowledge it gave us under wraps. I cautioned her against printing out the story if she looked it up in the newspaper's archives.

'If it's on paper, it goes into discovery,' I said. 'So, no paper.'

'Got it,' Jennifer said.

'Also, there was a man in the story, a witness named Art Schultz. He was retired from the EPA. We need to find him and bring him in as a witness. He'll be key.'

'But what happens when we put him on the witness list? The prosecution will be all over it and they'll figure out where we're going with this.'

Each side's witness list was included in discovery, and the court required an abbreviated summary of what every witness would testify to. Writing these so that they were accurate on face at the same time that they carried no hint of strategy or significance of the full testimony was an art form.

'There's a way around it,' I said. 'To camouflage it. Make contact with Schultz and get his CV. He was with the EPA, so he probably has a biology degree or something like that. Put him on the list and say he'll testify in regard to the material found under the victim's fingernails. He'll be our grease expert and will probably fly well below the prosecution's radar. But once we get him on the stand, we'll use him to connect what's under the nails to what's going on at BioGreen.'

'Risky, but okay,' Jennifer said. 'I'll work on it after the hearing.'

The judge stepped out from the door to her chambers and took the bench. She first apologized for being late, explaining that a monthly judges' luncheon had run long. She then got down to business.

'This is a continuation of a motion to compel discovery by the defense, and I believe, Ms. Berg, that I instructed you to investigate the matter of a missing wallet and to report back to the court. What have you found?'

Berg stepped over to the lectern to address the court. She looked pained as she adjusted the level of the microphone.

'Thank you, Your Honor,' she said. 'Simply stated, the wallet remains missing. Over the past two days, Detective Drucker has conducted an investigation and is here to testify if necessary. But the wallet was not found. The People concede that the video evidence presented by the defense Monday is conclusive in that regard — there does appear to have been a wallet in the victim's back pocket at the time the body was discovered in the trunk of the defendant's car. But it was not among the personal property that was later turned over to the LAPD at the coroner's office.'

'Have you determined when it was taken or by whom?' Warfield pressed.

'No, Your Honor,' Berg said. 'The procedure is that the body would have been transported to the coroner's office, where it would have been placed in the prep room. That's where clothing and property is removed and the bodies are prepared for autopsy, while the property is sealed and held for the police. In this case specifically, the body was discovered in the evening and therefore not delivered to the prep room until approximately two a.m. This means that autopsy prep would not have occurred until the morning.'

'So, the body would have just been sitting there unattended?' the judge asked.

'Not exactly,' Berg said. 'It would have been

moved to a large refrigerated crypt that is part of the coroner's office.'

'So, it was in with other bodies.'

'Yes, Judge.'

'Not isolated.'

'Not beyond being in a crypt where authorized access is required.'

'Did Detective Drucker check to see if there are any surveillance cameras in the area?'

'He did and there are no cameras.'

'So we have no way of knowing who may have gained access to this crypt and taken the wallet.'

'That is correct at this time.'

'At this time? Do you think that is going to change?'

'No, Your Honor.'

'What is it that the People suggest I do about this, Ms. Berg?'

'Your Honor, the People make no excuse for the loss of this property. However, it is a loss that impacts both sides equally. Neither the People nor the defense has the opportunity to access the wallet and whatever case information, if any, it contained. Therefore, it is the People's position that while we accept responsibility for the loss, the damage — if any — is equal.'

Warfield digested that for a few moments before responding.

'Something tells me that Mr. Haller is not going to agree with that assessment,' she said. 'Would the defense like to respond?'

I was up quickly and to the lectern almost before Berg had time to step away.

'Yes, Your Honor is exactly right,' I said. 'The

221

damage to the defense and prosecution can in no way be considered equal. The state sits fat and happy with the case just as it is, Your Honor. They have a body in the trunk of a car and they've charged the driver. No need to dig deeper than that. Case closed. They didn't even raise a question about the missing wallet until the defense did. They clearly weren't interested, because the wallet and what ID the victim was using could lead to what Sam Scales was up to on the last days of his life, and that might not fit with the neat package they have put together on me. It is clear, Judge, that the damage here is to the defense, not the prosecution.'

'Say I agree with you, Mr. Haller,' Warfield said. 'What is the remedy the defense seeks?'

'There is no remedy. The defense wants the wallet. That's the remedy.'

'Then, what is the penalty? There appears to be no evidence of sinister behavior by those involved in the investigation. The wallet appears to have been stolen by someone who had access to the body while it was in the custody of the coroner's office. The matter will certainly be referred for internal investigation by the coroner, but the court does not feel inclined to punish the prosecution for this unfortunate set of circumstances.'

I shook my head in frustration even though I knew this was heading toward the outcome I had expected and, based on the morning's discoveries, wanted.

'Your Honor,' I said. 'For the record, then, I want it noted that the investigation of the missing evidence carried out by the prosecution was conducted by the same detective who was in charge of protecting the crime scene and the evidence in this case.'

'So noted, Mr. Haller,' Warfield said. 'Any other matters before we adjourn?'

'Yes, Your Honor,' Berg said.

I relinquished the lectern to her and headed back to my seat, shaking my head as if frustrated by the judge's ruling.

'Excuse me, Ms. Berg,' Warfield said. 'Mr. Haller, I noted your demonstration. Are you upset with the court's decision?'

I stopped in my tracks.

'Your Honor, I'm just frustrated,' I said. 'I am trying to put together a defense and it seems that at every turn, I am thwarted. The People lost the wallet — by negligence or malfeasance doesn't really matter — and I will pay for it. That's all.'

'I advise counsel on both sides to keep their emotions and demonstrations in check,' Warfield said. 'Particularly when we go to trial. The court will have no patience for such outbursts then, not in front of a jury.'

'Judge, I would not call it an outburst. I was just — '

'Are you going to argue with the court now as well, Mr. Haller?'

'No, Your Honor.'

I continued to my seat and Warfield tracked me with her eyes in case I so much as frowned. Finally, she broke away and looked at the prosecutor.

'Ms. Berg, continue,' she said.

'Judge, yesterday we received the first witness list from the defendant,' Berg said. 'It had only two names on it — the defendant himself and his investigator. This from a defendant who has twice come before this court to complain about discovery issues, and he has the audacity to put just two names down on his witness list.'

Warfield looked like she was either weary of the constant cross fire between the prosecution and defense or was being hit with fatigue from the two martinis she'd probably had at the judges' lunch. I was sure the alcohol was what had inspired her to snap at me. Before I could object to Berg's complaint, Warfield held her hand up to me, indicating that she was not interested in my response.

'It's early, Ms. Berg,' Warfield said. 'We are still almost thirty days out, and there will be an update on the lists from both parties next week and every week after. Let's wait a bit before we panic about whom he plans to call. Anything of a more serious nature?'

'No, Your Honor,' Berg said.

'No, Your Honor,' I said.

'Very well,' Warfield said. 'Then we are adjourned.'

26

Having not had time to eat before the hearing, I went to the Little Jewel for a shrimp po'boy sandwich directly after court. I was joined by everyone on the defense team except Bosch. He was apparently off doing his own thing again and was incommunicado. I told the team that the defense had turned a corner with the case knowledge gathered in the last forty-eight hours and that it was time to start thinking in terms of presenting the case to a jury. We could clearly anticipate what the prosecution presentation would be, because it had not really changed since the start of the case. We could prepare for that but what was more important was preparing to tell our story.

A trial often comes down to who is a better storyteller, the prosecution or the defense. There is evidence, of course, but physical evidence is at first interpreted for the jury by the storyteller.

Story A: A man kills an enemy, puts the body in the trunk, and plans to bury it late at night, when there will be no one around to see.

Story B: A man is set up for the murder of a former client and unwittingly drives around with the body in the trunk until he is pulled over by police.

The physical evidence fits both stories. One might be more believable than the other when writ small. But a skilled storyteller can even the

225

scales of justice or maybe even tip them the other way with a different interpretation of the evidence. This was where we were now and I was starting to get the visions I got before all trials. Visions of witnesses on the stand, visions of me telling my story to a jury.

'We are clearly going for third-party culpability,' I said. 'And the guy we point the finger at is going to be Louis Opparizio. I doubt he pulled the trigger but he gave the order. So he is our fall guy and our number one witness. We need to find him. We need to paper him. We need to make sure he shows up for court.'

Jennifer Aronson shook her hands palms out like she was warding off a swarm of bees.

'Can we just back up?' she asked. 'Walk me through this like I'm a juror. What are we saying happened? I mean, I get it. Opparizio killed Scales or had Scales killed and then tried to frame you for it. But can we say yet exactly how this went down?'

'Nothing is exact at this point,' I said. 'And we have a lot of holes to fill — that's why we're meeting right now. But I can tell you what I think went down and what the evidence — once we have it all — is going to prove.'

'Yes, please,' Lorna said. 'I'm with Jen. I'm having a hard time seeing this.'

'Not a problem,' I said. 'Let's go through it slowly. A couple things to start with first. Number one is Louis Opparizio's enmity for me. Nine years ago I sandbagged him in court, revealing his mob connections and shady dealings in the foreclosure world. In that case, he

226

was a straw man. He was the shiny bait I put out in front of the jury and they went for it. Though he was not the killer I portrayed him as in court, he was involved in some shady shit, the government took notice, and he and his mob backers ended up forfeiting major millions when the Federal Trade Commission reversed a hundred-million-dollar merger he had just completed. I think all of that explains why he would hold a grudge against me. Not only did I expose him in public but I cost him and his mob backers a ton of money.'

'No doubt,' Cisco said. 'I'm surprised he waited until now to make a move against you. Nine years is a long time.'

'Well, maybe he was waiting until he had the perfect frame,' I said. 'Because I'm in a tight box.'

'That's for sure,' Lorna said.

'Okay, so the second building block of the case is the victim,' I said. 'Sam Scales, con man extraordinaire. Our story is that these two — Opparizio and Scales — intersected at BioGreen. They were bleeding the beast, operating the long con, when something went wrong. Opparizio had to take out Scales but also had to make sure the investigation came nowhere near BioGreen. So I became his fall guy. He somehow knew of my history with Scales and that it ended badly. He sticks Sam's body in my trunk and I go down for it while BioGreen stays clean and supposedly keeps pumping out that recycled fuel the government loves so much.'

I looked at the three faces around the table.

'Questions?' I asked.

'I have a couple,' Lorna said. 'First, what was the con they were pulling?'

'It's called *bleeding the beast*,' I said. 'Scamming the government — the beast, that is — out of federal subsidies for producing green gold: recycled oil.'

'Whoa,' Lorna said. 'Sounds like Sam really came up in the world. That's a long way from the Internet scams he was known for.'

'Good point,' I said. 'That is something that doesn't fit with what I know about him, but I'm just telling you my theory so far. He had green gold under his fingernails. One thing we do need to find out is whether Sam went to Opparizio with the scam idea, or was Sam simply recruited into the ongoing operation?'

'Any idea what the falling-out was?' Jennifer asked. 'Why was Sam killed?'

'Another hole we have to fill,' I said. 'And my guess is that the FBI is at the bottom of that hole.'

'They flipped him?' Cisco half asked, half suggested.

I nodded.

'I think it's something along those lines,' I said. 'Opparizio found out and Sam had to go.'

'But the smart move would have been to just make him disappear,' Cisco said. 'Why put the body anyplace where it could and would be found?'

'Right,' I said. 'That goes on the list of unknowns. But I think that simply disappearing Sam might have brought in more scrutiny from

228

the feds. Doing it the way they did would help insulate BioGreen and maybe make it look like it had nothing to do with the scam down there.'

'Not to mention Opparizio knew this was a good way to get back at you, boss,' Cisco added.

'Most of this is just theory,' Jennifer said. 'What's next? How do we turn theory into a solid defense?'

'Opparizio,' I said. 'We find him, serve him, and make sure the judge enforces the subpoena.'

'That only gets him to court,' Jennifer said. 'Last time you wanted him to take the Fifth, but this time you have to get him to actually testify.'

'Not necessarily,' I said. 'If we have the goods on him, it'll be about the questions we ask, not the answers. He can take the Fifth all he wants. The jury will hear the story in the questions.'

I turned my eyes to Cisco.

'So, where is he?' I asked.

'We've been on the girlfriend, what, five days now?' Cisco said. 'And no sign of him. We may need to shake things up. Throw a scare at her, create a need for her to see him.'

I shook my head.

'I think it's too early for that,' I said. 'We have some time. We don't want to subpoena him till pretty late in the game. Otherwise, Iceberg will be onto us.'

'She is already,' Jennifer said. 'She would have gotten copied on the FBI subpoena.'

'But my guess is she saw that as a shot in the dark,' I said. 'A fishing expedition to see if the feds had anything. Even the judge thought that. Anyway, I don't want to go for a subpoena yet.

That will give the prosecution too much time to cover our ground. So we need to find him first and then watch him until it's time.'

'That can be done,' Cisco said. 'But it will cost. I didn't realize we were talking about running this up to the trial.'

'How much?' I asked.

'We're running four grand a day with the surveillance package we've got out there now,' Cisco said.

I looked at Lorna, the keeper of the practice's bank accounts. She shook her head.

'We're four weeks out from trial,' she said. 'You'll need a hundred thousand to keep it going, Mickey. We don't have that.'

'Unless you go back to Andre La Cosse or Bosch,' Jennifer said. 'They got off easy on your bail but had been willing to pony up six figures each.'

'No on Bosch,' I said. 'I should be paying him rather than asking him for money. Lorna, see if you can set up a dinner between me and Andre. I'll see what he's willing to do.'

'Maybe Cisco can negotiate a discount?' Lorna said, looking across the table at her husband. 'Mickey is a repeat client, after all.'

'I can try for it,' Cisco said.

I knew that he probably got a piece of any business he brought to the Indians. So Lorna's suggestion hit him in his own wallet.

'Good,' I said.

'So, what about the FBI?' Jennifer said, changing the subject. 'The FOIA and subpoena went nowhere. We could formally go to the U.S.

Attorney with a Touhy letter. But we all know the feds can just sit on it, and it won't work with our timeframe.'

'What's a Touhy letter?' Cisco asked.

'Step one in a protocol for demanding a federal agent's testimony,' Jennifer said. 'Named after an Illinois convict whose case created it.'

'You're right, though,' I said. 'It'll take forever. But there might be an end run with the bureau. And if we make enough waves at BioGreen or at least threaten to, they may come to the table.'

'Good luck with that,' Jennifer said.

'Yeah, luck is what we need,' I said.

And that put a solemn cap on the meeting.

27

Wednesdays had always been my night with my daughter but things had shifted with law school. She had a torts study group that met at seven, so I was relegated to the early-bird special. We'd meet on campus or close by for a quick and early dinner and then she would go off to the law school and the group's meeting room.

I had Bishop drop me off at the gate on Exposition Boulevard. Before getting out, I handed sixty dollars over the seat to him.

'Pick me up here in two hours,' I said. 'Meantime, use that money to buy me a prepaid burner and then get yourself something to eat with the rest. If there's time after that, set up the burner. I'll need to make a call on it when I get back.'

'You got it,' Bishop said. 'You want to be able to text?'

'Not necessary. If it goes right, I'll make one call and receive another. That's it.'

I walked across campus from there to Moreton Fig in the student center. I found Hayley at an outside table near the towering tree the restaurant was named for. And to my surprise, she was sitting with her mother. They were on the same side of the table, so when I sat down I was facing them both.

'Well, this is a nice surprise,' I said. 'Good to see you, Mags.'

232

'Good to see you too. Are you going to eat?' Maggie asked.

'Uh, that's why I'm here,' I said. 'And to see our daughter.'

'Well, you don't look like you're eating,' she countered. 'You've been out of lockup for, what, a month? And it looks like you're still losing weight. What's going on with you, Mickey?'

'What is this, an intervention?' I asked.

'We're worried about you, Dad,' Hayley said. 'I asked Mom to come.'

'Yeah, well, try being charged with a murder you didn't commit,' I said. 'It wears you down, whether you're in jail or not.'

'How can we help?' Maggie said.

I paused before answering while a waitress brought us menus. Maggie refused a menu, saying she wasn't going to eat.

'You're here to tell me I have to start eating but you're not going to eat?' I said.

'I know these dinners are special,' Maggie said. 'For both of you — going all the way back to when you used to get pancakes at the Du-Par's that isn't there anymore. I just wanted to see you and ask how you're doing, then let you two be together.'

'You can stay,' I said. 'We would always make room for you.'

'No, I have plans,' Maggie said. 'I'm going to go, but you didn't answer my question. How can we help you, Mickey?'

'Well,' I said, 'you could start by telling your colleague, Iceberg, that she's so blinded by the idea of having me as a trophy on her shelf that she's not seeing the case for what it really is. A set — '

Maggie waved her hands to cut me off.

'I'm talking about what we could do outside the courtroom,' she said. 'This is an extremely awkward work situation, as you know. They've kept me far away from the case because of the conflict of interest, but I don't even have to see the case or the evidence to know there's no way you did this. Just as I know you're going to win the case. Hayley and I could never think otherwise. But you need to be *able* to win the case, and your physical health is key. And you look like shit, Mickey. I'm sorry, but I've seen you in court. Hayley said you got your suits altered, but you still look like skin and bones. You've got circles under your eyes . . . you don't look confident. You don't look like the Lincoln Lawyer we know and love.'

I was silent. Her words hit hard because I knew they were sincere.

'Thank you,' I finally said. 'I mean that. It's a good reminder. Act like a winner, you'll become a winner. That's the rule and I guess I forgot it. You can't act like a winner if you don't look like one. It's all about sleep, I think. It's hard to sleep with this hanging over me.'

'See a doctor,' Maggie said. 'Get a prescription.'

I shook my head.

'No prescriptions,' I said. 'But I'll figure something out. Should we order? You sure you can't stay? The food here is great.'

'I can't,' she said. 'I really do have a meeting

234

and I want you and Hay to visit. She was just telling me that she's learning more watching you in court than in the hallowed hallways of USC Law. Anyway, I'm going to go now.'

Maggie pushed back her chair.

'Thanks, Mags,' I said. 'It means a lot.'

'Take care of yourself,' she said.

And then she did a surprising thing. After leaning down and kissing Hayley on the cheek, she came around the table to kiss me as well. It was the first time in too many years for me to remember.

'Bye, guys,' she said.

I watched her go and was silent for a few moments.

'Do they really call her that?' Hayley asked.

'What?' I asked.

'Iceberg.'

'Yeah, they do.'

She laughed and then I did too. The waitress came and we ordered off the happy-hour menu. Hayley had lobster tacos and, inspired by Maggie's 'skin and bones' comment, I ordered the classic hamburger with grilled onions even though I'd had a late lunch.

During the meal, we mostly talked about her classes. She was at a stage where the law was a wonderful thing, with protections for all and equitable punishments for the offenders. It was an exciting time and I remembered it well. It was when ideals were set and goals attached to them. I let her talk and mostly just smiled and nodded my head. My mind was on Maggie. The things she had said, and the kiss at the end.

235

'Now you,' Hayley said at one point.

I looked up, a french fry ready to go into my mouth.

'What do you mean?' I asked.

'All we've been talking about is me and the theoretical world of law,' she said. 'What about you and the real world? How is the case going?'

'What case?'

'Daaad.'

'Just kidding. It's going well. We're coming up with some good stuff, I think. I'm beginning to see the trial come together. There was a football coach. I can't remember who it was — maybe Belichick, the Patriots guy. Anyway, he would call the first twelve plays of the game for the offense a couple days before the game even started. He'd look at film of the other team, study their habits, decide what he expected them to do on defense, and write out the plays. That's the place I'm getting to. I can see things falling into place — witnesses, evidence.'

'But you don't get to go until after the prosecution.'

'True. But I pretty much know what they're going to do. I mean, we're four weeks out, so there's plenty of time for things to change and maybe they surprise me. But right now I'm thinking about my case, not the state's, and I'm beginning to feel good about it.'

'That's great. I already talked to all of my professors and told them I needed to be there.'

'Look, I know you're with me on it, but you don't have to be there and miss school. Maybe come for openers and then I'll let you know if there's something you might want to see. Then the verdict and the celebration afterward.'

I smiled, hoping she would share my optimism.

'Dad, don't jinx yourself,' she said instead.

'Is that what they teach you at USC Law?' I said. 'How not to jinx a case?'

'No, that's third year.'

'Funny girl.'

We went our separate ways outside the restaurant. I walked off but then stopped to watch her make her way through the plaza. It was dark now but the campus was well lit. She walked with confidence and a fast step. I watched until she disappeared between two buildings.

Bishop was waiting for me at the appointed spot. I got in the rear passenger door. He handed a cheap flip phone over the seat to me as well as change from my sixty.

'Did you get something to eat?' I asked.

'I went over to the Tarn's on Fig,' he said.

'I had a hamburger, too.'

'Hit the spot. So, where to?'

'Just hold right here a minute while I make a call.'

On my real phone I googled the number for the FBI's Los Angeles Field Office and called it on the burner. It was answered by a male voice and a curt 'FBI.'

'Yes, I need to get a message to an agent.'

'There's nobody in right now. Everybody's gone home.'

'I know. Can you please get a message to

Agent Dawn Ruth?'

'You'll have to do that tomorrow.'

'It's an emergency call from a confidential informant. Tomorrow will be too late.'

There was a long pause and then he relented.

'Is this the number she needs to call?'

'Yes, and the name is Walter Lennon.'

'Walter Lennon. Got it.'

'Please call her now. Thank you.'

I closed the burner and looked over the seat at Bishop.

'Okay, drive. I want to be moving if she calls back. Harder to track us that way.'

'Anywhere?'

'Tell you what — head toward your place. I can drop you off tonight instead of you dropping me and taking an Uber.'

'You sure?'

'Yeah, go. I want to be moving.'

Bishop pulled the Lincoln away from the curb and started driving. He was soon on the 110 freeway going south. I knew he would connect to the 105 and turn west toward Inglewood.

We were in the carpool lane and making good time. As we took the exit to the 105, the burner phone started to buzz with a call. Caller ID was blocked. I flipped it open but didn't speak. Soon I heard a woman's voice.

'Who is this?'

'Agent Ruth, thanks for calling. It's Mick Haller.'

'Haller? What the hell are you doing?'

'Is this a private line? I don't think you want this recorded.'

238

'Yes, it's private. What exactly is this about?'

'Well, it's about Walter Lennon. And the fact that you called me back so quick pretty much confirms you know exactly who he is. Make that, was.'

'Haller, you have about three seconds before I hang up. Why are you calling me?'

'I'm taking a gamble, Agent Ruth. The other night when your partner Aiello wanted to throw me off the deck, you pulled him back. I've seen a lot of tape in my time of the good cop-bad cop routine, and I don't think that's what was going on there. You didn't like what he was doing.'

'I'm asking you one more time before hanging up: What do you want?'

'Well, for one thing, I want you to testify.'

I heard sarcastic laughter.

'And barring that,' I said, undaunted, 'I want you to tell me what was going on with Sam Scales aka Walter Lennon and BioGreen.'

'You're crazy, Haller,' Ruth said. 'You expect me to just throw my job away?'

'I expect you to do the right thing, is all. Isn't that why you became an FBI agent? I'm basing this on what happened the other night but I'm guessing that whatever is going on — this cover-up — you're not down with it. Your partner may be all in, but you're not. You know I didn't kill Sam Scales and you can help me prove it.'

'I'll say it again. You're crazy if you think I'm going to throw away my career for you. And, no, I *don't* know whether or not you killed Sam Scales.'

'Well, maybe you don't have to throw away your career. Maybe you can do the right thing and still keep it. I know this: your partner isn't keeping his.'

'What are you talking about?'

'He was going to throw me off the deck.'

'Please, you're exaggerating. He was over the top, I'll give you that, but you were pushing our buttons, Haller. And he wasn't threatening to push you over. That's totally insane.'

I didn't respond, so she kept going.

'Besides, it would be your word against two agents'. Do the math on that.'

'Is that why you guys always travel in pairs?'

She didn't respond. I pressed on.

'Look, Agent Ruth, for some reason I like you. It's not been my experience with feds, but like I said, you pulled him off me. So I'm going to do you a favor. I'm going to stop you from filing a false report on that incident when I make the complaint. It'll probably save your job and then maybe you'll do right by me.'

'I don't know what you're talking about now. This is — '

'Do you have a private email address? Give it to me and I'll send you something tonight. You'll know what I'm talking about then. I have a camera on the balcony, Agent Ruth. I caught the whole thing. It would be the word of two agents against a video. You would lose.'

There was a long silence and I looked out the window. I saw we were going by the new billion-dollar football stadium. Then I heard Ruth recite an email address. I snapped on the overhead light and wrote it down on a legal pad.

'Okay,' I said. 'I'll send you the video as soon as I get home and get steady Wi-Fi. Probably be an hour. Hopefully I hear something back from you and this whole thing can be avoided — for you and your partner.'

She disconnected without a further word. I put the burner into my jacket pocket and snapped off the overhead light.

'That video must be pretty good, huh?' Bishop asked from the front seat.

I stared at him in the darkness, his face catching a dim glow from the dashboard lights. I once again wondered about Cisco having cleared him as a possible spy for the prosecution. Either way, he didn't need to know my business.

'Nah,' I said. 'I was just bluffing.'

28

The next morning came quickly, thanks to a
7 a.m. hammering on the front door. Kendall
jumped out of bed first and then I sat up so fast
I thought I felt a muscle in my lower back
twinge.

'What is it?' she cried.

'I don't know,' I said. 'Just get dressed.'

I pulled on the pants I had discarded on the
floor the night before and grabbed a fresh shirt
out of the closet. I buttoned it as I walked
barefoot down the hall, the dread growing with
each step that I might be going back to Twin
Towers. Only the cops pounded on your door
this early.

I opened the door, and sure enough, there was
Drucker and another detective I didn't recognize. Behind them stood two uniformed officers.
Drucker was holding up a document I did
recognize, a search warrant.

'Hello, sir, we have a warrant to search these
premises,' Drucker said. 'May we come in?'

'Let's see what you've got,' I said.

I took the warrant, which was several pages
stapled together. I knew to skip through all the
preamble and the probable-cause statement to
get to the meat of what they were looking for.

'You want billing records,' I said. 'I don't have

242

any of that here. My office manager has all of the current stuff, and the rest is in storage.'

'My partner is serving a warrant at Ms. Taylor's residence,' Drucker said. 'And we have a third for your storage unit. I was hoping you would cooperate and meet us there to facilitate that search after this.'

I stepped back from the doorway and held my arm out, signaling them to enter. I noticed Kendall in the door to the hallway leading to the back. She was holding up my phone.

'It's Lorna,' she said.

'Tell her I know she's getting searched,' I said. 'I'll call her back in five.'

I turned to the four law officers now standing in my living room.

'I have a home office in the back,' I said. 'I assume you'll want to start there. But like I said, I don't keep billing records here. Lorna handles all of that.'

Drucker was not put off.

'If you could show us the way,' he said. 'We'll try to make this as painless as possible.'

They followed me down the hall. I saw that Kendall had retreated to our bedroom and closed the door. As we went by, I knocked on the door to get her attention.

'Kendall, I need to stay with these guys,' I said. 'Will you bring me some socks and my shoes?'

I then moved to the last door in the hallway, which led to a bedroom I'd converted into an office. There was a desk covered in paperwork and files.

'These are case files that contain privileged information you are not entitled to look at,' I said.

I reached down and started opening drawers in the desk so they would see they were mostly empty.

'Knock yourself out but, as you can see, no billing records,' I said. 'You're wasting your time and mine.'

I moved back around from behind the desk so there was room for the searchers. There was a couch in the office, where I slept on occasion. I sat down as Kendall entered with a fresh pair of socks and my black lace-up Ferro Aldo boots. She also handed me my cell phone.

'You people are unbelievable,' Kendall said. 'Why don't you just leave him alone?'

'It's okay, Kendall,' I said. 'They're wrong, but they're just doing their job. The sooner we let them get to it, the sooner they're out of here.'

Kendall left the room in a huff. I called Lorna back.

'Mickey, they're searching my records,' she said upon answering.

'I know,' I said. 'They can look at the billing. Just make sure they're not looking at privileged material.'

'I'm not letting them near that. But you know, all the stuff with Sam Scales is not here.'

'Detective Drucker is here. I told him that but they're going to do what they want to do.'

Lorna lowered her voice to a whisper for her next question.

'What does this mean, Mickey? What are they looking for?'

I hadn't really had time to think about those questions. I told Lorna I would call her back and disconnected. I then sat on the couch, unmoving, as I watched Drucker and the unnamed detective going through the drawers of my desk. The uniformed officers were milling about in the hallway. They were there to enforce the search if there was push back. But since I was cooperating, they had nothing to do but stand with their hands on their equipment belts.

I knew that Death Row Dana was shoring up her case. I guessed that this search was about accounts receivable and motive. They were looking for documentation that Sam Scales had stiffed me. They wanted my own records to prove it, and that told me that the murder-for-financial-gain charge was still in play.

A few minutes later Drucker closed all the drawers in the desk and looked at me.

'Let's check the garage,' he said.

'There's nothing in the garage,' I said. 'The California bar frowns on client records being stored in unsecured locations. You want to just skip all of this and go to my warehouse. I know what you're looking for, and if I have it, it's there.'

'Where's your warehouse?'

'Over the hill. Studio City.'

'Let's check the garage and then go.'

'Whatever.'

It was too early for Bishop to be around. After the garage was cleared — my first time being in there since the murder — I drove the Lincoln, and as I made my way north through Laurel Canyon, I thought about how many times I had chided clients for being cooperative with the people working to take away their freedom. *Do you think by being nice and helping them out you'll convince them you didn't do it? Not a chance. These people want to take everything away from you: your family, your home, your freedom. Do not cooperate with them!*

And yet here I was, leading a parade of police cars to the place where I kept the records of my practice and livelihood. This was the moment when I thought maybe I did have a fool for a client. Maybe I should have just told Drucker to fuck off and let him find the warehouse on his own, then cut the locks and figure out where the files were.

My phone buzzed and it was Lorna again.

'I thought you were going to call me back.'

'Sorry, I forgot.'

'Well, they're gone. I heard them say they were going to the warehouse.'

'Yeah, I'm heading there now.'

'Mickey, what are the chances they're going to finish their search and then arrest you on new charges?'

'I thought about that, but they let me drive my own car and lead them up here. No way Drucker would have done that if he had an arrest warrant in his pocket.'

'I hope you're right.'

'Have you heard from Jennifer yet today?'

'Not yet.'

'Okay, I'll call her to let her know what's going on. Hang in there, Lorna.'

'I just wish this would all be over.'

'Me too.'

I led the police brigade up Lankershim to the climate-controlled warehouse where I kept my records along with male and female mannequins and other props I had used at trials over the years. I also had two racks of suits there of various sizes that I kept for clients to wear in court and the third of my three Lincoln Town Cars. There was also an upright AMSEC gun safe for when I took firearms in trade for services rendered. As a condition of my bail, I could have no firearms, so I'd had Cisco take the guns to the home he shared with Lorna until the case came to an end.

The warehouse had a roll-up garage door, which I opened for the searchers. I then led them to a locked storage room within the warehouse, where I kept archived records in locked filing cabinets, in full compliance with California bar guidelines for securing client records. I used a key to unlock the first four-drawer cabinet.

'Have at it, gentlemen,' I said. 'This row contains the business records going back to '05, I believe. You will find the P and Os, the accounting and tax returns, all the financial stuff. That's what you are entitled to see under the scope of the warrant. The other drawers contain case files and they're off-limits — even the Sam Scales files.'

The room was too small for the whole group, which now included Drucker's partner, Lopes. I backed out of the room to where the uniformed cops stood and I hovered by the doorway, where I could keep a watch on the search.

There was a folding table in the file-storage room that I used when I had to look through old cases. The detectives remained standing but opened the files they were interested in on the table. If there was something they wanted to take, they placed it to the side.

With the three of them working it, the search was conducted quickly, and by the time they were finished, they had placed four documents aside to seize under the authority of the search warrant. I asked to see them.

'There is nothing in the warrant that directs me to share with you what we seize,' Drucker said.

'And there's nothing in there that directs me to cooperate with you,' I said. 'But I did. Whatever you take, it comes back to me in discovery anyway, Detective. So, why be a dick about it?'

'You know, Haller, you didn't have to be a dick yourself and rake me over the coals in public.'

'What? You're talking about the other day in court? If you think that's raking somebody over the coals, wait till you testify in front of the jury. Make sure you wear your Depends, Detective.'

Drucker gave me a smile without a note of humor in it.

'Have a good day,' he said.

He brushed by me, holding the documents to his chest so I could not get even a glimpse of them. Lopes and the unnamed detective followed him out. Then the whole entourage of detectives and uniformed escorts left the warehouse. I texted Lorna to let her know I had not been re-arrested. Yet.

29

Friday, January 17

The *Catalina Express* moved swiftly over the dark waters of the Pacific. The sun was just starting to dip behind the island that lay ahead of us. The wind was biting cold but Kendall and I faced it on the open deck, arms wrapped around each other. It was Friday afternoon and I had told Team Haller that I was disappearing for the holiday weekend. My bail restrictions prohibited me from leaving L.A. County without the judge's permission, so I chose a spot as far away as I could get without breaking the rules.

The boat docked at the pier in the Avalon Harbor at 4 p.m., and there was a chauffeured golf cart from the Zane Grey Pueblo waiting for us. It carried us and our one bag up the hill, the driver making small talk about the renovations recently completed at the historic hotel, which had once been the home of the author and the place where he had written several of his novels about the western frontier.

'He lived out here because he loved the fishing,' the driver said. 'He always said that he wrote so he could fish — whatever that means.'

I just nodded and looked at Kendall. She smiled.

'Did you know he was a dentist?' the driver asked.

'Who was?' I asked.

'Zane Grey,' he said. 'And that wasn't his real first name. His real name was Pearl — like the woman's name. No wonder he went by Zane. That was his middle name, actually.'

'Interesting,' Kendall said.

It was off-season and the hotel was nearly empty. We had the pick of several rooms, all named after the author's most popular novels. We took the *Riders of the Purple Sage* suite, not because I knew the book but because it had a view of the harbor and a working fireplace. I had been in the room before, many times, many years ago, with Maggie McPherson when we were still married.

Our plan was to stay in for most of the weekend and enjoy each other's company. No phones, no computers, no intrusions. We did, however, rent a golf cart from the hotel for sorties to restaurants and the grocery store down in the town.

The setup was great but there was something sad for me about the trip. I was feeling depressed and couldn't shake it. Kendall and I spent time in front of the fireplace talking and reminiscing and planning. And we made love the first two nights and on Sunday morning. But by Monday we had stopped talking about anything that mattered, and I sat most of the day in front of the flat-screen, watching CNN reports on the ongoing impeachment saga as well as the mystery virus in China. The Centers for Disease Control had announced that it was deploying medical staff to LAX to meet flights from Wuhan and check passengers for fever and other symptoms of illness. Those who were determined to be sick would be quarantined.

The news was a diversion. I had made a good show of it, turning my phone off and never pulling it out of the suitcase the whole weekend. But I couldn't take my mind off other things. The weight of what was ahead and the stakes involved was coming down on me.

I had the premonition that Kendall and I were spending our last days together, that her return to L.A. and our trying to rekindle our romance would ultimately be a failed experiment. I couldn't pinpoint exactly why this was. But thoughts intruded about Maggie and the meeting at USC that had briefly reunited our lost family. And the kiss. It was amazing to me how something so casual, quick, and unexpected could shake the fragile foundations of the relationship at hand.

30

Tuesday, January 21

When Tuesday Dawned with a gray overcast sky and heavy fog cover between the island and the mainland, it somehow seemed appropriate to me.

The dread that had steadily built through the weekend was confirmed shortly after I turned on my phone for the first time in three and a half days. Just as we were about to check out and head to the boat, I got a call from Jennifer Aronson.

'Mickey, where are you?'

'Catalina.'

'What?'

'Kendall and I went for the weekend. I told you. Anyway, we're about to head back. What's up?'

'I just got a call from Berg. They want you to turn yourself in. They dropped the current murder charge against you this morning, then got a grand jury indictment for murder with special circumstances — financial gain.'

That meant no bail. I remained silent for a long moment and thought about Drucker going through my Sam Scales files. What did he take? Was there something in my files that had led to this?

Kendall noticed the look on my face and

whispered, 'What is it?'

I shook my head. I would tell her after the call. At the moment I had to come up with a strategy for dealing with this.

'Okay,' I said. 'Call Warfield's clerk. See if you can get on the calendar in the afternoon. I'll turn myself in then and there. But we — '

'*What?*' Kendall shrieked.

I held a hand up to quiet her and continued with Jennifer.

'We ask for a probable-cause hearing on the special-circumstances allegation. This is bullshit.'

'But the grand jury indictment obviates a preliminary hearing. It presumes probable cause.'

'Doesn't matter. We need to get in front of the judge and convince her that this is a bullshit attempt by the prosecution to tilt the board and reset the game clock.'

'Okay, that's the angle. Speedy trial. I can work on that. You need to get back here and be ready to argue. I think this is one where you need to address the court.'

'Absolutely. You take probable cause and I'll take the speedy-trial argument. I'm on my way. Let me know if they're going to wait till the hearing or try to pick me up ahead of that. I've got the ankle monitor, so they can find me if they want to.'

'I'm on it.'

We disconnected and I turned to Kendall.

'We have to go. They're going to arrest me again.'

'How can they do that?'

'They dropped the original case, then went to the grand jury and got an indictment, and it all starts again.'

'You're going to jail?'

She put her arms around me and hugged me as though she wouldn't let them take me away.

'I'm going to do my best to get in front of the judge and argue against it. So we should go.'

The ride on the *Catalina Express* back to San Pedro was through a thick fog. This time Kendall and I stayed inside the cabin, sipping hot coffee and trying to remain calm. I walked her through the steps Berg had taken in turning me into a wanted man. Untrained in the law, Kendall said it was unfair even if it was a valid legal maneuver. And I couldn't argue with that. The prosecutor was using completely legal means to subvert a completely legal process.

The crossing was slowed by the thick blanket of fog and it was an hour before I heard and felt the boat's big engines thrum down as we slowly approached the harbor. I had not heard back from Jennifer and didn't know if I would be met at the dock by police who had tracked my monitor. I got up and moved to a forward-viewing window. If I was about to be arrested, I needed to prep Kendall on what to do and whom to call.

The fog started to thin as we entered the harbor, and I saw the green span of the Vincent Thomas Bridge appear in the mist. Soon I saw the ferry terminal, but I noticed no sign of law enforcement on the dock. The parking lot where I had left the Lincoln was not in view because of the terminal building. I returned to Kendall and handed her the keys to the Lincoln.

'In case they're waiting for me,' I said.

'Oh my god, Mickey! Do you think they are?' she said.

'Take it easy. I didn't see anybody on the dock and that's where they'd most likely be waiting. It'll probably be fine, but just in case, you have the keys and can drive back. But before you go anywhere, you call Jennifer and tell her what's happening. She'll know what to do. I'm going to text you her contact.'

'Okay.'

'Then call Hayley and tell her too.'

'Okay. I can't believe they're doing this.'

She started to cry and I hugged her and assured her that everything would be okay. Privately I wasn't as certain as I sounded.

We got off the boat and to the Lincoln without being stopped. My phone buzzed as we were getting in the car. It was Jennifer but I didn't answer. I was paranoid and felt like a sitting duck. I wanted to get out of the parking lot and onto the freeway. A moving target was always harder to get a bead on.

Once we were on the 110 going north, I called Jennifer back.

'We're on the calendar for three o'clock.'

'Good. And they aren't going to try to grab me in the meantime?'

'That's what Berg told the judge. You'll be allowed to surrender in her courtroom following a hearing at three.'

'Did Berg object to the hearing?'

'I don't know, but probably. But Warfield's clerk tipped me that the judge is a bit upset about this — about the bail part, since she set bail and now the D.A.'s trying to take it away. So we'll have that going for us when we go in.'

'Good. When and where do you want to meet beforehand?'

'I need time to work on points for your argument. How about one? We could meet in the cafeteria at the courthouse.'

I checked the dashboard clock. It was already ten thirty.

'One is good but not the courthouse. Too many badges around there, and somebody might try to be a hero and hook me up. Let's not get to the courthouse till it's time for the hearing.'

'Got it. Where, then?'

'How about Rossoblu? Since I might be back on a baloney diet after today, I'm going to eat some pasta for lunch.'

'Okay, I'll be there.'

'One more thing if you have time. Get a message to the twins who have been covering this for the papers. Make sure they know about the hearing. I'd do it but I want to be able to say I didn't if Berg accuses me of it again. Still, the media should be there to see this bullshit.'

'I'll call them.'

We disconnected and Kendall immediately spoke.

'I want to be with you in court.'

'That would be nice. And I'll call Hayley when we get home. I need to put on a suit and work a little bit on what I'm going to say to the judge, and then we'll go to lunch.'

I knew it was going to be a working lunch and Kendall shouldn't be there because she was outside the privilege circle. But I also knew that my freedom could be down to these last few hours. I didn't want to exclude her.

It took us almost an hour to get to the house. I parked at the curb next to the stairs, still not wanting to use the garage. Bishop was sitting on the stairs, waiting. I had told him Friday we would start at ten on Tuesday, and he had been waiting. I had forgotten about him.

Kendall went up the stairs while I got our suitcase out of the trunk.

'Let me help you with that,' Bishop said.

'You're my driver, not my valet, Bishop,' I said. 'You been waiting long?'

'Not too long.'

'Sorry about that. But you're going to have to wait another hour while I get ready and do some work inside. Then we'll head downtown. You might be driving Kendall back by herself.'

'What about you? I go back for you?'

'I don't think so. They're going to try to put me back in jail today, Bishop.'

'They can do that? You got bail.'

'They can try. They're the government. The beast. And the game is always rigged in the beast's favor.'

I lugged the suitcase up the stairs and through the front door. Kendall was standing in the living room, holding an envelope out to me.

'Somebody slid this under the door,' she said.

I took the envelope and studied it while rolling

the suitcase to the bedroom. It was a plain white envelope with nothing written on either side of it. The flap was not sealed.

After putting the suitcase on the bed for unpacking, I opened the envelope. It contained a single folded document. It was a photocopy of the face sheet of a Ventura County Sheriff's Department arrest report dated December 1, 2018. The suspect arrested on suspicion of fraud was identified on the form as Sam Scales. The summary stated that Scales had used the name Walter Lennon to set up a funding site to raise money for the families of victims killed in a mass shooting the month before in a bar in Thousand Oaks. I didn't need the arrest report to remember the incident at the Borderline Bar & Grill. A sheriff's deputy and twelve customers were killed. The money-raising scam appeared to be very similar to the one Scales went to prison in Nevada for.

I walked into the home office to the desk, where I had left my case files. I was sure that the Ventura County arrest was not on the rap sheet we had received in discovery from the District Attorney's Office. I opened the victim folder and found the arrest record. There was no listing of the arrest in December 2018.

Kendall followed me into the office.

'What is it?' she asked.

'An arrest report for Sam Scales,' I said. 'A case over a year ago in Ventura County.'

'What does it mean?'

'Well, it's not on the rap sheet the prosecution gave us in discovery.'

The face sheet of the arrest report was a form with various windows and boxes below the handwritten summary. Under the box where FRAUD had been checked off was another checklist where the box marked INTERSTATE had a slash through it. At the bottom of the list was a line where the author of the form had written 'FBI-LA.'

'Were they trying to hide it from you?' Kendall asked.

I looked up at her.

'What?'

'Was the prosecutor trying to hide that arrest from you?'

'I think they didn't know about it. I think the FBI came and scooped Sam up.'

Kendall looked confused but I did not explain further. My mind was racing ahead to the possibilities of what the arrest report could mean.

'I have to make a call,' I said.

I pulled my phone and called Harry Bosch. He answered right away.

'Harry, it's me. I'm meeting Jennifer for lunch downtown, then I have to go to court. Can you meet us? I have something you need to see.'

'Where?'

'Rossoblu at one.'

'Rossoblu? Where's that?'

'City Market South, off Eleventh.'

'I'll be there.'

I disconnected. I felt a push of momentum. The arrest report could confirm a lot of things about Sam Scales and the case. It could also be a way to penetrate the FBI wall.

'Who put that under the door?' Kendall asked.

I thought about Agent Ruth but didn't say her name.

'I think it was somebody who wanted to do the right thing,' I said.

31

In anticipation of my return to custody, the courtroom had three times the number of deputies usually on hand for a hearing involving a noncustodial defendant. They were posted by the door, in the gallery, and on the other side of the gate. It was clear from the start that no one was planning on my leaving the way I had come in.

My daughter had been unable to take me up on an invitation to lunch because of a class but now was in the front row of the gallery, directly behind the defense table. She sat next to Lorna, who sat next to Cisco. I hugged Hayley and spoke to each of them, trying to be encouraging even though it was hard for me to be encouraged myself.

'Dad, this is so unfair,' Hayley said.

'Nobody ever said the law is fair, Hay,' I told her. 'Remember that.'

I moved down the line to Cisco. He had not been to lunch and didn't know about the arrest report that had been slipped under my door. I had chosen Bosch to run with it because of his law enforcement pedigree. I believed he was better suited to make contact with the Ventura County sheriff's investigator who had arrested Sam Scales.

'Anything new?' I asked.

He knew I was talking about the surveillance

262

and the hopes of locating Louis Opparizio.

'Not as of this morning,' he said. 'The guy's a ghost.'

I nodded, disappointed, and then moved through the gate to the defense table, where I sat down alone and collected my thoughts. I had beat Jennifer to the courtroom from our lunch because she had to find parking in the black hole while I'd had Bishop drop Kendall and me at the front door. I looked at notes from our lunch meeting and rehearsed in my mind what I would say to the judge. I had never been nervous or intimidated in a courtroom. I had always felt at home and fed off the animosity that was usually directed at the defense from the prosecution table, the bench, sometimes even the jury box. But this was different. I knew that if I failed here, I would be the one who was escorted through the steel door into lockup. Before, when I was arrested, there had been no opportunity to argue my case before being booked. This time I had a chance. It was a long shot because the state was within the rule of law in making its moves. But that didn't make it right and I had to convince the judge of that.

My concentration broke when I noticed Dana Berg and her bow-tied second take seats at the prosecution table. I didn't turn to look at them. I didn't say good afternoon. This had gotten personal, with Berg repeatedly seeking to take away my freedom to prepare my case unfettered. She was now the enemy and I would treat her as such.

Jennifer slid into the seat next to me.

'Sorry, no parking in the black hole,' she said. 'I had to go down to a pay lot on Main.'

She seemed out of breath. The parking lot must have been more than a few blocks down Main.

'No worries,' I said. 'I'm ready to go.'

She turned in her seat to acknowledge our line of supporters, then turned back to me.

'Bosch not coming?' she asked.

'I think he wanted to get going,' I said. 'You know, head up to Ventura.'

'Right.'

'Listen, if this doesn't turn out the way we want it to and I go back to Twin Towers, you'll need to deal with Bosch on the Ventura thing. Make sure there's no paper. He's not used to how we work things on the defense side. No paper, no discovery. Okay?'

'Got it. But things are going to work out, Mickey. We're going to tag-team them and we are a damn good team.'

'I hope so. I like your confidence — even if the whole legislature and penal code is against us.'

I turned and made one more sweep of the gallery, making momentary eye contact with the two reporters who were in their usual places in the second row.

A few minutes later the deputy called the court-room to order as Judge Warfield came through the door to chambers and took the bench.

'Back on the record with *California versus Michael Haller*,' she said. 'We have new charges filed in the case, warranting a custody-and-arraignment hearing as well as a reading of the indictment. And we have a six-eight-six motion from the defense as well. Let's start with the charges.'

I waived a formal reading of the indictment.

'How do you plead?' Warfield asked.

'Not guilty,' I said crisply.

'Very well,' Warfield said. 'Now let us take up the issue of pretrial release or detention. And I have a feeling we are going to have a lot of back-and-forth between the lawyers today, so let's remain at our respective tables to reduce traffic and time. Please speak loudly and clearly when addressing the court so the record will be clear. What is the position of the People, Ms. Berg?'

Berg stood up at the prosecution table.

'Thank you, Your Honor,' she began. 'This morning, previous charges in this case were dropped after the Los Angeles County grand jury delivered an indictment of J. Michael Haller on a charge of first-degree murder under special circumstances outlined by the state legislature, to wit, murder for financial gain. It is the People's position that this is a no-bail offense and we are seeking detention pending trial. There is a presumption — '

'I'm well aware of what the law presumes, Ms. Berg,' Warfield said. 'I am sure Mr. Haller is as well.'

Warfield seemed annoyed by the state's effort to incarcerate me and also by having her hands tied in the matter. She appeared to write something on a document up on the bench. She took a few moments to finish before looking down at me.

'Mr. Haller, I assume you want to be heard?' she asked.

I rose from my seat.

'Yes, Your Honor,' I said. 'But first I'd like to know whether the state is seeking the death penalty under this new charge.'

'Good question,' Warfield said. 'That would change things considerably, Ms. Berg. Has your office decided to seek the death penalty in your case against Mr. Haller?'

'No, Your Honor,' Berg said. 'The People will waive the death penalty.'

'You have your answer, Mr. Haller,' the judge said. 'Do you have anything else?'

'Yes, I do, Judge,' I said. 'Legal precedent holds that once the death penalty has been taken off the table, this is no longer a capital case, notwithstanding that I face a sentence of life without parole. Ms. Berg must also convince the court that guilt is evident and the presumption thereof is great. In and of itself, the indictment is insufficient to prove that guilt is evident, and Ms. Aronson will further address this issue.'

Jennifer stood.

'Your Honor, Jennifer Aronson, representing Mr. Haller on this issue,' she said. 'Mr. Haller will argue the six-eight-six motion himself when that comes up. As to the indictment before the court, it is the defense's position that the prosecution has gone outside the bounds of fair play to deprive Mr. Haller of his freedom as he prepares to defend himself in this matter. This is no more than a ploy to handicap Mr. Haller's ability to defend himself by putting him in a jail cell, where he cannot work full-time on his defense, is in constant danger from other prisoners, and risks his health as well.'

She looked down at her notes before continuing.

'The defense also challenges the allegation of special circumstances in this case,' she said. 'Though we have not seen this new evidence that the prosecution claims will show Mr. Haller's financial gain from the murder of Samuel Scales, it is preposterous to think, let alone prove, that his death would in any way result in gain to Mr. Haller.'

Warfield was again writing when Jennifer finished, and Berg took the opportunity to respond. She stood and addressed the judge while the pen was still moving in her hand.

'Your Honor, the indictment by the grand jury precludes a preliminary hearing on the charges, and the state would object to turning this hearing into a determination of probable cause. The legislature is quite clear on that.'

'Yes, I know the rules, Ms. Berg,' Warfield said. 'But the legislature also gives a superior court judge in this state the power of discretion. I join Ms. Aronson in being troubled by this move by the prosecution. Are you prepared for the court to use its discretion and rule on bail in this matter without providing further support of probable cause?'

'A moment, Your Honor,' Berg said.

For the first time today, I looked over at the prosecution table. Berg was conferring with her second. It was clear that the judge, a former defense attorney, did not approve of the game Berg was playing to put me back in jail. It was put-up-or-shut-up time, no matter what she had been able to run by the grand jury. I saw the second open one of the files in front of him and take out a document. He handed it to Berg, who then straightened up to address the court.

'May it please the court, the People wish to call a witness in this matter,' she said.

'Who is the witness?' Warfield asked.

'Detective Kent Drucker. He will introduce a document that I am sure the court will see in support of probable cause regarding the special-circumstances allegation.'

'Call your witness.'

I had not seen Drucker earlier, but there he was in the front row of the gallery. He got up and went through the gate. He was sworn in and took the stand. Berg began by eliciting from him the details of the searches conducted of my home and warehouse, as well as the home of Lorna Taylor.

'Let's talk specifically about the records you searched at the warehouse,' Berg then said. 'What exactly were you looking at there?'

'These were nonprivileged files relating to the business of Michael Haller's law practice,' Drucker said.

'In other words, the billing of clients?'

'Correct.'

'And was there a file relating to Sam Scales?'

'There were several because Haller had represented him in a number of cases over the years.'

'And in searching these files, did you find any documents pertinent to your investigation of his murder?'

'I did.'

Berg then went through the formality with the judge of gaining approval to show the witness a document he had found in my files. I had no idea what it could be until the prosecutor dropped off a copy at the defense table after handing the judge's copy to her clerk. Jennifer and I leaned toward each other so we could read it at the same time.

It was a copy of a letter apparently sent to Sam Scales in 2016 while he was awaiting sentencing for a fraud conviction.

Dear Sam,

This will be the last correspondence from me and you will have to find yourself a new attorney to handle your sentencing next month — if you do not pay the legal fees agreed to during our meeting of October 11. My agreed-to fee for handling your case was $100,000 plus expenses with a $25,000 retainer. This agreement was made regardless of whether your case went to trial or was handled in disposition. It subsequently was handled by disposition and sentencing is set. The remainder of the fee — $75,000 — is now owed.

I have handled several prior cases involving you as a defendant and know that you keep a legal fund so that you can pay your lawyers for the good work they perform for you. Please pay this invoice or consider this the termination point of our professional relationship, with more serious action to follow.

Sincerely,
p.p. Michael Haller

'Lorna wrote this,' I whispered. 'I never saw it. Besides, it means nothing.'

Jennifer stood and objected.

'Your Honor, may I voir dire?' she asked.

It was a fancy way of asking if she could question the witness about the origin and relevancy of the document before the judge accepted it as a prosecution exhibit.

'You may,' Warfield said.

'Detective Drucker,' Jennifer began. 'This letter is unsigned, true?'

'That is true, but it was in Mr. Haller's files,' Drucker said.

'Do you know what the 'p.p.' before Mr. Haller's printed name means?'

'It's Latin for pro per-something.'

'Per procurationem — do you know what it means?'

'That it was sent under his name but he didn't actually sign it.'

'You said you found this in Mr. Haller's files. So it was never mailed?'

'We believe it is a copy and the original was sent.'

'Based on what?'

270

'Based on it being found in a file marked 'Correspondence.' Why would he keep a file full of letters he didn't send? It makes no sense.'

'What evidence do you have that this letter was ever mailed or delivered directly to Mr. Scales?'

'I assume it was mailed or delivered. How else would Mr. Haller expect to get paid?'

'Do you have any evidence that Mr. Scales ever received this letter?'

'Again, no. But that is not what is important about the letter.'

'Then, what is important about the letter?'

'Mr. Haller says he knows that Sam Scales kept a fund to pay his lawyer and he wanted another seventy-five thousand. That is motive to kill.'

'Do you suppose that Mr. Haller knew about the fund because Sam Scales told him?'

'That would make sense.'

'Did Sam Scales reveal to Mr. Haller where he kept that fund and how to access it?'

'I have no idea, but it would be covered under attorney-client privilege.'

'If you can't show that Mickey Haller knows where Sam Scales kept his money, how can you claim that he killed Sam Scales for his money?'

Berg had had enough and stood.

'I object, Your Honor,' she said. 'This isn't voir dire. Ms. Aronson is conducting a discovery deposition.'

'I can see what she is doing, Ms. Berg,' Warfield said. 'And she has made her point. Anything further, Ms. Aronson?'

Jennifer checked me and I gave a slight shake of my head, reminding her that a lawyer should always quit talking when she's ahead.

'No further questions at this time, Your Honor,' she said. 'It is clear from the detective's testimony as well as the document that it was not signed or written by Mr. Haller and has no relevancy to this hearing.'

'Judge, the relevancy is clear,' Berg countered. 'Whether or not it was signed by the defendant, it was sent by his office and it references a meeting he attended. It is clearly relevant because it speaks to the issues and motives surrounding this crime — that the defendant was owed money and knew that Sam Scales, the victim, had the money and wouldn't part with it. We have further documentation we are ready to present that shows the defendant filed a lien against the victim in furtherance of collecting his money. That lien is now lodged against the estate. If money is found, the defendant is in line to receive it, plus interest. He could not get Sam Scales to pay him in life — he hopes to collect from him in death.'

'Objection!' Jennifer yelled.

'Ms. Berg, you know better,' Warfield said. 'Leave your sound bites for the reporters, not this court.'

'Yes, Your Honor,' Berg said, her tone falsely contrite.

The judge dismissed Drucker from the witness stand. I knew it was fruitless. The judge would either be canny and object to what the prosecution was doing or let it slide. Warfield asked if there was any further argument and Berg demurred while Jennifer asked to address the court.

'Thank you, Your Honor,' she said. 'The court noted earlier that it has wide discretion over bail. The bail schedule is meant to protect the community as well as ensure that defendants accused of crimes are held to answer. To these points, I believe it is clear that Michael Haller is neither a threat to the community nor a threat to flee. He has been free on bond now for six weeks and he hasn't attempted to flee. He hasn't threatened the community or anyone associated with this case. In fact, he has sought and received the court's permission to leave the county and state and yet returned the same night. Your Honor, you do have discretion in the matter and it is in pursuit of a fair trial in this case that I ask that bond be carried over from the original charge and that Mr. Haller be allowed to remain free to defend himself.'

Berg's comeback was only to remind the judge that rules were rules. She said judicial discretion did not extend to the findings of a grand jury or to the legislature's decision to make murder for financial gain a no-bail charge.

She then sat down.

I didn't think we had a winning argument, but the judge built anticipation in the courtroom as she wrote notes before speaking.

'We'll hear the other motion before I make a decision on this matter,' she said. 'We are going to take a ten-minute break first and then we'll consider Mr. Haller's six-eight-six motion. Thank you.'

The judge quickly left the bench. And I was left with ten minutes to figure out how to turn things around.

32

It might have been my last chance to walk the halls of the courthouse, even ride the elevator down and step outside to enjoy a few moments of free, fresh air, but I remained at the defense table during the ten-minute break, which actually lasted twenty. I wanted to be alone with my thoughts. I even told Jennifer I didn't want her next to me when court resumed. She might have been hurt, but she understood my reasoning. It was me against the state, and while I would not be speaking to a jury, I wanted the judge to be reminded of the fact that I was one man standing alone against the power and might of the beast.

I composed myself to be ready at the ten-minute mark and then dealt with the anxiety of waiting in overtime. Finally Warfield came out and retook her position on the bench above everyone.

'Very well, back on the record,' she said. 'We have a motion from the defense to compel a speedy trial. Mr. Haller, I see you are now alone at the defense table. You will be arguing this motion?'

I stood up.

'Yes, Your Honor,' I said.

'Very well,' Warfield said. 'I hope we can be succinct. Proceed.'

'If it please the court, I will be succinct. What

275

the prosecution has done with its grand jury indictment is attempt to subvert the law and my constitutionally guaranteed right to a speedy trial. It's a shell game, Your Honor, played by the prosecution not in the furtherance of justice but in the gaming of it. There have been two constants since the very first minutes of this case. One is that I have steadfastly denied these charges and claimed my innocence. The other is my refusal under any circumstances to delay these proceedings for any amount of time.'

I paused for a moment and looked down at the notes I had scribbled on my legal pad. I didn't need them. I was on a roll. But I wanted the space so the judge could take in my argument in pieces.

'Since day one I have demanded my right to a speedy trial,' I continued. 'I have said put up or shut up to the state. I did not commit this crime and I demand my day in court. And as that day has drawn closer and the prosecution knows it's almost time, they have blinked. They know their case is weak. They know it is full of holes. They know I have innocence and reasonable doubt on my side and they have attempted to thwart my defense at every turn.'

I paused again, this time turning slightly to look back at my daughter and offer a wistful smile. No man should have his daughter see him in this position.

I turned back.

'Judge, every lawyer's got a bag of tricks — prosecutor, defense attorney, doesn't matter. There is nothing pure about the law when you

276

get inside a courtroom. It's a bare-knuckle fight and each side uses whatever it can to bludgeon the other. The constitution guarantees me a speedy trial, but by dropping the original charge and talking a grand jury into a new one, the prosecution is trying to bludgeon me in two ways: stick me in a jail cell so I am handicapped in preparing my defense, and restart the game clock so the state has more time to wield its power and might and shore up their losing case against me.'

This time I kept my eyes on the judge as I paused before the windup.

'Is it legal? Is it within code? Perhaps. I'll give them that. But is it fair? Is it in the pursuit of justice? Not a chance. You can stick me back in jail, you can delay the search for truth that a trial is supposed to be, but it won't be the right thing to do and it won't be fair. The court holds a lot of discretion in this regard and the defense urges you not to restart the clock. Let's get to the search for the truth now instead of later, instead of at the prosecution's convenience. Thank you, Your Honor.'

If my words had any impact on Warfield, she didn't show it. She didn't write anything down as she had during the earlier motion. She simply swiveled six inches in her high-backed, leather chair so that her gaze shifted from me to the prosecution table.

'Ms. Berg?' she said. 'Would the state like to respond?'

'Yes, Your Honor,' Berg said. 'I promise to be more succinct than the defense. In fact, Mr.

Haller made my argument for me. What we have done with the refiling of the case through grand jury indictment is firmly within the bounds of the law as well as something that happens routinely in this courthouse and courthouses across the country. It is not a do-over or a delay tactic. I am charged with seeking true justice for the victim of this cold-blooded murder. Through the grand jury and the presentation of evidence from the ongoing investigation, we have elected to upgrade the charges in the pursuit of justice.'

In my peripheral vision I saw Berg glance my way as she threw my own words back at me. I did not give her the satisfaction of a look back.

'Your Honor, the case against the defendant is strong and getting stronger as the investigation of this crime continues. That's what the defendant knows, that is what *he* is trying to subvert: a search for truth with all the evidence on the table. It is his hope that by hurrying into trial, he can stop the mounting evidence from crushing him. That won't happen, because the truth is inevitable. Thank you.'

The judge paused before speaking, possibly waiting to see whether I would stand to object or respond to Berg. She even swiveled her chair back toward me as if expecting it. But I held my ground. I had made my points and there was no need to restate them.

'This is a novel situation,' Warfield began. 'It has been my experience as a judge — and as a defense attorney in a prior life — that it is the defendant who most often seeks delays, seem-ingly in an effort to put off the inevitable. But not in this case. And so the arguments today give me pause. Mr. Haller clearly wants this behind him — no matter the outcome. He also wants to be free to build his case.'

The judge swiveled toward Berg.

'On the other hand, the state gets only one shot at this,' she said. 'There are no do-overs and therefore time to prepare is key. There are new charges in the case and the state bears the responsibility of being able to support those charges to a level far above the probable-cause threshold found by the grand jury. The burden of proof — proving guilt beyond a reasonable doubt — is just as heavy as the burden carried by the defense.'

The judge straightened her seat and leaned forward, clasping her hands together.

'The court is inclined in these matters to split the baby. And I will let the defense choose how that split is made. Mr. Haller, you decide. I will continue your bail with all the existing restrictions but you will waive your right to a speedy trial. Or I will revoke bail but refuse to change the case calendar, leaving the start of trial on this matter set for the eighteenth of February. How do you wish to proceed?'

Before I could stand and respond, Berg did.

'Your Honor,' she said urgently. 'May I be heard?'

'No, Ms. Berg,' the judge said. 'The court has heard all it needs to hear. Mr. Haller, will you make a choice, or would you like me to allow Ms. Berg to choose?'

I stood slowly.

'A moment, Your Honor?' I asked.

'Make it fast, Mr. Haller,' Warfield said. 'I am in an uncomfortable position that I will not hold for long.'

I turned toward the railing behind the defense table and looked at my daughter. I signaled her closer and she slid forward on her seat, putting her hands on top of the rail. I leaned down and put my hands on top of hers.

'Hayley, I want this over with,' I whispered. 'I didn't do this and I think I can prove it. I want to go in February. You going to be okay with that?'

'Dad, it was so hard when they had you in jail before,' she whispered back. 'Are you sure?'

'It's like what you and your mother and I talked about. I'm free right now, but inside I feel like I'm still locked up as long as this is hanging over me. I need it to be over.'

'I know. But I worry.'

From behind me I heard the judge.

'Mr. Haller,' she said. 'We are waiting.'

I kept my eyes on my daughter.

'It's going to be all right,' I said.

I quickly leaned over the rail and kissed her on the forehead. I then glanced at Kendall and nodded. I could tell by the look of surprise on her face that she expected more, she expected to be consulted. That I had sought my daughter's approval on this choice rather than hers might doom our relationship. But I did what I felt I had to do.

I turned back to the judge and announced my decision.

'Your Honor, I surrender myself to the court at this time,' I said. 'And I will be ready to defend myself on the charges on February eighteenth as scheduled. I am innocent, Judge, and the faster I can get to a jury to prove it, the better.'

The judge nodded, seemingly not surprised but concerned by my decision.

'Very well, Mr. Haller,' she said.

She made it official with rulings from the bench, but not without a final objection from the prosecution.

'Your Honor,' Berg said. 'The People ask that your ruling on the trial date be stayed while under review by the Second District Court of Appeal.'

Warfield looked at her for a long moment before replying. It is always a risky move to tell a judge you are appealing a ruling from the bench when you still have a whole trial before the same judge ahead of you. Judges are supposed to be impartial, but when you announce you are going to a higher court to complain that your lower court judge was in error, well, there are ways for that jurist to even the score down the line. A perfect example is what Judge Hagan did to me at my first appearance on this case. I had reversed him twice on appeal. He paid me back by slapping me with a $5 million bail. He all but winked and smiled at me when he did it. Berg was walking a similar line with Warfield now, and it looked like the judge was giving her a few seconds to reconsider.

But Berg waited her out.

'Ms. Berg, I'll now give you a choice,' Warfield finally said. 'I won't stay the ruling on the six-eight-six motion without staying the ruling on Mr. Haller's bail revocation. So if you want a stay while you appeal, then Mr. Haller remains free under the current bail arrangement until you get a ruling from the appellate court.'

The two women locked eyes for a tense five seconds before the prosecutor responded.

'Thank you, Your Honor,' Berg said coldly. 'The People withdraw the request for a stay.'

'Very well,' Warfield responded with just as much ice. 'Then I think we are adjourned here.'

As the judge stood up, the deputies in the room moved toward me. I was going back to Twin Towers.

33

I was placed back in K-10, the high-power module at Twin Towers where they housed inmates on keep-away status. The only problem I had with this was that I wanted to be kept away from the jailers more than from the jailed. The investigation that had followed the eavesdropping scandal had put the mark on me and I knew the potential that the jail deputies would get back at me physically had increased exponentially.

Bishop was long gone and I needed new protection. In a way, I held auditions. I spoke to a handful of men in the module the morning after my arrival, attempting to learn whom I might be able to trust, who might have greater enmity for the hacks than I did. I settled on a guy named Carew, who was physically impressive and being held on a murder charge. I didn't know the details of the case and didn't ask for them. But I learned that he had private counsel and I knew that a murder defense cost serious money. I offered him four hundred a week to watch my back and settled the negotiation at five hundred delivered weekly to his attorney.

The days in the jail fell into the same routine as the earlier stint, with my team coming in to conference most afternoons at three. It seemed

283

that our nets had already been cast and we were in the stage where we were looking through the catch and devising our strategy. My energy and outlook remained high. I was confident in the case. I just wanted to get to it.

The only break from the routine came three days after my re-arrest when I was taken to the visitors' center and sat down in front of my first ex-wife, Maggie McPherson. Her coming to see me embarrassed me and made my heart swell at once.

'Is anything wrong?' I said. 'Is Hayley all right?'

'Everything's fine out here,' she said. 'I just wanted to see you. How are you, Mickey?'

I was ashamed of my situation and my jailhouse blues. I could imagine how I must appear to her, especially after her taking exception to the way I had looked outside jail.

'All things considered, I'm okay,' I said. 'The trial's soon and this will all be over.'

'Are you ready?' she asked.

'More than ready. I think we're going to win this thing.'

'Good. I don't want our daughter to lose her father.'

'She won't. She's what keeps me going.'

Maggie nodded and said nothing more on it. I read the reason for her visit as her checking on my health and state of mind.

'It means a lot to me that you came here,' I said.

'Of course,' she said. 'And if you need anything, call me — collect.'

'I will. Thanks.'

The visit only lasted fifteen minutes but I came away from it feeling stronger. With family, as splintered as it was, behind me, I felt like I couldn't lose.

34

The silk suit felt good against my skin. It eased the itch from the prison rash I had developed over most of my body. I sat quietly next to Jennifer Aronson at the defense table and savored the moment of pseudofreedom and relief. I had been taken to court for a hearing requested by the prosecution, which was seeking sanctions for alleged foul play on the part of the defense. But no matter what the cause, I was happy to be pulled out of Twin Towers for any reason for any amount of time.

Over the years I'd had many incarcerated clients who exhibited and complained about prison rash. Visits to the jail clinic didn't cure it or explain it. Its origin was unknown. It had been suggested that the industrial detergent used on the jail bedding and laundry caused it, or that there was something in the material used in the thin mattresses in the cells. Others said it was an allergic reaction to confinement. Still others called it the manifestation of guilt. All I knew was that I didn't get it the first time around at Twin Towers and then I got it bad the second. The difference was that in between stays, I had been the root cause of another damaging internal investigation of the jail system. This made me think that the jail deputies were behind

286

it — that the rash that kept me itching and awake at night was a form of payback. They had spiked my food or my laundry or my cell in some way.

I kept this belief to myself to avoid being considered paranoid. My physical decline and weight loss was continuing and I wanted no one to add concerns about mental acuity to the question of whether I could adequately defend myself. Maybe it was the suit or maybe it was the courtroom. All I knew was that my preoccupation with the malady went away as soon as I left the jail and was put on the bus.

On the way over, the bus had passed two painted murals depicting Kobe Bryant. The famed Lakers basketball star had been killed with his daughter and others in a helicopter crash only ten days earlier and already the street memorials were up in solemn testimony to his transcending mastery of his sport to reach iconic status, in a city where the climb to that level was already so crowded.

I heard the soft thud of the courtroom door closing and turned to see that Kendall Roberts had entered. She gave a secretive wave as she came down the center aisle. I smiled. She moved down the first row and sat directly behind the defense table.

'Hey, Mickey.'

'Kendall, you didn't have to come all the way down. This probably is going to be a pretty quick hearing.'

'It's still better than the fifteen minutes they give you at the jail.'

287

'Well, thanks.'

'Also, I wanted to — '

She stopped when she saw Chan, the courtroom deputy, moving toward us to order me to stop communicating with people in the gallery. I held my hand up to signal that I was halting the violation. I turned forward and leaned toward Jennifer.

'Do you mind telling Kendall that I'll call her later when I can get to the phone in the module?'

'Not at all.'

Jennifer got up to whisper to Kendall and I went back to staring straight ahead and feeling the tension leak out of my muscles and spine. You never stopped looking over your shoulder in Twin Towers. I savored these moments when I didn't have to worry.

Jennifer returned to her seat. I finally came out of my reverie and got to work.

'So,' I said. 'What's the update on Opparizio?'

I had gotten the word during a team meeting Monday that the Indians had finally located him when they followed Jeannie Ferrigno to a rendezvous at a hotel in Beverly Hills. They dropped her and stayed with Opparizio, tailing him to a house in Brentwood that was held in an impenetrable blind trust.

'Same,' Jennifer said. 'They're ready to go with the subpoena when you give the word.'

'Okay, let's wait till next week. But if it looks like he might be getting ready to split town, we need to serve him. He can't get away.'

'We know, but I'll remind Cisco.'

'We also serve the girlfriend then and his two

other associates holding shares in BioGreen. And all of it on camera so we can show the judge if they don't show up.'

'Got it.'

I glanced over at the prosecution table. Berg was by herself today. No bow-tie backup. She was looking at a handwritten document and I guessed that she was rehearsing her argument. She sensed my gaze.

'Hypocrite,' she said.

'Excuse me?' I said.

'You heard me. You talk about tilting the board all the time and the prosecution not playing fair, and then you pull a stunt like this.'

'Like what?'

'I'm sure you know what this is about. Like I said and you heard, you're a hypocrite, Haller. And a murderer.'

I looked at her for a long moment and I could see it in her eyes. She was a true believer. She had me down as a killer. It's one thing when the cops think it — most of them can't see the difference between a defense lawyer and a defendant. But in the world of trial lawyers, I had for the most part encountered respect from both sides of the aisle. That Berg believed I was capable of putting a man in a trunk and shooting him three times was a reminder of what I was facing at the trial ahead: a true believer who wanted to put me away forever.

'You're so wrong,' I said. 'You're so blinded by the lies you've been told by — '

'Save it for the jury, Haller,' she said.

The verbal confrontation ended with Deputy

Chan announcing that court was coming to order. Judge Warfield stepped through the door at the back of the courtroom and took the bench. She quickly got down to business on *California versus Haller* and invited Berg to explain her request for sanctions against the defense. The prosecutor took the document she had been studying to the lectern with her.

'Your Honor, the defense in this case has repeatedly accused the People of playing unfair with discovery, and yet it is the defense that has engaged in deception all along,' Berg began.

'Ms. Berg,' the judge cut in. 'I don't need the preamble. Get to the point. If there is a discovery violation, please get to it.'

'Yes, Your Honor. On Monday, the latest witness lists were due from each side. And to our surprise, the defense actually put new names on their witness list. One name that stood out to us was Rose Marie Dietrich, whom the defense listed as the landlord of the victim in this case, Sam Scales.'

'Was this a witness the prosecution was not familiar with?'

'No, Your Honor, we were not familiar with her. I dispatched investigators to locate and talk to her and we learned that the reason she was not known to us is that Sam Scales used a false identity when he rented an apartment from her.'

'I'm not seeing the problem here as far as the defense goes, Ms. Berg.'

'Your Honor, the problem is in what Rose Marie Dietrich told us. She said that Mr. Haller and two of his investigators spoke with her three weeks ago about Sam Scales, who was using the name Walter Lennon when he rented the apartment. Additionally, she allowed Mr. Haller and his crew to look through the victim's belongings, which were stored in the garage of the property. Unaware that Mr. Scales had been murdered in October, Dietrich and her husband boxed his belongings when he seemed to disappear without paying rent for December. They stored his property in the garage.'

'This is all very interesting, but where is the infraction the People are seeking sanctions for?'

'Judge, the point is that the defense had access to several boxes of belongings, including documents and mail, and yet three weeks later, nothing has come to the People in discovery. They didn't put Rose Marie Dietrich's name on their witness list until this week in order to ensure that when the prosecution got to Ms. Dietrich, it would have no access to the property.'

'Why would that be, Ms. Berg?'

'Because they were turned over to the Salvation Army after the defendant and his crew visited Ms. Dietrich. It is quite obvious that the defense had a strategy to keep whatever information was in the victim's belongings from the People, Your Honor.'

'That is a lot of supposition. Do you have anything that backs that up?'

'We have a sworn statement from Rose Marie Dietrich that states unequivocally that she was told by the defendant that she could donate the property.'

291

'Then let me take a look at that.'

Berg dropped off a copy of the statement with me after handing one to the clerk for the judge. There was silence for a minute or so as Jennifer and I huddled together to read the witness statement at the same time as the judge.

'Okay, the court has read the document,' Warfield said. 'I'd like to hear from Mr. Haller on this matter next.'

I got up and went to the lectern as Berg abandoned it. I had decided on the bus ride over to go full-on sarcastic with my response as opposed to full-on outraged.

'Good morning, Judge,' I said good-naturedly. 'I would like to begin by saying that normally I would welcome any opportunity to leave the spare accommodations afforded me at the Twin Towers Correctional Facility, courtesy of Ms. Berg, to be in court, but this time I am baffled by the reason I'm here and the logic of her argument. It seems to me, Your Honor, that she should be seeking sanctions against her own team of investigators, not the defense.'

'Mr. Haller,' Warfield said in a tired tone. 'As I said to Ms. Berg, let's stay on point. Please respond directly to the discovery issue that the prosecution has raised.'

'Thank you, Judge. My response is to say there has been no discovery violation. I have no documents to turn over and I have hidden nothing from the prosecution. Yes, we went to the address in question and looked through the contents of the boxes stored there. I took nothing from those boxes, and I guarantee that

Ms. Berg's investigators asked Rose Marie Dietrich what we took. Unhappy with the response they got to that question, Ms. Berg chose not to include the answer in this piece of paper she claims is a statement of fact. It's got some facts listed here, Judge, but not all of them.'

'Judge?' Berg said, rising from her seat.

'Your Honor, I'm not finished,' I said quickly.

'Ms. Berg, you had your turn,' Warfield said. 'Let counsel finish and then you will get a chance to respond.'

Berg sat back down and started writing furiously on her legal pad.

'In closing, Your Honor,' I said. 'There is no subterfuge here. The court recalls that three weeks ago in a teleconference hearing that Ms. Berg was party to, I asked permission to leave the county and state. I assume the court reporter has a record of that hearing, and it will reveal that the prosecution asked specifically whom I was going to see at High Desert State Prison in Nevada. And I said I was going to visit the former cellmate of the victim in this case. If Ms. Berg or any of the many investigators at her disposal had bothered to follow up and talk to that man in Nevada, they would have gotten the same address and alias for Sam Scales that I got, and in fact could have beaten me to the location we're talking about here. Your Honor, again I say that this is nothing but sour grapes. The discovery obligations of the defense require that I turn over to Ms. Berg a witness list and copies of

293

anything I intend to offer into evidence. I have done that. I am not required to share with Ms. Berg my interviews, observations, or other work product. She knows that. But since day one, the prosecution's investigation has been lazy, sloppy, and shoddy. I am confident that I will prove that at trial, but the sad thing is, there shouldn't be a trial. The prosecution has — '

'Okay, let me stop you right there, Mr. Haller,' the judge said. 'I believe you have more than made your point. You can return to your seat now.'

'Thank you, Your Honor,' I said.

Usually when a judge tells you to sit down it means that all that needs to be said has been said and a decision has been made.

The judge swiveled in her chair and focused on Berg.

'Ms. Berg, do you recall the teleconference referred to by counsel?' she asked.

'Yes, Your Honor,' Berg said.

There was no emotion in her tone. She had taken the same cue I had when Warfield told me to sit down.

'It appears to me that the state had every opportunity to follow and find this location and the victim's belongings,' Warfield said. 'The court tends to agree with Mr. Haller that this is about work product and a missed opportunity, not about any gamesmanship on the part of the defense. Certainly nothing I would consider a violation of discovery.'

Berg stood but did not move to the lectern, a sign that her protest was going to be half-hearted, no matter what she had scribbled on her legal pad.

'He waited three weeks to put her on the witness list,' she said. 'He was hiding her importance. There should have been a written report about the interview and the search of the property. That is exactly what the spirit and intention of discovery is.'

I started to rise to object but the judge made a signal with her hand, gesturing me back into my chair.

'Ms. Berg,' the judge intoned, the first note of annoyance in her voice. 'If you are suggesting that Mr. Haller is under an obligation to document his investigation with reports of his moves and interviews just like a law enforcement agency and then immediately decide whether he will call Ms. Dietrich as a witness, then you must take me for a fool.'

'No, Your Honor,' Berg said quickly. 'Not at all.'

'Very well, then. We're done here. The motion for sanctions is denied.'

The judge looked over at the calendar that hung on the wall over the clerk's corral.

'We are thirteen days from jury selection,' she said. 'I am setting a hearing for next Thursday at ten a.m. for final motions. I want to handle everything on that day. That means, get your paperwork in with enough time for the court to consider it. I want no surprises. I will see you all then.'

The judge adjourned court and I felt the dread of incarceration return before Deputy Chan and his cohorts could even get to me.

35

Upon my second arrest I was placed back in a single-bed cell at Twin Towers. This time I had even graduated to the outside wall of the jail, which gave me a window — only four inches wide and escape-proof, but it had a partial view of the Criminal Courts Building just a few blocks away as the crow flies. It was enough of a view for me to want to stay in the cell with my eyes on the prize rather than congregate in the dayroom with the other keep-aways. And this, even though I had replaced Bishop with Carew.

So I was feeling safe and secure in the module. The problem was that there were no such protections on the jail buses that moved hundreds of inmates to and from court each day. Whom you rode with and whom you were chained to was mostly a matter of chance. Or so it appeared. No matter what measure I took to protect myself in custody, I was always going to be most vulnerable on the bus. I knew this for a fact because I'd had clients attacked on the buses. And I had seen fights break out and attacks staged while riding them myself.

After the hearing on the prosecution's motion for sanctions, I waited two hours in the courthouse jail before being shuttled onto a bus back to the Towers. I was cuffed fourth on a chain behind three other men and moved onto the bus. We were put into the second-to-last compartment and I was seated against the barred window in the forward-facing bench. The deputy checked us, closed the gate and locked it, and proceeded to fill the next compartment. I leaned forward to look across the man next to me to the prisoner seated on my row against the opposite window. I recognized him but not from the keep-away module. I couldn't place him. It could have been from court or a potential client meeting in which I didn't take the case. He was checking me out as I was checking him. And that fired my paranoia. I knew I had to keep a watch on him.

The bus exited the garage beneath the courts building and trundled up the steep grade to Spring Street. As it turned left, City Hall was on the right side, and several prisoners followed the tradition of flipping the finger at the seat of power. This of course could not be seen by anyone on the marble steps or behind the windows of the iconic building. The bus's 'windows' were actually slotted metal that allowed a confined view out but no view in.

I watched the man I was curious about hold his hand up and extend the fuck-you finger. He did it so routinely, without even looking out through the slots himself, that I knew he was a regular guest of the system. And that was when I recognized him. He was the client of a colleague whom I had once filled in for during a hearing before a judge. It had been a babysitting job, a minor hearing that involved a court appearance. Dan Daly had been stuck in a trial and asked me to handle it and I did.

Satisfied that I had answered the question and that the man posed no special threat, I relaxed and leaned back in my seat, tilting my head up to look at the ceiling. I started counting the days until the start of my trial and how soon I could reasonably expect to walk free after a not-guilty verdict.

It was the last thing I remembered.

36

Thursday, February 6

I could only open my eyes to narrow slices of light. It wasn't the harshness of the light that prevented me from opening them wider. It was physical impediment. I simply could not do it.

I was disoriented at first, not sure where I was.

'Mickey?'

I turned at the voice, recognized it.

'Jennifer?'

The one word set fire to my throat, the pain so sharp I grimaced.

'Yes, I'm here. How do you feel?'

'I can't see. What — '

'Your eyes are swollen. You burst a lot of blood vessels.'

I burst blood vessels? This didn't make sense.

'What do you mean?' I asked. 'How did I — *ahh*, it hurts to talk.'

'Don't talk,' Jennifer said. 'Just listen. We went over this an hour ago and then the sedation hit and you went out again. You were attacked, Mickey. On the jail bus after court yesterday.'

'Yesterday?'

'Don't talk. Yes, you've lost a day. But if you can stay awake, I can get them in here to do the testing. They need to check your brain function to see if there was anything . . . so we'll know if

299

there is any . . . anything permanent.'

'What happened on the bus?'

The pain.

'I don't know all the details and the sheriff's investigator wants to talk to you about it — he's waiting outside but I told him I was going to talk to you first. Basically, another man on the bus got his chain free and used it to choke you. He was behind you and wrapped it around your neck. They thought you were dead but paramedics revived you, Mickey. They say it's a miracle you're alive.'

'It doesn't feel like a miracle. Where am I?'

I was beginning to be able to manage the pain. Talking in a monotone, turning my head slightly to the left seemed to lessen it.

'County-USC — the jail ward. Hayley and Lorna and everybody wanted to come in to see you but you're on lockdown and they'd only let me in. I don't think you want them seeing you like this anyway. Better to wait till the swelling goes down.'

I felt her hand grip my shoulder.

'Are we alone in here?' I asked.

'Yes,' Jennifer said. 'This is an attorney-client meeting. There's a deputy outside the door but it's closed. Also, the investigator's out there, waiting to talk to you.'

'Okay, listen, don't let them use this to delay the trial.'

'Well, we'll see, Mickey. You need to be tested to make sure you — '

'No, I'm fine, I can tell. I'm already thinking about the case and I don't want to delay it. We have them where we want them and I don't want to give them time to catch up to us. That's it.'

'Okay, I'll object if they try.'

'Who was the guy?'

'What guy?'

'The one who choked me with the chain.'

'I don't know, I only got his name. Mason Maddox. Lorna put it through the conflict-of-interest app, and there were no hits. You have no prior history with him. He was convicted last month of three murders — I haven't gotten the case details yet. He was in court for a motions hearing.'

'Who's his lawyer? The PD?'

'I don't have that information yet.'

'Why'd he do it? Who put him up to it?'

'If the Sheriff's Department knows, they're not sharing it with me. I have Cisco looking into it and a call in to Harry Bosch.'

'I don't want to pull Cisco off trial prep. That could be the whole motive behind it.'

'No, because he tried to kill you and probably thought he did. You don't kill a guy to distract his investigators. I filed a motion with Warfield today asking her to issue an order reinstituting bail or ordering the sheriff to transport you by car to and from court. No more buses. Too dangerous.'

'That's good thinking.'

'I hope to get a hearing on it this afternoon. We'll see.'

'Is there like a hand mirror around here or something?'

'Why?'

'I want to see myself.'

'Mickey, I don't think you — '

'It's all right. I just want to take a quick look and I'll be fine.'

'I don't see a mirror, but hold on, I have something.'

I heard her unzip her purse and then she put a small square object in my hand. A mirror from a makeup case. I held it up to my face and managed to get a glimpse. I looked like a boxer on the morning after a fight — and a losing bout at that. My eyes were swollen and the rash of exploded blood vessels extended from the corners of my eyes and across both cheeks.

'Jesus,' I said.

'Yeah, not a good look,' Jennifer said. 'I still think you should let the doctor test you.'

'I'm going to be fine.'

'Mickey, there could be something and you should know.'

'But then the prosecution could know and they'll use it to ask for a delay.'

There was a brief silence as Jennifer considered that and realized I was right.

'Okay, I'm getting tired,' I said. 'Send in the investigator, let's see what he says.'

'Are you sure?' she asked.

'Yes. And don't pull Cisco off trial prep. When you hear from Bosch, put him on Mason Maddox. I want to know everything. There's got to be a link somewhere.'

'A link to what, Mickey?'

'A link to the case. Or the sheriff's wiretap investigation. Something. We have to look at everybody. The sheriff's, Opparizio, the FBI, everybody.'

'Okay, I'll tell the guys.'

'You think I'm paranoid, don't you?'

'I just think it's kind of far-fetched.'

I nodded. Maybe it was.

'Did they let you bring your phone in here?' I asked.

'Yes,' she said.

'Okay, take a picture of me. You might want to show it to the judge when you make your argument for protection.'

'Good idea.'

I heard her getting her phone out of her purse.

'I'm sure Berg will object to it,' she said. 'But worth a try.'

'If the judge knows there's a photo, she'll want to see it,' I said. 'Human curiosity.'

I heard her snap the shot.

'Okay, Mickey,' she said. 'Rest up.'

'That's the plan,' I said.

I heard her step toward the door.

'Jennifer?' I said.

I heard her steps come back to the bed.

'Yes, I'm here,' Jennifer said.

'Look, I can't really see yet, but I can hear,' I said.

'Okay.'

'And I hear doubt in your voice.'

'No, you're wrong.'

'Look, it's a natural thing. To question things. I think you —'

'It's not that, Mickey.'

'Then, what is it?'

303

'Okay, look, it's my father. He's gotten sick. I'm worried about him.'

'Is he in the hospital? What's wrong?'

'That's the thing. We're not getting straight answers. He's in a care home up in Seattle and my sister and I are not getting answers.'

'Is your sister there?'

'Yes, she thinks I should go up. If I want to see him before . . . you know.'

'Then, she's right, you need to go.'

'But we have the case — the trial. The motions hearing is next week and now this attack.'

I knew that losing her could be devastating to the case, but there was no choice.

'Look,' I said, 'you gotta go. You can take your laptop and there's a lot you can do from up there when you're not with your father. You can write motions, Cisco can get them to the court clerk.'

'It's not the same,' she said.

'I know it's not but it's what we can do. You need to go.'

'I feel like I'm leaving you all alone.'

'I'll figure something out. Go up there, see him, and, who knows, maybe he'll start feeling better and you get back down for trial.'

She didn't respond at first. I had said my piece and was already thinking of alternative ways to go.

'I'm going to think about it tonight,' Jennifer finally said. 'I'll let you know tomorrow, okay?'

'That's okay, but I don't think there is much to think about. It's family. Your father. You have to go.'

'Thanks, Mickey.'

I nodded.

I heard her steps again as she headed to the door. I tried to relax my throat and ease the pain. Talking felt like swallowing glass.

Then I heard Jennifer tell the investigator waiting outside the room that he could go in.

PART FOUR

BLEEDING THE BEAST

37

The world seemed to be on the edge of chaos. More than a thousand people were dead from a mystery virus in China. Almost a billion people were on lockdown there and American citizens had been evacuated. There were cruise ships out on the Pacific that were floating incubators of the virus, and no vaccine was on the horizon. The president was saying the crisis would pass, while his own virus expert was saying brace for a pandemic. Closer to home, Jennifer Aronson's father had just died in Seattle of an undiagnosed illness, and she was not getting any answers.

In L.A., it was the second day of jury selection in the trial of my life.

We had been proceeding at a rapid pace. The four days scheduled for voir dire had been cut in half by a judge who also felt that there was a coming wave. She wanted this trial over with before the wave hit, and while I wasn't comfortable hurrying to pick a jury, I was right there with the judge. I wanted this over. Some of the deputies at Twin Towers had started wearing masks and I took that as a sign. I didn't want to be in lockup when that wave the judge was worried about came in.

Still, picking the twelve strangers who would deliberate the case involved the most important decisions of the trial. Those twelve would hold my life in their hands, and the time allotted to choosing them had been chopped in half. This had caused me to take extraordinary measures to quickly try to find out who these people were.

Jury selection was an art form. It involved research, knowledge of social and cultural data, and, finally, gut instinct. What you want in the end is a panel of attentive people who are there for the truth. What you look for and hope to root out are those who view the truth through the prism of bias — racial, political, cultural, and so forth. And those with ulterior motives for serving.

The process begins with the judge weeding out jurors who have conflicts of schedule, can't sit in judgment of others, or can't grasp the meaning of legal tenets like reasonable doubt. It then moves to the lawyers, who may question jurors further to determine if they should be dismissed for cause — reasons of bias or background. The prosecution and defense are also given an equal number of peremptory challenges allowing them to dismiss jurors for unstated reasons. And that is where gut instinct most often comes into play.

All of this must be synthesized into decisions about whom to keep in and whom to kick out. That is the art — to finally arrive at a panel of twelve people you believe will be open to your cause. I fully admit that there is an advantage to the defense in that it has to win the belief of only one juror to be successful — one doubter of the state's case. One holdout for the defense can hang a jury and force the state to start over, or even reconsider whether to go forward with a second trial at all. The state must win all twelve hearts and minds to get a conviction. Still, the state's advantages beyond this one are so enormous as to make the defense's jury advantage negligible. But you take what you are given, and therefore jury selection has always been sacred to me, made all the more so this time because I was the defendant.

It was 2 p.m. and the judge was expecting — no, demanding — that a jury be empaneled by the close of court in three hours. I could push it into the next day, because the judge ultimately wouldn't want to enforce a demand that was potentially reversible on appeal. But if I did force the issue, there would be consequences down the line in terms of rulings from the bench.

Besides that, I was down to my last peremptory challenge and I knew there was no way I would be able to milk it for three more hours. We would fill the box before the courtroom went dark and the prosecution in the murder of Sam Scales would begin in the morning.

The good news was that the panel was largely set with jurors who I believed ranged on the defense meter from yellow — the middle ground — to deep green for pro-defense. Because of long-embedded and rightful distrust of police in minority communities, Black and brown jurors were always prized by the defense because they tended to view the testimony of police officers with suspicion. I had managed to

311

keep four African Americans and two Latinas on the panel, fending off Dana Berg's efforts to jettison the Blacks in particular. When one Black panelist revealed under questioning that she had once made a donation to the local Black Lives Matter organization, Berg first asked for the woman to be dismissed for cause. Making the request to an African-American judge took a certain level of courage, but it also underlined Berg's singular purpose in convicting me. When the judge denied the motion, the prosecutor then attempted to use a peremptory challenge. That was when I swung in with an objection that the move was based on race, a clear exception to the rules of peremptory challenges. The judge agreed and the juror was seated. The ruling put Berg on notice in regard to future efforts to sculpt the jury along racial lines but then allowed me to do just that.

It was a big win for the defense but the last round of challenges had left three new faces in the box and I had just one peremptory. All three were white — two women and one man. And this was where my extraordinary juror profiling came into play. Early the morning before, Cisco had posted himself in the First Street garage, where jurors were directed to park. At that point, a few hundred potential jurors had been summoned for jury duty. Cisco had no way of knowing who would end up on my panel but he took note of character-defining aspects of the people arriving: things like make and model of cars, registrations, bumper stickers, interior contents, and so on. A person driving a

Mercedes SL is going to have a different worldview from someone driving a Toyota Prius.

Sometimes you want the Mercedes on the jury. Sometimes you want the Prius.

After the first morning session with the hundred people called for the panel in my case, Cisco went back to the garage at lunch-time and then again at the end of the day. By his fourth time in the garage on Wednesday morning, he was recognizing people assigned to my case and building intel on many of them.

When court was back in session, he returned from the garage, sat in the gallery, and communicated what he knew about each potential juror to my co-counsel. I wasn't alone at the table but I wasn't with Jennifer Aronson either. My new co-counsel was Maggie McPherson. She had taken a leave of absence from the District Attorney's Office and answered my distress call. I could think of no one better to be sitting next to as I faced the most difficult challenge of my life.

You never want to use your last peremptory, because you never know who will take the seat of the potential juror you just dismissed. You could clear the way for a new face that is a prosecutor's dream, and you are left with nothing with which to stop it. So you always hold back the last peremptory for emergency circumstances only. I learned this the hard way as a baby lawyer when I was defending a man accused of assaulting a police officer and resisting arrest. I felt sure that the assault charge was bogus, an add-on by the arresting officer because of personal animosity.

313

The officer was white and my client Black. During jury selection I gambled with my last peremptory to kick out a potential juror who was yellow on my meter. There were still several African Americans in the courtroom pool waiting to be randomly called to the box. I figured my chances were almost fifty-fifty that one of them would get the call to take the open seat for questioning. The move paid off. A Black woman was called, but under questioning she revealed that she was the daughter of a retired law enforcement officer who had served in the Sheriffs Department for thirty-two years. I questioned her at length, trying to elicit an answer that would get her bumped for cause, but she maintained her stance that she could view the case impartially. The judge denied my request to dismiss her, so there I was, with a cop's daughter on my assault-on-a-police-officer jury and no peremptory to change it. My client went down on all charges and spent a year in a county detention center for a crime I believed he had not committed.

I followed my usual routine for charting and tracking jurors through the selection process. A plain manila file folder was open flat on the defense table. I had drawn what I called the icecube tray across both flaps: a long rectangle divided into fourteen squares for the jury of twelve and two alternates. Each cube was two inches square — the size of a small Post-it Note. I wrote the salient thoughts and details about each prospective juror in the cube numbered for the jury box seat the candidate occupied. As jurors were dismissed and new people took the seats, I used Post-its to cover the no-longer-needed details and start again. Charting everything on the file folder allowed me to flip it closed if inquiring eyes wandered over from the prosecution table.

The prosecution got to question the new additions to the panel first. And while Berg went through her routine questions, Maggie and I checked the texts coming to her laptop from Cisco, who had to disguise what he was doing because no one but the attorneys on the case was allowed to use electronic devices in the courtroom. Cisco hid his phone from the courtroom deputies by keeping it down on the bench next to one of his massive thighs.

To protect the anonymity of the jury in a criminal case, the prospective jurors were referred to by numbers given to them when they checked in at the jury coordination center on the first floor. Cisco's texts did the same.

17 parked in handicap — no tag.

That reference was to the male member of the new trio. It was an interesting piece of information but not something I would be able to go at directly without possibly giving away how I got the information. Revealing that I had an investigator scoping out potential jurors in the parking garage would not go over well with the judge or the California bar. It didn't go over well with Maggie McFierce either. She was getting a quick education in criminal defense and didn't always like what she was learning. But I wasn't worried. She was now co-opted by the attorney-client relationship.

I had watched number 17 stand up in the gallery when his number was called. He had squeezed past others out of the row and then moved to the jury box for questioning without showing any obvious physical difficulty or handicap. Of course, there were other possible unseen issues that could have resulted in his receiving a handicap tag. But it bothered me. If the man was a cheat, I didn't want him on the jury.

Cisco immediately followed his first missive with a text on one of the women.

68 should be 86ed. Trump 2020
bumper sticker.

This was good intel. Politics were a good window into a person's soul. If 68 was a supporter of the president, it was likely she was a law-and-order hard-liner — not good for a guy accused of murder. That this person would continue to support the president after the media had documented his many, many untruths was a factor as well. It was blind loyalty to a cause, and an indicator that truthfulness was not an important part of her framework.

I agreed with Cisco. She had to go.

On the third potential juror — number 21 — Cisco had limited intel.

21 drives a Prius. Extinction Rebellion

sticker on rear window.

I didn't know what an Extinction Rebellion sign was but I thought I understood the sticker's message. Both pieces of information were almost useless. Both could be indicators of a judgmental personality, particularly when it came to the environment and crime. I drove a gas-eating Lincoln and that would certainly come out in trial. And I was charged with a very violent crime while being a person who associated profession-ally with others charged with violent acts.

I kept an ear on the proceedings as Berg questioned the new candidates but I also huddled with Maggie as she pulled out the questionnaires the three had filled out when reporting for jury service.

Immediately I changed my mind about 21. I liked what I read. She was thirty-six years old, unmarried, lived in Studio City, and had a job as a prep chef at one of the upscale restaurants at the Hollywood Bowl. This told me she liked music and culture and chose to work in a place that had both. She also listed reading first among her hobbies. I didn't think anyone who was a reader could avoid coming across stories — nonfiction or fiction — that underscored the frailties of the American justice system, chief among them that the police don't always get it right and that innocent people are sometimes accused and convicted of crimes they didn't commit. I believed that would give 21 an open mind. She would listen closely to my case.

'I want her,' I whispered.

317

'Yeah, she looks good,' Maggie whispered back.

I moved on to the other two questionnaires. I saw that 68, the other female, was my age and had gotten married the same year she graduated from Pepperdine, a conservative Christian school in Malibu. Add all of that to the Trump bumper sticker, and I was convinced. She had to go.

Maggie agreed.

'You want to use the last challenge?' she asked.

'No, I'm going to question her,' I said. 'Try to get her bumped for cause.'

'What about the guy? There's nothing here.'

She was referring to 17. I scanned his questionnaire and had to agree with Maggie. Nothing on the single page drew a flag. He was forty-six years old and married, an assistant principal at a private school in Encino. I was familiar with it because Maggie and I had flirted with the idea of sending Hayley there for elementary school many years before. We took the tour and went to a parents' presentation but ultimately got a bad vibe. Most of the students came from well-to-do families. We weren't destitute by any means but Maggie was a civil servant and I was always chasing money cases. Some years were fat, some were thin. We thought the peer pressure on our daughter would be unhealthy. We enrolled her somewhere else.

'You remember this guy?' I asked. 'He would have been there when we looked at the place.'

'I don't recognize him,' Maggie said.

'I'll see what I can get on Q and A. You okay with my taking all three?'

318

'Of course. It's your case. I don't want you deferring to me.'

While Berg finished her canvassing of the jurors, I wrote notes on all three on Post-its and attached them to the corresponding squares on my ice-cube tray chart. I wrote in green for 21 and red for 68. For 17, I wrote a yellow question mark. Then I folded the file closed.

38

When it was my turn to question the people who might decide my future, the judge verbally cut me off at the knees before I even got to the lectern.

'You have fifteen minutes, Mr. Haller,' she said.

'Your Honor, we technically have three open seats and then the alternates to fill,' I protested. 'The prosecution just took way more than fifteen minutes to question these three.'

'No, you're wrong. I timed it. Fourteen minutes. I'm giving you fifteen. Starting now. You can use the time to argue with me or to question the jurors.'

'Thank you, Your Honor.'

I went to the lectern and started with number 68.

'Juror sixty-eight, I was looking at your questionnaire and didn't see what your husband does for a living.'

'My husband was killed in Iraq seventeen years ago.'

That brought a moment of silence — a collective holding of breath — as I retooled my approach. I could not let the jurors who were already seated see me treat the woman with anything but kid gloves.

'I'm sorry for your loss,' I said. 'And that I even brought the memory up.'

'Don't worry,' she said. 'The memory never goes away.'

I nodded. Though I had stumbled into this, I had to find a way to finesse my way out.

'Uh, on the questionnaire, you didn't check that you had been a victim of a crime. Don't you consider the loss of your husband to be in a way a crime?'

'That was war. That was different. He gave his life for his country.'

God and country — a defense lawyer's nightmare on a jury.

'Then he was a hero,' I offered.

'And still is,' she said.

'Right. He still is.'

'Thank you.'

'Have you been on a jury before, ma'am?'

'It was one of the questions on the form. No, I have not. And please don't call me ma'am. Makes me feel like my mother.'

There was a slight tickle of laughter in the courtroom. I smiled and pressed on.

'I will refrain from doing that. Let me ask you a question: If a police officer testifies to one thing and then a regular citizen testifies and says the opposite, whom do you believe?'

'Well, I guess you just have to weigh what each one says and try to figure out who's telling the truth. It could be the officer. But it might not be.'

'But do you give the police officer the benefit of the doubt?'

'Not necessarily. I would have to hear more about the officer. You know, who he is, how he comes across. Like that.'

I nodded. It was becoming clear that she was a Jury Judy — someone who wants to be on the jury and gives the right answer to every question whether or not it reflects her true sentiments. I am always suspicious of people who want to be on a jury, who want to judge others.

'Okay, and as the judge explained yesterday, you know that I am both the defendant and defense attorney in this case. If at the end of this trial you think that I probably committed the crime of murder, how do you vote in the jury room?'

'I would have to trust my instincts after weighing the evidence.'

'Which means what? How would you vote?'

'If I'm convinced beyond a reasonable doubt, I vote guilty.'

'Is thinking I *probably* did it convincing? Is that what you mean?'

'No, like I said, I would have to feel you are guilty beyond a reasonable doubt.'

'What does *reasonable doubt* mean to you, ma'am?'

Before 68 could answer, the judge cut in.

'Mr. Haller, are you trying to bait the juror?' Warfield said. 'She asked you not to call her that.'

'No, Judge,' I said. 'I just forgot. My Southern manners. I apologize.'

'That's all well and good, but I know you were born right here in Los Angeles, because I knew your father.'

'Just a figure of speech, Your Honor. I won't

say the offending word again.'

'Very well, continue. You're using up all your time on this one juror. I'm not giving you an extension.'

Fifteen minutes to interview the people who might decide your fate. I thought I had my first point of appeal should the trial not go the way I wanted it to. I turned my attention back to the woman in the jury box.

'If you could, can you tell us what you believe *reasonable doubt* to mean?'

'Just that there's no other possible explanation. Based on the evidence and your evaluation of it, it couldn't have been anybody else.'

I realized I wasn't going to be able to make any headway with her. She had her answers rehearsed. I had to wonder whether she had been following the case in the media.

'Yesterday morning the judge asked for a show of hands for anyone who had read about this case in the media. You did not raise your hand, correct?'

'That's correct. I had never heard of it before.'

I didn't believe her. She knew about the case and for some reason wanted to be on the jury. I checked my watch and moved on to Mr. 17. I had no choice.

'Sir, you are an assistant principal at a private elementary school, correct?'

'Yes, that's right.'

'I see on the questionnaire that you have a master's degree in education and are working on a doctorate.'

'Yes, part-time on the doctorate.'

'Is there a reason why you haven't chosen to teach at the university level?'

'Not really. I like working with younger kids. That's where I get my fulfillment.'

I nodded.

'It says you also coach the boys' basketball team at the school. Does that require a lot of physical activity on your part?'

'Well, I think the boys should see their coach as someone who can keep up with them. Someone in shape.'

'You do strength-training exercises with them?'

'Uh, sometimes.'

'You run with them?'

'I do laps in the gym with them.'

'What is your philosophy on sport? Winning is everything?'

'Well, I'm competitive, yes, but I don't think winning is everything.'

'What do you think, then?'

'I think winning is better than losing.'

That drew some polite laughter. And I changed the direction of my questions.

'Your wife. According to the info sheet, she is a teacher as well?'

'Yes, same school. We met there.'

'So I assume you carpool to school together?'

'No, I have the coaching after school, and she has a part-time job at a crafts store. So different schedules, different cars.'

'Do you think that there are serious crimes and not serious crimes?'

'Excuse me?'

'Do you think that there are some crimes that

324

shouldn't be considered crimes?'

'I don't really understand.'

'I guess I'm talking about the highs and lows. Murder — that's a crime, right?'

'Yes, of course.'

'And those who murder should pay for their crimes. You agree?'

'Of course.'

'What about smaller crimes? Crimes where there are no victims — should we bother with those?'

'A crime is a crime.'

The judge intervened again.

'Mr. Haller, do you intend to question juror twenty-one with the time you have left?' she asked.

I was annoyed at the interruption. I was building toward a decision with 17 and she shouldn't have interrupted.

'As soon as I'm finished here, Your Honor,' I said, my frustration clear in my voice. 'Can I proceed?'

'Go ahead,' Warfield said.

'Thank you.'

'You're welcome, Mr. Haller.'

I turned back to 17 and attempted to gather my splintered momentum.

'Sir, is a crime a crime, no matter how big or small?'

'Yes. Of course.'

'What about jaywalking? It's against the law but do you think it's a crime?'

'Well, if that's what the law is, then, yes, I guess it's a crime. A minor crime.'

325

'What about parking in a handicapped zone when you have no handicap?'

It was a gamble. All I knew about 17 was what I had read on the questionnaire and what I learned in the text from Cisco about his parking in a handicapped spot. I had to make a call on him but could only dance around the essential question: Was he a cheater?

We stared at each other in silent communication before 17 finally spoke.

'There might be a reasonable explanation for someone doing that,' he said.

There it was. He didn't believe he needed to play by the rules. He was a cheater and he had to go.

'So what you're saying is that — '

Warfield interrupted again.

'Your time is up, Mr. Haller,' she said. 'Counsel, approach.'

I cursed under my breath and turned away from 17.

We had been handling challenges at the bench so the objections to jurors — possibly embarrassing to them — were not made in open court. But when I got to the bench, I was too hot to worry about keeping my voice down.

'Your Honor, I need time to question the last juror,' I said. 'You can't arbitrarily set my time based on what time the state needed. That is patently unfair to the defense.'

Maggie had joined the conference at the bench. She now lightly touched my arm as the judge responded. It was a warning to tread carefully.

'Mr. Haller, your time management is not my problem,' Warfield said. 'I made it abundantly clear from the start of day yesterday, start of day today, and at the start of your most recent questioning of potential jurors: we are going to finish jury selection today and opening statements are tomorrow. We are now approaching three o'clock and we still have alternates to seat and I imagine at least one or two jurors. Your time was up. Now, does either of you have a challenge?'

Before Berg could say a word, I spoke.

'I would like to confer with counsel first,' I said. 'Could we take the afternoon break and then consider challenges?'

'Very well,' the judge said. 'Ten minutes. Step back.'

The lawyers returned to our tables while the judge informed the courtroom of the afternoon break. She sternly said that court would resume in ten minutes sharp. I slid into my seat and huddled with Maggie.

'This is crazy,' I said. 'Fifteen minutes to question three jurors? She's nuts, and this is reversible.'

'Look, you have to calm down, Mick,' Maggie said. 'You can't cross swords with a judge before the trial even starts. That's suicide.'

'I know, I know. I'll be calm.'

'Now, what are we going to do? We only have one challenge.'

Before answering, I looked over and saw that Berg was also huddling with her co-counsel — the bow-tie guy. I had an idea. I looked back at Maggie.

'How many challenges do they have left?' I asked.

She looked at a score sheet she was keeping. 'Three,' she said.

'I don't want to give up ours,' I said. 'I want to try something. I want you to go into the hall for the break. Don't come back until the ten minutes are up.'

'What?'

'Don't worry about the challenges yet. Just go.'

She tentatively got up and went out through the gate toward the door to the hall. I checked the prosecution table and then turned toward Chan, the courtroom deputy, and signaled him over. I opened my file, revealing the ice-cube tray chart. I quickly switched the Post-its I had used to mark jurors 21 and 17, putting the green light on the schoolteacher.

The deputy stepped over.

'I gotta use the can,' I said. 'Can somebody take me back?'

'Stand up,' he said.

I did as instructed. Chan handcuffed me and walked me to the custody door.

'You've got about five minutes,' he said.

'I only need two,' I said.

He led me into the secured holding area and into a cell where there was an open toilet. There were two men sitting on a bench in the cell, at this hour most likely waiting to be transported back to Twin Towers after their court appearances. I stood at an angle preventing them from seeing my business and urinated into the toilet while Chan waited in the hallway outside the cell.

I took my time washing my hands in the sink next to the toilet. I wanted to give the bow-tie guy enough time to see that I had left my chart open on the defense table.

'Let's go, Haller,' Chan said from outside the tank.

'Coming,' I said.

After I returned to my seat at the defense table, I closed the file and looked over at the prosecution table. Berg and her cohort were no longer talking but looking straight ahead and waiting for court to resume.

Soon several members of the jury pool were returning to the courtroom. Maggie came back to the defense table and sat down.

'So, what are we doing?' she asked.

'I'm going to try to get sixty-eight kicked for cause,' I said. 'And I'm hoping the state boots the teacher.'

'Why would they do that? He's perfect for them. I know I'd want him if this was my case.'

I flipped open the file and pointed to the Post-its. Maggie was staring at them, putting the ruse together when the judge returned to the bench and called counsel forward.

At the bench, the prosecution went first.

'Your Honor, the People will use a peremptory challenge to dismiss number seventeen,' Berg said.

I jerked my head back like I had been slapped and then shook it in disappointment. I hoped I wasn't overacting.

'You're sure?' Warfield asked.

329

'Yes, Your Honor,' Berg said.

The judge wrote a note down on a pad.

'Mr. Haller, anything from the defense?' she asked.

'Yes, Your Honor,' I said. 'The defense seeks the dismissal of juror sixty-eight for cause.'

'That cause being what?' the judge asked.

'Clear animosity exhibited toward the defense,' I said.

'Because she doesn't like to be called *ma'am*?' Warfield asked. 'I don't want to be called that either.'

'That and a generally combative tone, Judge,' I said. 'She clearly doesn't like me, and that is grounds for cause.'

'Your Honor, can I be heard on this?' Berg said.

'You don't need to be,' Warfield said. 'I'm denying the motion to dismiss for cause. My tally shows you have one last peremptory, Mr. Haller. You want to use it?'

I paused for a moment to consider. If I used my last peremptory, I would have nothing left while we sat the replacements for 68 and 17. I didn't want the Trumper on the jury but it was risky being unable to control the last two slots on the panel. The alternates would be handled separately, with additional peremptory challenges.

'Mr. Haller,' the judge said. 'I am waiting.'

I pulled the trigger.

'Yes, Your Honor,' I said. 'We thank and excuse juror sixty-eight.'

'And that is using your last challenge?' Warfield asked.

'Yes, Your Honor.'

'Very well, you can step back.'

I knew it would be useless to ask for additional challenges. Berg would oppose it and the judge, with her hard-line adherence to her schedule, would be disinclined to be generous. I returned to my place at the defense table and decided to dwell on the one good thing that had just happened. I had managed to get rid of two potentially problematic jurors with one challenge. I would never know whether leaving my chart open to the potential spying eyes of the prosecution table had played a part in the dismissal of the schoolteacher, but I had to think it did. I listened as the judge thanked and dismissed him along with the widow of the war hero.

For the moment, the chef from the Hollywood Bowl was secure.

The judge quickly referred to a list of numbers randomly selected by a computer and called the next two prospective jurors into the box.

We had little more than an hour to finish.

39

Thursday, February 20

It was time. It was Thursday morning at 10 a.m. and the trial would now move past the preliminaries to opening statements from the lawyers. The jury and alternates had been seated the day before without additional angst from me. My gamble with my last peremptory had paid off in that the final candidates for placement on the jury had not raised any serious flags for the defense. The jury was sworn in and we were good to go.

I felt comfortable with the overall panel. There were no known prosecution bogeys and three members of the jury I actually thought tilted toward the defense side of the scale. In most trials you are lucky if you get even one.

Still, my comfort with the jury was offset by the knot in my stomach. I was fully recovered from the attack on the bus, but the tension of a sleepless night had carried through into the day. I was nervous. I had tried many cases and I knew that anything could happen. It wasn't a comforting knowledge. I was fully prepared to engage in this battle, but I knew there would be casualties and I could not guarantee that the truth would not be among them. Innocent men were found guilty. I didn't want to be one of them.

An opening statement is merely a blueprint of the case to come. My strategy was a third-party-culpability defense. That was a legal way of saying somebody else did it and I was either intentionally framed or the police were so incompetent that they bungled the case and framed me in the process. I was fully aware that it would be awkward and possibly off-putting for me to stand in front of the jury and espouse this line of defense. This was why I had assigned the opening statement to Maggie McPherson. I wanted her to point to me and summon all her fierceness when she said I was innocent and that the state did not have a case that would prove guilt beyond a reasonable doubt.

At the same time, I didn't want Maggie saying much beyond that. When it came to opening statements, I was from the Legal Siegel school of law. He always said, save your powder, meaning less is more; don't reveal your case or its surprises until it's time to present your evidence. That's when it mattered. Legal Siegel also said that opening statements were not worth spending much time on because they would soon be forgotten as the prosecution presented its case, followed by the defense.

There was the option of withholding the defense's opening statement until the start of its case. I had taken that option on occasion in prior trials but I never liked doing it. I always felt it unwise to miss the opportunity to address the jury early on, no matter how briefly. Since we were starting this trial on a Thursday, I knew it would be six or seven days before the defense phase started, and that seemed too long to go without countering the state with my own view of the case.

I passed all this wisdom on to Maggie, though such advice was not remotely necessary for her. She had given and sat through more than her share of opening statements and already knew that less was always more.

However, this wisdom was apparently never part of Dana Berg's training. She stood before the jury first and delivered an opener that lasted almost ninety minutes. I would have preferred to sleep through it but I had to carefully monitor it and take notes. An opening statement was a promise to the jury of what you will present during your case in chief. It was unwise to promise something and then not deliver it. That was why I took notes. I would keep a scorecard, and as the case progressed I would be sure to point out to the jury where the state had failed to deliver on the goods promised.

Berg started by detailing the night of my arrest and the discovery of Sam Scales in the trunk of my car. This was where she made her first mistake, telling the jury that they would hear from Officer Roy Milton about how a routine traffic stop — started when he saw my car had no license plate — led to the discovery of the murder victim.

I wrote her words down verbatim because I would use them against Officer Milton when he was brought into court to testify. There was nothing routine about the traffic stop or anything else that night.

At an early point in her statement, Berg interjected a note about Sam Scales, describing him as a small-time grifter who never lived a life on the straight and narrow.

'In fact, Mr. Scales knew Mr. Haller because Mr. Haller was the attorney who defended him most often,' Berg said. 'But no matter what crimes Mr. Scales contemplated or committed, he did not deserve to be murdered in the trunk of his lawyer's car. You must remember that no matter what you hear about Sam Scales, he was the victim in this case.'

While Berg went long, she was also pretty straightforward, sticking closely to what she said the evidence in the case would show. There was a lot but it was all window dressing on the key elements of the case — that the victim was found in my trunk and that ballistic evidence would show that the killing took place in my garage.

There were a few times when I could have objected when Berg strayed from statement into argument, but I was mindful of perceptions. I didn't want the jury to see me as some sort of petty referee or interrupter, so I let the editorializing go. The prosecutor wrapped it up after eighty-five minutes with a summary of her summary, repeating the major points she promised to deliver during the trial and sounding a lot like a closing argument.

'Ladies and gentlemen, the evidence we will present over the next several days will show that Mr. Haller was engaged in a long-running dispute with Sam Scales over money. It will show that he knew that his best and only chance of

335

getting his money was to kill Sam Scales and draw it from his estate. And it will show beyond a reasonable doubt that he did indeed carry out that plan to kill Mr. Scales in the garage of his home. It would have been the perfect murder if not for the sharp eyes of a police officer who noticed a missing license plate on a dark street. I ask that you pay attention to the evidence presented and not be swayed by efforts to distract you from your very important job. Thank you.'

The judge called for a fifteen-minute break before the defense got its turn. I, of course, was going nowhere. I turned to scan the gallery as people got up to use the restrooms or just stretch their legs. I saw that the courtroom had gotten crowded as the case got underway — more media and more observers from both in and out of the courthouse. I saw several attorneys I knew and other courthouse workers. In the front row were my team and family. Cisco and Lorna. Bosch was there and had even brought his daughter, Maddie. She sat next to my daughter. I smiled at them now.

Kendall Roberts was not in the courtroom. After I was taken into custody, she had assessed her situation and decided to call it quits with me a second time. She had moved out of my house and left no forwarding address. I could not say I was left heartbroken. The strain the case had put on our relationship had been clear even before I was jailed for the second time. In fact, I couldn't blame her for extricating herself from it all. She had tried to tell me in person, coming to court

336

for one of my hearings, but the circumstances didn't allow it. So she had written me a note and sent it to the jail. And that was the last I had heard from her.

Toward the end of the break, Hayley got up and squeezed down the row until she came to the railing behind the defense table and in front of Cisco. Since I was a custody, I was not allowed to touch her or get close. But Maggie slid her chair all the way back to the rail.

'Thanks for being here, Hay,' I said.

'Of course,' she said. 'I wouldn't miss it for the world. You're going to win, Dad. And Mom. You're going to prove what I already know.'

'Thanks, baby,' I said. 'How's Maddie?'

'She's good,' Hayley said. 'I'm glad she made it. It's really good to see Uncle Harry too.'

'How long can you stay?' Maggie asked.

'I cleared the whole day,' Hayley said. 'I'm not going anywhere. I mean, my mom and dad on the same team — what could be better than that?'

'I hope it doesn't leave you behind in classes,' Maggie said.

'Don't worry about my classes,' our daughter, the future lawyer, said. 'Just worry about this.'

She gestured to the front of the courtroom, meaning the case.

'We're locked and loaded,' I said. 'Confident.'

'That's good,' Hayley said.

'Do me a favor and keep your eye on the jury,' I said. 'If you see anything, let me know during the breaks.'

'Like what?' Hayley asked.

'Like anything,' I said. 'A smile, a shake of the head. Somebody falling asleep. I'll be watching too. But we can use any read we can get.'

'You got it,' she said.

'Thanks for being here,' I said somberly. 'I love you.'

'I love you too,' she said. 'Both of you.'

She moved back to her seat, and Cisco and Bosch leaned forward to the railing to speak confidentially, even though I had to keep the same separation from them.

'We all set on everything?' I asked.

'We're good,' Cisco said.

Then he looked at Bosch for agreement and Bosch nodded.

'Good,' Maggie said. 'Looking at Dana's witness list, I'm guessing that the state's case will go to at least Tuesday. So we should be ready with subpoenas and everything else on Monday, just in case.'

'Done,' Cisco said.

'Good,' Maggie said.

People were returning to their seats. The break was almost over.

'Well, this is it,' I said. 'We're here. I want to thank you guys for everything.'

They both nodded.

'This is what we do,' Cisco said.

I turned back to the table and then leaned toward Maggie, who was already back to studying notes scribbled on a legal pad in front of her.

'You ready?' I asked.

'Of course,' she said. 'Quick and dirty.'

The courtroom settled and the judge came back to the bench.

'Mr. Haller,' she said. 'Your opening statement.'

I nodded but it was Maggie who stood up and went to the lectern. She carried her legal pad and a glass of water. We had not informed the judge or prosecution who would be making the opening statement for the defense. I picked up a note of surprise on Berg's face when she turned in her seat toward the lectern, expecting to see me. I hoped it would be the first of many times she would be caught off guard.

'Ladies and gentlemen of the jury, good morning,' Maggie said. 'My name is Maggie McPherson and I am co-counsel for the defense on this case. As you have been told by the court, the defendant, Michael Haller, is also representing himself in this trial. More often than not it will be Mr. Haller who stands here to question witnesses and speak to the judge. But for this opening statement we agreed that it would be best for me to speak on his behalf.'

I had a clear view of the entire jury box, and my eyes traveled from one face to another. First the front row and then the back. I saw real interest and attention but I knew this was the group's first exposure to the defense's case. I also knew that they might be disappointed by not getting the finer details in Maggie's speech.

'I am going to be brief here,' she said. 'But first let me say congratulations. You are all part of something that is sacred and one of the cornerstones of our democracy. In fact, no

339

institution in modern society is more democratic than a jury. Look at yourselves. You are twelve strangers randomly brought together for one purpose. You will elect a leader and each one of you will have an equal vote. Your duty is so important because you have the power to take away a citizen's life, liberty, and livelihood. It's an awesome and urgent responsibility. And once you carry out your charge, you disband and go back to your lives. There is nothing as important as the duty you have agreed to take on in this courtroom.'

When we were married, I had watched Maggie in trial dozens of times and she always riffed in opening statements on the democracy of the jury. There was no change here except that she now stood — for the first time — for the defense. After the preamble, she got down to the case at hand.

'So, now your work begins,' she said. 'Remember as you go, opening statements are basically all talk. Not evidence. Ms. Berg spoke to you for ninety minutes but she did not give you any evidence. It was just talk. The defense wants to get to the evidence — or in the state's case, the lack of evidence. We want to prove to you that the state has made a terrible mistake and charged the wrong man — an innocent man — with this crime.'

Maggie raised her hand and pointed to me at the defense table.

'That man is innocent,' Maggie McFierce said. 'And there is really nothing else to say. We don't have to prove his innocence in order for

340

you to return a verdict of not guilty. But I promise you we will.'

She paused to underline the emphatic statement and looked down at the notes on her legal pad.

'You are going to hear two stories in this trial,' she continued. 'The prosecution's story and our story. The prosecution will point the finger at the defendant. We will show that a man whose name the state will never mention and doesn't want you to even know is responsible for the death of Sam Scales. Only one of these stories can be true. We ask for your patience and diligence and hope that you will keep an open mind and wait for the defense's case. Again, only one story can be true, and you will choose it. Pay careful attention to the facts. But be aware that facts can be twisted. We will show that as we go. You all were given notebooks. Keep tabs on who is twisting the facts and who is not. Write it down so that when you go into the deliberations at the end of this trial, you know the facts and you know who told the truth and who didn't.'

Maggie paused to take a drink from her glass of water. It was a trial attorney's trick. Always take a prop like a glass of water to the lectern when giving an opening statement or closing argument. Taking a drink of water allows one to underline an important statement or to collect thoughts before proceeding.

After putting the glass down, she moved toward her closing.

'A trial is a search for truth,' she said. 'And in this trial you are the truth seekers. You must be unbiased and undaunted. You must question everything. Question everything every witness says from the stand. Question their words, question their motives. Question the prosecutor, question the defense. Question the evidence. If you do that, you will find the truth. And that is, that the wrong man sits now at the defense table while there is a killer out there still. Thank you.'

She took her glass and her pad and returned to the defense table. I turned to her as she sat down and I nodded.

'Great start,' I whispered.

'Thank you,' she whispered back.

'Better than I could ever do.'

She squinted like she wasn't sure what she had just heard was true.

But I meant it. It was true.

40

The prosecution is always tasked with establishing the timeline, presenting the evidence with a clear starting and ending point. It is linear storytelling and is sometimes long and laborious, but required. In order to get to the body found in the trunk of my Lincoln, Dana Berg had to tell the jury how it came to be that my car was stopped and the trunk opened. That meant she had to start with Officer Roy Milton.

Milton was called to the witness stand directly after the lunch break and Berg quickly set up through testimony where he was and what he was doing when he noticed my car had no rear plate and pulled me over. She then used Milton to introduce the videos from his car and body cam, and the jury had a visceral you-are-there experience in the finding of Sam Scales in the trunk of my Lincoln.

I carefully watched the jurors during the playing of the body cam. Some were clearly repulsed when the Lincoln's trunk came open and the body was revealed. Some leaned into it, fascinated, it seemed, by the discovery of the murder.

As the testimony proceeded, Maggie tracked what Milton was saying against a transcript of his testimony from the discovery hearing back in December. Any contradiction could be brought up and called out during cross-examination. But

Milton stuck close to the previous story, in some cases using the same wording — a sign that prior to trial he had been coached by Berg not to stray from what was already on the record.

Milton's sole purpose as a witness was to get the videos into evidence and in front of the jury. They were a powerful start to the case for the state. But then it was my turn to take on Milton in cross-examination. I had waited two months for this and my measured and polite questioning during the hearing in December would be a thing of the past. I adjusted the microphone on the lectern and went right at him with the first question. My goal was to rattle him in any way I could for as long as I could. I knew that if I succeeded, I would be rattling Dana Berg as well.

'Officer Milton, good afternoon,' I began. 'Can you please tell the jury who it was that told you to follow and then conduct a traffic stop of the Lincoln Town Car I was driving on the night of October twenty-eighth?'

'Uh, no, I can't,' Milton said. 'Because that didn't happen.'

'You are telling this jury that you received no prior notice or instruction to pull me over on a traffic stop after I left the Redwood Bar?'

'That is correct. I saw your car and noticed it had no plate and — '

'Yes, we heard what you told Ms. Berg. But what you are telling me and this jury now is that you received no direction to pull me over. Is that correct?'

'Correct.'

344

'Did you receive a radio call telling you to stop me?'

'No, I did not.'

'Did you receive a message on your car's computer terminal?'

'No, I did not.'

'Did you receive a call or a text message on your personal cell phone?'

'No, I did not.'

Berg stood and objected, saying that I was repeatedly asking the same question.

'The question has been asked and answered, Your Honor,' she said.

Warfield agreed.

'It's time to move on, Mr. Haller,' she said.

'Yes, Your Honor,' I said. 'So, Officer Milton, if I were to produce a witness at this trial who alerted you to the fact that I was leaving the bar, then that person would be lying, correct?'

'Yes, that would be a lie.'

I looked up at the judge and asked if the attorneys could approach the bench. She waved us up. I got there first and waited for Berg and McPherson to join.

'Judge,' I said. 'I'd like to set up my own playback of the videos from the patrol car and Officer Milton's body cam.'

Berg raised her hands palms up in a what-gives? gesture.

'We just watched the videos,' she said. 'Are we trying to bore the jury to death?'

'Mr. Haller, explain,' Warfield said.

'My tech guy has put them side by side on one screen and time-coordinated them,' I said. 'The

345

jury will see them simultaneously and be able to see what happens inside the car at the same moment as things are happening on the street.'

'Your Honor, the People object,' Berg said. 'We have no way of knowing whether these have been edited or altered by this so-called tech guy. You can't allow this.'

'Judge, we don't know if the prosecution edited or altered what they played for the jury,' I said. 'I will provide a copy to the prosecution and they can examine it all they want. If they find that it was altered, I'll turn in my bar ticket. But what's really happening here is that the prosecution knows just where I'm going with this, knows that it is indeed probative, and she simply doesn't want the jury to see it. This is a search for truth, Judge, and the defense has the right to put this before the jury.'

'I have no idea what he's talking about, Judge,' Berg said. 'The People still object based on lack of foundation. If he wants to play it during the defense phase, he can bring in his tech guy and try to establish foundation. But this is the state's case right now and he should not be allowed to hijack it.'

'Your Honor,' Maggie said. 'The prosecution has already laid the foundation by playing the videos to the jury. To allow the prosecution to play what it wants to show to the jury but prevent the defense from doing so would be a wholly unacceptable injury to the defense.'

There was a pause while the judge considered the intensity of Maggie's unexpected argument. It gave me pause as well.

'We're going to take the afternoon break early and I'll come back with my ruling,' Warfield said. 'Get your equipment set up, Mr. Haller, in case I allow it. Now step back.'

I returned to the defense table, pleased with our arguments, especially the strong hint from Maggie that preventing the defense from playing its video might be a reversible error.

The judge adjourned court for a fifteen-minute break. Maggie and I never left the defense table. I stayed because my only choice would be to go back into the courtside lockup. She did because she was connecting her laptop to the courtroom's audio-visual system. If we got the judge's okay, we would put the simultaneous videos on the big screen mounted on the wall over the clerk's station and across from the jury box.

While Maggie worked, I checked the courtroom and saw Hayley and Maddie Bosch holding fast, still in the same seats. I nodded and smiled and they did the same.

When the judge retook the bench, she immediately ruled that I could play the simultaneous videos. While Dana Berg offered another objection, I turned to Maggie.

'We all set?' I asked.

'Good to go,' she said.

'Okay, and where are the time codes?'

'Hold on.'

She opened her briefcase and looked through a stack of documents before pulling out a page that had the video time codes I needed in order to cross-examine Milton. I stood up and went to the lectern with the document and a remote control for the playback. The judge overruled Berg's objection and I began.

I explained to Milton that I would show him videos from both his car and his body cam running side by side in synchronized time. I began the playback at a point before Milton followed me and while I was still in the Redwood. The view from the patrol car's camera was through the windshield, looking west down Second Street to the intersection of Broadway and two blocks beyond to the tunnel. On the south side of Second the red neon sign that said REDWOOD was visible half a block up. The view from Milton's body cam was low because he was apparently sitting slumped in his car. The screen showed his car's steering wheel and dashboard. His left arm and hand were visible, the arm propped on the sill of the open driver's-side window and his hand draped over the top of the steering wheel.

I asked Milton to describe for the jury what he was seeing on the screen and he grudgingly obliged.

'Not much, if you ask me,' he said. 'On the left is the car cam and that is looking west down Second Street. Then on the right is my body cam and I'm just sitting in the car.'

The body cam was picking up the intermittent sound of the police radio in the patrol car. I let it play and checked my list of time codes. I then looked back up at the screen.

'Now, do you see the entrance of the Redwood up on the left side of Second Street?' I asked.

'Yes, I see it,' Milton said.

The door to the bar opened and out stepped two figures. It was too dark to identify them in the red glow of the neon. They spoke on the sidewalk for a few seconds and then one walked west in the direction of the tunnel, and the other went east, moving toward the camera.

This was followed by a low-level buzzing sound that clearly came from a cell phone. I used the remote to stop the playback.

'Officer Milton, was that you getting an email or a text on your cell phone?' I asked.

'Sounded like it,' Milton said matter-of-factly.

'Do you recall what the message was?'

'No, I don't. In the course of a night I could get fifty messages. I don't remember them all the next day, let alone three months later.'

I pushed the play button and the videos continued. Soon the figure walking east on Second Street stepped into the illumination from a streetlight. It was clearly me.

As I became recognizable in the light, the angle on the body cam changed as Milton apparently straightened up in his seat.

'Officer Milton, you seem to have gone on alert here,' I said. 'Can you tell the jury what you're doing?'

'Not really doing anything,' Milton said. 'I saw somebody on the street and was eyeballing him. It turned out to be you. You can read into that whatever you want but it didn't mean anything to me.'

'Your car is running at this point, correct?'

'Yes, that's standard.'

'Was that message on your phone an alert that

349

I was leaving the Redwood?'

Milton scoffed.

'No, it wasn't,' he said. 'I had no idea who you were, what you were doing, or where you were going.'

'Really?' I said. 'Then maybe you can explain this next sequence.'

I hit the play button and we watched. I checked the jury and saw all eyes on the screen. One witness into the trial and I had them riding with me. I could feel it.

On the screen I had turned the corner and then disappeared off camera as I headed to the parking lot to get into my Lincoln. Seconds ticked by with nothing happening but I didn't want to fast-forward. I wanted the jurors to know exactly what was going on here.

Then the Lincoln appeared in the patrol car cam as I drove into the left-turn lane on Broadway at Second. The car held there as I waited for the traffic signal to change.

On the body-cam video, Milton's right arm came up and pulled the transmission lever from park to drive. The move registered on the digital dashboard as a *D* appeared on the screen. I froze it there and looked at Milton. He still didn't look concerned.

'Officer Milton,' I said. 'On direct examination you told the jury that you did not decide to pursue my car until you saw that it was missing the rear plate. Can you see the rear bumper from this angle?'

Milton looked up at the big screen and acted like he was bored.

'No, you can't.'

'But it is clear from your own body cam that you just put your patrol car into drive. Why did you do that if you had not seen the rear bumper of my car?'

Milton was silent for a long moment as he contemplated an answer.

'I, uh, guess it was just cop instincts,' he finally said. 'So that I would be ready to move if I needed to move.'

'Officer Milton,' I said. 'Do you want to change any of your earlier testimony to better reflect the facts as they are seen and heard on the video?'

Berg sprang up from her spot to object to my badgering the witness. The judge overruled her, saying, 'I want to hear his answer for myself.'

Milton declined the opportunity to change his testimony.

'So, then,' I said. 'It is your sworn testimony that you were not there specifically to wait and target me. Do I have that correct?'

'That's right,' Milton said.

Now there was a defiant tone in his voice. That was what I wanted the jury to hear. The how-dare-you-question-me tone of the police state that at least some of them knew so well. A tone that I believed would trigger their suspicions that something here was not right.

'And you do not wish to change or correct your earlier testimony?' I asked.

'No,' Milton said emphatically. 'I do not.'

I paused for a moment to underline that answer and snuck a glance at the jury before looking down at my notes. I was sure Berg and Milton thought I was bluffing — that I was engaging in theatrics in implying that I had a witness in the wings who would further blow Milton and his story out of the water. But I didn't care about them. I was more concerned with what the jury thought. By implying as much, I had created an unspoken bargain with the jury. A promise. I would have to deliver on it or be held accountable.

'Let's jump forward,' I said.

I advanced the video to the point where Milton popped the trunk and discovered the body. I knew it was a risky move to show the body to the jury again. Any murder victim shown in repose after a violent end will draw sympathy from a juror and may kick-start instinctive needs for justice and revenge — all of which could be directed at me, the accused. But I thought the risk-reward balance would be in my favor here.

During her playback of the videos, Berg had kept the sound on a low setting. I did not. I set the audio at a level that could be clearly heard. When the trunk came up and the body was seen, there was Milton's very clear 'Oh shit,' followed by a stifled laugh that carried the unmistakable tone of gloating in it.

I stopped the playback.

'Officer Milton, why did you laugh when you found the body?' I asked.

'I didn't laugh,' Milton said.

'What was that, then? A guffaw?'

'I was surprised by what was in the trunk. It was an expression of surprise.'

I knew he had prepped for this with Berg.

'An expression of surprise?' I said. 'Are you sure you weren't gloating about the predicament you knew I would now be in?'

'No, that wasn't the case at all,' Milton insisted. 'I felt like a semi-boring night just got interesting. After twenty-two years, I was going to make my first arrest for homicide.'

'Move to strike as nonresponsive,' I said to the judge.

'You asked the question, he answered,' she responded. 'Overruled. Continue, Mr. Haller.'

'Let's listen again,' I said.

I replayed the moment on the video, turning the sound up louder. The gloating laugh was unmistakable, no matter how Milton tried to couch it.

'Officer Milton, are you telling the jury that you did not laugh when you opened the trunk and discovered the body?' I asked.

'I'm saying I might've been a little giddy, but not gloating,' Milton said. 'It was a nervous laugh, that's all.'

'Did you know who I was?'

'Yes, I had your ID. You told me you were a lawyer.'

'But did you know of me before you pulled me over?'

'No, I did not. I don't pay much attention to lawyers and all of that.'

I felt that I had gotten all I could out of the moment. I had thrown at least some suspicion on the prosecution's very first witness. I decided to leave it at that. No matter what came next, I

353

felt we had opened the trial with a strong showing of contesting the state's evidence.

'No further questions,' I said. 'But I reserve the right to recall Officer Milton to the witness stand during the defense phase of the trial.'

I returned to the defense table. Berg took the lectern and tried to mitigate the damage on redirect, but there wasn't much that could be done with the video evidence I had presented. She walked Milton through his story again, but he could not express a good and believable reason for his dropping the car into drive before he could have seen the rear bumper of my car. And the buzzing of the cell phone just prior to that had cemented in place the possibility that he had been told to pull me over.

I leaned into Maggie to whisper.

'Do we have the subpoena ready on his cell?' I asked.

'All set,' she said. 'I'll take it to the judge as soon as we adjourn.'

We were going to ask the judge to allow us to subpoena the call and text records from Milton's personal cell phone. We had planned to follow his testimony and the playing of videos with the subpoena so as not to show our hand to Milton or Berg. My guess was that if we got the cell records, there would be no call or text that matched up with the buzzing sound heard on the video we had just played for the jury. This was because I was pretty sure that Milton would have used a throwaway phone for work like this. Either way it would be a win when I brought him back to testify during the defense phase. If there was no record of a text to his registered cell, he would have to explain to the jury where the buzzing sound came from. And when I asked if he had a burner with him that night, his denial would ring false to the jury, who had clearly heard that unexplained buzzing sound.

Overall, I felt the Milton cross-examination had been a score for the defense, and Berg apparently already needed to regroup. With a half hour still to go in the court day, she asked Warfield to adjourn early so she could review evidence with her next witness, Detective Kent Drucker. She had anticipated that the defense's opening statement and cross-examination of Milton would both last longer than they had.

Warfield reluctantly agreed but warned both sides that they should expect full days of court and should plan accordingly with their witnesses.

Immediately after adjournment, Maggie went to the clerk with the subpoena for Milton's cell records. I waved goodbye to the rest of my team and my loved ones and was taken into the courtside holding tank. I changed from my suit into blues in preparation for being driven back to Twin Towers in a sheriff's patrol car. While I waited in the cell to be escorted down the security elevator to the prisoner loading garage, Dana Berg came into the holding area and looked at me through the bars.

'Way to go, Haller,' she said. 'Score one for the defense.'

'The first of many,' I said.

'We'll see about that.'

'What do you want, Dana? You come to tell

me you see the light and are dropping the charges?'

'You wish. I just wanted to come back and say, well played. That's all.'

'Yeah, well, it wasn't a play. It might be a game to you but it's life or death to me.'

'Then that's why you should savor today's win. There won't be any more.'

Having delivered her message, she turned from the bars and disappeared, heading back to the courtroom.

'Hey, Dana!' I called.

I waited and a few seconds later she was back at the bars.

'What?'

'The Hollywood Bowl chef.'

'What about her?'

'I wanted her on the jury. I switched the tags on my chart during the break because I knew you'd send your bow-tie guy over to steal a look.'

I could see the surprise momentarily move across her face. Then it was gone. I nodded.

'That was a play,' I said. 'But today? That was the real thing.'

41

Possibly it was in reaction to the Milton testimony the day before, but Dana Berg came to court Friday morning with a plan not just to even the score in the jury's ledger but to tip the scales permanently to the state's side. She had choreographed a day that would stack the blocks of evidence and motive against me so high that the jurors would be able to see nothing else and would go into the weekend with my guilt permeating their brains. It was a good strategy and I needed to do something about it.

Kent Drucker was the lead detective on the case. That made him lead storyteller as well. Berg used him to take the jury through the investigation at a leisurely pace. I could and did object on occasion but it all amounted to a buzzing of gnats. I could not disrupt the flow of one-sided, unchallenged information to the jury until I could cross-examine the witness. And it was Berg's goal to prevent that from happening until after the weekend.

The morning session was largely just nuts and bolts. She walked Drucker through the initial phase of the investigation, from his callout at his home out in Diamond Bar to the full crime scene investigation. She did the smart thing and owned all the mistakes that had been made,

357

revealing through Drucker that the victim's wallet had somehow gone missing from either the crime scene or coroner's office.

'And did you ever recover the wallet?' Berg asked.

'Not yet,' Drucker said. 'It's just . . . gone.'

'Was there an investigation into the theft?'

'There's an ongoing investigation.'

'And did losing the wallet hamper the homicide investigation?'

'To some extent, yes.'

'How so?'

'Well, we were able to identify the victim pretty quickly from fingerprints, so that was not an issue. But the victim's criminal history indicated that he changed IDs frequently and adopted a new name, address, bank account, et cetera with each new scam that he perpetrated. My thinking was that the wallet contained the documentation of whatever identity he was using at the time of the murder. That was gone and it would have been useful to have that from the start.'

'Did you eventually find that identity?'

'We did, yes.'

'How?'

'We learned it through discovery in this case. The defense team had that information and we eventually figured it out when they put the name of the victim's landlord on their witness list.'

'The defense team? Why would they have it ahead of the police?'

I objected, telling the judge that the question asked for speculation. But the judge wanted to

358

hear the answer and overruled. It emboldened Drucker, with long experience testifying in murder trials, to go a step too far.

'I'm not clear on how the defense got ahead of us,' he said. 'The defendant exercised his rights and stopped talking to us after his arrest.'

'*Objection!*' I bellowed. 'The witness has just disparaged my Fifth Amendment right to remain silent and not be compelled to testify against myself.'

'Approach the bench,' the judge said angrily, glaring at Berg as she walked to the side bar.

Maggie joined me at the bench. I could tell she was as angry as I was at Drucker's cheap shot.

'Mr. Haller, you have made your objection,' Warfield said. 'Are you requesting a mistrial?'

Berg interrupted to say, 'Your Honor, I hardly think that — '

'Be quiet, Ms. Berg,' Warfield snapped. 'You've been a prosecutor for long enough to know that you *must* instruct your witnesses never to comment on a defendant's right to remain silent after arrest. I consider this prosecutorial misconduct and will take it under advisement to be dealt with at a later time. For now, I would like to hear from Mr. Haller.'

'I'd like an instruction,' I said. 'In the strongest terms possible. I have a — '

'I'm capable of fashioning a suitable instruction, Mr. Haller,' Warfield said. 'But I want to make certain that you are waiving any request for further remedy.'

'I am not moving for a mistrial, Your Honor,' I

359

said. 'I am on trial for a crime I didn't commit. I am here for exoneration, not just acquittal. Even if the court were to grant motions for mistrial and to dismiss with prejudice based on prosecutorial misconduct, there would forever be a cloud of suspicion over me. I want my trial and I will be satisfied with a strongly worded jury instruction.'

'Very well,' Warfield said. 'Your motion is granted and I will instruct the jury. You can all step back now.'

Once we were all seated, the judge turned to face the jury.

'Members of the jury, Detective Drucker just now unfairly commented on Mr. Haller's constitutional right to remain silent,' she said. 'A bell once rung cannot be unheard, but I instruct you to disregard the comment and not to infer from it any evidence of guilt. The Fifth Amendment to the United States Constitution grants to any person accused of a crime the right to remain silent and not to be compelled to incriminate himself. This right is as old as this country. There are good reasons for it that are too numerous to review with you now. Suffice it to say that in this case, as you have heard, Mr. Haller is a criminal defense lawyer and he has a firm grasp on why an accused would not want to submit to an interrogation by his accusers. He was well within his rights to decline to speak following his arrest. Detective Drucker, on the other hand, ought to know better than to even mention the assertion of a constitutional right to remain silent. So, because it is so fundamental and important to our justice system, I repeat: Disregard the comment on Mr. Haller's post-arrest invocation of his right to remain silent, and do not infer from it any evidence of guilt.'

The judge then turned slightly to focus on Drucker. His face was already red from humiliation.

'Now, Detective Drucker,' she said. 'Do you need time to review with Ms. Berg how to testify without unconstitutional, unfair, and unprofessional comment?'

'No, Judge,' Drucker mumbled, staring straight ahead.

'Look at me when I address you,' Warfield said.

Drucker turned his whole body in the witness stand to look up at her. The judge's penetrating glare held his for what he must have considered an eternity. Then she turned the lasers on Berg.

'You may resume your inquiry, Ms. Berg,' she said.

Resuming her position at the lectern, Berg asked: 'Detective, do you know whether the defendant knew Sam Scales?'

'Over a period of years, Michael Haller appeared as counsel of record in almost every criminal case brought against Sam Scales. He had a long-term relationship with the victim and most likely knew his routines and practices.'

'*Objection!*' I said indignantly. 'Again, Your Honor, speculation.'

The judge pinned the witness with her scowl.

'Detective Drucker,' she said. 'You will confine your testimony to what you know from personal observation and experience. Do I make myself clear?'

'Yes, Judge,' the twice-chastened detective said.

'Continue, Ms. Berg,' Warfield said.

Berg was trying to turn an investigative failure on the part of the police into suspicion of the defense and the defendant. I knew I might be hanging a lantern on the suspicion the prosecution was throwing at me, but a few stern warnings from the judge to the prosecution were an unexpected victory, and they blended well with my strategy of exposing the investigation and prosecution as sloppy and unfair.

It was good to get these little victories in the midst of a long stretch of pro-prosecution testimony. You take them where you can get them. I soon returned to writing notes on my legal pad to remind myself to hit these strategy buttons harder during cross-examination — whenever that would finally be.

Berg continued to question Drucker right up until the lunch break and by then had only covered the first night's investigation. There was more to come in the afternoon session and it was becoming increasingly clear that I would not get my shots at the detective until after the weekend. I checked the jury as they were filing out of the box to leave for lunch. I saw a lot of stretching of arms and signs of lethargy. The chef even yawned. It was okay for them to grow tired of the prosecution's case, just as long as they hadn't already made a decision about me.

I took lunch in the courtside holding tank with

Maggie and Cisco. The judge had allowed them to bring food in to me during the lunch-break working sessions. Friday's meal came from Little Jewel and I devoured the shrimp po'boy like a man who has just been rescued from a life raft found floating in the middle of the Pacific. We talked about the case, though I had my mouth full most of the time.

'We need to knock this train off its tracks,' I said. 'She's going to run the clock out in the afternoon session, and then those jurors go home for the weekend with my guilt in their heads.'

'It's a filibuster,' Maggie said. 'That's what we call it in the D.A.'s Office. Keep the witness away from the defense for as long as possible.'

I knew that in the afternoon session Berg would probably move on to the part of the investigation that supported the charges against me. She would also start hitting on motive, and by the end of the day, her case would be practically complete. It would then be more than forty-eight hours before I got the chance to fight back in cross-examination.

Realistically, the afternoon session would last three hours. The lunch recess ended at 1:30 and no judge in the building would keep a jury past 4:30 on a Friday afternoon. I needed to cut a big chunk out of that three hours and somehow knock Berg's case delivery into next week. It wouldn't matter how much time she monopolized on Monday. I'd step up with cross-examination the minute it was over. It was the weekend I couldn't give her — two full days with

363

only one side of the story in a juror's mind was an eternity.

I looked down at what was left of my sandwich. The fried shrimp was delicately wrapped in a homemade rémoulade.

'Mickey, no,' Maggie said.

I looked up at her.

'What?'

'I know what you're thinking. The judge will never buy it. She was a defense attorney and she knows all the tricks.'

'Well, if I throw up on the defense table, she'll buy it.'

'Come on. Food poisoning — that's really bush league.'

'Then, fine, you come up with a way to delay Death Row Dana and knock her off her game.'

'Look, almost all her questions are leading. Start objecting. And every time Drucker gives an opinion, call him on it.'

'Then I look like a nitpicker to the jury.'

'Then I'll do it.'

'Same thing — we're a team.'

'Better looking like a nitpicker than like a murderer.'

I nodded. I knew objections would delay things but they would not be enough. They would slow Berg down but not stop her. I needed something more. I looked at Cisco.

'Okay, listen, your assignment once we get back out there is to watch the jury,' I said. 'Keep your eyes on them. They were already looking tired this morning and now they just ate lunch. Anybody starts nodding off, text Maggie and we'll put it in front of the judge. That'll buy us some time.'

'On it,' Cisco said.

'Meantime, did you check their social media since yesterday?' I asked.

'I'll have to check with Lorna,' Cisco said. 'She was watching all of that stuff so I was freed up for whatever you needed.'

Part of his backgrounding job on the jurors was to continue to gather intel on them. Through his work in the garage, he had been able to pick up names through car registrations and other means. He then parlayed that into monitoring their social-media accounts wherever possible for any references to the trial.

'Okay, call her before we start the afternoon session,' I said. 'Tell her to check. See if anybody's bragging about being on the jury, saying anything the court should know about. If there's something there, we can bring it up, maybe get a juror-misconduct hearing going. That would knock Berg's plan back till Monday.'

'What if it's one of our keepers?' Maggie asked.

She was talking about the seven jurors I had down as green on my sympathies chart. Possibly sacrificing one of them for a two-hour delay was a tough trade-off.

'We'll see when we get there,' I said. 'If we even get there.'

The discussion ended when Deputy Chan came to the holding-room door and said it was time to move me back into the courtroom to start the afternoon session.

Once court resumed, I started things off with an objection to Berg's ongoing use of leading questions in the examination of Detective Drucker. As I had anticipated, this brought a fierce response from Berg, who called the complaint unfounded. The judge saw merit in her argument.

'Defense counsel knows that to object well after the fact is not a sustainable objection,' Warfield said.

'If it please the court,' I said. 'My objection is to alert the court that this is happening as a matter of course. It is not unfounded and I thought a directive from the bench could put an end to it. However, the defense is more than fine making contemporaneous objections as we proceed.'

'Please do so, Mr. Haller.'

'Thank you, Your Honor.'

The dispute had taken ten minutes off the clock and knocked Berg a bit off her game as she returned Drucker to the witness stand and continued to question him. Not wanting to give me the satisfaction of a sustainable objection to the form of her questions, she took extra care and time with them. This was what I wanted and I hoped the slower pace might have the added bonus of fatiguing the freshly fed jury. If one dropped into slumber, I would be able to chew up more time by asking the judge for a directive to the jury.

But all of those efforts proved moot when, an hour into the afternoon session, Berg handed me all I needed to run the clock out myself. She had moved Drucker's testimony into an area exploring who Sam Scales was and what he might have been up to at the time of his murder. Drucker recounted how he had learned that Scales had been using the alias Walter Lennon and had found applications for credit cards and subsequent billing statements under the name and address last used by Scales. Berg then moved to enter the documents as prosecution exhibits.

I leaned toward Maggie and whispered.

'Did we get this stuff?' I asked.

'I don't know,' Maggie said. 'I don't think so.'

Berg walked copies to us after dropping duplicates off with the court clerk. I placed the pages on the table between Maggie and me and we quickly studied them. A murder case generates a tremendous number of documents and sometimes keeping track of it all is a full-time job. This case was no different. Plus, Maggie had come into the case, replacing Jennifer, only two weeks earlier. Neither of us had command of all of the paperwork. That had been more Jennifer's job than mine because I wanted to keep a minimal number of documents with me in the jail.

But I was pretty sure I had never seen these papers before.

'You have the discovery report there?' I asked.

Maggie went into her briefcase and pulled out a file. She located a printout with a one-line description of all documents received from the District Attorney's Office as part of discovery. She ran her finger down the column and then checked a second page.

'No, they're not here,' she said.

I immediately stood up.

'*OBJECTION!*' I said with a fervor I rarely used in a courtroom.

Berg stopped in mid-question to Drucker. The judge startled as if the steel door to the holding cell had been slammed with great force.

'What is your objection, Mr. Haller?' she asked.

'Judge, once again the prosecution has willfully violated the rules of discovery,' I said. 'The efforts to keep the defense from evidence to which it rightfully should have access has just been staggering in — '

'Let me stop you right there,' the judge said quickly. 'Let's not get into this in front of the jury.'

Warfield then told the jurors that court was adjourning for a short afternoon break. She asked them to be back in the assembly room in ten minutes.

We waited as the jurors slowly made their way out of the box and to the courtroom's exit. My anger grew with each second of silence. Warfield waited for the door to close behind the last juror before finally addressing the situation.

'Okay, Mr. Haller,' she said. 'Now speak.'

I moved to the lectern. I had hoped to manufacture a delay tactic that would push the most damaging part of Drucker's testimony into Monday, when I would be able to address and mitigate it in a timely manner. I didn't care whether the delay was legit, but I had just been handed a discovery violation that was as righteous as anything I could have imagined. I teed it up and swung hard.

'Judge, this is just incredible,' I began. 'After all the issues we've already had in discovery, they just go and do it again. I have never seen these documents, they are not on any supplemental discovery lists, they are a complete surprise. And now they're exhibits? They want the jury to see them but they never let me see them, and I'm the one being tried for murder here. I mean, come on, Judge. How can this keep happening again and again? And with no sanctions, no deterrent.'

'Ms. Berg, Mr. Haller says he hasn't received this in discovery. What is your response?' Warfield said.

I had been aware the entire time I was speaking that Berg was leafing through a thick white binder that had the word DISCOVERY on its spine. She was moving through it a second time, this time back to front, when the judge called her to answer. She stood and addressed the court from her table.

'Your Honor, I can't explain it,' she said. 'It was supposed to be in a discovery package delivered two weeks ago. I have someone checking the emails to defense counsel but this is the master list I'm looking at here and I don't see the documents in question on it. All I can say is that it was an oversight, Judge. A mistake. And I can assure the court that it was not intentional.'

I shook my head as though I was being offered

369

a deal on an ice-cube farm in Siberia. I was not impressed.

'Judge, *oops* is not a legal excuse,' I said. 'I am unable to evaluate the authenticity, relevance, or materiality of these exhibits, nor am I prepared to confront and cross-examine this witness about them. I have been severely prejudiced in my ability to prepare and present my defense. The state's lack of respect for my rights has to be corrected. Respect to the system, respect to the court, respect to the rules we all have to learn and must play by.'

The judge pursed her lips as she realized the discovery violation was confirmed and had to be dealt with.

'All right, Mr. Haller, taking counsel at her word, the violation appears to be a mistake,' she said. 'The issue now, however, is how to proceed, and that depends on what this evidence means to the People's case and the ability of the accused to confront the testimony and evidence against him. Ms. Berg, what is the relevance and materiality of this evidence and testimony? To what issue does it relate?'

'These are documents relating to Sam Scales alias Walter Lennon's finances and bank accounts,' Berg said. 'They are relevant to the defendant's motive for killing him. They are crucial to the People's case for special circumstances.'

'Mr. Haller,' Warfield said. 'Would you please look at the documents provided to you and tell me how long you will need to review and investigate them?'

370

'Judge, I can tell you right now that I will need at least the weekend, possibly more, because the banks are closed over the weekend and my ability to investigate will be limited. But that is only one of the issues. These documents and the testimony related to them ought to be excluded from evidence. The prosecution, in its zeal to — '

'We're losing the day, Mr. Haller,' the judge said. 'Please get to the point.'

'Exactly,' Berg chimed in. 'Judge, it is clear that counsel is engaged in tactics to delay the testimony of my witness. He would like nothing better than — '

'*Your Honor*,' I cut in loudly. 'Am I missing something? I'm the victim here, and the prosecution is now trying to blame me for her malfeasance, intentional or otherwise.'

'It was a *mistake*!' Berg yelled. 'A mistake, Judge, and he's trying to make it look like the end of the world. He — '

'All right, all right!' the judge yelled. 'Everyone just settle down and be quiet.'

In California, judges don't use gavels — it's supposed to be the kinder, gentler justice system — or surely the hammer would have just come down hard. In the silence that followed the judge's outburst, I saw her eyes rise above the lawyers in front of her to the clock on the rear wall of the courtroom.

'It's now after three o'clock,' she said. 'Tempers are running hot. In fact, you both are bringing far more heat than illumination to this proceeding. I'm going to bring the jury back in and send them home for the weekend.'

371

Berg hung her head in defeat as Warfield continued.

'We'll take this matter up Monday morning,' she said. 'Mr. Haller, I want a submission from you to my clerk on remedies by Monday, eight a.m. You will copy Ms. Berg by email with a draft of your submission by Sunday evening. Ms. Berg, you too will file your submission as to why this evidence should not be excluded or why other proposed sanctions would be inappropriate. As I have repeatedly said in this courtroom, I take the rules of discovery very seriously. There are no honest mistakes when it comes to discovery. It is the backbone of case preparation, and the rules must be rigorously and jealously adhered to. Any infraction, whether intentional or not, must be seriously dealt with as a violation of the accused's fundamental right to due process. Now let's bring the jury back in here so they can get an early start on the weekend.'

I moved back to the defense table and sat down. I whispered to Maggie.

'Talk about falling in shit and coming up smelling like a rose,' I said.

'Glad now that I didn't let you claim food poisoning?' she said.

'Uh, that falls under attorney-client privilege, not to be mentioned ever again.'

'My lips are sealed. I'll write the motion and get it in. What about sanctions?'

'I feel like we just got them. Her putting this over till Monday is a home run for us.'

'So, no sanctions?'

'I didn't say that. You never miss an

opportunity for sanctions against the state. That's just too rare to pass up. But I don't want a mistrial, and if what the Iceberg says is true about the evidence being crucial to her case for special circumstances, the judge won't exclude it. Let's think about it some — we have the weekend. I'll take the printouts and read it all over tomorrow, maybe get some ideas. Can you come to Twin Towers on Sunday to meet?'

'I'll be there. Maybe meet Hayley for lunch first.'

'Good. Sounds like a plan.'

The door to the assembly room opened and the jurors began filing down the two rows of seats in the box. It was the end of day two of prosecution's case and by my count I was still ahead.

42

They didn't start moving me to one of the attorney conference rooms until almost three o'clock. The runner who took me down was wearing a mask that matched the green of his uniform. That told me that the face covering had been officially distributed by the Sheriffs Department, a sign that the coming wave was a real threat.

When he walked me through the door of the interview room Maggie was already there and waiting. And she, too, wore a mask.

'Are you kidding me?' I said. 'This thing is real? It's coming?'

She didn't say anything as the deputy led me to a seat and removed the handcuffs. He then recited the rules.

'No touching,' he said. 'No electronic devices. The camera's on. No audio, but we'll be watching. If you get up from the chair, we're coming in. Understood?'

'Yes,' I said.

'Understood,' Maggie said.

He left the room then and locked the door behind him. I looked up at the camera mounted in the corner of the ceiling. Despite the scandal and internal investigation that I had tipped off, it was still in place and we were expected to take it on faith that no one was listening to our conversation.

'How are you, Mickey?' Maggie asked.

'I'm worried,' I said. 'Everybody's wearing masks but me.'

'Don't you have TV in the module? CNN? People are dying in China from this virus. They think it is probably here.'

'They changed shifts in the bubble, and the new people in there with the remotes only give us ESPN and Fox News.'

'Fox has its head in the sand. They're just protecting the president, who still says everything's going to be fine.'

'Well, if he said it, it must be true.'

'Oh, yeah, sure.'

I saw that she had some documents spread out on the table in front of her.

'How long have you been here?' I asked.

'Don't worry about it,' she said. 'I got work done.'

'Did you see Hayley today?'

'Yes, we ate lunch at Moreton Fig. It was nice.'

'Love that place. Miss it. Miss being with her.'

'You're going to get out of here, Mickey. We have a strong case.'

I just nodded to that. I wished that I could see her whole face so I could read her better. Was she just giving me a pep talk, or did she really believe what she was saying?

'You know, I don't have it, whatever it is,' I said. 'The virus. You don't need to wear the mask.'

'You might not know if you have it,' she said.

'Anyway, it's not you I'm worried about. It's the air recirculation in this place. They're saying the jails and prisons are going to be vulnerable. At least you're not on those buses going back and forth from court anymore.'

I nodded again, studying her. The mask accentuated her dark, intense eyes. Those eyes had been what first pulled me toward her twenty-five years ago.

'Which way do you think Hayley's going to go?' I asked. 'Prosecution or defense?'

'Hard to say,' she said. 'I don't know, actually. She'll make her own decision. She did say she's not going to classes this week. She wants to watch the trial full-time.'

'She shouldn't. She'll fall too far behind.'

'I know. But there's too much at stake for her. I couldn't talk her out of it.'

'Hardheaded. I know where she gets that.'

'Me too.'

I thought I detected a smile behind the mask.

'Maybe she'll go into criminal defense and we could have a family law firm,' I said. 'Haller, Haller, and McFierce, Attorneys-at-Law.'

'Funny,' she said. 'Maybe.'

'Do you really think they're going to take you back after this? You've betrayed the tribe, crossed to the dark side, all of that. I'm not sure they let you do that on a temporary basis.'

'Who knows? And who's to say that I want to go back? I see Dana in that courtroom and I really ask myself, do I want that anymore? I don't know. Once they moved me out of Major Crimes to make room for the young hard chargers like her, I knew my career . . . it wasn't exactly over but it had . . . plateaued. It wasn't important anymore.'

'Oh, come on. Environmental protection? What you do is still important.'

'If I have to go after one more dry cleaner for dumping chemicals down the storm sewer, I think I'll just kill myself.'

'Don't kill yourself. Come partner with me.'

'Funny.'

'I mean it.'

'That's okay.'

I took that as a hit. Her quick no reminded me of what had gotten between us and ended things, despite our daughter inextricably binding us together for life.

'You always thought I was dirty because of what I do,' I said. 'Like it rubbed off on me somehow. I'm not dirty, Mags.'

'Well, you know the saying,' she said. 'Lie down with dogs . . .'

'Then what are you doing here?'

'I told you. No matter what I think about what you do, I know you and I know you didn't do this. You couldn't have. And, besides, Hayley came to me. She asked me to help you. No, she told me. She said you needed me.'

I hadn't known any of that. That stuff about Hayley was new and it cut me to the bone.

'Wow,' I said. 'Hayley never said anything to me.'

'The truth is, she didn't have to tell me,' Maggie said. 'I wanted to do it, Mickey. I mean that.'

377

A silence followed that. I nodded my thanks. When I looked up, Maggie was pulling the elastic straps off her ears and removing the mask.

'Should we get down to business?' she said. 'They only gave us an hour.'

'Sure,' I said. 'Anything back yet on Milton's phone?'

'They're stringing that out but I'll go to the judge if I have to.'

'Good. I want to burn that guy's ass.'

'We will.'

'Sanctions?'

She wore no lipstick and I guessed that she had wanted to keep the makeup off her mask. Seeing her face now, I got that pang in my chest. She had been the only one who ever did that to me. Mask or no mask, makeup or no makeup, she was beautiful to me.

'I say we go big or go home,' she said. 'We tell the judge to put bail back on the table.'

I snapped out of my reverie.

'As a sanction?' I said. 'I doubt Warfield would go for that. The trial will be over by the end of this week. She won't let me out just to possibly yank me back in if there's a guilty verdict. And then I don't think I want to put up a bond for what might amount to just four or five days of freedom.'

'I know,' Maggie said. 'The judge won't go for it and it's a losing argument, but that's just it. It's an argument and we start the week with it and Dana has to expend all her Monday-morning energy on it.'

'Takes some of the wind out of her sails,' I said.

'Exactly. It's a big distraction from her trial plan.'

I nodded. I liked it.

'Smart,' I said. 'Let's do it.'

'Okay,' Maggie said. 'I'll write it up and get it to all parties before six. Tomorrow I'll handle the argument too.'

I had to smile. I admired how Maggie was justifying her McFierce reputation on both sides of the aisle and for my benefit.

'Perfect,' I said. 'What do we ask for when Warfield shuts us down?'

'Nothing,' she said. 'We just bank it.'

'Okay.'

She seemed pleased that I did not push back on her plan.

'So, where are we on everything else?' I asked.

'Opparizio,' Maggie said. 'He knows something is up and left town yesterday. By car. Cisco had his guys on him.'

'Don't tell me he left the state. Vegas?'

'No, he probably thought he'd be tracked there easy. He drove to Arizona. Scottsdale. He checked into a resort out there called the Phoenician. Cisco will go out tomorrow and hit him with the subpoena.'

'What if he knows that he doesn't need to respond to a subpoena from another state? It's probably the reason he left.'

'Something tells me he doesn't and he left town because he was feeling the heat. He's gotta know there's a trial in the murder he's

379

responsible for. Best to get out of town till it's over. Anyway, Cisco said they'll video the whole thing, make it an airtight service looking totally legit. The question is, what day do you want him here?'

We had to think about that. We had Dana Berg's witness list and from that could extrapolate how long her case might take to put before the jury. We had already delayed things Friday with Drucker, but before that, the prosecutor had been stringing out his testimony in an attempt to run it up to the weekend. Berg would likely shift strategy now and move more quickly with him, trying to build momentum. She then had a deputy coroner on her wit list, the lead crime scene investigator, and then a few ancillary witnesses to follow.

'I'm thinking Dana has two days left at the max,' I said.

'I'm thinking the same,' Maggie said. 'So we go with Opparizio on Wednesday?'

'Yeah, Wednesday. Good. Means I'll be telling my side of this in less than seventy-two hours. Can't wait.'

'Me neither.'

'And our other witnesses are set?'

'They're all good to go. I have the retired EPA guy — Art Schultz — flying in Wednesday morning. The rest are all local. So we should have everybody on hand, and you can put them on in whatever order we decide works best.'

'Perfect.'

'Depending on what we get on the phone records, you can slip Milton in anywhere or make him the grand finale. Have Moira from the bar and then him as a one-two punch at the end.'

I nodded. It was good to set up witnesses so that we could handle any surprises or no-shows. Nothing would annoy Warfield or any judge more than having the jury ready but no witnesses to present to them. We needed to avoid that at all costs.

'What's our contingency if Opparizio doesn't come back or sends a lawyer to quash?' I asked.

'I've been thinking about that,' Maggie said. 'We could go to Warfield for a bench warrant. That'll work across state lines. We'll just have to get the locals out there to scoop him up.'

'That could delay things for days.'

'That's why we play to Warfield. No one wants this trial over with more than you. But she's second on that list, and we'll make her see that she's got to use her power to bring Opparizio in. He's the centerpiece of the defense case. This could be reversed if we don't get the opportunity to put him on the stand.'

'Well, let's hope it doesn't come to that.'

There was a pause in the conversation and then I pointed it down another difficult track.

'What about the FBI?' I asked. 'Have we given up on that?'

'No, not yet,' Maggie said. 'I've talked to some people over there — sneaking into my office and using the phone. It helps to have the D.A.'s Office come up on their caller ID — they actually take the calls. I'm just trying to get an off-the-record sit-down with Agent Ruth.'

'That's a long shot.'

'I know but I think if I can just talk to her, I can work something out. I know she'll never get permission to testify, but if she would agree to just come and sit in court when it's our turn to tell the story, we might win her over.'

'To do what, testify without the bureau's permission?'

'Maybe. I don't know.'

'That would be fantastic. But no way.'

'You never know. She's already helped you once. Maybe she'll do it again. We just need to find a way for her to do it. I think she might come to court anyway to see what comes out about Opparizio and BioGreen.'

'Well, send her an embossed invitation. We'll save her a front-row seat. But I think it'll be a seat that doesn't get used.'

It appeared we had covered everything. The week ahead would determine the future of my life. I felt confident in Maggie and myself and our case. But the dread was still there. It never went away. Anything could happen in court.

Maggie picked up her mask and started looping the straps behind her ears. Even with the elastic the loops were too tight and pulled her ears slightly forward. In that moment I saw our daughter when she was younger and her ears were one of her most pronounced features.

'What?' Maggie asked.

'What?' I said.

'What are you smiling at?'

'Oh, nothing. Your mask sort of pulls your ears out. It reminded me of Hay. Remember when we

382

used to say she had to grow into her ears?'

'I do. And she did.'

I nodded at the memory and watched Maggie cover her smile.

'So,' I said. 'Who are you dating these days?'

'Uh, that's none of your business,' she said.

'True. But I want to ask you out. I don't want it to be a problem.'

'Really? Why? Ask me out where?'

'Next Sunday — one week from tonight. We go out and celebrate the big NG. I'll take you to Mozza.'

'You're certainly confident.'

'I have to be. It's the only way to go. You in or out?'

'What about Hayley?'

'Hayley too. The whole firm — Haller, Haller, and McFierce, bringing new meaning to *family law*.'

Maggie laughed.

'Okay, you're on.'

She gathered the paperwork and got up. She knocked on the steel door and then turned back to me.

'Stay safe, Mickey.'

'That's the plan. You, too.'

The door was opened by a deputy, this one without a mask, and I watched her go. I realized after the door closed that I was falling in love again with Maggie McFierce.

43

I was already in place at the defense table when Maggie arrived. She dropped a folded Metro section from the *Times* in front of me as she pulled her chair out.

'I take it you haven't seen the paper,' she said.

'Nope,' I said. 'I asked that it be delivered with my breakfast every morning but it never comes.'

She tapped her finger on a story at the bottom corner of the page. The headline said it all: 'Sheriff: Inmate Acted Alone in Assault on 'Lincoln Lawyer.''

I started scanning the story but Maggie summarized it as I read.

'They say that Mason Maddox acted completely on his own when he attempted to kill you. No one put him up to it and the Sheriffs Department comes out squeaky clean, even though it was the sheriff's office that handled the investigation.'

I stopped reading and tossed the paper onto the table.

'Bullshit,' I said. 'Then why'd he do it?'

'That story says he told investigators he mistook you for another inmate he had a grudge against,' Maggie said.

'Yeah, well, like I said — '

'Bullshit.'

'I'm still going to sue their asses when I get out of here.'

'That's the spirit.'

The conclusion of the investigation was not surprising but it made me feel more vulnerable. If the attack by Maddox had been orchestrated as payback by deputies in the jail, there was nothing to stop them from trying again. The first effort had been whitewashed — so would be the second.

I didn't get much time to dwell on it. Judge Warfield soon took the bench, and the jury remained in the assembly room while the hearing on the discovery issue that was revealed Friday continued. Maggie McFierce made a strong argument for reinstatement of bail as a sanction against the prosecution but it went down without Dana Berg's even having to respond. Warfield simply rejected it out of hand with a simple 'We're not doing that.'

The judge then asked if the defense wanted to entertain other sanctions. Maggie declined and the issue was left open, meaning it might come into play and give the defense an edge down the line if there was a tight ruling involving judicial discretion. The hope was that the judge would remember the prosecution's unremedied violation of discovery and tip her discretion our way.

Detective Kent Drucker was returned to the witness stand, and the prosecution took up where it had been forced to leave off Friday. As I had expected, Berg shortened her questions and picked up her pace, using the morning session to take Drucker through the post-crime scene investigation. This included the search of my home the morning after I was arrested, which led to the discovery of the blood and the bullet on the floor of my garage.

To me this was the most damning evidence in the whole case but also the most confounding. To believe I was innocent, you had to believe that I slept through the murder that occurred right below my living space and then unknowingly drove around with the body in my trunk for a day. To believe I was guilty, you had to believe I went out and drugged and abducted Sam Scales, or had someone do it for me, then put his body in the trunk of the Lincoln and shot him before spending the next day with his body still in the trunk while I drove to and from the courthouse. Either way was a hard sell. And both the prosecution and defense knew it.

At one point Berg put several blow-up photos of my house on easels in front of the jury box to help build the case for the guilty scenario. The house was located on a hillside that sloped down from the rear of the property to the front. At street level was the double-wide garage. Stairs to the right went up to the residential space above, which included the front deck, where I had been confronted by agents Aiello and Ruth. The front door led into the living room and dining room, which were directly over the garage. In the back were my bedroom and my home office.

Berg moved Drucker through some testimony involving their testing of gunshots with and without various sound suppressors, so-called silencers, and with the garage door open or closed, in an effort to determine if someone could have broken into the garage, put a drugged Sam Scales into the trunk, and then shot him multiple times without my hearing it from above.

Before Berg could ask the detective what his conclusions were, I objected and asked for a sidebar. The judge told us to approach.

'Judge, I know what counsel is doing,' I began. 'She's going to ask him if all of this testing with gunfire could be heard upstairs, but the witness is not an expert in ballistics or the science of sound. He can't give an opinion on this. No one can. There are too many factors not accounted for. Was the TV on? Was the stereo on? What about the washing machine and the dishwasher? You see, Judge? You can't allow this. Where was I in the house when this was supposedly happening? In the shower? Asleep with earplugs in? She is trying to rebut a defense position before we have even put up a defense.'

'Counsel makes a good point, Ms. Berg,' Warfield said. 'I'm inclined to stop this line of questioning.'

'Your Honor,' Berg said. 'We've gone down this path for the past twenty minutes. If I'm not allowed to finish, the state will be unfairly held in a bad light by the jury. The witness is describing efforts made by the police to see if the suspect could actually be innocent. What happens during the defense phase when Mr. Haller trots out the tired tunnel-vision defense? He'll accuse Detective Drucker of only focusing on his guilt to the exclusion of possibly exculpatory evidence. He can't have it both ways.'

387

'You make a good point as well, Ms. Berg,' Warfield said. 'We are going to take the lunch break now and I'll have a ruling on the objection when we come back at one sharp.'

Court was adjourned and I was led back to the courtside holding cell for the hour break. Maggie didn't join me there for almost a half hour, finally coming in with a sandwich Lorna had picked up at Cole's, as well as news from Arizona.

'They got him,' she said. 'He was staying in his suite, having food brought in, and they thought they were going to have to door-knock him with the subpoena, when he ventured out to the pool. They got him in a bathing suit and bathrobe.'

'Tony Soprano,' I said, recalling that the television mobster liked to lounge around the pool in a bathrobe.

'Exactly what I thought.'

'They get it on video?'

'The whole thing. I have it on my phone. I can show you in the courtroom but they wouldn't let me bring it in here.'

I unwrapped my sandwich. It was roast beef on a roll. I took a bite and spoke with my mouth full.

'Good. So we have Opparizio for Wednesday — if he shows up.'

I took another bite. The sandwich was delicious, but then I noticed she wasn't eating.

'You want some of this?' I asked. 'It's great.'

'No, I'm too nervous to eat,' Maggie said.

'What, about the trial?'

'What else?'

'I don't know. I just didn't think Maggie McFierce ever got nervous.'

'You'd be surprised.'

'So, who is Opparizio using these days? Back during the Lisa Trammel case, he used Zimmer and Cross to try to quash our subpoena. They failed. I heard he fired them right after that.'

'As far as we can tell from documents we've located on BioGreen, he uses the firm of Dempsey and Geraldo for a lot of his stuff. Whether they provide criminal defense, I don't know.'

'Interesting.'

'Why?'

'I've run up against them before. They rep a lot of cops. Especially Dempsey. Looks like with Opparizio they're at the other end of the spectrum.'

Maggie pursed her lips and I knew she was considering something.

'What?' I said.

'Just thinking, is all,' she said. 'I'd like to get a list of their clients who are cops. See if there's a connection to Officer Milton.'

'You can get that.'

'They're not going to just give it to me.'

'No, but you have access to the county courts database. Put their names into it, and you'll get hits on every case they're involved with.'

'I took a leave, Mickey, remember? I could get fired if I did that.'

'You told me yesterday you were sneaking in to use your office phone.'

'That's different.'

389

'How's — '

Deputy Chan opened the cell door and told us it was time to go back to court. Maggie and I dropped the conversation there.

Once we were back at the defense table, Maggie pulled her phone and played me the video she had received from Cisco in Scottsdale. She had the sound down low but I could hear enough. And I could tell from Opparizio's contorted and red face that he was angry at being served with the subpoena. He was equally upset with the camera recording the event. He lunged at it, his bathrobe flapping open and his flour-white gut hanging over his board shorts. The man behind the camera — one of Cisco's Indians — was lighter on his feet and the lens swiftly moved out of range of Opparizio's swinging hand without ever losing him in the frame.

The reference to Tony Soprano had been spot-on and I wondered if Opparizio himself embraced the resemblance.

After missing the camera, Opparizio followed the momentum of his swinging arm and turned back toward Cisco. Opparizio took two steps toward him while Cisco calmly stood his ground. I saw his shoulders and arms tense. So did Opparizio. He thought better of his move and stopped in his tracks. He went with the finger instead of the fight, pointing it at Cisco's face and yelling an empty threat at him. At no point did Opparizio say anything about the subpoena being invalid when served in another state. He clearly didn't know.

Maggie cut the video as Chan announced that court was coming to order.

'That's the end,' she whispered. 'He runs back to his room after cussing Cisco out.'

She dropped the phone into her briefcase as Judge Warfield took the bench.

Before bringing the jury back in, the judge ruled on the objection I had made.

'Ms. Berg, you have accomplished what you set out to show,' she said. 'Detective Drucker has testified to the experiments at the defendant's house, but his opinions about what the experiments mean are irrelevant. You will move on to another area of inquiry.'

Another minor victory for the defense.

The jury was brought in and Detective Drucker returned to the stand. Berg completed eliciting his direct testimony an hour into the afternoon, ending with a line of questioning designed to outline the motive for my killing Sam Scales: money.

Through Drucker's testimony about the search of my records at my warehouse, she introduced the letter I had sent Scales in a final effort to collect the money he owed me. The letter was entered into the record as a state's exhibit without my objection. I didn't want to keep it from the jury. It was my belief that it cut both ways, and that would become clear when I put on my defense.

Through her questioning, Berg tried to make it seem to the jury that the letter was a key piece of evidence that I had tried to conceal by burying it in records hidden in a massive warehouse full of other possessions and junk.

'Where exactly did you find this letter in Mr. Haller's warehouse?'

'There was a small closet toward the back of this place. The door was kind of hidden behind a rack of clothes. But we found it, and inside we found some file cabinets. The drawers were full of files and didn't really seem to be in any order. We found a file on Sam Scales and the letter was inside it.'

'And when you read the letter, did you recognize it as potential evidence in the case?'

'Yes, right away. It was a demand — a final demand — for money that Haller believed he was owed.'

'Did you perceive the letter as a threat to Sam Scales?'

Maggie hit my arm and nodded toward the witness stand. She wanted me to object before Drucker could answer — giving an opinion on what should be a jury decision. But I shook my head. I wanted Drucker's answer so that I could turn it against him when it was my time.

'Yes, definitely a threat,' Drucker said. 'It says right in the letter that this was the final request before serious action would follow.'

'Thank you, Detective,' Berg said. 'Now the final thing I want to do is have you introduce a video in which you spoke to the defendant, but in his capacity as his own lawyer. Do you recall that conversation?'

'I do.'

'And it was video-recorded?'

'Yes.'

'Let's play that for the jury.'

Maggie leaned in to me.

'What is this?' she whispered.

'His last try to get me to confess,' I whispered back. 'I told him to fuck off.'

The video was played on the big wall screen over the clerk's station. It was from an interview room at Twin Towers. I had already been jailed for a week or so when Drucker and his partner, Lopes, came to see me to tell me what they had and to see if I would roll over.

'We see you're going to defend yourself on this thing,' Drucker said. 'So, we're here today to talk to you as a lawyer, not as the defendant, okay?'

'Whatever,' I said. 'If you're going to talk to me as a lawyer, you should have a prosecutor with you. But you've had your head up your ass on this from the beginning, Drucker. Why do I get the dumbest pair of detectives on the squad who can't see what this is?'

'Sorry we're so dumb. What is it we aren't seeing?'

'It's a setup. Somebody did this to me and you bought it hook, line, and sinker. You're pathetic.'

'Well, that's why we're here. I know you said you won't talk to us, and that's your right. So we're telling you, the attorney of record on this, what we've got and what the evidence shows. Maybe it changes your 'client's' mind, maybe it doesn't. But now is the time if you want to try to talk to us.'

'Go ahead, tell me what you got.'

'Well, we've got the body of Sam Scales in the trunk of your car. And we can prove through

393

ballistics and other evidence that he was killed in your garage when you were supposedly upstairs twiddling your thumbs.'

'That's bullshit. You're trying to bluff me. You think I'm that stupid?'

'We've got blood on the floor and ballistics — we found the slug on the floor of your garage, Haller. You did this and we can prove it. And I gotta tell you, it looks like it was planned. That's first-degree and that's life without parole. You have — your client has — a kid. If he ever wants to see that kid again outside a prison, now is the time for him to come in and tell us exactly what happened. Was it heat of the moment, a fight, what? You see what I mean, Counselor? Your client is fucked. And there is a small window here where we can go see the D.A. to explain this and get you — uh, him — the best deal possible.'

There was a long beat of silence on the video as I just stared at Drucker. I realized that this was what Dana Berg wanted the jury to see. The hesitation looked like I was considering the offer from Drucker — and wouldn't only a guilty man pause to weigh the choice? That, of course, was not what I was doing. I was trying to think of a way to elicit more information about the case. Drucker had just mentioned two key pieces of evidence that at the time were new to me. Blood and ballistics — a bullet slug found in my garage. I wanted to trick out more from him, and that was what the pause was all about. But the jury would not read it that way.

'You want me to make a deal?' I said on the

video. 'Fuck your deal. What else you got?'

Drucker clearly smiled on the video. He knew what I was doing. He had given up all he was going to.

'Okay,' he said. 'Just remember this moment, when we gave you the chance.'

Drucker started to get up from the table. Berg ended the video.

'Your Honor,' she said. 'At this time I have no more questions for Detective Drucker but I request leave to bring him back for further testimony as the state's case progresses.'

'Very well,' Judge Warfield said. 'It is a little too early to take the afternoon break. Mr. Haller, Ms. McPherson, do you have questions for this witness?'

I stood and moved to the lectern.

'Your Honor,' I began. 'Detective Drucker will be a key witness during the defense phase of the trial and I'll defer the bulk of my questions until then. But if I may, I will ask the witness a few questions now regarding the testimony he's given since the lunch break. There were things said that were incomplete and inexcusable and I don't want them to languish in the minds of the jurors for even a day.'

Berg stood up immediately.

'Judge, I object to the characterization of the witness and his testimony,' she said. 'Counsel is trying to — '

'Sustained,' Warfield said. 'You inquire, Mr. Haller. You do not argue. Keep your tone and opinions to yourself.'

'Thank you, Your Honor,' I said, acting as

though there had been no rebuke.

I checked the notes I had scribbled on a yellow pad just a few minutes before.

'Okay, Detective Drucker,' I began. 'Let's talk about this letter you say you interpreted as a threat to violence.'

'I called it a threat,' Drucker said. 'I didn't call it a threat to violence.'

'But isn't that what you are really saying, Detective? We're here because this is a murder case, correct?'

'Yes, this is a murder case. No, I did not say the letter was a threat to violence.'

'You didn't say it, but you want the jury to make that leap for you, correct?'

Berg objected, saying I was already badgering the witness three questions into the cross-examination. The judge told me to watch my tone but said that the witness could answer the question.

'I am stating facts,' Drucker answered. 'The jury can draw whatever conclusion or connection they see fit.'

'You said this mysterious closet where you found this letter was hidden behind a rack of clothes, correct?' I asked.

'Yes, there was a stand-up rack of clothes that obscured the door and that we had to move.'

'So, now it's obscured and not hidden?'

'Is that a question?'

'This rack of clothes that hid or obscured the closet door — was it on wheels, Detective Drucker?'

'Uh, yes, I believe so.'

'So when you said you and your fellow searchers had to move it, you mean you just rolled it out of the way, correct?'

'Yes.'

'And, by the way, was I present at this search?'

'You were.'

'But you didn't mention that earlier in your testimony, did you?'

'No, it didn't come up.'

'And was I not the one who told you to move the rack of clothes to get to the closet where I kept my financial records?'

'I don't recall that.'

'Really? You don't recall coming to my home with your search warrant and my volunteering to take you to my warehouse, where I kept the records you wanted to search?'

'You did agree to meet us at the warehouse and open it for us so we wouldn't have to break the lock.'

'Okay, and once we were there and you found this so-called hidden closet, did I not tell you what file drawer to look in for communications between me and Sam Scales?'

'I don't remember it that way, no.'

'Well, how many file cabinets were in the storage room, Detective?'

'I don't remember.'

'More than one?'

'Yes.'

'More than two?'

'I don't remember how many there were.'

I disengaged from Drucker and looked up at the judge.

'Objection, Your Honor,' I said. 'The witness is unresponsive to the question asked.'

'Answer the question, Detective,' the judge told the detective.

'There were more than two,' Drucker said. 'There may have been as many as five.'

'Thank you, Detective,' I said. 'Did you search all five of those filing cabinets?'

'No. You said most of them contained client files and were covered by attorney-client privilege. You refused to unlock them.'

'But I unlocked the filing cabinet containing my financial records, isn't that right, Detective?'

'I don't remember whether it was locked.'

'But you remember that you were prohibited from searching some filing cabinets but not the one you searched, is that correct?'

'I suppose that is correct.'

'So, first you didn't remember that I showed you the filing cabinet containing my financial documents, but now you admit that in fact I did show you where to search for my financial records. Do I have that right, Detective?'

'Objection!' Berg shouted.

Warfield raised her hand to cut off anything further.

'This is cross-examination, Ms. Berg,' she said. 'Impeachment of the witness's credibility is a proper issue of inquiry. Answer the question, Detective.'

'You did direct us to the filing cabinet,' Drucker said. 'I apologize for my misstatement. I was not visualizing the events as I experienced them.'

'Okay, let's move on here,' I said. 'You said you searched the cabinet, found the file on Sam Scales, and removed the document now marked as state's L. Do I have all that right?'

'Yes.'

'Did you look for or take any other documents during the search of my records?'

'Yes. There were two earlier letters to Sam Scales of similar nature — asking for money.'

'You mean asking him to pay his legal bills?'

'Yes.'

'Did they include threats to violence if he did not pay?'

'Not that I recall.'

'Is that why they have not been introduced in court today?'

Berg objected and asked for a sidebar. I was on a roll with Drucker and didn't want to lose momentum. I withdrew the question, negating the objection and need for a sidebar, then pressed on.

'Did you take anything else from my storage files, Detective Drucker?'

'No. The warrant covered only financial communications between you and the victim.'

'So, you did not ask the judge who signed the warrant for permission to check my tax returns to see if I had written off the Sam Scales debt as a business loss?'

Drucker had to think for a moment before answering. This was completely new information to be considered.

'It's a simple question, Detective,' I prompted. 'Did you — '

'No, we did not ask for tax returns,' Drucker said.

'Do you think if you had known that this debt was turned into a tax deduction, it would have mitigated your belief that it was the motive behind the killing of Sam Scales?'

'I don't know.'

'Do you think it might have been good information to have as you investigated the case?'

'All information is good to have. We like to throw out a wide net.'

'But not wide enough in this case, correct?'

Berg objected to the question, saying it was argumentative. The judge sustained the objection, and that was what I wanted. I didn't want Drucker to answer the question. It was meant for the jury.

'Your Honor,' I said. 'I have no further questions at this time but will be calling Detective Drucker back as a defense witness.'

I returned to the defense table while Berg called her next witness. Maggie gave me the nod for my first swing at Drucker.

'Good stuff,' she said. 'Should I have Lorna go to the warehouse and pull the tax return? We could use it as a defense exhibit.'

'No,' I whispered. 'There is no deduction.'

'What do you mean?'

'You wouldn't know this because you've spent your life in public service. Same with Berg and same with Drucker. Even the judge was a public defender before she got elected. But a private attorney can't deduct unpaid fees as a business loss. The IRS won't allow it. You

400

just have to eat the loss.'

'So it was a bluff?'

'Pretty much. About as much bullshit as them saying that letter I sent Sam was a threat to kill without really saying it.'

Maggie leaned back and stared straight ahead as she computed this.

'Welcome to criminal defense,' I whispered.

44

Linear, Methodical, Routine — Dana Berg was following textbook case delivery. The prosecution usually had such advantages in terms of its wealth and reach that that was usually all it took. The state overwhelmed with its power and might. Prosecutors could afford to be unimaginative, even stodgy. They trotted out their cases to the jury like furniture instructions from Ikea. Step-by-step with big illustrations, all the tools you needed included. No need to look elsewhere. No need to worry. And at the end you have a sturdy table that is both stylish and functional.

Berg ran out the afternoon with testimony and video from the lead criminalist who had been in charge of the crime scene and then the deputy coroner who had conducted the autopsy on the victim. Both witnesses were part of the building blocks of the state's case, even if they offered no evidence that directly implicated me. With the criminalist, I passed on the opportunity to ask questions. There was nothing to be gained there. With the coroner, Berg ran her direct examination past the usual 4:30 p.m. cutoff for testimony. Judge Warfield liked to use the last half hour of the day to dismiss the jury with warnings about avoiding media reports and discussing the case on social media or anywhere else, and then to check with the lawyers for any new business to consider.

But I stood up to address the court before she could do it.

'Your Honor, I have only a few questions for the witness,' I said. 'If I can get them in today, the prosecution can start tomorrow with a new witness and Dr. Jackson will be able to go back to his important work at the coroner's office.'

'If you're sure, Mr. Haller,' the judge responded, a suspicious tone in her voice.

'Five minutes, Judge. Maybe less.'

'Very well.'

I went to the lectern with only my copy of the autopsy report and nodded to the witness, Dr. Philip Jackson.

'Dr. Jackson, good afternoon,' I began. 'Can you tell the jury if it was your opinion that the victim in this case was obese?'

'He was overweight, yes,' Jackson said. 'I'm not sure he would be considered obese.'

'How much did he weigh at autopsy?'

Jackson referred to his own copy of the autopsy report before responding.

'He weighed two hundred six pounds,' he said.

'And how tall was he?' I followed.

'He was five foot eight.'

'Are you aware that the National Institutes of Health table of desired weights for adults places the maximum optimum weight of an adult male five foot eight in height at one hundred fifty-eight pounds?'

'Not off the top of my head, no.'

'Would you like to review the table, Doctor?'

'No. That sounds about right. I don't dispute it.'

403

'Okay. How tall are you, Dr. Jackson?'

'Uh, six foot even.'

'And your weight?'

As I expected, Berg stood and objected on the grounds of relevancy.

'Where are we going with this, Judge?' she asked.

'Mr. Haller,' the judge said. 'We are going to adjourn and take this up in the — '

'Your Honor,' I interrupted. 'Three more questions and we'll be there. And the relevancy will be clear.'

'Hurry, Mr. Haller,' Warfield said. 'You may answer the question, Dr. Jackson.'

'One ninety,' Jackson said. 'Last I checked.'

There was a slight murmur of laughter from the jury box and gallery.

'Okay, so you're a relatively big guy,' I said. 'When it came time during the autopsy to examine the victim's back for injuries, did you turn the body over yourself?'

'No, I had help,' Jackson said.

'Why is that?'

'Because it's difficult to move a body that weighs more than yourself.'

'I imagine so, Dr. Jackson. Who helped you?'

'As I recall, Detective Drucker witnessed the autopsy and I enlisted his help in turning the body over.'

'Judge, I have no further questions.'

Berg had no redirect and Warfield moved to adjourn court for the day. As she gave the jury the routine warnings, Maggie reached over and patted my hand.

'That was good,' she whispered.

I nodded and liked how she had touched me. It was my hope that the five-minute cross-examination of Jackson would leave the jury with something to think about as they went home for the night.

So far, Berg had offered nothing in the way of testimony or evidence that explained how I had gotten Sam Scales, who was essentially built like a mailbox, into the trunk of my car in order to shoot him. The possibilities ranged from my having an accomplice to help move an incapacitated Sam into the trunk to my drugging him and then ordering him into the trunk at gunpoint before those drugs took effect. I didn't know whether Berg was planning to avoid the issue altogether or if something was coming further down the line in her presentation.

But for the moment, at least, I had control of the issue. And it was a bonus that my weight loss since my initial arrest had now reached nearly thirty pounds, leaving me at least fifty pounds lighter than Sam Scales at death. I had checked the jury during my final questions to Jackson and several were looking at me instead of the witness, most likely sizing up whether I could have manhandled the 206-pound mailbox into the trunk of my car.

Going to trial is always a gamble. The prosecution is always the house in this game. It holds the bank and deals the cards. You take any win you can get. As Deputy Chan came to collect me and take me back into courtside holding, I felt good about the day. I had spent less than fifteen minutes cross-examining the state's witnesses but felt I had scored points and put a hit on the house. Sometimes that was all you could ask for. You plant seeds that help keep jurors thinking and that hopefully sprout and bloom during the defense phase of the trial. For the third trial day in a row, I felt momentum building.

I changed into my blues in the holding cell and waited for a runner to come get me and take me down to the dock. Sitting on the bench, I thought about where Dana Berg would take the trial next. It seemed to me that the case had largely been delivered to the jury through Drucker.

Tomorrow would certainly center on my garage. The state's wit list included another criminalist, who had handled the search there the morning after the killing, a DNA expert who would testify that the blood collected from the floor of the garage came from Sam Scales, and a ballistics expert who would testify about the analysis of the bullet evidence.

But I couldn't help thinking that there was going to be something else. Something not on a list. An October surprise, as members of the defense bar liked to call a sandbagging by the prosecution.

There was a clue to something coming. I had noticed that Kent Drucker left the courtroom after his testimony concluded. He was not replaced by his partner, Lopes, which meant that Berg was flying blind through the rest of the afternoon — no case detective on hand in case she needed documents or a refresher on aspects of the case. This rarely happened in a murder trial and it told me something was up. Drucker and Lopes were working on something. It had to be case-related, because they would have been taken out of the homicide rotation once the trial started. I was sure there was an October surprise coming.

This was how the rules of fairness in trial procedure were subverted. By putting off the investigative work on a witness or piece of evidence until trial is underway, the prosecutor can claim that it was a newfound witness or piece of evidence and that is why there was no forewarning to opposing counsel. The defense did it as well — I'd had people poised to drop a subpoena on Louis Opparizio, who would be my own October surprise. But there was something inappropriate and unfair about it when the prosecution, which held all the power and all the cards, did it. It was like the New York Yankees always getting the best players because they had the most money. It was why my favorite team in baseball was whatever team was playing the Yankees.

My thoughts were interrupted when the runner came to the holding cell to escort me down to the prisoner transport dock in the courthouse basement. Twenty minutes later I was in the back of a sheriff's cruiser being driven solo back to Twin Towers, courtesy of the order from Judge Warfield. I noticed that the driver was a different deputy from the one who had driven me that morning and last week. This driver seemed familiar to me but I couldn't place him. Between the jail and the courthouse I had seen so many different deputies in the past four months that there was no way I could remember them all.

After we pulled out of the courthouse complex and onto Spring, I leaned forward to the metal grille that separated the driver from the rear compartment, where I was locked into a plastic form-fitting seat.

'What happened to Bennet?' I asked.

I had noted the name on the new guy's uniform when he was putting me into the car. Pressley. It, too, was familiar but not enough for me to place it.

'Assignment change,' Pressley said. 'I'll be driving you the rest of this week.'

'Sounds good,' I said. 'Have you worked in the keep-away module lately?'

'No, I'm in transport.'

'Thought I recognized you.'

'That's because I've sat behind you in court a few times.'

'Really? This case?'

'No, this goes back. Alvin Pressley is my nephew. You had him as a client for a while.'

Alvin Pressley. The name, followed by a face, came back to me. A twenty-one-year-old kid from the projects caught slinging dope with enough quantity in his pockets to qualify for a big-time prison sentence. I was able to score him a better deal: a year in the county stockade.

'Oh, yeah. Alvin,' I said. 'You stood for him at the sentencing, right? I remember his uncle was a deputy.'

'I did.'

408

Here was the hard question.

'So, how's Alvin doing these days?'

'He's doing good. That was a wake-up call for him. Got his shit together, moved out to Riverside to get away from all the crap. He lives with my brother out there. They got a restaurant.'

'Good to hear.'

'Anyway, you did right by me with Alvin, so I'm going to do right by you. There's people in the jail not happy with you.'

'Tell me about it. I know.'

'I'm serious now. You gotta watch your back in there, man.'

'Believe me, I do know. You're driving me because I got choked out by a guy on the bus. You know about that?'

'Everybody knows about that.'

'What about before? Did people know that was going to go down?'

'I don't know, man. Not me.'

'The story they put in the paper today was bullshit.'

'Yeah, well, shit happens like that when you're making waves. Remember that.'

'I've known that my entire life, Pressley. Is there something you want to tell me that I don't know?'

I waited. He said nothing, so I tried prompting him.

'Sounds like you took a risk asking to drive me,' I said. 'Might as well tell it.'

We turned off Bauchet Street and into the inmate-reception garage at Twin Towers. Two deputies came to the car to get me and move me back up to the keep-away module.

'Just watch yourself,' Pressley said.

I had long assumed I was a target for any number of the forty-five hundred inmates held inside the jail's octagonal walls. Anything could spur violence — the cut of your hair, the color of your skin, the look in your eyes. Getting warned about the deputies charged with keeping me safe was another matter.

'Always,' I said.

The door opened and a deputy reached in to unlock my cuffs from the seat and then pull me out.

'Home, sweet home, asshole,' he said.

45

The morning session in court had not gone well
for the defense. Through crime scene analysis,
DNA, and ballistics, prosecution witnesses had
convincingly offered proof that Sam Scales had
been shot to death in the trunk of my Lincoln
while it was parked in my garage. While the case
was missing the murder weapon, and none of the
evidence could put me in the garage pulling the
trigger, it was what defense attorneys call
common-sense evidence. The victim was killed
in the defendant's car in the defendant's garage.
Common sense dictates that the defendant was
responsible. There was, of course, room in that
chain of circumstances for reasonable doubt, but
sometimes common sense was an overriding
factor in a juror's decision. And whenever I had
checked the faces of the jurors during the
morning session, I never saw any skepticism.
They were paying rapt attention to the parade of
witnesses that wanted to bury me in guilt.

Two of the witnesses I did not even bother to
question on cross. There had been nothing in
their testimony I could attack, no loose thread I
could use to unravel their claims. With the
ballistics expert, I thought I scored a point when
I asked if any of the bullet slugs recovered in the
case showed markings from a silencer being used

on the weapon. His answer, as I knew it would be, was that sound-suppression devices do not come into contact with the discharged bullet, so it is impossible to tell if such an attachment was on the murder weapon.

But then Dana Berg took the point away and scored her own when she used my question on redirect to bring out from her expert the fact that sound suppressors do not reduce the report of a gunshot to anything even approaching silence.

I likened going into courtside holding during the lunch break to going into the locker room at halftime. My team was down and I felt the weight of dread as Deputy Chan led me into the holding cell. After securing me, he would bring Maggie McPherson in with lunch, and I was sure we would dissect the morning session to see if there was any way to repair the damage when we moved into the defense phase of the trial.

But those thoughts disappeared like smoke after I went through the steel door from the courtroom and was directed by Chan down the hallway to the attorney-client room. I immediately heard a voice echoing off the steel and concrete walls. A female voice. As we passed the holding cells on either side, I looked through the bars on the right and saw Dana Berg sitting on a bench in the cell. I remembered now that she had gotten up from the prosecution table the moment the judge had left the bench. Now she was in the holding cell, but it wasn't her voice I'd heard. It was coming from another woman but I could not see her because the cell extended to the right along a concrete wall beyond the barred door.

I knew the voice. I just couldn't place it.

Chan delivered me to the attorney-client room.

'Hey, who's that Berg is with?' I asked casually.

'Your old girlfriend,' Chan said offhandedly.

'What girlfriend?'

'You'll find out soon enough.'

'Come on, Chan. If I'm going to find out, you might as well tell me.'

'I actually don't know. It's all on the down-low. All I heard was that she was brought down from Chowchilla.'

He slid the solid steel door closed behind me and I was left alone with the single clue as to who was in the cell with Berg. Chowchilla was up in California's Central Valley and the location of one of the biggest women's prisons in the state. While my client list ran 80 percent or more male, I had a few female clients in the prison system. I usually didn't track my clients once they were adjudicated and sent off to prison, but I knew of one former client who, last I heard, was serving a fifteen-year stretch for manslaughter in Chowchilla. It was her voice, distorted by echoes off steel and concrete, that I now recognized.

Lisa Trammel. She was the October surprise.

The door slid back open to allow Maggie to come in with the bag containing our lunch. But I had just lost my appetite. After the door banged closed again, I told her why.

'They've got a witness they're bringing in and we need to fight it,' I began.

'Who?' Maggie asked.

'You hear the voices in the other cell? That's her. Lisa Trammel.'

'Lisa Trammel. Why do I know that name?'

'She was a client. She was charged with murder and I got her off.'

I saw the prosecutor in Maggie react.

'Jesus, now I remember,' she said.

'They just brought her down from Chowchilla to testify,' I said.

'About what?'

'I don't know. But I know the voice and I know she's in there with Dana Berg. Her case was the one I hung on Opparizio in court. He was the straw man. I got him to take the Fifth.'

'Okay, let's think about this.'

Maggie started opening the bag and taking out wrapped sandwiches Lorna had ordered from Nickel Diner. Lorna knew I liked their BLT and that was what I got.

Maggie held her sandwich up to take a bite but first said, 'Come on, Mickey. They don't bring somebody down from Chowchilla on a whim. There's something. Think.'

'Look, you have to understand that she's a liar,' I said. 'A good liar. She had me convinced nine years ago when we went to trial. I mean, totally convinced.'

'Okay, so what can she lie about that will help the prosecution here?'

I shook my head. I didn't know.

'It could be anything,' I said. 'She was a

longtime client. I handled her foreclosure defense, then the murder. She was a lot like Sam Scales, a skilled liar who eventually played me and never —'

I snapped my fingers as I got it.

'Money. Like Sam, she didn't pay me. Berg is going to use her to support motive. She's going to lie about the money, say I threatened her or something.'

'Okay, I should handle this out there. First the objection, then the cross if she's allowed to testify. It will look bad you going after her.'

'Agreed.'

'So tell me everything I need to know.'

Thirty minutes later lunch was over and I was returned to the courtroom. Cisco, back from Arizona, was standing at the railing. It looked like he had something urgent to say. I spoke to Chan as he was removing my handcuffs.

'All right if I talk to my investigator here?'

'Make it fast. The judge is ready to come out.'

I stepped over to the rail so we could speak confidentially.

'Two things,' Cisco said. 'First, we lost Opparizio in Scottsdale.'

'What do you mean?' I said. 'I thought your guys were going to stay with him.'

'They were. They set up on his room and were ready to go whenever he made a move but he never did. I just got a call. Housekeeping cleared his room this morning. He's gone. His car is still there but he's gone.'

'Damn it.'

'Sorry, Mick.'

415

'Something's going on. Tell them to keep looking for him. He might come back for his car.'

'They're on the car. They're also trying to figure out how he got out of the room. They had cameras set up in the hallway.'

'Okay, what's the other thing?'

'Well, you remember Herb Dahl, that sleazeball movie producer who got hooked up with Lisa Trammel back in the day?'

'What about him?'

'He's sitting out in the hallway by the courtroom door. I think he might be here as a witness.'

I nodded. The picture was becoming clearer.

'They also brought Lisa down from Chowchilla,' I said. 'She's in holding and ready to go too.'

'They weren't on the wit list,' Cisco said.

'Yeah, it's an October surprise. Listen, I just thought of something. Step out and call Lorna, tell her to pull the Lisa Trammel file and bring in the letters she's sent me over the years. Get them to Maggie ASAP. That means you might have to wait out on Spring Street for her.'

'You got it.'

'And let me know as soon as you hear something on Opparizio.'

'Will do.'

Cisco headed out of the courtroom. I got to my seat just as Deputy Chan announced that court was in session and the judge emerged from chambers. Maggie stood up as I sat down, a signal to the judge that there was business to attend to before bringing in the jury. I didn't get

416

a chance to tell her about Herb Dahl or the hate letters Lisa Trammel had sent me from prison. I looked over at the prosecution table and saw Berg follow Maggie in rising to her feet.

'Back on the record,' Warfield said. 'Ms. McPherson, I saw you standing first. Do you wish to address the court?'

'Yes, Your Honor,' Maggie said. 'It has come to the defense's attention that the state is going to introduce a witness that is not on any list the defense was given. This witness is a convicted killer who has lied under oath in the past and will do so again today if she is allowed to testify.'

'Well, this is all news to me,' Warfield said. 'Ms. Berg, I see you standing as well. Do you wish to address this issue?'

'Yes, Your Honor,' Berg said.

While Berg identified Lisa Trammel as the witness and gave her argument for putting her on the stand, I tugged on Maggie's sleeve and she bent down to hear me whisper.

'She's got a backup witness out in the hallway,' I said. 'A movie producer named Herb Dahl. Lisa and Dahl were in cahoots against me during the trial.'

Maggie just nodded, then straightened back up and refocused on Berg's statement to the judge.

'It is pattern evidence, Your Honor,' Berg said. 'Evidence of prior bad acts in terms of how the defendant treated his clients, demanding money from them and then making threats and carrying out those threats when no money was exchanged. Additionally, I have a second

417

witness named Herbert Dahl, who has firsthand knowledge of these activities and was threatened over money by Mr. Haller as well.'

'You still have not addressed why these witnesses are suddenly appearing in my courtroom today without notice to the defense or the court,' Warfield said. 'I know Ms. McPherson's next argument — that the defense has been sandbagged by this. I think it is a very valid argument.'

Berg disagreed, saying there was no sandbagging because Trammel and Dahl were not even known to her until Saturday, when she opened a letter Trammel had sent from prison after seeing a television report about the Sam Scales case. The prosecutor offered the letter, including the postmarked envelope, to the judge for examination. She handed a copy to Maggie for us to share.

'Judge, that letter arrived on my desk last Wednesday,' Berg said. 'You will see it is postmarked the day before. As you know, we were in trial last week. I had no time to go through the mail. I did that on Saturday and found the letter. I immediately contacted Detective Drucker and we drove up to Chowchilla to talk to Ms. Trammel and gauge her potential as a witness. We heard her story and believed it was something the jury should hear — if we could find a way to back it up. She had given us the name Herbert Dahl. While Ms. Trammel was being transported down here yesterday, Detective Drucker finished his testimony and then went to interview Mr. Dahl.

There is no subterfuge here, no sandbagging. We brought these witnesses to the attention of the court as soon as they were determined to be truthful and important for the jury to hear.'

While Maggie pushed back, I studied the letter. It laid out a onesided story of how badly I supposedly had treated Lisa Trammel. She blamed me for putting her in prison and leaving her penniless. She claimed that I operated on greed and the constant need for media adoration — the two qualities that I believed best described Lisa herself.

In the end, Maggie could not swing the judge. Warfield ruled that Trammel and Dahl could testify and it would be up to the jury to decide whether they were truthful and if their stories had any merit.

'However,' Warfield said, 'I will grant the defense ample time to prepare for these witnesses if necessary. Ms. McPherson, how long would you need?'

'May I confer with counsel?' Maggie asked.

'Of course,' the judge said.

Maggie sat down and huddled with me.

'I'm sorry,' she said. 'I should have been able to stop this.'

'No worries,' I said. 'You did your best. But don't worry. The prosecution just made a big mistake.'

'Really? It seems to me that she just got her way.'

'Yes, but we can use Trammel to open the door to Opparizio. Then we destroy her on the stand.'

'So, how much time to prepare?'

'None. Let's go right at her.'

'Are you sure?'

'I just told Cisco to get Lorna to pull the file on Lisa Trammel. I think we may be able to counter their October surprise with our own little surprise.'

'Good. Tell me more.'

46

I had heard Lisa Trammel's voice but had not seen her in courtside holding. She was now walked into the courtroom by Deputy Chan. I saw a woman who was almost unrecognizable to me. Her hair had turned gray and was cropped short in a man's cut. Her paper-white skin seemed to be stretched over her bones, as she looked to be half the weight of the woman I had known and defended a decade before. She wore a baggy orange jumpsuit and had a blurry blue prison tattoo — a line of stars — arching over her left eyebrow. All eyes from the jury were on this curiosity as she stood to be sworn in.

Once Trammel was seated on the witness stand, Dana Berg moved to the lectern and began to draw out her story.

'Ms. Trammel, where do you currently reside?'

'I'm at the Central California Women's Prison in Chowchilla.'

'And how long have you been there?'

'Uh, six years. Before that, I spent three down at Corona.'

'That's a prison, too, in Corona?'

'Yes.'

'Why are you incarcerated?'

'I was sentenced to fifteen years for manslaughter.'

'And what were the details of that crime?'

'I killed my husband. It was an abusive

relationship and I ended it.'

I was watching the jurors more than I was watching Trammel. How they reacted to her would influence how Maggie would conduct her cross-examination. For the moment, they were attentive, even having just come from lunch. Trammel was enough of a change of pace to keep them interested and alert. I noticed that the Hollywood Bowl chef was leaning forward and sitting at the edge of her seat.

'Are you familiar with the defendant in this case, Michael Haller?' Berg asked.

'Yes, he was my lawyer,' Trammel said.

'Can you point him out for the jury?'

'Yes.'

Trammel pointed at me and for the first time our eyes locked. I saw the hate burning behind hers.

'Can you tell us about that relationship?' Berg asked.

Trammel was slow to break her stare away from me.

'Yes,' she said. 'I hired him about eleven years ago to try to save my home. I was a single mother of a nine-year-old son and I had gotten behind on the mortgage and the bank was foreclosing on me. I hired him to help me after I got a flyer in the mail.'

Trammel had come to me during the wave of foreclosures that swept across the country following the 2008 financial crisis. Foreclosure defense was the growth sector in law and I signed on like many other criminal defense lawyers. I made a lot of money, kept several people in their homes, and unfortunately met and agreed to defend Lisa Trammel.

'Did you have a job then?' Berg asked.

'I was a teacher,' Trammel said.

'Okay, and was Mr. Haller able to help you?'

'Yes and no. He delayed the inevitable. He filed papers and challenged the bank's actions, and he delayed things more than a year.'

'And then what happened?'

'I was arrested. I got accused of killing the man at the bank who was taking away my home.'

'What was his name?'

'Mitchell Bondurant.'

'And were you put on trial for the murder of Mitchell Bondurant?'

'Yes.'

'And who was your attorney?'

'It was him. Haller. The case got a lot of attention. In the press, you know. And he, like, begged me to let him defend me.'

'Do you know why that was?'

'Like I said, the case got a lot of media attention. It was free publicity for him and that was the deal. I didn't have any money for a lawyer, so I said yes.'

'And the case went to trial?'

'Yes, and I was found innocent.'

'You mean not guilty?'

'Yes, not guilty. By the jury.'

Trammel turned and looked at the jury as she said this last part, as if to say, *a jury believed me before and you must believe me now.* My eyes scanned down the two rows of jurors — their eyes all on Trammel — and then continued into the crowded gallery. I saw my daughter watching with rapt attention as well.

'Did there come a time when you had a financial dispute with Mr. Haller?' Berg asked.

'Yes, there did,' Trammel said.

'And what was that about?'

'There was a movie producer who had attended the trial and was interested in making a movie about the case. Because of the foreclosure angle, it was a story that spoke to the time and people would be interested, especially because I was innocent, you know?'

'What was the movie producer's name?'

'Herb Dahl. He had a deal at Archway Pictures, where he brought them projects. He said they were interested in the movie.'

'And how did that become a dispute with Mr. Haller?'

'Well, he told me he wanted to get paid. Halfway through the trial, he said he wanted part of the movie money.'

I slowly shook my head at the lie. It was an involuntary response, not meant for the jury. But Berg noticed and turned her attention from Trammel to the judge.

'Your Honor, could you please instruct Mr. Haller not to make demonstrations distracting to the jury?'

Warfield looked at me.

'Mr. Haller, you know better,' she said. 'Please refrain from showing reaction to the testimony.'

'Yes, Your Honor,' I said. 'But it's hard not to react to lies about your — '

'Mr. Haller,' the judge barked. 'You know

424

better than to make such a comment as well.'

The judge closed her mouth in a tight line as she probably considered slapping me with a contempt citation. She thought better of it.

'You've been warned,' she finally said. 'Proceed, Ms. Berg.'

'Thank you, Your Honor,' the prosecutor said. 'Ms. Trammel, did Mr. Haller tell you how much money he wanted?'

'Yes,' Trammel said. 'A quarter million dollars.'

'And did you agree to pay him that?'

'No. I didn't have it, and Herb Dahl said I would be lucky to get half of that as an up-front payment from the studio for my story.'

'How did Mr. Haller respond to that?'

'He threatened me. He said there would be consequences if I didn't pay him what he deserved.'

'What happened next?'

'I was found not guilty and I told him a deal was a deal. He got good publicity for the case, especially when I was found innocent. I said that he would probably get paid when they made a movie because they would need to use his name and what he did at the trial and all.'

'Did he accept that?'

'No. He said that there were consequences and I would be sorry.'

'Then what happened?'

'The police came to my house with a search warrant and they found my husband. He was buried in the backyard. I had buried him after he died. I was afraid that nobody would believe me

425

about the abuse and that I would lose my son.'

Trammel was tearful now. It could be heard in her voice rather than seen on her face. To me it was all an act. A good one. Berg underlined the moment with a strategic pause and I saw the jury watching the witness closely, looks of sympathy on some of their faces, including the Hollywood Bowl chef.

This was an unmitigated disaster.

I leaned toward Maggie and whispered.

'This is so much bullshit,' I said. 'She's an even better con artist now than she was back then.'

At that moment, I thought I saw sympathy on Maggie's face as well. It made me not want to turn to see my own daughter's face.

'Did Mr. Haller represent you in the new case involving your husband's death?' Berg asked.

'No, no way,' Trammel said. 'He was the one who told them I had buried Jeffrey. I needed somebody I could — '

'Objection, hearsay,' Maggie said.

'Sustained,' Warfield said. 'The answer is no. The jury will disregard the rest of the answer.'

Berg retooled for a moment, obviously looking for a way to get to the answer she wanted — that I had ratted out Trammel when she wouldn't pay me. It wouldn't be much of a leap from that to believing I would kill Sam Scales when he didn't pay me.

'Did there come a time when you began to suspect that you could not trust Mr. Haller as your attorney?' she asked.

'Yes,' Trammel said.

426

'And when was that?'

'When they found my husband's body and I got arrested for murder. I knew he had told the police.'

'I object again,' Maggie said. 'Assumes facts not in evidence. Ms. Berg is trying to put something in front of the jury that is pure speculation. There is no record anywhere that Mr. Haller or any member of his staff broke the rules of the attorney-client relationship, yet the prosecution persists in —'

'You told them!' Trammel yelled, pointing her finger at me. 'You were the only one who knew. This was the payback —'

'*Silence!*' Warfield yelled. 'There is an objection before the court and the witness will remain silent.'

The judge's voice had cut Trammel off like an ax coming down. She paused and looked at all parties before continuing.

'Ms. Berg, you need to school and control your witness on what is hearsay and what is not,' she said. 'One more improper outburst and you will both be held in contempt.'

She turned to the jury.

'The jury will disregard the statements of the witness,' she said. 'They are hearsay and not evidence.'

She turned back to the attorneys.

'You may continue, Ms. Berg,' she said. 'Carefully.'

As attention in the courtroom returned to Berg, I heard a low whisper from behind and turned to see Cisco offering a file across the rail.

I tapped Maggie on the arm and signaled her to take the file. She immediately opened it on the table between us.

Meanwhile, Berg was only too happy to end her direct examination of Trammel. She had gotten the message to the jury that I was vindictive when it came to money.

'Your Honor, I have nothing further for this witness,' she said.

The judge threw it to the defense, and Maggie asked for a brief recess before she questioned the witness. The judge gave us fifteen minutes and we spent the time reading the correspondence that had come in from Trammel over the years.

When court reconvened, Maggie was ready. She got up with her legal pad and went to the lectern. She came out aggressive.

'Ms. Trammel, have you ever lied to the police?' she asked.

'No,' Trammel said.

'You've never lied to the police?'

'I said no.'

'How about under oath? Have you ever lied under oath?'

'No.'

'Aren't you lying right now under oath?'

'No, I — '

Berg objected, saying McPherson was badgering the witness, and the judge sustained the objection, telling Maggie to move on. She did.

'Isn't it true, Ms. Trammel, that early on, you agreed to share any movie revenues from your story with Mr. Haller?'

'No, he wanted publicity, not money. That was the agreement.'

'Did you kill Mitchell Bondurant?'

Trammel involuntarily pulled back from the witness-stand microphone as the question came out of the blue. Berg stood and objected again, reminding the judge that Trammel had been found not guilty in the Bondurant case.

'Everyone knows that a not-guilty verdict is not a finding of innocence,' Maggie argued.

The judge ruled that Trammel could answer the question.

'No, I did not kill Mitchell Bondurant,' she answered pointedly.

'Then, was it established at trial who did?' Maggie asked.

'There was a suspect named, yes.'

'Who was that?'

'A man named Louis Opparizio. A Las Vegas mobster. He was brought in to testify, but he took the Fifth because he didn't want to.'

'Why was Louis Opparizio a suspect in Mr. Bondurant's murder?'

'Because they had shady dealings together and Mr. Bondurant had contacted the FBI about it. There was an investigation starting and then Mr. Bondurant got killed.'

'After you were found not guilty, was Opparizio charged with the crime?'

'No, he never was.'

We now had Opparizio on the trial record and known to the jury. If nothing else came out of Maggie's cross, that was the one thing we could take into the defense phase and work with.

429

But Maggie wasn't finished. She asked the judge for a moment and then walked to the defense table, where she retrieved the letters that had been in the Trammel file. She had planned it that way. She wanted Trammel to track her movements as she went to pick up the loose pages. She wanted Trammel to know what was coming.

'Now, Ms. Trammel, you clearly blame Mr. Haller for your current situation in prison, correct?' she asked.

'I've owned what I did,' Trammel said. 'I didn't go to trial. I pleaded guilty and have taken full responsibility.'

'But you blame Mr. Haller for the police finding your husband's body buried in the backyard, do you not?'

'I thought the judge said I can't answer that.'

'You can speak for yourself. You can't speak for him.'

'Then, yes, I blame him.'

'But isn't it true that you are the one who has threatened Mr. Haller and repeatedly told him that there would be consequences for his actions?'

'No, that's not true.'

'Do you remember writing Mr. Haller a series of letters from prison?'

Trammel paused before answering.

'It was a long time ago,' she finally said. 'I don't remember.'

'What about more recently,' Maggie pressed. 'Say, a year ago. Did you send a letter from prison to Mr. Haller?'

'I don't remember.'

'What is your inmate number at the prison in Chowchilla?'

'A-V-one-eight-one-seven-four.'

Maggie looked up at the judge.

'Judge, may I approach the witness?' she asked.

After receiving permission from the judge, Maggie handed an envelope to Trammel and asked her to open it and remove the letter that was inside.

'Do you recognize that as a letter you sent last April ninth to Mr. Haller?' she asked.

Berg stood to object. She couldn't know what was in the letter but she knew it was bad.

'Your Honor, I have not been shown the document,' she said. 'It could be from anyone.'

'Overruled,' Warfield said. 'You'll get your chance when Ms. McPherson is done authenticating the letter through this unexpected witness, Ms. Berg. You may continue, Ms. McPherson.'

'Is that your prisoner number on the outside of the envelope, Ms. Trammel?' Maggie asked.

'Yes, but I didn't write it there,' Trammel said.

'But that is in fact your signature at the end of the letter, correct, Ms. Trammel?'

'It looks like it, but I can't be sure. It could be forged.'

'Please examine these four other letters and confirm that they also bear your signature and inmate number.'

Trammel looked at the letters put down in front of her.

'Yes,' she finally said. 'It looks like my

signature, but I can't be sure. There are a lot of women in prison who are there because they forged signatures on checks.'

'And you say it is possible that they forged letters to your attorney over a span of nine years?' Maggie asked.

'I don't know. Anything is possible.'

Except it wasn't, and Maggie was destroying her.

'Your Honor,' she said. 'The defense offers in evidence what will be marked as defense exhibits A through E.'

Maggie handed the exhibits to the clerk to be marked.

'If further authentication is needed, Mr. Haller's office manager can testify to receiving the letters and securing them over the years in a file,' she said.

'Let's take a look at these letters,' Warfield said.

I trailed Maggie to the bench for the sidebar. The judge quickly scanned the original letters while Berg was handed copies.

'As an officer of the court and a prosecutor for twenty-plus years, I can represent to the court that the state prisons do not allow inmates to send letters anonymously,' Maggie said. 'That was why her inmate number was written on the return address of each envelope.'

'Even if the letters are from her, there is a relevancy issue here, Judge,' Berg said.

'Oh, they're relevant all right, Ms. Berg,' the judge said. 'She just sat there and accused the defendant of threatening her over money. The exhibits are admitted. Ms. McPherson, you may proceed.'

We returned to our positions and Maggie approached the witness stand. She put another letter down in front of Trammel.

'Ms. Trammel, did you write this and send it to Mr. Haller from Chowchilla?' she asked.

Trammel looked at the letter and took a long time to read it.

'The thing is,' she said, 'I was diagnosed as bipolar at the inmate-reception center nine years ago, so sometimes I kind of slip into a fugue and do things I don't always remember doing.'

'Is that your inmate number on the envelope?'

'Yes. But I don't know who put it on there.'

'Is that your name on the letter?'

'Well, yes, but anybody could have written that.'

'Could you read the letter to the jury, please?'

Trammel looked at Berg and then at the judge, hoping someone would say she didn't have to read what she had sent to me.

'Go ahead, Ms. Trammel,' Warfield said. 'Read the letter.'

Trammel looked at the letter for a long moment before finally beginning to read.

'*Dear Asshole-at-law,*

Just wanted you to know that I haven't forgotten about you. Never. You ruined everything and you will one day answer for it. I have not seen my son in six years. Because of you! You are a piece of shit to the end. *You call yourself a lawyer but you are nothing. I hope you have found God because you will need him.'*

I watched the jury as she read it. I could see that Trammel's credibility disintegrated with each word she read. And some of that probably rubbed off on Berg. The prosecutor sat at her table, realizing that she had been blinded by greed. Greed for one more piece of evidence against me. She had heard Trammel's story through Drucker and thought it was the thing that would slam the prison door shut on me.

But her October surprise turned into a December dud. She didn't even bother to call Herb Dahl into the courtroom to testify. He was told to go home.

It was unclear whether the misstep with Lisa Trammel would have much impact on the jury, especially after the morning's delivery of conclusive evidence about Sam Scales being killed in my garage while I was apparently on the premises. Either way, by the day's end, Berg felt good enough about her case to bring it to an end. Whatever potential witnesses she still had in the wings, she decided to hold them for rebuttal and a big finish.

'Your Honor,' she said, 'the state rests.'

47

I spent a restless night in my cell, listening to the random echoes of desperate men calling out in the dark. I heard steel doors bang and incongruous laughter from the deputies on the midnight shift. At times my body shook in physical reaction to the gravity of the moment. How could I sleep when I knew the next two days would determine the rest of my life? When deep down I knew that, should things go wrong, I would choose not to live this way for very long? I would make my escape one way or the other and I would be free.

Incarceration does that. Makes you think about what is beyond the last wall. They can take your belt and shoelaces away but they can't stop you from going over it. I've had three clients go over that wall in the weeks after conviction. Now that I had personally experienced the prospect of long-term incarceration, I understood their choice and respected it. I knew it would be my choice as well.

Deputy Pressley got me to the courthouse early and I was in courtside holding, waiting for trial to begin, when Maggie and Cisco were allowed back for a precourt conference. I could tell by their faces that there was bad news.

'Still no sign of Opparizio?' I guessed.

'No,' Maggie said. 'It's worse.'

'He's dead,' Cisco said.

'We have to rethink everything,' Maggie said. 'We need to reset the order of wit — '

'Wait a minute, wait a minute,' I said. 'Back up. What happened? What do you mean he's dead?'

'They whacked him,' Cisco said. 'His body was found last night. He was dumped on the side of the road near Kingman.'

'That's on the road up to Vegas. How did this happen when twenty-four hours ago your guys supposedly had him locked down?'

'Remember I told you they had a camera on his door? They reviewed the tape this morning, and Opparizio got room service Monday night. No big deal, he took all his meals in. But this time his dinner was rolled in on a cart with a tablecloth on it.'

'That's how they got him out?'

'Yeah, hidden in the cart. I think a guy posing as a room-service waiter whacked him in the room, put him under the cart, and wheeled him out. He had intercepted the food delivery at the service elevator. My guys found the real room-service guy at his apartment. He admitted he got paid to turn over his red jacket and go home. The guy was drunk as a skunk.'

'So how did this . . . room-service hit man know where he was?'

'I figure Opparizio called somebody and revealed that he'd been hit with our subpoena. They told him they'd get him out of there and set up the room-service gag. Only then they whacked him.'

436

'Why?'

'Who knows? They probably didn't want to risk him testifying. They knew he was compromised.'

I looked at Maggie to see if she had a take.

'It could be any number of reasons,' she said. 'It's safe to say he became a liability. But we can't dwell on that, Mickey. This changes everything. What is our defense now? How do we point the finger at Opparizio when he's dead?'

'What about Bosch?' I asked. 'Does he know about this?'

'I told him,' Cisco said. 'He's got contacts in Arizona and Nevada from his LAPD days. He was going to make some calls, see what he could find out.'

I sat in silence for a long moment. I was brooding, trying to figure out how to reboot a third-party-culpability defense without the third party. I knew that Opparizio's death did not change the defense theory, but as Maggie had said, it made it harder to point a finger at him.

'All right,' I finally said. 'We need to get through today and then regroup and see where we are tonight. Who do we have who's ready to go?'

'Well, we've got Schultz, the EPA guy,' Maggie said. 'He got in last night. I told him we probably were going to hold him till tomorrow but we can get him ready for today. He's just over at the Biltmore.'

'Do it,' I said. 'We also have Drucker. We can put him on first. Then go with the EPA guy.'

'We supposedly have the Ventura County

437

detective who arrested Sam the last time coming in today,' Cisco said. 'Harry talked him into it. But that's not a subpoena, so I'll believe it when I see him. And we have Moira from the Redwood and the Rohypnol expert on subpoena. As soon as we're done here, I'll see who's out in the hallway.'

'What about Opparizio's girlfriend?' I asked.

'We served her the same night we papered Opparizio,' Cisco said. 'She's supposed to come in Thursday, but now with him dead, she probably split and is hiding. We took the eyes off her to put them on Opparizio, so . . . '

'We don't know where she is,' I finished. 'So we don't have her unless she decides to honor the subpoena. I would put the chances of that at zero.'

'We also have you,' Maggie said.

'I wasn't going to testify,' I said.

'Well, you may have to now,' she said. 'Without Opparizio to pin the tail on, we're probably going to need you to pull it all together.'

'If I testify, who knows what Death Row Dana will bring up,' I said. 'My whole history will be out there. The pills, the rehab, everything.'

'I'm not worried,' Maggie said. 'You can hold your own against her.'

I was quiet for a few moments while thinking it through.

'All right, let's start with Drucker and then the others,' I finally said. 'Hopefully we won't have to decide about me till tomorrow. What about Ruth, the FBI agent?'

'I've called, left messages,' Maggie said. 'I'll keep trying.'

The door opened and Deputy Chan stuck his head in and gave us a five-minute warning. I stood up to go but then thought of something.

'What about Milton? Did we get the cell records?'

'Yes, I was going to tell you about it later,' Maggie said. 'I didn't want to pile on the bad news. We got the records but they don't help.'

'Why not?' I asked.

'He did get a text at the exact time on the video,' Maggie said. 'But it was from another Metro cop in the civic center surveillance that night. He was just asking when they were going to eat and where.'

'Any chance they dummied it up?' I asked.

'The documents we received look legit,' Maggie said. 'We can check for tampering but we aren't going to be able to do anything with it this week.'

'Okay, so I guess we drop it,' I said.

'The problem is, the same stuff goes to Dana in discovery,' Maggie said. 'She won't drop it. You can count on her introducing it in rebuttal.'

That was bad news and I now wished I hadn't brought it up. Between losing Opparizio and handing the prosecution some solid rebuttal evidence, the defense was stumbling before it was even out of the gate. I knew that going head-to-head with Drucker again was going to be a challenge, but I needed to put a couple hits on the house.

Five minutes later, I was at the defense table

when Judge Warfield entered and took the bench. She seated the jury, then looked down at me and told me to call my first witness. She seemed slightly surprised and disappointed when I called Kent Drucker. I think she thought recalling a prosecution witness was a weak way to start my case.

Drucker seemed surprised himself. He had been sitting in the gallery but now proceeded through the gate and to the witness stand, stopping by the prosecution table to retrieve the murder book in case he was called on for details he didn't quite remember.

The detective was reminded by the judge that he was still under oath from his first round of testimony.

'Detective Drucker, how many times did you search my home?' I asked.

'Twice,' Drucker said. 'The day after the killing and then in January, when we searched it again.'

'And how many times did you search my warehouse?'

'Just the once.'

'My other two Lincolns?'

'Once.'

'Now, would you describe these searches as thorough?'

'We try to be as thorough as possible.'

'You *try*?'

'We are thorough.'

'If you were so thorough in the search of my house, why did you need to search it a second time?'

'Because the investigation was ongoing and as new information was gathered, we realized that we needed to search again for different evidence.'

'Now, one of the state's experts testified yesterday that ballistic markings on the bullets that killed Sam Scales indicated that the murder weapon was a twenty-two-caliber Beretta handgun. Do you agree with that?'

'Yes, I do.'

'And after all the thorough searches of my properties and cars, did you find such a weapon?'

'No, we didn't.'

'Did you find any ammunition for such a gun?'

'No.'

'Your experts also testified yesterday that there was convincing evidence that the murder of Sam Scales occurred in the garage located below my house. Do you agree with that?'

'Yes.'

'The coroner testified that time of death was between ten o'clock and midnight. Are you in agreement with that estimate?'

'Yes.'

'Did you conduct a canvass of the neighborhood where the murder occurred?'

'Not me personally, but we did conduct a canvass.'

'Who conducted it?'

'Other detectives and patrol officers at the direction of my partner.'

'How long did that take?'

441

'It was about three days before we talked to everyone on the block. We had to keep going back until we got to everyone.'

'You were being thorough, yes?'

'Yes, we had a checklist of every house on the block and we made sure we spoke to someone from every address.'

'How many said they heard gunshots between ten and midnight on the night of the murders?'

'None. No one heard anything.'

'And based on your experience and knowledge, did you draw a conclusion from that?'

'Not really. There could have been a lot of factors.'

'But you are sure, based on the evidence, that Mr. Scales was killed in my garage?'

'Yes.'

'Do you assume the garage door was closed during the time of the killing to help prevent the gunshots from being heard?'

'We considered that but it's speculation.'

'And you don't want to speculate in a murder case, correct?'

'Correct.'

'Now, without revealing any results, you told the jury during your earlier testimony that the LAPD conducted sound tests in the garage, correct?'

'Yes, we did.'

'Again, not getting into any results, did you measure the sound of gunfire from inside the house?'

'I'm not sure I understand.'

'When you were test-firing guns in my garage,

442

did you have anyone upstairs in the bedroom to determine if those shots could be heard?'

'No, we did not.'

'Why not?'

'It just wasn't part of our investigation at that point.'

My hope was that Drucker's answers would give credibility to the possibility that I had slept through the killing of Sam Scales in the garage below my house.

'Okay, let's move on,' I said. 'Did your canvass of the neighborhood produce any reports of other sounds or unusual occurrences at the time of the murder?'

'One neighbor reported hearing the voices of two men arguing the night of the shooting,' Drucker said.

'Really? But you did not tell the jury about that during your earlier testimony, did you?'

'No, I did not.'

'Why is that? Wasn't two men arguing on the night of the killing important to the case?'

'After we received the toxicology report from the medical examiner, we determined that it was unlikely that Sam Scales was conscious at the time of the killing.'

'So the neighbor who heard two men arguing was wrong or lying?'

'We believe she was mistaken. It could have been a TV she heard, or the time could have been different. It wasn't clear.'

'So you discarded it and didn't bother telling the jury.'

'No, it wasn't discarded. It was — '

443

'Is that what you do, Detective? If something doesn't fit with your theory of the case, you just hide it from the jury?'

Berg objected for a variety of reasons and Warfield sustained them all, admonishing me to let the witness finish his answers.

'Go ahead, Detective,' I said. 'Finish your answer.'

'We evaluate every potential witness,' Drucker said. 'We found the information from this witness not to be credible. No one else heard an argument, and there was an indication that the witness may have been confused about the night in question. We have not hidden anything from the jury.'

I asked the judge for a moment and then walked over to the defense table, where I leaned down to whisper to Maggie.

'Do you have that arrest report from Ventura?' I whispered.

Maggie was ready with the report and handed me a file.

'Okay,' I said. 'Anything else I should get on the record before the big finish?'

Maggie thought for a long moment before responding.

'I don't think so,' she said. 'I think it's time to go for it.'

I nodded.

'Is Schultz here yet?' I asked.

'Cisco texted,' she said. 'He's out in the hallway and ready to go.'

I held up the arrest report.

'What about this guy Rountree?' I asked.

'He's out there, too, sitting with Harry,' Maggie said. 'But so far the bartender is a no-show.'

'All right, then. Depending on how this next part goes, I might take Detective Rountree next.'

'Sounds good. And by the way, don't be obvious about it but Agent Ruth is sitting in the back row.'

I stared at Maggie for a long moment. I didn't know what to make of the FBI agent's presence. Was she here to watch and report? Or had the death of Louis Opparizio changed things?

'Mr. Haller?' the judge said. 'We're waiting.'

I nodded once to Maggie and walked back to the lectern. My focus returned to Drucker.

'Detective, you testified earlier that Sam Scales was using the name Walter Lennon at the time of his death. True?'

'Yes, if I testified to it, it's true. You don't have to ask again.'

'I'll remember that, Detective. Thank you. What else did you learn about Walter Lennon?'

'Where he lived. Where he supposedly worked.'

'Where was it that he supposedly worked?'

'He told his landlord he worked at a refinery called BioGreen near where he was living in San Pedro. We could not confirm that.'

'Did you try?'

'We went to BioGreen. They had no record of a Walter Lennon or Samuel Scales as an employee. The head of HR did not recognize a photo of Sam Scales.'

'You left it there?'

'Yes.'

'Do you know what BioGreen does?'

'It's a refinery. It recycles oil. Makes clean fuel.'

'Would the oil it recycles be considered grease?'

Drucker hesitated as he realized that he had just stepped into a hole.

'I don't know,' he finally said.

'You don't know,' I said. 'Did you ask?'

'We were talking to the personnel manager. I doubt she would know the answer to that question.'

I almost smiled. Drucker was coming off as defensive and trying to turn an obvious shortcoming in his investigation into pushback against me.

'Thank you, Detective,' I said. 'Can you tell me if you have ever heard the phrase *bleeding the beast?*'

Again, Drucker took time to think.

'I can't say I have,' he said.

'Then we'll move on,' I said. 'Can you tell the jury what part in this case Louis Opparizio played?'

'Uh, no, I can't.'

'Do you know that name?'

'Yes, I've heard it.'

'In what context?'

'It came up in this case. A witness mentioned it yesterday, and prior to that, people were talking about the methods of distraction you would use and that I should be ready for.'

'Well, I don't want to distract you, Detective,

446

so we'll move on. Can you tell the jury, did you research the criminal record of Sam Scales after he was identified as the victim?'

'Yes, of course.'

'And what did you find?'

'That he had an extensive record as a con man and a fraud. But you know about that.'

Drucker was now getting surly, but that was okay with me. It meant I was getting under his skin. That wasn't a bad thing.

'Can you tell the jury the details of his last arrest?'

Drucker opened the murder book.

'He was arrested for running a fraudulent online fundraising scheme for victims of the music festival shooting out in Las Vegas,' Drucker said. 'He was convicted and — '

'Let me stop you right there, Detective,' I said. 'I asked about the last time Sam Scales was arrested, not convicted.'

'They're one and the same. The Vegas case.'

'What about his arrest in Ventura County eleven months before his death?'

Drucker looked down at the open murder book in front of him.

'I have nothing on that,' he said.

I opened the file Maggie had given me. The moment was precious. I knew I was about to put another hit on the house — a big hit — and it was a moment any trial lawyer would savor.

'Your Honor, may I approach the witness?' I asked.

The judge granted permission and I walked forward with the arrest report that had been anonymously slipped under my front door. I handed a copy to the clerk and then one to Dana Berg before putting a third copy down in front of Drucker. As I made my way back to the lectern, I casually checked the gallery, nodded surreptitiously to my daughter, and looked beyond her to the back row. I saw Agent Dawn Ruth. We locked eyes for a moment before I turned back to face Drucker. I knew I had to move quickly because as soon as Berg confirmed that a copy of the arrest report was not in the defense's discovery file, she would raise holy hell.

'What is that, Detective Drucker?' I asked.

'It looks like an arrest report from the Ventura County Sheriff's Office,' he said.

'And who is the arrestee?'

'Sam Scales.'

'Arrested when and for what?'

'December first, 2018, for operating a fraudulent online fundraiser for victims of a mass shooting in a bar in Thousand Oaks.'

'This is a standard arrest form, correct?'

'Yes.'

'At the bottom of the form, there are a series of boxes that are checked. What do they indicate?'

I checked the prosecution table. Berg's bow-tied second was looking through files.

'One is marked 'interstate fraud,'' Drucker said.

'And what does the reference to 'FBI-LA' mean?' I asked quickly.

'That the FBI's office in L.A. was notified of the arrest.'

'Why did this arrest not come up on your search of Sam Scales's criminal record?'

'He probably wasn't charged and the arrest wasn't put into the computer.'

'Why would that happen?'

'You'll have to ask the Ventura sheriff's about that.'

'Is this what you would see when someone who is arrested agrees to cooperate with the authorities in some way?'

'Like I said, you'd have to ask Ventura about that.'

I checked the prosecutors again. Bow-tie was whispering to Berg now.

'Isn't this standard operating procedure for law enforcement?' I asked. 'To arrest someone for one crime in order to leverage their cooperation in a bigger investigation of a bigger fish?'

'I don't know anything about this arrest,' Drucker said in an annoyed tone. 'You have to ask Ventura. It was their case.'

In my peripheral vision I saw Berg start to stand to object.

'Sam Scales was an FBI informant, wasn't he, Detective Drucker?' I asked.

Before Drucker could reply, Berg made the objection and asked for a sidebar. The judge checked the clock on the back wall and decided to take the midmorning break. She said she would hear Berg's objection in chambers during the break.

As the jurors filed out, I returned to the defense table and sat down. Maggie leaned toward me.

449

'You got it in,' she whispered. 'No matter what happens now, the jury knows he was an informant.'

I nodded. That was the big finish. That was the hit on the house.

48

Judge warfield was upset and Dana Berg was livid. Neither bought my explanation for the discovery violation. That was when Maggie McFierce stepped up, willing to take the fall so the defense — my defense — could move on unscathed.

'Judge, this is my fault,' she said. 'I dropped the ball on this.'

Warfield looked at her suspiciously.

'Do tell, Ms. McPherson.'

'As you know, Mr. Haller lost his co-counsel and I agreed to step in. It was late in the game and I have been playing catch-up, familiarizing myself with the evidence, the defense theory, and the prosecution's case. Things have fallen through the cracks. As Mr. Haller has explained, the origin of the police report in question is unknown. It was slipped — '

'I don't believe that for a second,' Berg cut in. 'And if that is what you're going to spin, you should never come back to the office and they should never take you.'

'Ms. Berg, let her finish,' Warfield said. 'And don't make it personal when you have the opportunity to respond. Continue, Ms. McPherson.'

'As I was saying,' Maggie said. 'The origin of this document was unknown and, frankly, questionable. It had to be confirmed and we had

451

an investigator on it. He confirmed it and it was moved into the case presentation file at the beginning of the week. I have been in court all week and organizing the defense presentation at night. There was a miscommunication between Mr. Haller and myself. It didn't help that he is incarcerated and not available to me at a moment's notice. It was my understanding that we were not going to introduce the arrest report until later in the week and that would give me time to turn copies over to the state and the court today. All of that changed this morning when we learned from our investigator that Detective Rountree from the Ventura County Sheriff's Department was in town today and could testify.'

There was a slight pause as we waited for the judge to react to the explanation. But Berg reacted first.

'This is such bullshit,' she said. 'They planned it this way from the start so my detective would be blindsided in front of the jury.'

'He wouldn't have been blindsided if his investigation was as thorough as he claimed,' I said.

'Hold it right there,' Warfield said. 'We're not going to turn this into a boxing match. And Ms. Berg, I would check that language unless you want to be the only one who leaves here with sanctions.'

'Your Honor, you can't be serious,' Berg erupted. 'You're giving them a pass on this?'

The outrage was clear in her voice.

'What would you have me do, Ms. Berg?' the

452

judge asked. 'The document is clearly of importance to this case. What's your solution? Withhold it from the jury because of the defense's misdeeds, intentional or not? That is not going to happen. Not in my courtroom. This is a search for truth, and there is no way on God's green earth that I am keeping the document or the defense's investigation of it from the jury. Look at yourself, Ms. Berg — this is evidence that should have been brought forward by the state. And if I find out that this is something the D.A.'s Office did have and deep-sixed, then we will really see some sanctions.'

Berg seemed to shrink two sizes in her seat under the judge's withering comeback. She dropped off the offensive and immediately moved to her own defense.

'I can assure you, Judge, that neither I nor the D.A.'s Office knew a thing about this until it was brought up in court by the defense,' she said.

'That is good to hear,' Warfield said. 'And let the court remind you that there have been multiple violations of discovery by the People resulting in no sanctions and just one instruction to the jury. I am willing to make an instruction in this matter but would be concerned that it would accentuate the cause of the defense in bringing this document forward.'

The judge was saying she was willing to tell the jury that the defense broke the rules, but that admonishment might serve to simply underline the importance of the arrest report.

'That won't be necessary,' Berg said. 'But,

453

Your Honor, once again, rules have been intentionally broken and the defense should not simply be allowed to walk away. There should be consequences.'

Warfield looked at Berg for a long moment before speaking.

'Again, what would you have me do, Ms. Berg?' she asked. 'You want counsel cited for contempt? You want them fined? What is the appropriate financial penalty for this?'

'No, Your Honor,' Berg said. 'I think the penalty should be the witness. Counsel mentioned that the Ventura County detective was in town and would testify. I request that the court disallow his testimony as — '

'The defense objects to that,' Maggie said. 'At minimum, we need Detective Rountree to authenticate the report. He also needs to explain what happened with the FBI. He has driven down all the way from — '

'Thank you, Ms. McPherson,' Warfield cut in. 'But I think Ms. Berg has come up with an equitable solution to this trespass on the rules of discovery. The report comes in as a defense exhibit but not the witness.'

'Your Honor,' Maggie pressed. 'How do we explain to the jury the significance of what happened?'

'You're a smart lawyer,' Warfield said. 'You'll find a way.'

The answer left Maggie speechless.

'I think we are finished here,' Warfield said. 'Let's go back out and, Mr. Haller, you can continue your examination of the detective.'

'Your Honor,' I said, 'I think I am finished with the detective and ready to move on.'

'Very well,' Warfield said. 'Ms. Berg can cross-examine if she wishes. Court will resume in ten minutes.'

We filed out of chambers and headed to the courtroom, Berg sullenly following Maggie, me, and Deputy Chan, a required part of the procession since I was in custody.

'I hope you can live with yourself after this,' Berg said to Maggie's back.

Maggie turned to her without breaking stride.

'I just hope you can,' she said.

When court resumed, Berg had a handful of questions for Drucker but she stayed away from the Ventura County arrest and did little more than some clarification work on the detective's previous answers. In the meantime, Maggie went out into the hallway to tell Detective Rountree that he had driven a long way from Ventura for nothing, and to prep Art Schultz and bring him in when Drucker finally stepped down.

By prior agreement, Schultz was to be Maggie's witness. I wanted her to play it like a prosecutor and use Schultz to bring out the details of the crime that I believed were at the heart of the case.

Schultz was a Trojan horse. He had been added to our witness list as a retired biologist with the Environmental Protection Agency who would discuss the material found beneath the victim's fingernails. This was to make him appear inconsequential. The hope was that Berg's investigators wouldn't bother or would be stretched too thin with other case priorities to speak to him in advance of his testimony. That had worked and now he was going to take the stand, where Maggie would use him to plant the tent pole that would hold up the defense theory and case.

Schultz looked like he had retired early, possibly to move into a career as an expert witness on all things EPA-related. He was early to mid fifties, trim and fit, with a deep tan. He wore steel-rimmed glasses and a wedding band.

'Good morning, Mr. Schultz,' Maggie began. 'Can we begin with you telling the jury who you are and what you do for a living?'

'I'm retired now but I spent thirty years with the Environmental Protection Agency,' Schultz said. 'I was in the enforcement division and primarily worked in the West, my last office being in Salt Lake. I stayed there when I retired three years ago.'

'Are you a biologist by training?'

'Yes, I am. Have degrees from UNLV and the University of San Francisco.'

'And you were asked to analyze the material found under the fingernails of the victim in this case, is that correct?'

'Yes, it is.'

'And what did you identify the material as?'

'I agreed with the findings of the medical examiner that is was a mixture of materials. There was chicken fat and vegetable oil. A small percentage of sugarcane. It was what we called feedstock. Restaurant grease is basically what it is.'

'When you say 'we,' Mr. Schultz, whom do you mean?'

'My colleagues in EPA enforcement.'

'And you dealt with feedstock — restaurant grease — in EPA enforcement?'

'Yes. I was assigned to enforcement of regulations regarding the EPA's biofuel program. That program is about renewable fuel — recycling feedstock into biodiesel fuel. It is a program designed to reduce our national dependence on oil from the Middle East.'

'And so, why was there a need for enforcement?'

Berg stood and objected, spreading her hands and expressing her puzzlement at what this line of questioning had to do with the case at hand.

'Your Honor,' Maggie responded. 'I'm asking for the court's indulgence. It will become critically clear very soon what this has to do with the killing of Sam Scales.'

'Proceed, Ms. McPherson, but get there soon,' Warfield said. 'The witness may answer the question.'

Maggie repeated the question. I had positioned myself so I could watch most of the jurors. So far no one appeared bored, but we were moving into a stage where the leaps between the steps of the defense case were getting wider. We needed their full attention and patience.

'Enforcement was needed because where there is money, there is always going to be fraud,' Schultz said.

'Are you talking about government money?' Maggie asked.

457

'Yes. Government subsidies.'

'How did that work? The fraud, I mean.'

'It's a costly process. Waste fuel, feedstock, whatever you want to call it, has to be collected before it even gets to the refinery. You don't pump it out of the ground like crude oil. It is collected through recycling centers, trucked to the refinery, then processed, sold, and shipped back out. To encourage the conversion of refineries to biofuel, the government started a subsidy program. Basically, the government pays the manufacturer two dollars a barrel for manufacturing biofuel.'

'What would that mean in terms of, say, a tanker truck full of renewable fuel?'

'A tanker truck carries about two hundred barrels. So that would be four hundred dollars paid to the refinery every time the truck leaves with its payload.'

'And that's where the fraud is?'

'Yes. My last big case was in Ely, Nevada. A refinery up there. They were running a scheme, running the same oil in and out of the plant. They had a fleet of tankers that were going in and out with the same cargo. They would change the labeling only. In basic terms, it would say 'feedstock' coming in and 'biodiesel' going out. But it was the same stuff, and they were collecting four hundred dollars a pop. They were running twenty-five trucks and were taking a hundred thousand dollars a week off the government.'

'How long did that go on?'

'About two years before we got onto them.

458

The U.S. government lost about nine million on the deal.'

'Were there arrests and a prosecution?'

'The FBI came into it and shut it down. There were arrests and people went to prison, but they never caught the main guy.'

'And who was that?'

'Unknown. The FBI told me it was run by the mob out of Vegas. They used somebody as a front to buy into the refinery and then the fraud started.'

'Did this scam have a name?'

'The scammers called it 'bleeding the beast.''

'Do you know why it was called that?'

'They said that the U.S. government was the beast. And it was so big and had so much money that it would never notice what was being bled off in the scam.'

Berg stood again.

'Objection, Your Honor,' she said. 'This is an interesting story, but how does it tie into Sam Scales being found shot to death in the defendant's garage and then found in the trunk of the defendant's car?'

I had to admire Berg for mentioning the two key elements of her case in her objection, reminding the jurors to keep their eyes on the prize.

'That is the question, Ms. McPherson,' Warfield said. 'I have to admit I am growing a bit weary, waiting for things to connect here.'

'Your Honor, just a few more questions and we will be there,' Maggie said.

'Very well,' Warfield said. 'Proceed.'

I heard the soft bump of the courtroom door closing and turned to check the gallery. Agent Ruth was gone. I guessed that she knew what at least one of the two last questions to Schultz was going to be.

'Mr. Schultz, you called this the last big case you were involved in,' Maggie said. 'When was it?'

'Well,' Schultz said, after pausing to remember the details, 'as far as we know, the fraud started in 2015, and we caught on and closed it down two years later. The prosecutions of some of the lower-level players came after I retired.'

'Okay, and you said that when the fraud was discovered, you notified the FBI. Correct?'

'Yes, the FBI took it over.'

'Do you remember the names of the case agents who handled the investigation?'

'There were a lot of agents but the two they put in charge of it were from here in L.A. Their names were Rick Aiello and Dawn Ruth.'

'And did they tell you the case you were involved in was unique?'

'No, they said it was happening at refineries all over the country.'

'Thank you, Mr. Schultz. I have no further questions.'

49

The testimony from Art Schultz was key to our case, but more than anything, it was his last few answers that really put us in play. The mention of the FBI agents by name gave us some leverage and we intended to use it. With Opparizio dead, it might be my only way to an NG.

While I watched Dana Berg complete a perfunctory cross-examination of the retired EPA biologist, Maggie McFierce went out into the hallway with her laptop to compose a court order that we would submit to the judge for consideration. She was back by the time Berg was finished with Schultz. I stood and said the defense needed to address the judge outside the presence of the jury and the media. Judge Warfield considered the request, then reluctantly sent the jurors off to an early lunch and invited the lawyers to her chambers.

As usual, because of my custody status, Deputy Chan came into chambers with us and positioned himself by the door.

'Judge,' I said while we were still choosing seats and sitting down. 'Can I ask that Deputy Chan be posted outside the door? Nothing personal with him, but what we are going to discuss here is pretty sensitive.'

The judge stared at me for a long moment. I knew she didn't have to be reminded of the investigation that was instigated by this court

461

into illegal eavesdropping and intel-gathering activities by Chan's department. But before she could speak, Berg objected to my request.

'It's a safety issue, Your Honor,' she said. 'Mr. Haller might be in his finest suit but he is still in custody and charged with murder. I don't think there should be any time that he is not under the supervision and control of the Sheriffs Department. I personally am not comfortable with the deputy outside the room.'

I shook my head.

'She still thinks I want to escape,' I said. 'I'm two days away from notching a not-guilty on this case and she thinks I'm planning to flee. Shows how clueless she is.'

The judge held up her hand to stop me from going on.

'Mr. Haller, you should know by now that personal attacks will get you nowhere in my court,' she said. 'And that includes my chambers. Deputy Chan has been assigned to my courtroom for four years. I trust him completely. He stays, and what you say here will not be leaked or distributed other than through the official record.'

She nodded to the court reporter, who was at her usual spot in the corner with her stool and steno machine.

'Now,' Warfield continued. 'What are we doing here?'

I nodded to Maggie.

'Judge,' she said, 'I just wrote and sent an order to your clerk for your signature. It's a petition for a writ of habeas corpus ad

462

testificandum, ordering one of the FBI agents just named in court to appear and give testimony.'

'Hold on,' Warfield said.

She picked up her desk phone, called her clerk, and told him to download and print three copies of Maggie's order and bring them to chambers. She then hung up and told Maggie to continue.

'Judge, we want you to order FBI agent Dawn Ruth to appear in court to give testimony,' Maggie said.

'Didn't I sign a subpoena for the FBI a month ago?' the judge asked.

'And they ignored it as the federal government can and is wont to do,' Maggie said. 'Standard operating procedure at the fed. That's why we want you to issue the writ. It will be difficult for the U.S. Attorney and Agent Ruth to ignore you, especially if the writ should go to warrant.'

This last part was a hint. Should the judge issue the writ, she could give it some teeth. The U.S. Attorney could ignore it or tell Agent Ruth not to respond to it. But if failure to comply resulted in an arrest warrant, then Agent Ruth and the U.S. Attorney would be vulnerable to being taken into custody as soon as they strayed outside the federal building and onto territory where Judge Warfield held jurisdiction. It would be a bold move, but Maggie and I had guessed that Warfield was the kind of judge who would be up for it.

'The People object,' Berg said. 'This is all part of a carefully orchestrated attempt to distract the jury from the evidence. This is Haller's specialty, Your Honor. He does it in every case, every trial. It's not going to work here, because it's a con. Call it the 'bleeding the beast' con. But it has nothing — *nothing* — to do with the evidence.'

'This is not a distraction, Judge,' I said, cutting in before anyone else could speak. 'Agents Rick Aiello and Dawn Ruth were just named by a witness in front of the jury. Agent Ruth was in the courtroom before that, keeping tabs on this case. Every one of those jurors — '

'Wait just a second, Mr. Haller,' Warfield said. 'You know Agent Ruth by sight?'

'Yes,' I said. 'She and Aiello confronted me at my house when my team started digging into this. They are the agents who went to Ventura County to take Sam Scales off the hands of the Sheriff's Department up there.'

That was just an educated guess on my part, but it seemed logical, since I was sure the leaked arrest report had come from Ruth. I pressed on.

'We now have Ruth's and Aiello's names on the record and out in front of the jury,' I said. 'They are expecting to hear from at least one of them, and the defense is entitled to their testimony.'

'They also have the name Louis Opparizio,' Berg said. 'Are we going to see him?'

I turned to look at Berg. She had a smirk on her face. It was a slip. She obviously would have known that Opparizio was on our witness list and that Warfield had signed a defense subpoena for him. But to already know that Opparizio was dead was a major tell. It meant that the

464

prosecution had been tracking Opparizio to a greater extent than I had thought. It also meant that Berg had been lying in wait and was ready to make a move to prevent his appearance or to neutralize him if he was allowed to testify. Her slip of the tongue had allowed me a glimpse behind the curtain.

All of this apparently passed by Maggie in the heat of the moment and she pressed on with her argument.

'Your Honor,' she said, 'it is your obligation to ensure that the defendant has a fair trial. That can't happen here without the testimony of the FBI. This is the whole case. The only alternative is to dismiss the charge.'

'Yeah, right,' Berg said sarcastically. 'That's not happening. Judge, you can't do this. This is a giant distraction. They just want to put the FBI out there to draw the jury away from the truth. You can't —'

'You don't speak for the court, Ms. Berg,' Warfield said. 'Let me ask the obvious question here. The agents were referenced in testimony regarding a three-year-old fraud case in Nevada. Where is the relevancy to this case?'

'They told Schultz that this was happening all over the country,' Maggie said.

'The defense will show through the agent's testimony and other evidence that the Nevada case is more than relevant to the murder of Sam Scales,' I added. 'We will show that Sam Scales was involved in a copycat scheme at BioGreen at the Port of Los Angeles.'

'But Detective Drucker testified that he could

not confirm that Sam Scales even worked there,' Warfield said.

'That's exactly why we need Agent Ruth to testify,' I said. 'She can confirm it, because she's the one who sent him in there as an informant. He was working for them and that's what got him killed.'

I noticed that Maggie had turned in her seat and was looking at me. I knew I was revealing more than I should, and promising more than I could deliver. But I instinctively felt that this was the key moment of the case. I needed to get Agent Ruth on the stand and was willing at this point to say anything to get her there.

'Your Honor,' Maggie said. 'It's a third-party-culpability case and getting Agent Ruth to testify is how we get there.'

Berg shook her head.

'You can't be seriously considering this,' she said. 'This is as thin as a spider's web. You can see right through it. There is nothing here but conjecture. No evidence, no testimony that remotely links whatever is going on at BioGreen with the murder of Sam Scales in his garage!'

She punctuated her objection with a finger pointed at me.

There was a pause while Warfield considered all arguments, and then she ruled.

'Thank you for your arguments,' she said. 'I'm going to sign the writ ordering Agent Ruth to appear at ten o'clock tomorrow morning. This time I will transmit it to the U.S. Attorney and I will remind him that he has to leave the building at the end of the day, and when he does, he's on my turf. Additionally, I will tell him that this case has garnered a lot of media attention and I can guarantee that the reporters in the courtroom tomorrow will hear my thoughts on the FBI and the U.S. Attorney if they do not comply.'

'Thank you, Your Honor,' Maggie said.

'Judge, the People still object to this,' Berg said.

'Your objection was overruled,' Warfield said. 'Do you have something else?'

'Yes, a running objection,' Berg said. 'With all due respect, since the start of this trial, the court has continuously ruled in a way that has been prejudicial to the People.'

That brought a stunned silence to the room. Berg was accusing the judge of shucking her impartiality and favoring the defense with her rulings. As a jurist who came out of the defense bar, Warfield would be particularly sensitive to such a charge. Berg was baiting Warfield into an outburst that might prove the objection.

But the judge seemed to compose herself before responding.

'Your running objection is noted but overruled,' she said calmly. 'If counsel's statement is intended to try to inflame or intimidate the court, be assured that you have failed in the effort and that the court will continue to make rulings impartially and independently based on the law and applied to the case.'

Warfield paused there to see if Berg had another comeback, but the prosecutor remained silent.

'Now, is there any other business to discuss?'

Warfield asked. 'I would like to get this order out and then have some lunch.'

'Your Honor,' Maggie said, 'we have lost our main witness for today and — '

'And who was that?' Warfield asked.

'Louis Opparizio,' Maggie said.

'Was the subpoena delivered?' Warfield asked.

'Yes, it was,' Maggie said.

'Then why isn't he here?' Warfield asked.

'He was murdered,' Maggie said. 'His body was found yesterday.'

'*What?*' the judge yelped.

'Yes,' Maggie said. 'In Arizona.'

'And does this have anything to do with this case?' Warfield asked.

'We think so, Your Honor,' Maggie said.

'Which is why you need the FBI to come in and testify,' Warfield said.

'Yes, Your Honor,' Maggie said. 'And other than Opparizio, we had only one other witness scheduled for today — Detective Rountree, whom you disallowed.'

'Are you saying you have no other witnesses to your case?' Warfield asked.

'We have only one: Mr. Haller,' Maggie said. 'And we don't want him to testify until after we possibly hear from the FBI and Agent Ruth. He would be our last witness.'

Warfield looked pained. She clearly didn't want to lose the afternoon.

'I seem to recall more names on your witness list,' she said.

'That is true but the course of the trial has dictated changes to our strategy,' I said. 'We've dropped some witnesses just this morning. We had a toxicology expert good to go today but Detective Drucker and the deputy medical examiner already covered the same ground. We had the landlord on subpoena but Detective Drucker covered her information as well.'

'I seem to recall you had a bartender on your list,' Warfield said.

I hesitated. We had described Moira Benson on the witness list as someone who would testify to my not drinking at the NG celebration and being totally sober when I left it. But that had been a disguise to hide the real value of her testimony. What she had actually been going to tell the jury was that she had gotten a phone call at the Redwood on the night of the party, and an anonymous caller had asked whether I had left yet. At the time, I had paid the tab and was moving toward the door, slowed by handshakes and thank-yous from the well-wishers who had gotten their nightly alcohol intake on me. She told the caller I was heading to the door. Under the defense theory, that call resulted in a text to Milton, alerting him that I was leaving. But now, with the cell records we had received, we couldn't complete the one-two punch the defense had hoped for. It didn't mean it didn't happen that way. The cell records could have been doctored, or Milton could have gotten a text on a burner. But we couldn't move the supposition from theory to fact and I couldn't put the bartender on the stand.

'Her testimony is also unneeded based on recent records we acquired,' I said.

469

The judge thought for a moment and decided not to inquire any further about the bartender.

'So, all you have left is the FBI, which we don't know about, and Mr. Haller,' she said.

'And it would really change our strategy if he had to testify before we heard from Agent Ruth,' Maggie said.

'*If* we hear from Agent Ruth,' Warfield said.

'Judge, this is ridiculous,' Berg said. 'They had no strategy. This whole thing about Ruth came up today.'

'Counsel is wrong,' Maggie said. 'The FBI has been on our radar from the start. And we always planned to end with Mr. Haller's forceful denial of the charge. We would like to keep it that way.'

'Very well,' Warfield said. 'I'm going to let the jury go for the day. Hopefully tomorrow we will hear from the FBI and then the defendant. Either way, you would all be advised to use the time we are not in session this afternoon to work on closing arguments. You may be giving them tomorrow afternoon.'

'Judge, we will be introducing evidence in rebuttal,' Berg said. 'And possibly a witness, depending on tomorrow's testimony.'

'That will be your prerogative,' Warfield said.

I noticed that Berg had stopped addressing Warfield as *Your Honor*. I wondered if the judge noticed too.

'I think we are done here,' Warfield said. 'I will see everyone back in court at one o'clock, when I will dismiss the jury.'

Moving back to the courtroom through the hallway outside the judge's chambers, I walked up behind Berg, who was leading the way this time.

'You knew Opparizio was dead before we went in there,' I said. 'If it was all just a choreographed attempt to distract the jury, why were you so on top of him?'

'Because I can see you coming from a mile away, Haller,' Berg responded. 'And we were ready for Opparizio, dead or alive. You obviously were not.'

She kept walking at speed and I slowed down so Maggie could catch up.

'What was that about?' she asked.

'Nothing,' I said. 'Just more bullshit. So, what do you think our chances are with the writ?'

'Getting an agent on the stand?' Maggie said. 'Somewhere between zero and zero. I think this is going to come down to you up there and winning the jury over. So be ready and be at your best.'

We walked in silence after that. I knew that whatever the risks were that lay ahead, they were all on me.

50

With the Jury sent home and the courtroom dark, Maggie McPherson and I were allowed to work in the attorney-client room in courtside holding until it was time for my private shuttle back to Twin Towers.

We got a lot done. Rather than focus, as the judge had suggested, on a closing argument, we worked on questions for the final two witnesses — Special Agent Dawn Ruth and me. And this was most critical with Agent Ruth because it was the questions that would most likely contain the information we wanted to get to the jury. We anticipated that if we were lucky enough to get Ruth on the stand, she would at best be a reluctant witness. We wouldn't ask, *Was Sam Scales an FBI informant?* We would ask, *How long was Sam Scales an FBI informant?* That way, the jurors would get the information we needed them to hear, whether or not the actual questions were answered.

It was agreed that I would question Ruth — if she responded to the judge's writ — and Maggie would, of course, question me. She convinced me during the work session that I had to testify. Once past that hurdle, I embraced the idea and started thinking about the questions and answers we were composing together.

I stayed in my suit as we worked, not wanting to spend that time with Maggie in prisoner's

472

garb. It was a little thing, and she probably didn't even care, but I did. Besides our daughter, she had always been the most important woman in my life, and I cared what she thought of me.

I knew there was a camera on us the whole time and touching was forbidden, but at one point I couldn't help myself. I reached across the table and put my hand on hers as she was trying to write down one of the questions she would ask me the next day.

'Maggie, thank you,' I said. 'No matter what happens, you were here for me and it has meant more than you'll ever know.'

'Well,' she said. 'Let's get the NG — as you like to call it — and everything will be all right.'

I withdrew my hand but it was too late. A voice came from the speaker box next to the camera and told me not to touch her again. I acted like I didn't even hear it.

'Still thinking about going back to the D.A.'s Office after this?' I asked. 'Now that you've seen behind the curtain of high-stakes defense work?'

I was smiling good-naturedly, wanting to take a small break.

'I don't know,' she said. 'I'm sure the bosses are getting a steady diet of complaints about me from Dana. The well may be poisoned — especially when we win. Maybe I could get used to sticking it to the man.'

She said it with full sarcasm. But she smiled and I smiled back.

At 4 p.m. I got a fifteen-minute heads-up from Deputy Chan that I was being moved to the shuttle and I had to lose the suit. Maggie said she was going to go.

'When you get out of here, call Cisco,' I told her. 'Get a copy of the video with the room-service guy in Arizona and bring it to court tomorrow. We might need it.'

'Good idea,' she said.

Twenty minutes later I was in the back of a cruiser being driven to Twin Towers by Deputy Pressley. He took the normal route from the courthouse, crossing the 101 freeway on Main Street and dropping down Cesar Chavez Avenue to Vignes Street.

But at Vignes, instead of turning left toward Bauchet Street and the jail, he turned right.

'Pressley, what's up?' I said. 'Where are we going?'

He didn't answer.

'Pressley,' I repeated. 'What's going on?'

'Just calm down,' Pressley said. 'You'll find out soon enough.'

But his answer didn't calm me. Instead, high concern gripped me. The stories about sheriff's deputies committing or orchestrating atrocities in the jails had permeated the local justice system. Nothing was unimaginable. But fact or fiction, the stories all took place inside the jail, where the situations were controlled and unseen by outside witnesses. Pressley was taking me away from the jail and we were driving behind the Union Station railway complex, bouncing over tracks and entering a maintenance yard where the workers had punched out at five sharp.

'Pressley, come on, man,' I said. 'You don't

474

have to do this. I thought we had an understanding. You told me to watch my back. Why are you doing this?'

I was leaning forward as far as the seat belt and the cuff lock between my legs would allow me. I saw a slight smile crack across his face and I realized he had played me. He wasn't a sympathizer. He was one of them.

'Who put you up to this, Pressley?' I demanded. 'Was it Berg? Who?'

Again, only silence from my abductor. Pressley pulled the car into an open work bay covered with a corrugated and rusted metal roof. He then hit the release on the rear door locks and got out of the car.

I tracked him as he walked around the front of the car. But he stopped there and looked back at me through the windshield. I was puzzled. Was he going to pull me out, or what?

The rear door across from me opened and I turned to see Special Agent Dawn Ruth slide onto the plastic seat next to me.

'Agent Ruth,' I blurted out. 'What the fuck is going on?'

'Calm down, Haller,' she said. 'I'm here to talk.'

I turned and looked through the windshield again at Pressley. I realized I had read him completely wrong just now.

'And I should ask you the same question,' Ruth said. 'What the fuck is going on?'

I looked back at her, regaining some of my composure and cool.

'You know what's going on,' I said. 'What do you want?'

'First of all, this conversation didn't happen,' she said. 'If at any time you try to say it did, I will have four agents ready to alibi me and you will look like a liar.'

'Fine. What exactly is the conversation?'

'Your judge is out of control. Ordering me to appear to testify? That's not going to happen.'

'Fine, don't show up. Then you can read about it in the *Times*. But if you ask me, that's no way to keep an investigation under wraps.'

'And you think testifying in open court is?'

'Look, if you cooperate, we can choreograph your testimony. We can protect what you need to protect. But I need to get on the record that Sam Scales was an informant and Louis Opparizio found out and had him whacked.'

'Even if that's not what happened?'

I looked at her for a long moment before responding.

'If that's not what happened, then what did?' I finally asked.

'Think about it,' she said. 'If Opparizio thought Sam was an informant, would he still go on running the scam at BioGreen? Or would he have killed Sam and closed up shop?'

'Okay, so you're saying the seam's been ongoing — even after Sam got killed. So the bureau's operation is also ongoing.'

I tried to put it together but couldn't.

'Why was Sam killed?' I asked.

'You probably knew him better than anybody,' Ruth said. 'Why do you think?'

It clicked.

'He was running his own scam,' I said. 'On the

476

bureau and Opparizio. What was it?'

Ruth hesitated. She was steeped in a culture that never gave away secrets. But now was the time — in a conversation that would and could be denied.

'He was running a skim,' Ruth said. 'We found out after he was dead. He secretly started his own oil distro company. Incorporated, registered with the government. He was running tankers back and forth to the port, but half the subsidies were going to him.'

I nodded. The story was easy to pick up from there.

'Opparizio found out and had to whack him,' I said. 'He didn't want an investigation to come to BioGreen and he saw an opportunity to settle a score with me.'

'And I'm not going to testify to any of this,' she said.

'There's no reason not to. Opparizio is dead, in case you didn't hear.'

'You think Opparizio was in charge of this? You think he was the target? He was running one operation. We're watching six refineries in four states. Ongoing operations. Opparizio wasn't giving the orders, he was following them. And that's why it was easy for them to decide he had to go. His freelancing vendetta with you showed poor business judgment and that's not tolerated by these people. At all. You think he snuck off to Arizona to avoid a subpoena? Don't be silly. He was hiding from them, not you.'

'You were watching him too?'

'I didn't say that.'

Through the windshield I could see Pressley pacing in front of the car. I had a feeling that we were on a clock. This was an unsanctioned stop.

'Does he work for you, too?' I asked. 'Pressley? Or do you have something on him?'

'Don't worry about him,' Ruth said.

My thoughts returned to my own situation.

'So, what am I supposed to do?' I said. 'Sacrifice myself? Take a conviction so your case goes on? That's crazy. You're crazy if you think I'll do that.'

'We had hoped that our investigation would be at the arrest phase before your case even made it to court,' she said. 'We would then square it. But that didn't happen — you refused to delay the case. A lot of things that were supposed to happen didn't.'

'No fucking kidding. Let me ask you one thing. Were you watching when they killed Sam? Did you guys just let it happen — to protect your case?'

'We would never let something like that happen. Especially just to protect a case. They grabbed him inside the refinery. We had nobody else inside. We didn't know he was dead until the LAPD ran his prints after finding his body in your trunk.'

Through the windshield, I saw Pressley start signaling to Ruth. He pointed to his watch and then twirled a finger in the air. He was telling her to wrap it up. When we were crossing the 101 earlier, he had used the cruiser's radio to report that he was moving his prisoner to Twin Towers.

It wouldn't be long before they noticed we had not arrived.

'So, why didn't you just go to the LAPD or the D.A.'s Office and lay this all out?' I asked. 'You could have told them just to back off of me, and none of this would have happened.'

'That would have been a little difficult to do with Sam being found in your trunk in your garage and the media storm that followed,' Ruth said. 'This whole thing has been an unavoidable clusterfuck from the start.'

'And you ended up with a guilty conscience. That's why you slipped the Ventura arrest report under my door.'

'I'm not saying I did that.'

'You don't have to. But thank you.'

Ruth opened her door.

'So, what happens tomorrow?' I asked.

She looked back at me.

'I have no idea,' she said. 'It's out of my hands, that's for sure.'

She exited and closed the door, then walked off to the rear and I didn't bother to turn to watch her go. Pressley quickly got in behind the wheel. He backed out of the work bay and headed out of the yard the way we had come in.

'Sorry, Pressley,' I said. 'I panicked before and read you wrong.'

'Not the first time that's been done,' he said.

'You an agent or just working with them?'

'Think I'd tell you?'

'Probably not.'

'So, if anything comes up at the Towers about us being late, I'm going to say I pulled over because you were getting sick.'

I nodded.

'I'll back that up,' I said.

'They won't even ask you,' he said.

We were back on Vignes Street. Through the windshield I could see Twin Towers up ahead.

51

In the morning they woke me early and put me in the escort cruiser before eight o'clock. No one at the jail told me why.

'Pressley, you know why I'm going over so early?' I asked. 'Court won't even be open for an hour.'

'Not a clue,' Pressley said. 'They just told me to get you there.'

'Any fallout from the little detour home last night?'

'What detour?'

I nodded and looked out the window. I hoped that whatever this was, Maggie McPherson had been alerted.

When we got to the courthouse, I was passed off to a runner who took me into the lockdown elevator and used a key to operate it. That was when I began to fill in the blanks. I was usually taken to the ninth floor, where Judge Warfield's courtroom was located. The runner turned the key next to the button for the eighteenth floor. Every trial lawyer in the city knew that the main District Attorney's Office was located on the eighteenth floor of the Criminal Courts Building.

Off the elevator I was ushered into a locked interview room that I assumed was used to

481

interview criminal suspects when they agreed to cooperate. It was not a good practice to let agreements like that sit. People change their minds — both criminal suspects and lawyers. If somebody facing a tough charge or a tough sentence makes the quiet offer in court to provide substantial assistance to authorities, you don't set up an appointment for the next day. You take them upstairs and extract whatever information there is to extract. And it happened in the room that I was now sitting in.

Handcuffed to a waist chain and still in my blues, I sat in the room alone for fifteen minutes before I started staring up at the camera in the corner of the ceiling and yelling that I wanted to see my lawyer.

This drew no response for another five minutes and then the door opened and the runner was there. He escorted me down a hall and through a door. I entered what looked like a boardroom — most likely where policy was set and prosecutors and supervisors discussed big cases. Ten tall-back chairs stood around a large oval table, and most of them were occupied. I was led to an open seat next to Maggie McPherson. I either recognized most of the people gathered around the table or could guess who they were. On one side sat Dana Berg, along with her bow-tied second, as well as John 'Big John' Kelly, the District Attorney, and Matthew Scallan, who I knew to be Berg's boss and head of the Major Crimes Unit. In that capacity he had also formerly been Maggie's boss until they moved her to the

Environmental Protection Unit.

Lined up across the table from the state prosecutors were the feds. I saw Agent Ruth and her partner, Rick Aiello, along with the U.S. Attorney for the Southern District of California, Wilson Corbett, and another man whom I did not recognize but assumed was a midlevel prosecutor most likely overseeing the BioGreen investigation.

'Mr. Haller, welcome,' Kelly said. 'How are you today?'

I looked at Maggie before answering and she gave a slight shake of her head. It was enough for me to understand that she did not know what this was about either.

'I just spent another night in your wonderful accommodations at Twin Towers,' I said. 'How do you think I feel, Big John?'

Kelly nodded like he knew that would be my response.

'Well, we think we have some good news for you, then,' Kelly said. 'If we can come to an agreement on some things here, we're going to drop the case against you. You could sleep in your own bed tonight. How would that be?'

I took a scan of the faces in the room, beginning with Maggie's. She looked surprised. Dana Berg looked mortified, and Rick Aiello looked the way he did the last time I had seen him on my front porch: angry.

'Dismissed?' I asked. 'A jury has been sworn in. Jeopardy has attached.'

Kelly nodded.

'Correct,' he said. 'You cannot be retried

483

under the double jeopardy clause. No do-overs. It's done. Over.'

'And what are the things we would have to come to an agreement on?' I asked.

'I'll let Mr. Corbett take that one,' Kelly said.

I knew little about Corbett other than that he'd had no experience as a prosecutor before being appointed U.S. Attorney by the current president.

'We have a situation,' he said. 'We have an ongoing investigation that reaches far deeper than you know. It doesn't end with Louis Opparizio. But to expose even a small part of it in a court case would imperil the larger case. We need you to agree to be silent until the larger case is completed and adjudicated.'

'And when will that be?' Maggie asked.

'We don't know,' Corbett said. 'It is ongoing. That is all I can tell you.'

'So, how would this work?' I asked. 'Charges are just dropped without explanation?'

Kelly took back the floor. I was staring at Dana Berg as he spoke.

'We would move to dismiss the charges as contrary to the public interest,' he said. 'We will state that the District Attorney's Office has come into information and evidence that casts grave doubt on the validity and justice of our case. What that information and evidence is will remain confidential as part of an ongoing investigation.'

'That's it?' I said. 'That's all you say? What about her? What does Dana say? She's been calling me a murderer for four months.'

484

'We want to draw as little attention to this as possible,' Kelly said. 'We can't grandstand this and still protect the federal investigation.'

Berg was staring down at the table in front of her. I could tell she was not down with this plan. She was a true believer in her case until the end.

'So, that's the deal?' I said. 'Charges dropped but I can never say why, and you people never say you were wrong?'

No one responded.

'You think you're making an accommodation,' I said. 'You think this is a deal where you let a murderer walk for the greater good.'

'We're not passing judgment,' Kelly said. 'We know you have information that could be detrimental to the greater good should it come out.'

I pointed to Dana Berg.

'She is,' I said. 'She passed judgment when she put me in jail. She thinks I killed Sam Scales. You all do.'

'You don't know what I think, Haller,' Berg said.

'I pass,' I said.

'What?' Kelly said.

Maggie put her hand on my arm to try to stop me.

'I said, I pass,' I responded. 'Take me down to court. I'll take my chances with the jury. I get a not-guilty from them, and I'm clean and clear. And I can tell the whole world how I was set up right under the FBI's nose and then railroaded by the D.A.'s Office. I like that deal better.'

I used my legs to start pushing my chair back

and turned to look for the deputy who had brought me in.

'What do you want, Haller?' Corbett asked.

I looked back at him.

'What do I want?' I said. 'I want my innocence back. I want it said that your new information and evidence clearly exonerates me of this charge. I want either you, Big John, or Dana to say that. First in a motion to the court, then to the judge in open court, and then I want it at the press conference on the courthouse steps. If you can't give me that, then I'll get it from the jury and we have nothing to talk about.'

Kelly looked across the table at his federal counterpart. I saw the nod and the transmission of approval.

'I think we can accommodate that,' Kelly said.

Berg leaned back abruptly as though she had been slapped across the face.

'Good,' I said. 'Because that's not all.'

'Jesus Christ,' Aiello said.

'I want two more things,' I said, ignoring Aiello and looking directly at Kelly. 'I want no backlash on my co-counsel. She goes back to work for you after this. No pay cut, no job change.'

'That was already going to be the case,' Kelly said. 'Maggie is one of our best and — '

'Great,' I said. 'Then it won't be a problem for you to put it in writing.'

'Michael,' Maggie said. 'I don't — '

'No, I want it in writing,' I said. 'I want all of this in writing.'

Kelly slowly nodded.

'You'll get it in writing,' he said. 'What's the second thing?'

'Well, I think we made a convincing case in court that Officer Roy Milton was waiting for me that night four months ago,' I said. 'His story about the missing license plate is bullshit. I was framed for this, and then I was beaten and nearly killed while my name and reputation were repeatedly dragged through the mud. The LAPD will never investigate this, but you have a Public Integrity Unit. I will be filing a complaint and I don't want it moth balled. I want it investigated to a conclusion. This could not have gone down without inside help, and Milton is the starting point. I'm sure there is a link somewhere to Opparizio — I'd start with his lawyers — and I want to know what that link is.'

'We'll open a file,' Kelly said. 'We'll investigate in good faith.'

'Then I think we're good,' I said.

Berg shook her head at my list of demands. Maggie saw me focusing on Berg and put her hand on my arm again, hoping to hold me back. But it was my moment and I couldn't let it pass.

'Dana, I know you'll never believe this was a frame,' I said. 'A lot of people won't. But maybe someday when the feds run this investigation out to the end, they'll take the time to show you where you and the LAPD went wrong.'

For the first time, Berg turned and looked at me.

'Fuck you, Haller,' she said. 'You are scum and no deal you make will ever change that. I'll see you in the courtroom. I want to get this over

487

with as soon as possible.'

She got up from her seat then and left the room. There was a long silence. I spent most of it with my attention on Agent Ruth. I wanted to help her but I didn't want to throw her under the bus for having helped me.

'Are we finished here?' Corbett asked, putting his hands on the arms of his chair and pausing before pushing himself up.

'I have something for the agents,' I said.

'We don't want anything from you,' Aiello said.

I nodded to Maggie.

'We have a video,' I said. 'It's got your killer on it. The man who killed Opparizio and snuck his body out of the hotel in Scottsdale. We'll get it to you. Maybe it will help.'

'Don't bother,' Aiello said. 'We don't want your help.'

'No,' Ruth said. 'We'll take it. Thank you.'

She looked at me and nodded. I could tell her words were sincere and that at least one person in the room did not believe they were setting free a murderer.

52

An hour later I was in my suit and stood in the courtroom before Judge Warfield. She had dismissed the jury but said they could stay if they wanted to and they all did. Dana Berg had, in a reluctant but carefully worded statement, reported to the court that new evidence of a confidential nature had come to light that exonerated me of the charges. She said the District Attorney's Office was withdrawing the charge with prejudice and would expunge my arrest record.

Maggie McPherson stood next to me while my daughter and the members of my team stood behind me. Despite an admonishment from the judge to contain emotions, people in the courtroom clapped as the prosecutor finished her announcement. I looked over to the jury box and saw that the Hollywood Bowl chef was one of them. I nodded. I'd had her down correctly on my scorecard.

Now it was the judge's turn.

'Mr. Haller,' Judge Warfield said. 'A grave injustice has been committed against you and it is the court's sincere hope that you can recover from this and continue your career as an officer of the court and defender of the rights of those who stand accused. Now that you have had this experience yourself, perhaps you will be better suited to serve in this capacity. I wish you all the best, sir. You are free to go.'

'Thank you, Your Honor,' I said.

My voice cracked as I said it. The magnitude of what had happened in the last two hours had left me shaking in my suit.

I turned and put my arms around Maggie, then reached back to my daughter. Soon the three of us were in a single embrace with the courtroom railing awkwardly between daughter and parents. I followed this with handshakes and smiles with Cisco and Bosch. I said nothing, because words were hard. I knew that would all come later.

53

Friday, February 28

We waited a day before hosting a celebration at the Redwood. By then the word had gotten out through press conferences and the media that I had been cleared of all charges and exonerated. It seemed appropriate to gather in the place where all the upheaval in my life had started. There were no invitations and no guest list. It was an open invitation to the courthouse set — with Lorna's company credit card held at the bar for the tab.

It got crowded quickly but I had made sure that the defense team got the big round table in the back reserved just for us. I sat there like a godfather in a mob flick, surrounded by my capos and receiving the well-wishes and handshakes of those who had come to the party to celebrate a rare win for the defense.

The drinks were flowing, though I maintained my sobriety, drinking orange juice on the rocks with a few maraschino cherries thrown in for style. Moira, the bartender, relieved at not having had to testify, was calling the concoction the Sticky Mickey, and it caught on, though most of the others in the bar were taking theirs with a couple shots of vodka in the mix.

I sat between my two ex-wives, Maggie McFierce to my left and our daughter next to

491

her, Lorna on my right followed by Cisco. Harry Bosch was directly across the table from me. For the most part I was quiet, just taking it all in and occasionally holding my drink up to clink glasses with a friend leaning over Bosch's shoulder to say well done.

'You okay?' Maggie whispered to me at one point.

'Yeah, I'm great,' I said. 'Just getting used to it being over, you know?'

'You should go away. Go somewhere and clear your mind of all of this.'

'Yeah. I was thinking of going out to Catalina for a few days. They just reopened the Zane Grey and it's really nice.'

'You've been there already?'

'Uh, online.'

'I wonder if they still have that room with the fireplace we used to get.'

I thought about that — the memory of when we were together and we'd go to Catalina for weekend getaways. There was a good chance that our daughter had been conceived there. Had I ruined the memory by taking Kendall there?

'You could come with me, you know,' I said.

Maggie smiled and I saw the shine I remembered so well in her dark eyes.

'Maybe,' she said.

That was good enough for me. I smiled as I looked out at the crowd. They were all there for the free booze. But also for me. I realized I had forgotten about Bishop. I should have invited him.

I then noticed that Cisco and Bosch had their

heads together and were talking in serious tones.

'Hey,' I said. 'What?'

'Just talking about Opparizio,' Cisco said.

'What about him?' I asked.

'You know, why they hit him,' Cisco said. 'Harry says they had to.'

I looked at Bosch and tilted my head back. I wanted to hear his take. I had told no one about my conversation with Agent Ruth in the back of Deputy Pressley's cruiser.

Bosch leaned as much as he could across the table. It was loud in the bar and not the proper setting for yelling murder theories out loud.

'He let personal business get in the way of the real business,' Bosch said. 'He should have taken care of Scales cleanly. Whacked him, buried him, put him in an oil barrel and dropped it in the channel. Anything but what he did. He used the situation — whatever it was — to try to settle an old score with you. That was his mistake and it made him vulnerable. He had to go, and the thing is, he knew it. I don't think he was out in Arizona hiding from you and a subpoena. He was hiding from a bullet.'

I nodded. The former homicide detective was very close.

'You think they found him through us?' I asked. 'Followed us out there to him?'

'You mean followed me,' Cisco said.

'Don't feel bad,' I said. 'I sent you out there.'

'About Opparizio?' Cisco said. 'I don't feel a thing about that guy.'

'It could've been the way,' Bosch said. 'He could have made a slip himself. Told his

493

girlfriend or somebody. Made a call.'

I shook my head.

'That room-service trick,' I said. 'That tells me the hitter knew we were there watching him. I think they used us to get to him.'

I thought of the video the Indians had taken and that I had turned over to Agent Ruth. The room-service hit man was white, maybe forty years old, with thinning red hair. He didn't look menacing. He looked nondescript. He looked like he belonged in the red room-service jacket he had used to bluff his way into Opparizio's room.

'Well, too bad,' Maggie said. 'He tried to pin a murder rap on you, Mickey. Just like Cisco, I have a hard time coming up with any sympathy for Louis Opparizio.'

The conversation shifted to speculation about who the federal target was and most agreed it was probably a corporate mobster, someone from the Las Vegas casino world who had been backing the biofuel play. But all of that was above our pay grade. I could only hope that one day Agent Ruth would call me and say, 'We got him.' Then I would know the identity of the man ultimately responsible for almost destroying my life.

Soon I was back to just enjoying the moment and watching the people in the bar. Eventually my eyes fell on a woman standing at the bar and I excused myself from the table to join her.

'Have you tried the Sticky Mickey?' I asked.

Jennifer Aronson turned and saw it was me. A broad smile broke across her face. She pulled me

494

into a hug and held me.

'Congratulations!'

'Thank you! When did you get back?'

'Today. As soon as I heard, I knew I had to get back here for this.'

'Once again, I'm sorry about your father.'

'Thank you, Mickey.'

'How did everything go afterward?'

'It was all right. I ended up being nursemaid to my sister, who got sick.'

'But you're okay?'

'I feel fine. But enough about me. Cisco told me that Maggie is a natural-born defense lawyer. That true?'

'Yeah, she was great. But it's not going to stick. She's going back to the D.A.'

'She's a lifer, I guess.'

'And you know, you did all the groundwork, Bullocks. I wouldn't be standing here free if you hadn't been there for me.'

'That's nice to hear.'

'It's true. Come sit at the table with us. The team's all there.'

'I will, I will. I just want to move around a little bit, say some hellos. So many people are here from the courts.'

I watched her push through the crowd and start giving friends hugs and high fives. I stepped back toward the bar so I could lean my back against it and take in the whole scene. I looked across the room and realized that few of those in front of me were truly celebrating that I was innocent and had defeated the forces against me. Most of them simply believed I had beaten the case, that I was not guilty by the legal standard, which didn't at all mean I was innocent.

It was a moment that seared me. I knew then how I would always be looked at in the courtroom, in the courthouse, in the city.

I turned toward the bar and saw Moira.

'Can I get you something, Mick?' she asked.

I hesitated. I looked at all the bottles lined against the mirror at the back of the bar.

'No,' I finally said. 'I think I'm fine.'

Epilogue

There were no paper towels or toilet paper. No bottled water, and not a single carton of eggs. I was giving a running commentary to Maggie over my cell, holding the handwritten list she had prepared with contributions from Hayley. So many items on the list were already gone. Long gone. I had started just grabbing what I could.

'What about pinto beans?' I asked. 'I just got four cans.'

We were speaking via my Bluetooth earpiece, leaving both my hands free to grab things from the shelves.

'Haller, what are we going to do with pinto beans?' she asked.

'I don't know,' I said. 'Nachos? There's nothing here. I just need to get whatever's left and then we'll have to make do with it. And I still have a lot of stuff at the house. Have you checked the pantry against this list?'

I spotted a lone jar of Newman's Own spaghetti sauce on the pasta shelf but another shopper swooped in and grabbed it first.

'Shit,' I said.

'What?' Maggie asked.

'Nothing. I missed out on some Newman's Own.'

'Just go to produce, see what's left. Get stuff

497

for salads. Then come back. This is too crazy.'

Crazy was an understatement. Chaos had descended. But in the midst of it, there was at least a calm center for me. My family was together for the first time in too many years to count. We had decided that the three of us would shelter together until the threat of the virus passed. Even with my home office converted into a bedroom for my daughter, my house had the most space and the biggest buffer zone around it compared with Hayley's apartment or Maggie's condo. The nuclear family would ride out the plague together and now it was down to the prep work. It was my second supermarket stop, the first having been equally disappointing. Still, I had earthquake supplies at the house and a mostly stocked pantry. It was just the wish list my girls had put together that I was missing. Red wine, good cheeses, and a few of the ingredients for Maggie's recipes.

I managed to fill the cart with things I was sure we would never use and none of the things that we would. Maggie stayed on with me the whole time. She had gone home with me at the end of the celebration at the Redwood and we traded sleepovers at each other's place until we settled on staying at my place. The relationship felt new and good and I often told myself that if the trade-off was four months of fear and turmoil to have Maggie back in my life, then that was a deal I'd make any day of the week.

'Okay, that's it,' I said. 'I'm getting in line now.'

'Wait, did you get orange juice?' she asked.

'Yes, they actually had orange juice. I got two cartons.'

'No pulp?'

I looked into the cart at what I had grabbed.

'Beggars can't be choosers,' I said.

'Great,' Maggie said. 'We'll make do with pulp. Hurry back.'

'I'm going to hit the ATM and then I'll head home.'

'Why? You won't need money. Everything's shutting down.'

'Yeah, well, cash will be king if the financial institutions go down and plastic no longer works.'

'Mr. Optimistic. You really think that could happen?'

'This year proves that anything can happen.'

'True. Get cash.'

And so it went. I waited nearly an hour to get through the checkout line. Near-hysteria was no doubt upon us now. I was glad to have my family close, though I feared what would happen to us if things got truly desperate.

It was so crowded in the parking lot that a car pulled up while I was unloading the cart and waited for my space.

'This place is a mess,' I said to Maggie. 'It's going to get out of hand.'

The guy waiting was holding up the cars behind him. Somebody honked but he didn't move. So I tried to go faster, putting the bags into the trunk of the Lincoln.

'What was that?' Maggie asked.

'Some guy wants my space — he's holding everybody up,' I said.

I turned my head at the sound of another honk and noticed a man with dark hair and slumped shoulders pushing a cart in my direction. A black mask covered the lower half of his face. He had only a single brown bag sitting in the cart's child seat. I did a double take because the bag said Vons and this was a Gelson's. I looked at the man again and thought he looked familiar. The way his hands were spread on the cart's push bar, the forward hunch, the droop of his shoulders.

In that moment I recognized him. The man in the video who was pushing the room-service cart into Louis Opparizio's hotel room in Scottsdale. His hair was different now, but the shoulders were the same.

It was him.

I stepped back from the trunk and looked around for an escape route. I had to run.

I shoved my cart forward to crash into his, then ran down the length of my car and into the next driving lane. I glanced back over my shoulder as I cut to my right. I saw that he was coming, pulling a gun from the Vons bag as he ran after me.

I kept going and cut sharply between two more cars and into the next driving lane over. Two quick gunshots sounded and I ducked low and kept my feet moving. I heard glass shatter and the impact of the bullet on metal but I felt no impact to my body.

Maggie's voice came sharply in my ear.

'Mickey, what's happening? What is going on?'

Then there were shouts behind me punctuated by another car horn.

'FBI! Freeze!'

I didn't know who was yelling at whom. But I didn't freeze. I lowered my head even more and kept running. And then more shots came — this time a loud and fearsome volley of overlapping shots from powerful weapons. I looked back again and saw no sign of the man from the video. I changed angles and saw him on the ground as four armed men and a woman moved in on him. I recognized the woman as Special Agent Dawn Ruth.

I stopped running and tried to catch my breath. Only then did I register Maggie's voice in my ear.

'Mickey!'

'I'm okay, I'm okay.'

'What happened? I heard shots!'

'Everything's all right. The guy from the video, the one who killed Opparizio, he was here.'

'Oh my god.'

'But so was the FBI. I see Agent Ruth over there. They got him. He's down on the ground. It's over.'

'The FBI? Were they following you?'

'Uh, either me or him.'

'Did you know, Mick?'

'No, of course not.'

'You better not have.'

'I just told you — I didn't. Look, everything's fine but I have to go. They're signaling me over. I probably have to give a statement or something.'

'Just get home soon, please. I can't believe this.'

I needed to go but didn't want to hang up without comforting her.

'Look, this means it's over. Everything. It's over.'

'Just come home.'

'As soon as I can.'

I disconnected the call and walked back to where the group was gathering around the man on the ground. He wasn't moving and nobody was bothering with CPR. Agent Ruth saw me and moved away from the pack, meeting me halfway.

'Is he dead?' I asked.

'Yes,' she said.

'Thank god.'

I looked over at the body. The gun I had seen was on the ground next to it. The scene of the shooting was being cordoned off.

'How did you know?' I said. 'You told me it was over. You said they wouldn't come after me.'

'We were just taking precautions,' she said. 'Sometimes these people don't like to leave loose ends.'

'And I'm a loose end?'

'Well . . . let's just say you know things. And you did things. Maybe he didn't like that.'

'So, it was just him? He did this on his own?'

'We don't know that for a fact.'

'What *do* you know? Am I still in danger? Is my family in danger?'

'Your family is fine, you're fine. He probably waited until you were away from the house because your family's there. Just calm down. Give me a day or two to assess and I'll call you.'

'What about now? Do I give a statement or something?'

'You should just go. Get away from here before people start to recognize you. We don't want that.'

I looked at her. Ever the protector of her case.

'How is the investigation going?' I asked.

'It's moving,' she said. 'Slowly but surely.'

I nodded toward the body.

'Too bad you won't be able to get him to talk,' I said.

'Guys like him never talk,' Ruth said.

I nodded and she walked off. The crime scene was beginning to draw a crowd. People wearing masks. People wearing rubber gloves and face shields. I then went to my car, finding the trunk still open but my haul of groceries still in their bags intact.

I closed the trunk and checked the rear bumper, a habit born of recent experience. The license plate was there as it should be, its six letters announcing my fate and my standing to the world.

NT GLTY

I got in my car and drove home to shelter.

Acknowledgments

The author gratefully acknowledges the help of many people in the research, writing, and editing of this novel. They include Asya Muchnick, Bill Massey, Emad Akhtar, Pamela Marshall, Betsy Uhrig, Terrill Lee Lankford, Rick Jackson, Linda Connelly, Jane Davis, Heather Rizzo, Dennis Wojciechowski, and John Houghton. A great debt of thanks goes to legal eagle Dan Daly as well as Roger Mills, Rachel Bowers, and Greg Hoegee.

We do hope that you have enjoyed reading this large print book.

Did you know that all of our titles are available for purchase?

We publish a wide range of high quality large print books including:
Romances, Mysteries, Classics
General Fiction
Non Fiction and Westerns

Special interest titles available in large print are:
The Little Oxford Dictionary
Music Book
Song Book
Hymn Book
Service Book

Also available from us courtesy of Oxford University Press:
Young Readers' Dictionary
(large print edition)
Young Readers' Thesaurus
(large print edition)

For further information or a free brochure, please contact us at:
Ulverscroft Large Print Books Ltd.,
The Green, Bradgate Road, Anstey,
Leicester, LE7 7FU, England.
Tel: (00 44) 0116 236 4325
Fax: (00 44) 0116 234 0205

Other titles published by Ulverscroft

FAIR WARNING

Michael Connelly

Jack McEvoy is a reporter with a track record in finding killers. But he's never been accused of being one himself. Jack went on one date with Tina Portrero. The next thing he knows, the police are at his house telling Jack he's a suspect in her murder. Maybe it's because he doesn't like being accused of a crime he didn't commit. Or maybe it's because the method of her murder is so chilling that he can't get it out of his head. But as he uses his journalistic skills to open doors closed to the police, Jack walks a thin line between suspect and detective — between investigation and obsession — on the trail of a killer who knows his victims better than they know themselves . . .